FROZEN EDEN

To Pam

Enjoy! Love
Sarah Barling

FROZEN EDEN

An Eden County Mystery

SARAH BEWLEY

LEVEL
BEST BOOKS

Author Photo Credit: Pat Payne

First edition

ISBN: 978-1-68512-562-2

Cover art by Level Best Designs

This book was professionally typeset on Reedsy.
Find out more at reedsy.com

For Dr. James Sunwall, my mentor and friend. I miss you.

Praise for Frozen Eden

"Eden County, Florida is no paradise for Sheriff Jim Sheppard. An unprecedented ice storm has struck, and he's found one person shot and another nearly frozen to death. As Sheppard tries to unravel the chaos enveloping Eden, he finds himself in pursuit of a woman that no one is eager to face. Things heat up as Sheppard and his crew, including a son he desperately wants to keep from following in his law enforcement footsteps, chase down answers. This page-turner will have you racing to *Frozen Eden*'s on-fire finish."—Albert Waitt, author of *The Ruins of Woodman's Village* and *Flood Tide*

"Sarah Bewley's *Frozen Eden* is like strapping into a fast car on an icy road. While driving dangerous speeds, you slip and slide and never know where the story will take you. The setting is so real you read it and shiver. Pick it up, you won't be disappointed."—David Putnam, bestselling author of the Bruno Johnson series

"Sarah Bewley's *Frozen Eden* works both as a banger of a story and as a master class in using dialogue to move the story forward and simultaneously reveal character. Both familiar and fresh, Bewley's cast of characters will appeal to fans of Robert B. Parker's Jesse Stone series as well as to fans of the late Charles Willeford's Hoke Moseley series. An absolute blast of a story."—Bobby Mathews, Anthony-nominated author of *Magic City Blues*, *Living the Gimmick*, and *Negative Tilt*

Chapter One

Sheriff Jim Sheppard parked on the shoulder of the highway and got out of his car. The cold wind stung his ears and made his eyes water. He looked across the highway and saw Bobby Dale wearing a hat that had fuzzy ear flaps that snapped together under his chin. For a moment, Jim wondered if he could pull rank and convince Bobby to loan him the hat. Then he shook his head and walked on to where Deputy Dee Jackson was standing, the turf under his boots crackling.

Dee Jackson stood on one side of Highway 27 while Deputy Bobby Dale stood on the other. Dee shook her head, "They close I-75 at the Georgia line because the roads are iced, and all the idiots decide to take 27."

Jim could see Bobby Dale's breath fogging the air around his head.

"How long has Bobby Dale been out here?" asked Jim.

"He took the night shift so Buck could go home and get some sleep. Buck had been out here for nearly twenty-four hours," said Dee.

"I was afraid of that. Bobby looks beat. I think maybe I'll cover here until this afternoon and give everyone a chance to get some rest," said Jim. "We are stretched way too thin, and I need to keep someone on the county roads. I don't want to think what Highway 98 looks like if I-75 is closed."

"I could take it," said Dee.

"And how long have you been up?" Jim asked.

Dee laughed, "I slept from yesterday afternoon until about 10 pm, so I'm doing all right."

The deep rumble of a diesel engine could be heard in the distance. "Damn, we've got semis running on 27?" said Dee.

Just as the semi came into view, it lost traction and went into the northbound lane. The driver slowed and tried to correct, and the big truck slid back into the southbound lane. Jim and Dee could both hear the tires slipping on the ice as the truck slid sideways, the trailer whipping the truck around to face north and being dragged down the highway.

The trailer seemed to be moving in slow motion. He could see the driver's horrified face through the passenger window of the truck. He had just enough time to think, Oh hell.

Something slammed into Jim from the side and carried him down the embankment and into the ditch. He heard the shriek of metal hitting metal, and something big and dark passed over Jim's head.

All he could think as he watched it go by was that the trailer had hit him and his car. Suddenly he was lost in the falling and rolling and finally coming to a stop in the frozen mud at the bottom of the ditch.

He was face down. He turned his head so he could breathe. He was pinned down. He waited for the pain to set in. He could feel the cold, but it had to be adrenaline keeping him from feeling what surely had to be fatal injuries. Or maybe he was dead?

"Sheriff?"

Dee Jackson sounded close. Jim raised his head slightly and realized the weight lying across him was his deputy.

"Dee?"

"Yes, sir," she said. "Give me a second. She rolled off him and sat on the frozen ground."

He slowly sat up, recognizing that his ribs were going to be sore and his left shoulder felt bruised. However, he was not dead, and so the rest he could live with. Literally.

He looked at Dee. "Did you just tackle me?"

Dee's broad smile was bright on her dark face, "Yes, sir."

Jim laughed. "Damn."

She pointed behind him. "Figured better me than that."

Jim turned and saw his patrol car crumpled against a line of pine trees. It had taken the bark off two trees and broken off the final one just below head height. The car had settled onto the ground upside down.

Beyond it was the trailer of the semi, broken axle resting on the icy road, the cab of the truck facing northbound in the middle of Highway 27. The driver was still in the cab. He stared at Jim, then slowly opened his door and climbed down. He took one step and slipped, feet flying up into the air and landing on his ass on the frozen pavement.

"Shit fire and save the matches," the man shouted.

Bobby Dale carefully made his way out to the driver. "Sir, can you get up?"

"Fuck if I know."

Bobby Dale reached out his hand, and the driver took it. He tried to raise himself into a sitting position, but let out a yell and let go, dropping back to the road.

"Oh, hell no," he said. "You get me an ambulance, cause I have broken something important."

Bobby Dale looked over to Jim. "I'll call an ambulance."

Jim waved him off. Bobby Dale headed back to his car and his radio. Jim turned back to Dee.

"You going to ticket the poor bastard?"

"You bet I am," she responded. She stood up stiffly. "I'm going to hurt for a week, and any chance we had of raises this year just disappeared with your car."

She helped Jim to his feet. This was a hell of way to start off the week leading up to Christmas.

It took a couple of hours to get the ambulance, the tow trucks, and everything taken care of so that Jim and Dee could leave. The driver probably had a broken hip.

Jim mournfully watched his car disappear slowly south on 27 on the flatbed tow. He had rescued his thermos of coffee, his first aid kit, and a set of emergency flairs from the sedan once it had been righted. He stood in the middle of the road with his thermos hanging from his hand.

The rest of his gear had been stowed in the trunk of Dee's patrol car. She'd agreed to give him a ride back into town. A hand rested on his arm just above his elbow. "Come on, Sheriff. Let me take you back into town. You ought to let Doc take a look at you."

Jim turned to Dee and sighed.

Dee patted his arm. "You're looking a little forlorn there, Sheriff."

"The insurance isn't going to come close to buying another patrol car. Not even something used," he said.

Dee shrugged. "Maybe the County will kick in enough to replace it."

Jim rolled his eyes. "Yeah, right."

Dee turned Jim around, and they headed for her car. The road had been cleared. Bobby Dale would continue the patrol. There really wasn't anything else to be done except go back into Warren and let Doc check him out. He was pretty sure that Dee had cracked a couple of his ribs, tackling him into the ditch.

Dee turned the heat to its highest setting and Jim's face tingled as it began to warm up. It felt uncomfortable. Jim couldn't remember it ever being this cold during the daylight hours. The temperature for the past day and a half hadn't gotten above 20 degrees, and it didn't look like it would change any time soon.

Dee slowed as they got close to a DOT utility shed. Damn, she had good eyes. The door to the shed was broken, and a bicycle lay on the ground in front of it.

"I could wait..." Dee said, "Come back after I get you into town."

"Nope, we'll check it out now," said Jim.

She pulled up next to the bike, and they both got out of the car. It was then they could see that the bike had been run over. The tires were warped, with broken spokes. One of the pedals had broken off and lay on the ground next to it.

"Hells bells," said Jim.

They hurried to the shed and pushed the door open. The crooked door hung and scraped on the rough concrete floor, but finally gave enough for them to both step inside.

Jim froze at the sight, but Dee quickly went to the two figures. A young black woman lay on the floor, her head resting on the legs of a young white man. Jim recognized him immediately. Bailey Braden. Blood had soaked and then frozen on his jeans and the floor beneath him.

Bailey's face was bright red beneath his dark watch cap, and his eyelashes were frost-covered. Streaks down his face, that must have once been tears, covered skin that looked burned. He had on a jacket and gloves. His hands cradled the woman's head gently. She had a bullet hole in her forehead, and her face was slack with death.

Dee put her hand against Bailey's face. "He's breathing."

Jim moved quickly and squatted down next to him. "Bailey? Bailey, it's Sheriff Jim. Can you hear me?"

Bailey turned his head a bit, his eyes opened, and he seemed to track Jim's voice.

"My fault," he whispered.

"What?"

"My fault."

"We've got to get him to the doctor and now. He's hypothermic. Help me move him," said Dee.

Jim and Dee went to take the young woman's head out of his hands and Bailey wailed and struggled clumsily, "No, no, can't leave her alone!"

They both stopped for a moment, Bailey panting between them. Then Dee said, "Bailey, she won't be alone. I'll stay here with her. You go with Sheriff Jim, okay?"

"Don't leave her," he said softly.

"I won't. I promise. I'll stay right here with her."

The silence was filled with Bailey's panting breath; then he let Dee take the young woman's head from his hands and lay her down on the concrete.

Jim got behind Bailey and put his hands under his arms and lifted him slowly to his feet. It made his ribs ache, but he had to get Bailey to his feet. Bailey wailed again, but this time in pain. They had no way to know how long he'd knelt there holding the young woman.

Dee nodded toward the door. "Get him in the front seat, keep the heat on high and give him some of that sweet coffee of yours. There's a blanket in the trunk, put it over him. After you've done that, you head straight to

Doc's. Get Bobby Dale over here. I'll take care of the scene."

Jim nodded. "You'll be all right?"

"Yeah, it's cold, but I'm not going to be in trouble before Bobby Dale gets here."

Bailey stumbled and Jim had to more or less carry him, but he got him into the front passenger seat, wrapped in the blanket. He closed the door, got into the driver's seat and pulled his thermos out. The coffee in it was still warm, and it was milky and sweet. He held the cup to Bailey's lips, and he sipped at it slowly. Then he raised his hands and took the cup, finishing it."

"More?" he asked softly.

"Sure," Jim said. He poured more coffee into the cup and let Bailey drink it. He called Bobby Dale on the radio as he pulled out onto the road into town.

With the roads iced up, it would take an ambulance at least forty-five minutes to reach them, and nearly an hour to get to Gainesville and the hospital. Bailey's best hope was Doc's. Jim pulled onto the shoulder and drove on the grass. It was safer than trying to get any speed on the icy road. He called Junior on the radio to get him to call Doc, then the Florida Department of Law Enforcement. They needed Bud Peterson and his crime team. He had no idea how Bailey Braden had ended up in that utility shed with a dead woman, but he would have to find out.

When Jim pulled up behind Doc's office, he got out of the car and banged on the back door. He didn't dare take Bailey in through the front. One look at his condition, the frozen blood on his jeans, and the gossip would be out of control before they got him back to an examination room.

The back door was opened by Ryan Edwards, Doc's partner. He wasted no time, "Where is he? Doc wants me..."

It made sense. Before Ryan moved to Warren, Florida and became Doc's partner he'd been a trauma specialist in the ER at one of the top hospitals in Washington, D.C. A brain injury left him aphasic and unable to function in the fast-paced world of a hospital. However, his skills were excellent and with Filly Ellis, world's smartest nurse working with him, he was a perfect fit for the small rural practice.

Jim and Ryan went to the car, where Jim opened the passenger door. Bailey, slumped in the front seat, and still balanced the cup from Jim's thermos with his hands.

"Bailey, this is Doc Ryan. He's going to help you."

Bailey nodded and fumbled the cup. Jim took it and set it on the dash, then curled his arm around Bailey and helped him out of the car. His legs gave out immediately, and Ryan grabbed him from the other side, and between them they carried the blanket-wrapped man inside through the back door.

They quickly moved into an examination room, and Ryan directed Jim to help him get Bailey undressed. He moaned when they pulled the blanket away. Even though the room was warm, it was clear that Bailey couldn't feel it.

Ryan efficiently stripped Bailey's bloodied jeans, jacket and sweatshirt. Then he had Jim help Bailey lie down. With incredible gentleness he loosened the frozen gloves from Bailey's hands, and then his socks from his feet. The last to go were his white briefs, which had also been soaked with blood.

The clothing was all laid aside on a table, and Filly entered the room carrying several warmed blankets and three bags of IV fluid. She handed one to Jim. "Put it up against his groin," she said as she put the other two bags beneath his armpits. Then she covered him with the blankets.

Ryan set up an IV line with warm saline going into Bailey's right arm. He pressed Bailey's hands and feet under the warmed blankets.

Filly took Bailey's watch cap off and replaced it on his head with a swath of warmed towels. Jim caught sight of the ragged, short hair of the young man. It looked dark and stiff.

Bailey started to shiver. Ryan smiled. "You're doing good, Bailey... Want something to drink?"

Bailey's teeth chattered, but he managed to get out, "More coffee?" in a hoarse whisper.

Filly looked at Jim. "Is he talking about that sweet stuff you call coffee? You fed that to the poor boy?"

Bailey nodded.

Jim blushed. "Yeah."

Filly turned to head out the door. "I'll see if I can replicate that garbage."

Ryan reached under the blankets to check the temperature of Bailey's feet. He held them softly, bending the foot at the arch slightly and checking the color of his toes. "I think we may be lucky. It looks like you got to him in time."

Filly returned with a cup of milky coffee and more warm saline bags. Ryan pressed them against Bailey's feet and hands under the blankets.

"We'll need to change the blankets...I want to leave the base...but keep switching out the top...for warmed ones."

"I'll take care of it." Filly handed Jim a paper evidence bag and nodded toward Bailey's abandoned clothes. "I'm assuming you'll be needing those."

"Yeah," Jim said. Ryan took the bag from Jim and carefully placed the clothing and shoes in it. "Can I try to talk to him?"

Ryan nodded. "He'...lucid, but hi...processing may be slow."

"Thanks."

Jim pulled a rolling stool up next to the examination table. He took the cup of coffee and helped Bailey drink a bit of it. "Bailey, can you tell me who the woman is?" he asked.

Bailey took a shuddering breath, then said, "Noel. Like Christmas."

"Bailey, you said it was your fault. Did you hurt Noel?"

Bailey shook his head slightly, "Never hurt Noel."

"Do you know who did hurt her?"

Tears began to roll from Bailey's eyes down the sides of his face.

"Did you find her like that?"

Bailey sipped at the coffee but didn't answer.

"Don't you want me to find out who did this to Noel?"

The tears fell faster, but still, he said nothing. He turned his head away from the coffee.

Ryan came up next to Jim. "Bailey, you're going to need to pee soon. I have a... thing you can use. You let me kno—"

"Need it now."

"Okay." Ryan motioned for Jim to take the bag of clothing and step outside. Jim walked out into the hallway and found Filly Ellis waiting for him.

"Why's he got all that blood on his clothes?"

"I can't talk to you about it, Filly."

"Like hell you can't. I've known Bailey Braden all his life. What happened?"

"We found him with a dead black woman."

Filly gasped and stepped back from Jim. "Who is she?"

"He says her name is Noel, like Christmas."

Filly was silent for a moment, then she shook her head. I don't know of a single woman in Eden County named Noel."

Jim shrugged. "Me either, but that's who Bailey says she is. Maybe he'll talk to you. He closed up tighter than Dick's hatband on me."

Filly looked at the closed door. "Not likely. Bailey talks, but he doesn't say much of anything."

That was true. Jim knew the one thing that was most obvious about Bailey was that he could find lots of things to say, and the vast majority of it was designed to keep you from asking him questions. He was full of smart aleck remarks but avoided talking about anything serious. Bailey Braden was cheerful and friendly, which made absolutely no sense to anyone who knew anything about his life.

"I need to get back to the scene. You and Ryan let me know if there's anything more he says about the woman."

Filly snorted. "Are you completely unaware of doctor/patient confidentiality?"

Jim gaped at her.

Filly tapped at the examination room door and then disappeared inside.

Chapter Two

Filly took the urinal and left the room. Ryan used a clean piece of gauze to wipe the tears from Baileys face, and his running nose. He reached under the blankets to touch Baileys hand. The flesh was still too cold. He started to move his hand back and Bailey grabbed it and held on.

"Are you in pain, Bailey?" Ryan asked.

Bailey shook his head. "Feels good."

Ryan reached beneath the blanket with his other hand and held Bailey's cold fingers between his hands. "Your hands and feet...hurt as you warm up."

Bailey nodded a little.

"I'm sorry your friend is dead," Ryan said.

Bailey made a small noise.

"Noel is a pretty name."

"Sh...sh...she...pretty."

Ryan couldn't help but think of Danielle. She had not been pretty. She'd been beautiful. Her short black curls and large brown eyes, and skin the color of bitter-sweet chocolate. He hadn't seen her dead, and for that he was glad. She would always be alive in his memory."

"My wife was from France," he said to Bailey. "Her parents were from... Africa...the Ivory Coast. She died, too."

Bailey's eyes turned to Ryan. Noel...really smart."

Ryan smiled. "Noel is Christmas in French."

Tears began to run down the sides of Bailey's face again. Ryan wiped at them to keep them from flowing into his ears. He closed his green eyes and turned his face away from Ryan.

Chapter Three

When Jim arrived back at the crime scene, Bobby Dale and Dee sat in Bobby Dale's car waiting for the FDLE crime scene team. Jim had been gone over an hour, and normally they'd have been there by now. But there was no sign of them, yet. Both deputies got out and greeted Jim.

"Any word on when Bud will be here?"

Dee shook her head. "They said they'd get here when they got here."

"Did you look around?" Jim asked.

Dee nodded. "Whatever ran over Bailey's bike, it was heavy. The frame is broken. Bullet that killed the girl was a through and through, which means it's probably in the walls, and she was definitely killed here. Any place else and there wouldn't have been blood and brains all over the floor and wall."

Bobby Dale had his hands in his armpits trying to keep the warm. Their winter gear was not enough for weather in the twenties. "Bailey going to be all right?"

"Yeah, Ryan says he will."

"He say anything about the girl?" Dee asked.

"Said her name was Noel like Christmas."

"You don't think Bailey did it?" Bobby Dale asked.

Jim shook his head. "Bailey said she was his friend, so no, I don't think he shot her. Someone else was here."

The sound of an engine could be heard in the distance. They all turned to the north and around the bend came the FDLE van. It bumped along the shoulder of the road, and still as it came around the curve the tires slipped and the van began a slow slide toward them.

"Oh, hell no!" said Dee, and she pulled Jim back from the side of the road.

The van slid up and came to a quiet stop. All three of them let out a huge sigh of relief.

The driver's door opened, and Bud Peterson got out. His breath fogged around his head like smoke from a cigarette. He had his travel mug in his hand, and unbelievably Jim could hear the slosh of iced tea in it. Bud took a long sip at his tea and the fog lessened slightly. "You picked a hell of a day to have a murder." He looked around and one technician had left the van and begun getting equipment out of the back. "Just bring what we'll use first, Angie. Otherwise shit's likely to start freezing on us."

A female voice made an affirmative noise from the back of the van. Bud waited for Angie and when she came around the van she had a case of equipment and two sets of blue booties for them to put over their shoes.

Bud looked down at Jim and Dee's boots. "So you've tromped all over my crime scene, I see."

They looked down and saw that there were traces of blood visible on their boots.

"I heard there was someone alive when you got here. They still alive?"

"Yeah. Hypothermic, but the young doc is taking care of him."

Bud grimaced. "Nasty. All right. Let's get to it."

He and Angie walked to the door, put on the booties and went inside. Their movements could be heard because of the bare concrete floor and the cold clear air.

"Bobby Dale, I'm sorry, but could you go on back to the highway and see if you can keep whatever fools decide to drive today from killing anyone? Dee and I will stay here."

"I got it, Sheriff," said Bobby Dale as he saluted Jim, then went to his car and pulled away. Jim and Dee got back into her car. She took the driver's side without saying anything and Jim figured she had the right. It was her patrol car. They kept the car running so they would have the heat. Dee cracked a window so they'd hear if Bud called for them.

"You think maybe Bailey was seeing this Noel?" Dee asked.

13

"I don't know. But I haven't seen him cry since he was seven."

"Maybe him being with her is what got her killed."

Jim studied the side of Dee's face. She looked out the windshield at the FDLE van. Her expression was unusually neutral.

"You mean like a hate crime?"

"Could be."

Jim thought about it a moment. Eden County had its racial divides, but there were also at least a dozen biracial couples he could think of off the top of his head.

The first time Jim saw Bailey Braden he was sitting on the roof of the elementary school. Jim had been a deputy working under his father at the time, and he'd been called to the school because no one could figure out how to get Bailey down. Every time the custodian put up a ladder, Bailey jumped to another wing, scaring the bejesus out of everyone. So they'd stopped trying to get someone up to him and called the Sheriff's Office hoping they'd have a better idea.

His father had told them he'd send Jim. He had a son a year younger than Bailey, and he thought it possible Jim might be able to talk to the boy better than the other deputies.

When Jim arrived the principal and custodian were standing a short distance from the one-story roof where Bailey sat. The principal had simply pointed to Bailey.

Jim had walked up to the side of the building and looked up at the scrawny child. His face was a mess of tears and snot. He squatted at the edge of the roof with his arms tight across his thin chest and his fists clenched tight.

"Hi," Jim had said. "How'd you get up there?"

Bailey had shrugged. "Climbed."

"You use a ladder?"

Bailey shook his head. His dark hair was shaggy and ragged, and his broad face and flat nose made him look like a tiny prizefighter who'd seen better days.

"Then how'd you do it?"

"There's cracks in the wall up above the water fountain. I climbed up on it until I could get to the cracks. Then when I got to the edge of the roof, I pulled myself up."

"You must be strong."

"I am."

"Why'd you go up there?"

Bailey snuffled. "They put me in the wrong class. I did first-grade last year. They put me in it again, and when I tried to go where my class was, they told me I couldn't be with them."

Jim's heart kind of broke at that. "They explain why?"

The boy shrugged again. "Said I got held back 'cause I didn't do good enough last year."

"Didn't anybody tell you that before you got here today?"

The boy shook his head.

"Well, that's just not right," said Jim. "Why don't you come down here? I'll make the principal apologize for not letting you know before."

"I want to be with my class. I don't want to be with the little ones."

Jim thought about it for a moment. The school was so small there was only one first-grade class. Which meant it was Michael's class.

"Well, you know, my boy, Michael, he's in that class. I know he could use someone older to help him out. Show him how school works. Maybe you'd consider being his helper for me? Sure would make me feel better about him being here."

Bailey's eyes narrowed. "You telling me the truth?"

"Cross my heart. Michael Sheppard's my son. He's in the first-grade class."

Bailey wiped his snotty face on his shirt. Then he stood up. "Okay. Can you catch?" he asked.

Jim said, "Sure," and then was surprised to see Bailey leap off the roof. He was sure he let out a bleat of terror at the small boy jumping, but he did manage to catch him.

As he held Bailey in his arms the boy said, "You catch good."

* * *

"You still with me, Sheriff?" asked Dee.

Jim realized he'd been lost in the memory of that first meeting. It had always amazed him that Bailey had trusted him enough to jump into his arms. But that was Bailey. By the time Bailey and Michael were in high school, Bailey was two grades behind him. He'd finally dropped out the year Michael had graduated.

"Yeah, just thinking about Bailey."

They heard a whistle from the door of the utility shed and saw Bud Peterson waving for them to come in.

As they stepped into the little room they saw that the technician had bagged the body.

"Found the bullet that killed her in the wall over there," Bud said.

There was a circle drawn around the hole in the concrete block.

"We go digging for it right now, we're going to tear it all the hell up. Think the county will kick up a ruckus if I take a Sawzall to the wall and take out most of that block?"

Jim looked at the bare concrete block. "Do it. I'll deal with the county."

"I'll let you know what we find once we get it back to the lab. We've sure as hell got enough blood and tissue samples. Think any of it belongs to anyone other than the victim? Your live one injured?"

"Just nearly frozen," Jim said.

"Nothing surprising about that," Bud muttered.

"Anything else?" Jim asked.

"A puddle of frozen urine right in the middle of all that blood. We'll be able to get DNA, but it's probably the guy you found," said Angie.

Jim winced. God only knows how long poor Bailey had knelt there holding the dead woman.

"No guns here. Did find a casing over next to the wall. We're taking the body back to the morgue for the Medical Examiner. We'll also take the bicycle with us. Everyone's trying to stay off the roads. Fortunately for you, I'm dedicated." Bud laughed.

Angie snorted.

"I know you're not a doctor, but can you give me an idea how long the body's been here?" Jim asked.

Bud looked at Angie. "Liver temp and rigor suggest not more than about five or six hours. You found her a couple of hours ago?"

Dee looked at her watch, "One hour and fifty-six minutes."

Angie nodded. "Then I'd say when you found her, she'd been here four, maybe five hours, not much more than that."

"Thanks," Jim said. "I appreciate the dedication."

Bud laughed out loud. "Damn right. We'll get back to you when we know more. Bullets deform like all hell when they hit concrete, so we may not get much off it other than the caliber. The casing may give us more."

Jim and Dee helped Angie and Bud get the body out to the van, and then wrap the broken bicycle in plastic and put it in the van, as well as the bag that contained Bailey's clothes. They'd need to be tested, too.

The wheels on the van spun a little before they caught and then Bud made a U-turn and headed south, going to Gainesville to drop off the body.

Dee and Jim walked back into the shed and looked at the discolored concrete.

"Whoever shot the girl didn't kill Bailey. You suppose he wasn't here when she was shot?" asked Dee.

Jim sighed. "Bailey's scared. He wouldn't talk about it when I tried to question him at Doc's."

A dead woman they only knew as Noel, like Christmas, Bailey Braden nearly dead from cold, and temperatures not expected to get above twenty for the next four to six days. Yeah, thought Jim, this Christmas was definitely not looking like an easy one.

Dee shivered. "I think we better keep Bailey out of sight for a while, don't you?"

Jim realized she was right. It hadn't occurred to him. Whether Bailey would talk to him or not, it would be better to keep him tucked away until they could figure out why he was still alive. "Ah, hell's bells," said Jim.

Chapter Four

As Bailey's body temperature rose, he shivered violently on the table. Filly and Ryan took turns sitting with him, changing out the warmed saline bags and blankets. His temperature rose steadily, which was a good sign. The fact that he could urinate and cry were both also excellent signs.

His face and hands seemed to have suffered the most. Ryan kept a careful eye on his fingers, watching for the color to go dusky which would be a precursor to them turning black and gangrenous. The frostbite on his face was bad. The tracks of his tears were not as bad as other areas because the salty tears had protected his skin.

Fortunately, the kid had an almost flat nose, which protected it from freezing as quickly, so the main tissue that would be damaged was across his high cheekbones, which were directly under his eyes, where he had cried copiously. His genetics would keep him from losing too much tissue to frostbite, and thus keep his scarring to a minimum.

Though Ryan was pretty sure that the kid didn't give a damn about any of that. He was overwhelmed with sorrow. Tears leaked down the sides of his face and soaked his hair and filled the creases of his ears. He drank the sweet milky coffee and warm soup he was offered but hadn't said more than a handful of words to them.

Ryan pressed the thermometer into Bailey's ear. The machine beeped and the temperature read 92.5. Ryan sighed with relief. When he'd come in his body temperature had been 81. Ryan had seen people survive lower temperatures, but not without full-scale hospital intervention. What they'd done here was more like field medicine in a war zone. He was damned relieved that it had worked.

"Is there someone…to call…?" Ryan asked.

Bailey shook his head and said, "N-n-no."

"Honey," said Filly, "why don't I send Claire over to your place to get you some clothes? Would that be all right? For her to go into your place?"

Bailey looked confused. "My clothes?"

"We had to give them to Sheriff Jim, honey," Filly replied.

"O.k…kay."

Ryan pressed a reassuring hand to Bailey's shoulder, then he and Filly left the room.

"You know where he lives?" Ryan asked.

"He has a room over the laundromat. I'll send Claire over to get him some clothes."

"Does he have family…?"

Filly shook her head. "He has family, but you don't want to be calling her. China Braden won't be any help."

Filly didn't wait to tell him more, just moved on down the hall to cover the phones while she sent Claire out. As Ryan watched her go, Doc came out of one of the examination rooms. He looked at Ryan, then asked softly, "How's he doing?"

"Good. He's good."

Doc swallowed. "Glad to hear that. Heard from Jim?"

Ryan shook his head.

Doc nodded. "Figures. I can't help thinking," then he stopped speaking. "Never mind."

"What?" Ryan asked.

"Doesn't make sense. Girl must not be a local, but she was with Bailey? He's never been anywhere he can't get on his bicycle."

"Why?"

"Bailey's…" he stopped. "He's not stupid. In fact, the kid can be damned clever, but he couldn't learn. Don't know why."

"No one tested him?"

19

Doc laughed, but it wasn't with humor. "China Braden had a fit. Everyone backed down."

It was clear Doc wasn't going to say anything else. Ryan motioned back to the door which led back to Bailey. "I'll go keep an eye on him." He turned and went back into the room.

Bailey Braden lay still on the table. His chest rose and fell as he breathed, and tears continued to track the sides of his face. But he made no sound and the only other movements were the shivers of his body as he slowly warmed up.

Chapter Five

Jim and Dee did another search around the outside of the shed and across the grass where Bailey's bike had been. They didn't find anything, not even cigarette butts, which were generally plentiful around sites used by the road crews. This weather had kept pretty much everyone except emergency personnel off the roads and in their homes.

They got back into Dee's car, and she turned the heat on and set the fan to high. The blast of not-freezing air felt good on Jim's face.

"The safest place for Bailey will be with me," Jim said. "I have the extra room. He knows Michael. I don't want him with civilians."

"Michael's a civilian," Dee said.

Jim rolled his eyes. "Yeah, but he doesn't want to be."

Dee said nothing in return. He knew she was well aware of his feelings about Michael having decided to study Criminology and Law. They'd had more than one heated discussion about it in his office.

"Okay, so you take him to your home. When you're not there, we put someone in the house, right?"

Jim nodded. "I don't want it to be obvious."

Dee agreed. "Your car is down. Whoever goes to pick you up, you take their car for the day."

Dee, Jim thought, was always smarter than him. Perfect.

Once they got back to the Sheriff's Office, things fell into a rhythm that was familiar to Jim. Junior gave him a quick update on everything on the board for the day. Dee sat down to write her report. Jim headed straight to his office and called Doc's. Filly answered the phone, which surprised him.

21

"Where's Claire?" he asked.

"Hello to you, too, Sheriff," Filly responded. "She's gone to get Bailey some clothes. She'll be right back."

"How's he doing?"

"He's warming up. Keeps crying and won't talk, but he's warming up."

"Keep him there until I can come get him."

"He's not going anywhere. He's not up to walking out of here on his own. What's going on?"

Jim rubbed his face, trying to figure out what he could or should say to Filly. Finally, he spoke, "We think whoever killed the young woman probably knows Bailey was there. I don't want to take a chance on him being found by whoever it was." Jim heard Claire's voice. She had returned from getting Bailey's change of clothes.

"He'll be here," Filly said. Then she hung up.

As Jim sat back in his chair, Junior appeared in the doorway to his office. 'I went through the schedule, and I've got your day guards in place. I'm pulling coverage off Windsor Ridge and putting them in your house until further notice. Whoever is covering the county roads west of there can make a pass through twice a day."

'Thanks. That makes sense. Just don't..."

"Don't let the Colonel know his patrol has been pulled off. Gotcha," Junior interrupted. Then he turned and left.

Dee grinned from the doorway. "I think he likes screwing with the Colonel's patrol."

Jim smiled, "Don't we all."

She dropped into the chair across from his desk. "Bud called. He's running the woman's prints. He'll let us know if he comes up with something. So far there's no missing persons report that matches her."

Jim sighed. "It's early, yet. Her family might not even realize she's not coming home."

"We'll get an ID. She was well dressed. Her nails were manicured. She's no street person."

Jim heard the phone ring in the office. Junior answered it, and after a

22

moment called out, "Sheriff, I think you should take this."

Jim picked up his extension as the call transferred to him. It was Annie from the library. "Jim, I've got a car in the parking lot of the library and the woman it belongs to isn't here. She should be here."

"Wait a minute, Annie, maybe she's getting coffee or something."

"No, she's always here. She gets her coffee in Gainesville before she comes. She meets Bailey Braden here every Tuesday and Thursday morning before he has to be at work at the Magnolia. She's been tutoring him."

"Hang on, Annie," he said. He punched the button to put the phone on speaker. "This young woman who's been tutoring Bailey, is she black?"

"Yes," said Annie. "Why?"

"Don't let anyone touch that car. We'll be right there."

"All right."

Jim cut the connection. "Call Bud Peterson. Tell him to get back over here."

Dee was already out of her chair and on her way to the outer office. "Junior," she called. "Get hold of Manny and tell him to meet me and the Sheriff at the library."

Jim began grabbing his gear. Dee was right. Manny Sota was one of the few deputies they had who wouldn't mess with the scene before they got there, and he would also prevent anyone else from messing with it. Jim might not have the largest force in the state of Florida, but he did have some of the sharpest deputies anyone could want.

Chapter Six

Filly came in with Bailey's clean clothes. They were wrapped in a towel to retain the heat from the dryer. She'd heated them up so they would help warm his body. She set them on the counter next to Ryan."

"You want me to help him dress?" she asked.

Bailey made a protesting sound from the examination table.

"Bailey, honey, you don't have a thing that I haven't seen before."

Ryan smiled when Bailey made another noise of protest. "...I'll help."

Filly snorted. "You men folk act like we're interested in your dangly bits." Then she left the room.

Ryan reached under the blankets and felt Bailey's hand. It was still cool to the touch, but the color was good. When Ryan moved his fingers, he got the same protesting noise from Bailey.

"That hurts?"

Bailey nodded.

"Let's see if you've got some socks here. If you put on some warm... it might make you feel a little better. Your hands and feet must be stinging."

"Yeah." Bailey's voice was soft and ragged.

Ryan opened the towels and a wave of warmth washed up into his face. He pulled a pair of white tube socks out of the pile and turned to the examination table. He lifted the blankets off Bailey's feet and quickly put the socks on him, pulling them up onto his legs. He rolled the blanket back down.

Bailey sighed with pleasure at the feel of the warm socks.

Ryan raised the head of the examination table a bit more. "Do you want to try...more clothes, or would...wait?"

"More," said Bailey.

Ryan took his time, uncovering only enough of the young man to get the piece of clothing on. Claire had brought underwear, sweat pants, a long sleeve t-shirt, and a flannel shirt to go over that. There were no gloves, so Ryan wrapped his hands in the towels that had held the warmed clothes. A normal shade of pink was coming back into Bailey's ears and face.

"Something to drink?"

"Coffee?" Bailey asked.

"Don't call it that in front of Filly. She'll be offended."

Bailey smiled for the first time. "Miz Ellis likes her coffee like she likes her men," he said softly.

Ryan barked out a surprised laugh. "Oh my God, ...I'm going to tell her...you said that."

"That's okay. She told me."

"I'll be right back."

Ryan stepped out into the hallway, closing the door behind him. Filly was about to head into an exam room. "Is Bailey all right?" she asked.

"He's fine. He...more coffee."

Filly shook her head. "That is not coffee. It's melted ice cream."

Ryan smiled. "Bailey says you like...coffee...like your men."

Filly threw her head back and laughed. "He remembers that, huh? Depend on that boy to remember the only inappropriate thing I ever said in front of him. I made a fresh pot of coffee about thirty minutes ago. There's half and half in the refrigerator. I had Claire pick some up when she went to get his clothes."

"Thanks. Call me...if Doc needs...with patients."

"I'll let you know. You know I'm not shy." Filly went on into the exam room and Ryan went down the hall to the small area they generously referred to as the staff room. It held a microwave, two refrigerators (the small one for food, the large one for the lab), a coffee maker, and a sink.

The coffee was hot, and Ryan filled half a large mug, then the rest with half and half. He spooned four spoonfuls of sugar into it. He'd seen Jim make his coffee dozens of times since he'd rented the apartment over Jim's garage. Ryan had taught Jim's son, Michael, the term kinderkaffee to refer to the sweet mix.

When he returned to the room with the mug, Bailey sat up slowly.

"Whoa!..." Ryan said. "I...hold...your hands..." Ryan held the mug close while Bailey's hands stayed under the blankets. He drank greedily from the mug. "You like...this...Sheriff's coffee?"

"It's good," mumbled Bailey.

Ryan smiled. "Well, that makes two of you who like it."

Chapter Seven

The Volkswagon Beetle was dark blue with a gray interior. The Florida tag was from Pinellas County. Annie came out of the library when Jim and Dee got out of her car. Manny had his cruiser parked behind the Beetle so no one could approach it without going by him. Manny nodded at Jim and Dee.

"Jim, what's going on?" asked Annie as she walked up to him. "Where's Noel?"

"I'm sorry, Annie. I can't really tell you, but I think she may be dead."

"Oh my Lord," Annie said softly. "I need to find Bailey Braden. Right away."

"We already found him, Annie. He's safe. He's at Doc's office."

Annie shook her head. "He's…He was crazy about her. She taught him to read, Jim. He got his GED because she helped him and they were both so happy."

Dee stepped up, "So they were involved?"

Annie smiled and tears started running down her face. "They were thick as thieves. She met him at the Magnolia House. Found out he couldn't read and took it upon herself to teach him. She's been tutoring him here at the library for close to eight months. I don't think they knew I knew, but I saw them a couple of times in the stacks kissing."

"Jesus," whispered Jim. "No wonder he wouldn't leave her."

Jim looked at Dee and stepped and stepped away. Dee took over. In the rush to get Bailey help, he hadn't thought about anything other than saving him. Baily Braden had been Michael's friend since they were 6 and 7 years

27

old. He knew Bailey too well. He could not be involved in the investigation. Without even speaking, Dee knew why he'd stepped aside. This would have to be her case.

"Do you know her last name?" Dee asked.

"Noel Williams," Annie answered. "She's in school in Gainesville at the university. She's in some kind of special education or testing program. She did a practicum at the elementary school testing the kids here last year. That's how she came to be in town. She was tutoring some of the kids in the library after school."

"Do you know where her family is?"

Annie shook her head. "No, but it's probably on the paperwork for the car. I know she was going home for Christmas and she and Bailey made plans to meet today. I think they were going to exchange gifts."

"Thanks, Annie. I appreciate your help."

Jim moved to take Annie's arm and she pulled away from him. "I'm fine. You do your job. I've got work to do." She quickly walked away and back into the library.

Jim's shoulders dropped. Dammit. He knew that Annie wouldn't talk to anyone. She knew how precious information was in a case like this. But she would mourn alone, and that hurt him. Annie White didn't have any family anymore.

"You should take my car and go pick up Bailey. Take him home. I'll have Manny or someone bring me by later to get it," said Dee.

"You'll keep me in the loop," Jim said.

"You'll read the reports no matter what."

Jim nodded. "Thanks."

Chapter Eight

Doc's office seemed unusually silent when Jim walked in the front door. Claire sat at the desk, but the waiting room was empty. She looked up and smiled, "Afternoon, Sheriff!"

"How are you doing, Claire?"

She shrugged. "Be better if it wasn't so dang cold outside. It's freezing my tootsies every time I have to go outside. And my house does not have the insulation to deal with this!"

Jim smiled, "I don't think anyone's house around here has the insulation to deal with this cold. I think we're definitely having a white Christmas this year."

Claire snorted. "White Christmases are for Yankees. I never had one, I don't need one, and I dang sure don't want one!"

Doc walked out from the hallway into the waiting room. "You here to pick up Ryan's patient?"

"Yes. But I need to talk to all of ya'll about this. Is Filly still here?"

"I'll get her and Ryan," Doc said and walked back toward the exam rooms.

"Michael's home from college, isn't he?" asked Claire.

Jim nodded. "He'll be here until right after New Year's. Then he goes back to Gainesville."

"He still planning on being a deputy?"

Jim sighed. "I can't talk him out of it."

Claire laughed. "I think the Sheriff gene skipped a generation, sir. You may not like it, but I don't think Michael's ever wanted to do anything else."

Jim shook his head. "I keep hoping that after baseball in the spring, he'll get some attention from the Major Leagues. I think that's the only thing that would change his mind."

"He does love playing baseball.

"Almost as much as he loves driving me nuts."

Doc, Filly, and Ryan walked into the waiting room and stood by Claire's desk. "What's up, Jim?" asked Doc.

"Dee Jackson is taking over the case of our dead woman. She and I both think that Bailey probably knows more about the killing than he's willing to tell us, and we don't want anyone knowing where he is. I'm taking him to my house since I'm not going to be working the case, and I'm asking you all to not say anything to anyone about Bailey being here, or anything you heard from him."

Filly pointed a finger at Jim, "This better be just a regular procedure because if you think any of us would talk about a patient or where he's going to be, I'm going to have to come over there and kick your ass real fast."

"Regular procedure," Jim lied.

Doc nodded, "I call bullshit, but we hear you." He turned to Ryan. "You go on home with Jim. No sense in keeping the office open. I'll take calls tonight in case someone needs us."

Ryan nodded. "Thanks. I'll...him ready, ...out the way we brought him in?"

Jim agreed. "I'll bring the car around back. Do you want to follow me to the house?"

Ryan shook his head. "Didn't drive. Walked...roads...icy. I know better... no snow tires or chains."

"You should have shared that knowledge with me," said Claire. "I think I slid all the way here this morning."

Filly made a rude noise and disappeared into the back.

"I'll be taking you home," said Doc to Claire. "I drove the truck in this morning, and its knobby tires handled the ice pretty well. I don't want you sliding off the road on the way back."

"Thanks, Doc!"

Jim waved to both of them and then headed outside. Dee's car had already gotten cold between the time he'd parked and now. He shivered and set the heat to high. He pulled around the back and left the car running as he got out and banged on the door.

Filly opened the door and Doc and Ryan walked out with Bailey. He walked slowly between them. "Back door, Jim. He's…need help," said Ryan.

"Got it!" Jim opened the car door and Ryan slid in, then Doc helped him get Bailey into the seat next to him. Ryan pulled him close, where his body heat would continue to warm Bailey.

"You keep them both safe," said Doc.

"I promise," answered Jim.

Doc and Filly disappeared back into the clinic, but not before Filly pointed at Jim with an "I'm watching you" signal.

Jim got back into the car, shivering.

"You shaking…scared of Filly?" asked Ryan.

"Anyone not scared of Filly is a fool," muttered Jim.

Bailey snickered, which surprised both of them.

"Are you laughing at me, Bailey Braden?" asked Jim.

Bailey snickered again and nodded. "Filly'll kick everyone's ass."

"That she will," said Ryan, pulling him closer.

Chapter Nine

Ryan knew Bailey would make it when he snickered at Jim. His body relaxed with that knowledge. He hated losing a patient more than just about anything in the world. The young man who'd arrived hypothermic scared him. Bailey had barely spoken and cried hard enough that dehydration had been a danger. It cheered him considerably to hear him snicker.

"I think you're high on sugar," said Ryan.

Bailey shook his head. "Like Sheriff Jim and Filly," he said.

Jim laughed softly. "Don't be laughing at me. You're scared of Filly, too, Bailey Braden!"

Bailey shook his head. "She loves me," he said softly. Then his eyes filled with tears again. "Noel loved me, too."

Ryan pulled him closer. "It's not your fault."

Tears streaked down Bailey's cheeks. "Is," he said. "Is." He took a shuddering breath.

"We can talk about it later, Bailey," said Jim.

Bailey shook his head. "Can't."

Ryan could see Jim's shoulders rising with tension. He hoped he wouldn't start an argument with Bailey right now. They needed to let him rest and get some food into him. Other than soup and ice cream coffee, Bailey probably hadn't eaten anything since breakfast.

Bailey snuffled a little and wiped his face on his sleeve. Jim clearly heard because his shoulders lowered fractionally. There would be no questioning in the immediate future.

After Jim parked in the driveway behind Michael's truck, they both helped Bailey walk into the house. As usual, the front door was unlocked. Ryan would never quit marveling that in Warren, locking your doors was the exception to the rule rather than the rule. He had never lived anywhere he felt safe not locking his door. And he still hadn't broken the habit. He didn't think he ever would. Too many things had happened during his time in Warren.

Michael met them in the living room. When Bailey saw him, he reached out. Michael stepped forward and put his arms around Bailey. "Hey Bailey B, how's my best friend?" he asked.

Bailey buried his face against Michael's chest.

"Are you wiping your snotty nose on my shirt?" asked Michael.

"Maybe," Bailey answered softly.

"Bailey is going to be staying with us for a bit," Jim said.

Michael looked at his father and caught the serious look. He nodded. "Well, c'mon, Bailey B, let's get you all settled in the back bedroom. Then I can tell you all about how I'm going to kick ass this spring in baseball. We've got a hell of a team at UF this year. We're going to win it all."

Bailey leaned against Michael and they walked together down the hall. Michael, a good head and a half taller than Bailey had no trouble at all supporting his weight as they moved.

When the heard the door to the bedroom shut, Jim seemed to wilt. Ryan grabbed his arm, "Are you all right?"

"I'm worn out. It's been a hell of a morning."

"Want to tell...a cup of hot cocoa?"

"God, that actually sounds good. Bailey drank all my coffee."

Ryan laughed. "He's...jacked up...sugar and caffeine...not coming down... for days."

Jim shook his head. "The kid needed it. I'm glad you knew what to do to save him. I was scared shitless he was going to die when we found him."

"I think if you hadn't found him...started getting him...warm... hypothermia...bad shape. Your kinderkaffee...did him good. Lots of sugar and cream...he wanted to drink it...it tasted good."

Jim rolled his eyes at him. "My coffee tastes great, to anyone who has tastebuds. I think yours are dead from all the black coffee you drank for years in the ER."

Ryan laughed. "Possibly true."

Jim took a chair at the table in the kitchen and Ryan pulled the milk out of the refrigerator and started to make hot chocolate the way Jim had taught him. He remembered how surprised Jim was that he didn't know how to make it with fresh milk, cocoa, and sugar. He'd patiently explained the process as he walked him through it. "Can you tell…what happened?" Ryan asked.

Jim sighed. "Close as I can figure, someone killed the black woman and Bailey was either there, or found her right after it happened. I'm thinking he was there because something heavy ran over his bike. It was outside the building all busted up."

Ryan stirred the milk and added in the cocoa slowly. "I've seen him… Magnolia, I never saw him in the office."

"I doubt Bailey's been to see Doc since he was a kid. When his grandparents were alive, they took care of him. His mother never could be bothered. She was 15 when she had him, and I think the night she gave birth was probably the last time she spent much time with him. Her parents took him away from her."

"Damn." The milk began to bubble and form a slight skin. He took it off the burner and poured it into two mugs.

He brought the sugar to the table and set it in front of Jim along with the hot chocolate. He didn't believe he'd ever get the sugar balance right enough to suit the man.

Jim took a sip of the chocolate, eyed Ryan, and pushed the sugar away. "Surprise!"

Ryan laughed. "You're kidding, right?"

Jim shook his head. "Nope. I've been cutting back. Except for the coffee."

This time Ryan rolled his eyes.

Michael walked into the kitchen and went straight to his father. "Bailey was leaving Warren with Noel today. She was taking him home to meet her parents. They were going to get married by New Year's."

Jim nearly spit out his cocoa. "What the hell?"

"They were meeting at the library and then leaving. She had planned it all out."

"We need to get him to talk to Dee."

Michael shook his head. "He won't talk to her or you."

"But he told you," Jim said.

"Yeah, I told him if I said anything it would be hearsay and no one would act on it."

"Did he tell you who killed her?"

Michael shook his head. "Says he doesn't know."

"Damn. Then I need you to talk to Dee. It gives her a starting point. Maybe the girl's family knows something."

"Nope. I'm going to make him a sandwich. I promised him I wouldn't tell Dee. That I'd only tell you. He trusts you."

Michael went to the refrigerator and pulled out sliced turkey and a tomato. Then he grabbed the bread. He started to leave the kitchen.

"Hey, where are you going with that?"

"I'm making Bailey B. a sandwich. Figured I'd take the stuff and see if I could get him to eat more than one. You better call Dee."

Michael left the kitchen.

Jim and Ryan both sat, letting their cocoa grow cold.

"He's…be a great cop," said Ryan.

Jim glared at him. "I swear to God, if he doesn't get drafted to play professional baseball, I'm going to have to kill him."

"Yeah, right," muttered Ryan, drinking his cocoa.

Chapter Ten

J im squeezed his mug of cocoa so hard he thought he might break it, and he didn't care if he did. Michael seemed determined to cause him to have a damn heart attack or stroke or something. Half the time they talked these days, it felt like his head might explode. He missed the days when they'd been on the same page, but he also thought Michael had never been on the same page. He just hadn't wanted to piss off his father.

Ryan ignored Jim's arguments with Michael. He wondered if that irritated Michael the way it did him. They truly did not agree on the path Michael wanted to take. The only thing they had agreed on was the potential for Michael to be drafted by some Major League Baseball team. If Michael did get drafted, he'd give it a shot. If he didn't… Well, that just didn't bear thinking about.

"You're turning purple and…cracked your mug," said Ryan.

Jim looked down. The mug was in one piece.

"Well… you are…purple," said Ryan.

Jim growled. He didn't mean to growl, but that was the sound that had come out of him.

"Stop it. He's great at centerfield… A stroke means you never…see him play."

"Oh, fuck you," muttered Jim.

"No thanks…heterosexual over here…going…Bonehead out…," said Ryan and he put his mug into the sink and left.

Jim pushed his mug aside. Ryan and Michael both were determined to drive him into an early grave. They could deny it all they wanted, but he knew they collaborated about Michael's desire to be hired into the department. It would be over his dead body. Michael needed a life away from Warren. He needed to get out into the world and see that there were other opportunities. If baseball didn't provide it, Jim would find another way for it to happen. Michael would not spend his life in Eden County.

Jim got up and grabbed the receiver for the wall phone and dialed his office. Junior's high thin voice answered the phone, "Sheriff's Office."

"Junior, I need you to radio Dee and have her come to my house after Bud Peterson's finished. Tell her I've got some information she needs."

"Yes, sir. I'll have Manny bring her over soon as they're done. I think FDLE sent someone else this time."

"Oh. I guess I'm so used to Bud, I just think he's going to be the one all the time."

"I understand, Sheriff. It's weird having someone else. Manny said it was a woman, and that she and Dee were not hitting it off."

"Oh boy," muttered Jim.

"Yes, sir."

"Thanks, Junior. Everything else quiet?"

Junior laughed, a strange wheezy sound that Jim found amusing. "We got a bunch of cars in ditches all along 27. Whiteshaw's Towing is making a killing, and the Bambi Motel has completely filled up."

"Oh, Lord," said Jim. "I take it the motel out by the highway is already full, too?"

"Yes, sir. I don't know what people are thinking. The Highway Patrol closes I-75, so they all take off on the old two lanes. You'd think they'd know better."

Jim sighed. "Christmas and family make people do crazy things."

"Yes, sir, it does. You going to be staying home the rest of today?"

"Maybe. Since I have Dee's car and she's going to want it back."

"All right. I'll let you know if something blows up or something."

Jim hung up the phone and went to sit on the couch, and had to shift to make himself comfortable. His bruises had bruises.

He'd never seen a freeze like this one. If the Highway Patrol hadn't closed

I-75, it would have made his life a whole lot easier. Then he thought about Bailey and the young black woman in that DOT box. If I-75 had been open, he probably wouldn't have been out on Highway 27 with Dee and Bobby Dale. Bailey would have died in that place, holding the head of the poor girl he'd loved.

"Shit," he said.

Chapter Eleven

For reasons that still weren't completely clear to him, Ryan found himself standing beside Dee Jackson's patrol car in the parking lot of the County Library. He'd been in the backyard with Bonehead when Jim had asked him to drive to the library and pick up Dee. Which thinking about it, probably meant Jim had some ulterior motive for asking him.

Manny Sota wandered over, leaned against the car, and offered Ryan a cup of coffee. "Annie made it and brought it out. It's not bad."

Ryan took it because at least it would keep his hands warm.

"Where's the Sheriff?"

"Home," said Ryan.

Manny nodded. "Makes about as much sense as everything else going on today." Manny pointed to the two women standing by the Volkswagen Beetle. "I'm figuring unless this woman finishes up her search of the car in the next ten minutes, Dee's going to shoot her."

"Why?"

"Hell if I know. But they've been sniping at each other since she started. I'd consider taking Dee's gun away from her, but I'm afraid she'd shoot me."

They watched the two women glare at each other as the evidence was photographed and put into evidence bags by the other woman.

"Is this Dee's first...murder?"

Manny shook his head. "She seems to be taking it more personal."

"Because the woman was in love with a...white man?"

Manny side-eyed Ryan. "I did not know that."

Ryan swallowed. "Whoops."

"Huh," said Manny. "I think you're on to something. Mackey does spend a lot of time up here in Eden County for a deputy from Levy County."

Ryan made the motion of locking his lips and tossing away the key.

"Let's see… 98 to 2001. You suppose she's just stringing him along?"

"I think I like my testicles, …not going to…think about Dee Jackson's love life. Jim says…she can do…with a knee."

Manny nodded. "It is her specialty. I think it's how she handcuffs 'em all so easy."

Ryan leaned toward Manny, "Jim says he thinks Mackey…likes it."

"That's just twisted," mumbled Manny.

"Yeah," replied Ryan.

"Why are you driving Dee's patrol car?"

"Jim told me to bring it to her…tell her…information."

"Information?"

"I've…said WAY too much."

Dee stomped over to where Manny and Ryan were standing. "What the hell are you doing here, Edwards?"

"Jim…you the car, and tell you…"

Dee waved at Manny. "Go back to whatever you were doing. She's probably going to put a plastic bag over the car before she leaves so that none of us local yokels can touch it and mess with her evidence," Dee said.

She walked around to the driver's side of the car and opened the door. "Are you coming, Edwards?"

"Yes, ma'am!" said Ryan.

Manny rolled his eyes at Ryan and grinned. "You might need a cup. I can see if I can rustle one up for you."

Ryan snorted in disgust and pulled open the passenger door. "You're… menace, Sota."

Manny walked away laughing.

The heat blasted out of the vents. Dee stepped on the gas and practically burned rubber leaving the library parking lot. "All right," said Dee. "What did Michael find out from Bailey?"

"Bailey said…planned to get married…and he was going with her."

"Yeah, that's pretty much what the evidence in the car says. Her phone was in the car and she'd been texting with her mother. She told her she was bringing Bailey down to meet them and that they were going to get married."

"Did her mother know…he's white?"

Dee spit out, "Yes."

"My wife didn't tell her parents before…"

Dee cocked her head toward Ryan. "You divorced?"

"Widower."

"Cancer?"

"Her throat…cut. She bled out."

"Fuck."

"Yeah."

"Where were you?"

"Unconscious. Baseball bat." He touched the scar that was just visible on his forehead.

"Double fuck. Where did this happen?"

"Parking garage in DC."

"I am really sorry, Dr. Edwards."

"Ryan."

"Dee."

"Thank you, Dee."

They drove in silence for a moment.

"I've got the address of Noel Williams' apartment. Dr. Sullivan will be there after the tow for the car arrives. Possibly after she stops for coffee and something to eat. I think that I should do her the favor of clearing the apartment prior to her arrival. Just to make sure it's safe for her to do her job."

Ryan smiled, turning his head down so that hopefully Dee Jackson wouldn't see the smile. "Want…company?…for safety?"

Dee laughed. "Sure. For my safety."

The trip into Gainesville went quickly despite the road conditions and

Dee pulled up outside an older apartment building. A young woman in the office had the key ready for them. She took them upstairs to a one-bedroom apartment on the north side of the building.

She unlocked the door and stood back. "Just let me know when you finish and I'll lock it back up," she said. Dee waited until she had gone back to the stairs before she pulled her gun, motioned for Ryan to stand back, and pushed the door open.

She quickly moved through the small apartment, making sure the place was unoccupied. When she finished she came back to the front door and motioned for Ryan to come inside. She closed the door behind them. She pulled two pairs of gloves from her pockets and handed one set to Ryan. "Put those on, but try not to touch anything."

Ryan took off his shoes and left them by the door. Dee watched him and laughed. "You're probably leaving dog hair from your socks."

Ryan shook his head. "Nope."

He walked into the kitchen. The refrigerator was empty except for a gallon of ice cream in the freezer and a couple of bottles of bubbly water. There were no dishes in the sink, and the shelves were organized and spare.

"...Must not cook...," said Ryan.

Dee answered from behind him. "Or she plans well. They were going away."

He pointed to the lack of spices and the boxes of cereal. "...Don't think so..."

Dee went into the bathroom. He could hear her checking the medicine cabinet and pulling back the shower curtain.

He made a circuit of the small living room. Noel had good taste in furnishings. The room looked comfortable, the bookcase featured textbooks and a handful of paperback novels, most of which were horror. That surprised him. He wouldn't have thought a young woman getting a masters in education would like horror. Then he saw the shelf above had several books by Ntozake Shange and Nikki Giovanni.

Noel's taste in books had definitely run toward poetry. Which meant that the horror...?

Maybe the horror novels weren't hers. He pulled one out of the bookshelf and saw that Bailey Braden's name had been printed boldly on the inside cover. "Book number 3" was written beneath his name.

Dee came out of the bedroom. She had a hardback notebook which she was putting in an evidence bag. "Found this in the bedroom. It's dated from January of this year. It goes through September."

"Diary?" Ryan asked.

"I have never seen one quite like this. Notes about her day, and then several long passages musing about her relationships with sorority sisters, boyfriends, and her identity as a black woman and a teacher. I think it may have been the beginning of a book more than a diary. There are several photographs tucked into the pages. Several of Bailey Braden, but in the earlier pages there is another young man. Matt Wetherford. Looks like she broke off with him about five months ago."

Ryan handed Dee one of the horror books. "Bailey...books he read..."

"Book 3. How many are there?"

He pointed to the shelf and Dee counted. "Six. Pretty impressive for someone who couldn't read when she met him."

"One...a month...?" Ryan said.

"Right about the time she broke off with the young Mr. Wetherford. I imagine he had no idea why."

Ryan nodded. "You...taking...?"

Dee nodded. "Yep. She'd just be turning it over to me later. If she thought I needed it. The current one is probably in her stuff in the car. I'll see how long it takes Dr. Sullivan to release that to me."

Dee went to the front door and Ryan followed her. He picked up his shoes and followed her in the hallway. As he put his shoes back on, Dee knocked at the doors of the other three apartments along the hall. No one answered.

"Probably all students. Everyone's gone for the holidays," said Dee.

They went back to the manager's office and the young woman said she'd be sure to lock it up. Dee and Ryan walked out to her patrol car in the parking lot.

"All right, let's get you back to your dog," said Dee. "I appreciate your

protection."
Ryan laughed.

Chapter Twelve

"Hi, Sgt. Jackson!" Michael said.

"Hey, Michael," answered Dee.

"Sheriff," said Dee.

Jim motioned for her to come on inside and Ryan followed her. "It take this long to process the car?"

"No, Ryan and I took a drive into Gainesville so I could check out Noel Williams' apartment."

"Find anything?"

"Sort of a diary. She wrote about Bailey. Figured it was worth looking over," said Dee.

"What's Dad going to do while you're doing that?"

"He's going to sit his butt in his office and handle paperwork," said Dee.

"Yeah, I'm going to sit in my office and do paperwork. I don't have a car."

"What happened to your car, Dad?"

Dee laughed. "His car is flat as a pancake. Got slammed into a bunch of pine trees by a semi-trailer. Way past saving."

Ryan looked back at Jim. "What?"

"I wasn't in it," said Jim. "It was parked. The semi jack-knifed on the road and slid into it. Took out about three big pines."

"Who's going to protect Bailey B.?"

"Dee figures that a deputy can come each day to the house. I'll take the deputy's car and then return it at the end of their shift and be in the house to watch over Bailey the rest of the time."

"Who...investigates?"

"Sgt. Jackson," said Jim.

Ryan looked from Dee to Jim. "Oh!"

"You have a problem with that, Dr. Edwards?"

Ryan blushed. "No, ma'am. None…"

"Good."

Michael laughed. "I think everyone's afraid of you, Sergeant."

Dee snorted. "They damn well better be. I don't carry a gun because I think it's decorative." She caught Jim's eye. "You're going to be in for the night. I'll get someone sent out to you tomorrow. When you get in the office, you can read my report and let me know if Bailey's given Michael any more information."

"Yes, ma'am," said Jim.

Ryan looked at Dee. "Are you working…by yourself? You should…back you up. Someone shot that woman…"

"Yes, I'm very aware of that. I saw her."

"Ms. Williams…someone…looking for Bailey."

"Likely," she said.

"Another deputy…with you? …you know?"

Jim hmmmed. "Not a bad idea, Dee. You're probably going to need to go down to Tampa to interview the family, see if they had any idea who might want Noel dead."

"And just who are we going to spare to go traipsing around the state with me?"

Ryan raised his hand.

"Put your hand down, Dr. Edwards. What do you have to say?" said Dee.

"I'm off…I could go…to Tampa."

The silence was so severe that they could hear the wind blowing outside.

"It's going to be a death call," Dee said.

"I'm a doctor…done that."

She looked at Jim.

"Wouldn't hurt," said Jim.,

Dee sighed. "All right. I'll take you with me, but you don't talk unless I tell you to, and you do not ask questions unless I ask you to, and you do not eat anything smelly in my car."

Ryan nodded. "Understood."

"I'll pick you up at 6," said Dee. "Bring coffee." She turned on her heel and left through the front door.

Jim smiled. Dee wasn't happy, but it would be good for her to have someone with her. Plus it gave him someone who could report to him what had happened, who'd heard and seen exactly what had been said by everyone. Dee's reports were good, but the woman could be a little spare when it came to details.

Michael nudged Jim's shoulder. "Guess you will be doing paperwork tomorrow."

Jim nodded. "Looks like it."

Chapter Thirteen

R yan checked on Bailey when Michael went in to wake him up. His color was much better and his temperature was normal. Bailey still wanted to be bundled up like Santa Claus, but that was mostly mental. He'd eventually realize he'd gotten fully warm.

"How… you feeling, Bailey?"

"Tired. Sad," Bailey mumbled.

Michael sat on the edge of the bed with one arm wrapped around Bailey's shoulders. Michael leaned his head against Bailey's. "It's okay to be sad."

"He's right," Ryan said. "It is okay…Michael will listen…or me. You…tell us anything."

Bailey shrugged. "Nothing to say."

Michael shook him a little. "I don't think that's true. But you can talk to me, and say as much or as little as you want. Just don't tell me something I can't tell my dad."

Bailey nodded. "Okay."

Michael had a gift for getting people to talk. Ryan had told him things he hadn't even told his parents almost from the first minute he met him. Michael felt safe. He had a way of creating a safe space around him for virtually anyone.

Ryan had watched him lead his baseball team to a state championship in his senior year of high school. He knew all his teammates and their weaknesses and strengths. They trusted him to help them use their abilities in the best way.

From what Ryan had heard, he was still doing that at the University. Ryan had considered him a friend since Michael was 16, which amazed him. He seemed older than he was and he certainly had a maturity that Ryan didn't see in many college-aged people.

In fact, Ryan knew that he'd been a complete idiot at the same age. He wanted to be a doctor, but that didn't keep him from doing incredibly stupid things with his fraternity brothers over Spring Break in his senior year. Luck and white privilege had kept him out of trouble. He damn well knew the truth of that.

Michael, on the other hand, spent his spring breaks doing volunteer work. Ryan had done exactly as much volunteer work as required to get into medical school, and nothing else. Jesus, he'd been a jerk.

Ryan pointed at Bailey. "You…if you start feeling bad, …Michael will get me. All right?"

Bailey nodded.

Jim was in the living room with a cup of coffee idly watching the news out of Gainesville.

"Anything about Noel Williams?"

Jim shook his head. "Fortunately, no. Our favorite reporter, Sheila Ward, took her mother to Miami for Christmas, and no one from Gainesville has picked it up, yet."

"…coffee left?"

Jim moved his head toward the kitchen. Ryan found the pot was hot and nearly full. He might regret it in a few hours, but the heat of the drink would feel good right now. He'd gotten chilled to the bone while waiting for Dee. He went back into the living room and dropped down on the end of the couch.

"What's…topic?"

"I-75 being closed at the state line. They say it could be Christmas Eve or even Christmas Day before it opens up again."

"That's not…help your guys."

"Nope. Every idiot heading south is going to take US 27."

"Fun, fun," said Ryan. "Do …need…check you?"

"I'm fine. Bruised, but nothing else."

They both sipped at their coffee and watched the sports news. The news ended with an ad for Mariah Carey's "Home for the Holidays."

"Oh, hell no," said Jim and he turned the tv off.

"You don't like Mariah?" Ryan asked.

"I'd rather be beat in the head with a hammer than watch a Christmas music special."

Ryan laughed. "Scrooge."

"This has been a hell of a day."

Ryan nodded. It had been. A young woman was dead, and Bailey Braden could have died if Jim and Dee hadn't found him. Ryan sighed.

"What are you sighing about?" asked Jim.

"I know...feels."

"I know you do," said Jim.

"Losing...love... You don't get over it."

"Did he say anything when you were with him?"

"Just...tired and sad...nothing to say."

Jim closed his eyes and rubbed his forehead. "Bailey is a chatterbox. If he has nothing to say, that means he's either scared or protecting someone."

"Why...protect...killed Noel?"

Jim shook his head. "Maybe if it had something to do with Noel. Something that would hurt her family or reputation. Bailey's sensitive about stuff like that, and he loved her." Jim was silent for a moment. "Or it has something to do with his mother. He loves her, too."

"Filly doesn't...like her."

Jim nodded. "Not many people do. China Braden has spent most of her life crossing the line that's going to make her life end very badly. Her parents kept her out of trouble when they were alive, but once they were gone, she's upped the ante every year."

"Poor Bailey."

"Yeah. Yeah, he's the big loser in anything having to do with his mother." Jim looked at Ryan, seeming to study his face.

"What...you thinking?" asked Ryan.

"You volunteering to go with Dee to talk to Noel Williams' family. You haven't spent a lot of time around Dee. What made you do it?"

"You...couldn't...the investigation."

"So you're doing this for me?"

Ryan rocked his head back and forth a little. "Maybe...a little. Mostly... wasn't a good idea...go alone."

"She wouldn't be going alone. I'd send someone with her."

"Oh." Ryan found himself blushing. "I can...I mean I don't have...I'll stay here. Help you watch Bailey."

Jim smiled and laughed. "Oh, hell no. You offered you're going. You're going to tell me everything that happens, and if you're off until New Year's Eve, you can maybe go with her to Gainesville and when she talks to Bailey's mom."

Ryan felt the blood drain from his face. He had set himself up to be Jim's proxy, with Dee Jackson, the toughest deputy in the entire Eden County Sheriff's Department. A department that included numerous veterans, including Manny Sota who had been a sniper in Iraq. Dee Jackson had been Military Police. She had spent her military career rousting rowdy Marines and investigating crimes committed under the circumstances of battle in a foreign country.

"Oh God," Ryan moaned.

Jim laughed loudly and put his hand on Ryan's shoulder. "Yeah, it's going to be tough, but you're definitely the man for the job."

"Jim, Dee...eat me alive...screw up this investigation."

Jim grinned. "Yes, she will. So you better mind her. Remember, you do what she says and keep your mouth shut unless she says she wants you to speak. You'll be fine."

Ryan put his head in his hands. What had he done?

Chapter Fourteen

Ryan left to take Bonehead for a walk. The dog loved the cold weather, but it got dark early, so Ryan usually took him over to the high school and walked him around the schoolyard. There weren't many people on the road, but Ryan wasn't one to take chances. Bonehead was always enthusiastic about walks, and he'd been hyper in the cold.

Jim saw Michael walk Bailey to the bathroom, then get him a towel, washcloth, and some sweats to put on. Bailey probably needed a good hot shower. He'd been soaked in the girl's blood when they found him. She had lived for a while after being shot, but he doubted she'd have been conscious. Jim was glad about that.

Michael came into the living room and dropped down on the couch, bouncing Jim a little. The boy weighed more than Jim these days, and he was a good three or four inches taller.

"I told Bailey he'd feel better if he took a good hot shower. He says he still feels cold."

"I think he might have died if Ryan hadn't been here," Jim said.

Michael rubbed the top of his head.

"Got a headache?"

"Yeah," he said. "I can't get Bailey to tell me anything. I warned him that I'd have to tell you, so he's shut up tighter than a tick."

"Want something for the headache?"

"How about food, a soda, and a couple of aspirin."

"You got it."

Jim walked into the kitchen and Michael followed him. "Help me listen for the water cutting off. If it doesn't happen in the next twenty minutes, I'll need to go check to see if he fell asleep in the tub," Michael said.

Jim checked the refrigerator. "How about grilled cheese and tomato soup?" he asked.

Michael's stomach growled.

"I'll take that as a yes. Do you think Bailey will want to eat?"

Michael shrugged. "I don't know, Dad. I've never seen him like this. He ought to eat, so go ahead and fix something for him. If he doesn't eat it, you and I can split it."

Michael opened a cabinet and pulled out a bottle of aspirin. He dumped two into his hand. Jim pulled a can of cola out of the refrigerator and handed it to him. Michael popped it open and the fizz sounded loud in the kitchen.

Jim could hear the shower running. It hadn't been long enough for Michael to check on Bailey, yet. He worried, though. Bailey had taken care of himself for years. He was a man, nearly twenty-one years old, and making his own way. Limited as it was. But if it was true, and Noel had taught him to read, if her death didn't destroy him, she'd given him two big gifts. One was love and the other was a path to something other than being a busboy at the Magnolia restaurant for the rest of his life.

As Jim put the sandwiches on plates, he heard the shower cut off. He looked at Michael and he nodded. "I'll go check on Bailey."

Jim put the sandwiches back in the pan and covered them, setting them on the back of the stove. The soup was hot and ready to eat.

When Michael returned with Bailey, they each took a seat at the kitchen table. Jim quickly put a sandwich on each plate, then filled two bowls with soup and set them in front of the young men. He got his own sandwich and bowl of soup and sat down with them.

Bailey's eyes stayed down on the food. He ate slowly.

Michael's eyebrow was raised at Jim, and he tilted his head toward Bailey. It made him think of a quote from an old cartoon series that his father used to quote, "That boy's about as subtle as a hand grenade in a bowl of oatmeal."

Jim set his sandwich down and spoke to Bailey. "How are you feeling?"

Bailey shrugged and didn't answer. He just continued to doggedly eat his sandwich and soup.

"The guest room is yours for a while. Michael and I both think you should stay here at least until after the holidays."

Bailey's eyes rose to meet Jim's. "Why?"

"We want to make sure you're safe."

Bailey shook his head. "Doesn't matter. Noel's gone."

Michael reached over and put his hand on Bailey's arm. "It does matter. She wouldn't want anything to happen to you. We don't want anything to happen to you. Whoever killed her, Dee will find them."

Bailey shook his head. "No."

"What do you mean, Bailey?" asked Jim.

"I was too late. Noel was dying when I got there. I rode as fast as I could. They just left her there to die alone."

"Who left her to die?" asked Jim.

Bailey shook his head.

"If you know something you should tell me," Jim said. "I saw your bike, Bailey. Someone ran over it. Someone else was there."

Bailey shook his head. "I heard someone come back. They didn't come in. They waited a little bit and then left."

"What did it sound like?" asked Michael. "Car? Truck?"

Baily looked at Michael. "Big. Deep motor sound, had to be a big truck." He closed his eyes and they were all quiet. "Diesel. It was a diesel engine. Chugged, you know how they do that?"

"Yeah, Bailey. I do. So probably a diesel truck," said Michael. He glanced up at Jim and Jim nodded.

"Thanks, Bailey. I'll tell Dee that. It will help."

Bailey finished his sandwich. His soup bowl sat on the table empty. He set his bowl on his plate and got up from the table. "I'll wash the dishes."

"You don't have to do that," Jim started.

Bailey interrupted him. "I do. I need to do something. Can't...can't keep sleeping. I just dream about her." He went to the sink, plugged it, and began to run water into it.

Michael got up from the table carrying his plate and bowl over. "I'll dry. I know where things go," he said.

Jim quietly got up from the table. He needed to talk to Dee, and her shift was over. She would be home by now.

Chapter Fifteen

The heat blasted against Ryan's body in Dee Jackson's patrol car. Her dress uniform looked crisp, if not particularly warm. Ryan had on his overcoat from his years in DC, with gloves, thick socks on his feet, and a scarf. He had a tuque in his pocket, but he'd made the decision to try not to put it on his head until after they had seen Noel Williams' family. It tended to flatten his hair, and he wanted to look professional and reassuring to them.

He'd handed Dee a travel mug of coffee, and he had his own reliable exactly one-cup mug. When she'd called the night before to set the time she'd pick him up, he'd asked her how she took her coffee. Her response had made him laugh.

"I take it like a good black woman. Dark and just a little sweet," she'd said.

She'd shown up exactly when she'd said she would, which he'd expected. He'd been downstairs waiting outside between the garage and Jim's house. When he got into the car the first thing she'd said was, "You are dressed like a true Yankee."

"I am...Yankee," he said.

"That coat wool?"

"Yes."

"Lord a mercy, I have never seen a man wear a coat that long."

"It's...sensible," said Ryan.

Dee nodded. "Yep, for a Yankee like you. This is not Florida winter. This is some Yankee shit that has been brought down upon us. We're taking US 98 down to Tampa. I'm staying the hell off Highway 27. I'd like to get to

Tampa and back alive," said Dee.

"You're...driver," Ryan said.

The silence lay heavily on them for a minute.

"How's Jackie?" asked Ryan, desperate to find a neutral topic of conversation.

"Gorgeous, smart, and perfectly trained," said Dee.

"Figures."

Dee laughed. "She's way too smart to be anything but perfectly trained. That dog also reads people like no person I've ever met. She manipulates Tim something awful. But the man is a closet romantic."

Ryan laughed. "He seemed...nice... I've talked to him."

"So how's Bonehead?"

"...Happier... Michael's home... m ...Jim...poor subs... for Michael."

"Bites the hand that feeds him, huh?"

"Sometimes...doesn't like fish. Doc gave fish...twice. He nipped me...the second time."

"You ever think to stop feeding it to him?"

"...Off menu permanently."

Dee chuckled as she made her way onto US 98 and began heading south. The road looked deserted, except for the occasional semi. Dee drove below the speed limit. Ryan knew it wasn't so she could spend more time with him.

"I hope we'll get down to where there is no ice soon. I do not like this shit."

"Things good...with Tim?"

"Really?"

"...wrong?

The tires slid for a moment and then gripped the road again. Dee let out a relieved sigh. "No, not wrong."

A loaded silence followed.

"I want to ask you something and if you don't want to answer, just tell me so," Dee said.

"I will."

"Did you fall in love with her because she was different? I mean, did her being black make her exotic or something?"

Ryan shook his head and stared out through the windshield. "No…She was funny, smart…I took her out…realized this…woman I wanted to marry… Had to convince her."

"You should know pretty much everyone knows you were married to a black woman."

"How?"

"Junior's daddy, Senior, told Junior that Filly told him you were married to a black woman and that she'd died in the attack that left you with brain damage."

Ryan looked at Dee with surprise. "What?"

"Filly and Senior are brother and sister. Filly tells Senior things and Senior repeats them to Junior."

"…that family and names!"

Filly laughed. "Started with Filly and Senior's daddy. He thought Senior sounded distinguished and Filly sounded pretty. Senior figured he'd name his son after himself, but instead of calling him Senior, Jr., he just called him Junior."

"Weird."

"Says the man with a dog named Bonehead."

Dee and Ryan both laughed.

"Tim says he fell in love with me when I put Billy Dustin on the ground in less than a minute. He thought that was cool, and he decided right then that he was going to get me to go out with him."

"You…scare the crap…me," said Ryan.

Dee nodded. "You're a sane man. I'm not so sure about Tim Mackey."

Chapter Sixteen

Deputy Waylon Forest showed up at Jim's house just before 8 am. He knocked on the front door. When Jim opened it Waylon said quickly, "Junior said Dee said I'm supposed to come here, let you take my car and I'm to stay here all through my shift and protect a witness."

"Yes, that's right. Come on in and have a cup of coffee while I go brush my teeth."

Jim took the Deputy into the kitchen. Michael and Bailey were still eating. "Good morning, Deputy Forest," said Michael.

"Morning. Hey Bailey, you doing all right?" Waylon asked.

Bailey shrugged. "I'm alive. Better than being dead."

"True fact," said Waylon and he sat down and took the cup of coffee Jim offered him.

Jim headed down the hall to the bathroom. He knew that Michael would handle the interactions and keep Bailey and the Deputy from coming to odds. Damn, it made things easier having Michael here. He just had a knack for helping people get along.

* * *

Junior had the desk well under control as usual. Buck Neville had a stranger sitting next to a desk in the bullpen. The man had a huge knot on his forehead, but otherwise seemed fine. What was odd was that Jim had no idea who the man was. That didn't happen in Eden County, and now it had happened twice in two days.

59

"What's going on?" Jim asked Junior softly.

Junior looked over at the man and grinned. "Mr. Henderson there stopped at the Motel 27 out on the highway and got into it with Wayne Wilbur about him not having a room available. He took a swing at Wayne and Wayne clocked him with his clipboard."

"Wayne pressing charges?"

"No. Buck felt sorry for him and he's calling Elsie to see if she'll put him up for the night. Doc said he's got a concussion and he shouldn't drive."

"Elsie going to do it?"

"Yeah, but she's arguing with Buck about whether he's going to take the guy to her or she's going to pick him up."

Jim nodded and headed on into his office. If Buck Neville thought he was going to win an argument with Elsie Sanborne, Eden's unofficial official caretaker, he was not thinking clearly.

A short time later Jim heard the Duster pull up in front of the Sheriff's office. Elsie marched into the office wearing an orange fleece covered with a camouflage down vest. "Mr. Henderson?" she called out.

The man stood up. He had a rolling suitcase next to him.

"Elsie Sanborne, Mr. Henderson. Let me get you back to the house so you can rest. Looks like Wayne gave you a big ol' goose egg."

"I deserved it. I was being a jerk," said Mr. Henderson sadly.

"Stressful times, sir. Stressful times."

As they started for the front door, Junior exclaimed, "Ms. Elsie, are those snow tires?"

That got Jim out of his chair and into the main office. Elsie Sanborne laughed. "Yes, they are. Ordered those special through McClain's."

Jim had to ask, "Why?"

Elsie turned to him and grinned. "Jim Sheppard, there will never be a day that I can't make it through the weather to be where I'm needed. We had a freeze near as bad as this one when I was a child. Figured it was likely to happen again someday."

Elsie escorted Mr. Henderson out of the office and got him and his luggage settled into the orange Plymouth Duster. The car had been Danny

Sanborne's pride and joy, and Elsie had made it her mission in life to keep it in vintage condition. Jim knew it was a memorial of a sort to the man she had married.

"I wonder how much snow tires would cost for my Lincoln," said Junior.

Jim didn't answer. But he knew that McClain's was going to be ordering a brand new set of snow tires for a 1998 Lincoln Navigator. Jim sighed and just went back into his office to finish working on next month's schedule.

Chapter Seventeen

Very little conversation interrupted the drive to Tampa. The traffic on the road was light and once they were south of Levy County the roads were clear of ice. Other than a couple of stops for coffee and bathroom breaks, they made good time down US 98 to where it joined with 19 and went down into the Tampa area.

"Can I help... directions?" asked Ryan, once they arrived in Tampa proper.

Dee handed over directions she had printed out. "We're going to Hyde Park. A very nice area of this lovely city, and right outside of the University of Tampa."

"...a tour?"

Dee laughed. "Yeah, it's pretty down here. The first time I saw this campus I thought it was one of the coolest places ever. It's got those onion-top buildings. You'll see."

Sure enough, Ryan could see the minarets as they got closer to the neighborhood. "Wow."

"Used to be a fancy hotel for Victorian types to spend the winter. I don't know when it became a college. It's always been one since I've been around."

The only places Ryan had seen in Florida before he moved to Eden County had been in South Florida, Ft. Lauderdale to be exact. His research into North Florida before his move enlightened him to the fact that there was a huge difference in the two parts of the state. "Florida...different," said Ryan.

Dee nodded. "I like Eden County. It may be a little barren in some ways, but I like the trees and the river and how quiet it is. At least unless you go near one of the camping areas in the middle of the summer. Then you get bombarded with Lynyrd Skynyrd and a lot of drunken whooping."

"Here's our turn," said Ryan. Dee turned right, heading south on South Boulevard, and then took another right and they found themselves on Tesla Avenue. The street was lined with trees and manicured lawns. The houses varied from brick two-stories to small bungalows. Dee pulled the car up in front of a handsome two-story home. Christmas lights glowed around the eaves and a huge wreath decorated the door.

"Do they know...?" asked Ryan.

"It's against procedure. However, since we know they were expecting Noel yesterday, I'm sure they will be here. I would be."

The two of them looked at the lovely house and the silence held as they opened their car doors and exited out onto the sidewalk in front of the home. As they walked up the walkway to the house the front door opened. A stocky dark-skinned man stood in the doorway. He wore a long-sleeved dress shirt, open at the neck, and dark gray slacks.

Ryan felt the hair on the back of his neck stand up. The stoic look the man wore reminded him far too much of Danielle's father the last time they had seen each other.

When they reached the step up to the front door the man raised his chin and spoke, "You're here about Noel."

"Yes, sir," answered Dee. "Deputy Dee Jackson, Eden County Sheriff's Office. This is Dr. Ryan Edward."

"She's dead."

"Yes, sir. She is."

The man stepped back and waved them into the foyer. The house smelled of holiday cooking. Little touches of Christmas decorations sat on small tables. A woman stood in the doorway to another room. "Anita, these people have come to talk to us about Noel."

Tears filled the woman's eyes, but she didn't tremble. "Come sit down, please," she said. She led them into a living room with furniture in shades of green and cream. It seemed as formal as the man who had met them at the door.

Ryan and Dee took a seat a short distance apart on the couch. The man and his wife sat opposite them on a smaller loveseat. The delicate coffee table between them made a poor barrier for the news they carried.

"I'm Nehemiah Williams. My wife is Anita. Noel's brother and sister have not arrived yet for the holidays. What can you tell us that we can share with them about Noel?"

Dee held her uniform hat on her lap. "I'm very sorry, I am here to notify you that your daughter is dead."

"Murdered?" Anita asked.

"Yes, ma'am."

"What about her young man?"

"He's in protective custody. We are concerned for his safety."

"Do you know who killed her?" asked Nehemiah.

"No, sir. We do not. We were hoping that perhaps you could shed some light on what was happening with your daughter recently," said Dee.

Anita spoke first, "Noel and I were texting. She was getting ready to leave Gainesville and go to Warren to pick up Bailey. They planned to be married before New Year's. She said that once she got to Eden County she would have limited service, but that she would keep her phone on. She wanted to text when they left so we would know when to expect them. They thought if they left early, before his shift at the restaurant was to start that no one would realize they'd left until they were already gone."

Dee made quick notes in a small notebook. "They expected possible trouble?"

The woman nodded her head and tears began to run down her face. "Noel said someone had seen them together outside the library, and that Bailey was worried."

"I spoke with Bailey earlier this week," said Nehemiah.

Anita looked surprised. Dee waited for the man to say more.

"He called the house while you were out shopping. He told me he was concerned for Noel, but that she insisted she would come and pick him up. He had offered to bicycle to a point out of town, but she said no. He said someone named Finley had seen them together, and he could not make her understand how dangerous it might be for her. He asked me to talk to her."

Anita gasped. "Did you? Did you talk to her?"

He nodded. "She told me she would be all right. I explained that Bailey had called, and she said that she'd have a conversation with Bailey about that later. She said she was not going to change her plans because of some ignorant redneck who 'might' have seen them."

He shook his head. "Noel was proud and strong, and she refused to be afraid."

Anita looked at Dee Jackson. "I'm sure you know how she felt."

"Yes, ma'am. I do."

Nehemiah took his wife's hand. "Can we help Bailey? Noel loved him, and we know he loved her very much."

"I don't think there's much you can do right now," said Dee. "Bailey told you Finley had seen them?"

"Yes. He was clear about that. He said that he didn't know Finley's last name. That no one had ever used it. He said Finley liked to make trouble."

"Thank you. That will help. I'm glad that Bailey spoke to you. He hasn't told us about Finley, but I'm sure that we'll be able to find out who he is. If he's responsible for Noel's death, we will arrest him." Dee took a breath, "The Sheriff of Eden County is Jim Sheppard. He's a good man and I will ask him to keep you up to date. I will also be sure that the Medical Examiner has your names and phone number so he can contact you himself."

"Thank you. Bailey Braden is a good man. He has got a good heart, and he's smart. I know he's not educated, but he's smart. All he wanted to do was love and protect Noel. I can assure you of that," Nehemiah said.

Dee stood up and reluctantly Ryan stood up with her. As she started for the door, Ryan stopped and held out his hand to Nehemiah Williams. As they shook, Ryan spoke slowly, carefully finding the words he wanted to say. "My deepest...condolences, sir. Bailey...found Noel. He...with her. He couldn't... He would not leave...her... She was not alone."

Anita reached out and touched Ryan's hand. "Thank you."

Nehemiah stood up and put is other hand on top of Ryan's. "Yes, thank you. I'm glad she wasn't alone. I'm sure that her spirit knew Bailey was there with her."

Ryan followed Dee out to her car. She started the car quickly and pulled away from in front of the house.

"I'm sorry…without you saying I could," said Ryan.

"Shut up, Ryan. You did more than I could do. You gave them some comfort."

Dee gunned the engine and they headed back to the north.

Chapter Eighteen

Junior appeared in Jim's office doorway. He had a big smile on his face. Junior generally smiled, but this one made Jim suspicious. He narrowed his eyes at Junior, who smiled even bigger. "I got a text message."

Jim rolled his eyes. Richie Libby had connected with several local businesses, and they had expanded the number of cell towers in Eden County to a grand total of twelve. The minute the towers were built, cell phones had started appearing in the populace. As far as Jim could see it was just one more way to keep poor people poor. He refused to give in and still used the radio to communicate with the deputies spread out through the county.

Junior, however, had invested in a phone just in the last month and was unsettlingly enamored of it.

"And?" Jim said.

"It was from Doc Edwards."

That made sense. Ryan bought a phone as soon as the roaming fees stopped on his plan. He used it mostly for when he was on-call, so he didn't have to stay in his apartment over Jim's garage.

"And?" Jim said.

"Bailey Braden called Noel Williams' father and told him that someone named Finley had seen him and Noel at the library together and that he was worried. He wanted her dad to convince her to let him meet her outside of town. But she wasn't having it."

Junior raised his phone and read, "She said she wasn't going to change her plans because of one ignorant redneck who might have seen them."

"Finley first or last name?" asked Jim.

"First name. He told Mr. Williams he didn't know the guy's last name."

"Huh." Jim ran the name through his mind and he couldn't connect it to anyone he knew.

"I did a search on the first name in our records. We've never arrested anyone with the first name Finley."

"Ryan say anything else?"

"He said they're going to Gainesville now because Dee found the professor who was supervising Noel Williams' graduate program. She wants to talk to the woman. She also has a possible lead on a sorority sister who was going to be in Gainesville over the holidays to stay with her boyfriend."

Jim wondered if he should try to talk to Bailey about this Finley. Or maybe Michael would know the guy.

"It's pretty close to lunchtime," said Junior.

Jim rolled his eyes. "Okay, what is it you want?"

"Sweet Ella's is running a special on their pulled chicken sandwiches."

"Got it. I'll bring you lunch, you cover the office. Deal?"

"Yes, sir, Sheriff!"

Jim stopped at Sweet Ella's on his way home, figuring that maybe barbecue would get Bailey to talk a little more freely. If not to him, maybe to Michael. He had Junior's lunch as well and took it inside the house to tuck into the oven so it would stay warm until he got back to the office.

Waylon Forest practically followed his nose to Jim while he was in the kitchen. He came in sniffing. "Did you buy Junior Sweet Ella's?" he asked.

"Yours is on the table."

Waylon whooped and plopped down in one of the wooden chairs. "Oh my Lord, it's pulled chicken and sweet potato fries. Sir, you have made my day."

Jim shook his head and walked down the hall to see where Michael and Bailey were. He found them lounging on the bed in Jim's room, with the smaller TV turned on to a Christmas cartoon.

"I brought lunch," Jim said leaning against the bedroom door. "Sweet

Ella's pulled chicken and sweet potato fries."

Michael's stomach audibly growled.

"I'll take that as a yes to lunch."

Bailey laughed and rolled off the bed. "I'll eat, too."

"Good. Let's all go before Deputy Forest starts foraging among the other lunches."

Bailey moved past Jim in the doorway. When Michael came close, Jim reached out and pulled him into a one-armed hug. "How is it going?"

Michael made a see-sawing motion with his hand. "He's up and down. I turned on the cartoon because I thought it would make him laugh. He likes Cindy-Lou Who."

Bailey had disappeared down the hall into the kitchen. They could hear him talking with Deputy Forest. Jim held the back of Michael's neck, feeling the short hair bristle against his hand. He used a lot less product these days and no longer looked like he had perpetual bedhead. Jim liked it better.

"What's going on, Dad?"

"Do you know someone with the first name of Finley?"

Michael thought for a moment. "Doesn't sound familiar."

"Bailey called his girlfriend's father and told him he was worried that Finley had seen him with Noel."

Michael nodded. "You want me to ask him about Finley."

"Only if you think you can do it without scaring him off. We need to keep Bailey safe. I'm afraid if we push, he'll take off."

"He probably would. I'll let you know."

Jim pulled Michael to him again and took a deep breath, getting the scent of his son in his head. The smell had changed over the years as he grew and matured. But the basic smell of son, family, was always there underneath. "Promise me you won't let Bailey talk you into doing something stupid," he whispered.

"Dad," Michael hugged him back. "I don't do stupid anymore. I just do ill-advised."

Jim smiled, knowing Michael could feel it against the side of his face. "Well, don't be doing anything ill-advised, either. Okay?"

"Okay."

They walked down the hall, going to rescue their lunches from Waylon Forest and Bailey.

Chapter Nineteen

Ryan found himself drifting into silence as he listened to the tires on the pavement. It wasn't until he felt the car slip a little and the crack of ice under them that he and Dee spoke to each other again.

"I hate this weather," muttered Dee.

"I'll have to say I haven't missed it," said Ryan. "I had this…in the closet. I'd…forgotten…gloves and tuque in…pockets."

"Tuque? That's what you call a stocking cap?"

"Stocking cap? That's…a tuque?" Ryan responded.

They grinned at each other. There hadn't been much to raise their spirits on this trip. The visit with Noel Williams' parents had been damned depressing.

"Where to…?" asked Ryan.

"Professor's house. She was pretty upset about the news, and wanted to help if she could."

"Then…sorority sister?"

Dee shuddered.

"Wait, what…?"

"Sororities make me itch."

Ryan worked to suppress his laugh. "Wow… No sorority?"

Dee cut her eyes toward Ryan. "Yeah, like they want a sister that just got back from Iraq where she served in the Military Police during Desert Storm. They were looking for experience in handling POWs and refugees."

"Sorry."

"Frat boy."

"Yes... Legacy for Sigma Chi."

"Am I supposed to be impressed?" Dee asked.

"Very," said Ryan.

Dee snorted. "Right. Rich white boys."

"Very rich white boys," said Ryan. "And I...the worst. Thought I was...hot shit."

"And you don't think you're such hot shit anymore?"

Ryan laughed out loud. "Danielle...fixed..."

"So the doctor didn't cure himself?"

Ryan shook his head. "No, the...smart...woman did. Put me in my place."

"Good for her."

"Yes," said Ryan.

Dee reached over and patted Ryan on the leg.

Ryan smiled as Dee focused on the road. The road definitely got worse the closer they got to Eden and Alachua Counties. The temperature had dropped considerably in the past hour. Dee slowed as the ice became heavier on the pavement. She stayed with the two-lane roads and brought them into Alachua County from the southwest. When they hit 441 the road went completely to shit. Dee slowed to a crawl and they made their way into town and to an older neighborhood in the northwest. The houses were mostly frame. A few had been maintained well, while others had fallen into disrepair.

They pulled up to a smaller home with a chain link fence and a paved drive. The house itself was painted a faded orange. Dee parked on the street in front of the house.

"Keep my mouth shut... Let you do...talking," Ryan said.

"It's almost like you're listening to me," said Dee.

She opened the gate and they started up the paver walkway. The front door to the house opened when they were about halfway up the walk. The woman who stepped out of the house was tall with short hair, no make-up, and a dignified bearing.

When they reached the porch, Dee handed the woman her card and spoke, "Dr. Oluco, we spoke yesterday. I'm Sergeant Dee Jackson from the Eden

County Sheriff's Office."

"Come in, Sergeant." She looked at Ryan. "And this man?"

"Dr. Ryan Edwards of Eden County. He saved the life of the young man who loved Noel."

The woman nodded. "Please, come in. I have coffee."

"Thank you," said Ryan.

The living room of the house was warm and welcoming. The space had woven art on the walls and Ryan noticed a large, rather crude wooden carving on a pedestal in one corner. Dee stopped in front of it. "Is this...?"

Dr. Oluco smiled. "Yes, an original Jesse Aaron. I was very fortunate. A friend had one he'd acquired many years ago when Jesse first began his work. When he died, I found out he had left it to me. He knew how envious I was of it."

Ryan studied the sculpture. The wood was rough, the image of the face broad, but strangely expressive. "I like it."

"Your Doctor is a clever man," said Dr. Oluco to Dee.

Dee smiled. "He knows which side his bread is buttered on."

Dr. Oluco threw her head back and laughed loudly. "I like you, Dee Jackson. You, too, Dr. Edwards. Please, have a seat. I'll get the coffee."

Once they had settled onto the couch and Dr. Oluco in an overstuffed chair, Dee began her questions about Noel Williams.

"Yes, Noel talked to me a great deal about Bailey. She met him when she was having lunch at this restaurant, The Magnolia. She began chatting to him whenever she was there. I think he appealed to her. Noel had a soft spot for a certain type of young man. She particularly liked young white men of that type," said Dr. Oluco.

"What type was that?" Dee asked.

"Kind men. Men of sweet temperament and gentle ways. She found them to be very rare and very special. Bailey also had a gift for making her laugh. When she discovered that he could not read, she offered to teach him. She spoke of how he said he was 'too stupid to learn' and that she would prove to him that this was not true. Noel believed that everyone could learn. Each at their own level, but they could learn."

"I've been told she met him weekly at the library in Warren, and that she successfully taught him enough for him to pass his GED. "

Dr. Oluco laughed. "Oh yes. Once she taught him to read, there was no stopping him. He wanted to learn everything. He read book after book, going from primers to young adult in a matter of just a few months. He understood math more than reading. She said he studied hard, worked very hard every night after he finished work, and that within six months he was at a high school comprehension of all the basics. Despite his idea that he was too stupid, he had obviously learned some things from being in school. He knew his basic math and had memorized the multiplication tables. Words were hard, numbers easier. They didn't form sounds that defied his comprehension. I believe her testing of him indicated dysgraphia and language processing disorder."

Ryan remembered a child he'd once treated in the ER. "Language processing disorder? That can be...head trauma."

Dr. Oluco looked at him, searching his face for something. Her eyes settled on the scar that trailed out of his hairline onto his forehead. "Aphasia?" she asked.

Ryan nodded. "Yes."

"And you continue to practice medicine?"

"I...trauma specialist. Now I treat colds...diabetes, things."

She nodded. "You made a remarkable recovery."

"I worked hard," he said.

Dee looked at Ryan, her eyes narrowed as though she was reading his face.

"Noel didn't know what caused Bailey's problems. He said he didn't remember his childhood very well and had no idea about whether he'd been born premature."

Dee turned back to Dr. Oluco. "Noel have any suspicions?"

"Noel was very perceptive of small behavioral hints. She believed he had been abused, and possibly was still being abused. She said he had bruises sometimes that he claimed he'd gotten bussing tables or riding his bike."

Dee said, "I imagine she was right. China Braden has never been known for her good qualities, and she's had a series of boyfriends who had records for assault, among other things. She likes them mean."

"China Braden. His mother?"

"Yes," said Dee.

"Noel did not know about her. Bailey talked about his grandparents. They are both dead?"

"They raised him, and he lived with them until he was about 17. They both died within months of each other. China inherited the house and moved into it. Bailey moved out. He's lived in an apartment over the laundromat since then."

Dr. Oluco thought for a moment. "Noel was going to marry this young man."

"That's what we were told," said Dee.

"This all makes sense. This is why he was scared for her."

Ryan couldn't stop himself from interrupting, "She told you about Finley?"

Dr. Oluco shook her head. "When they decided to get married, Noel brought him here for me to meet. She wanted my blessing. He asked me to explain to Noel why they needed to be careful in Eden County. I never heard any names, but he was worried, and Noel brushed it off. She's a... was a child of this century and privileged. She believed that she could protect herself. That no one would dare to hurt the child of a physician and a professor at the University of Tampa."

Dee Jackson shook her head. "She didn't pay attention."

"No, she didn't. And she didn't listen. I know she is dead. I knew that from her parents. How did she die?"

"She was shot at close range."

Dr. Oluco began to shed tears, but her voice didn't shake. "Such a great loss to the world. She would have been an amazing teacher. She would have been a good wife to Bailey. He was perfect for her. White, cute, and damaged."

There was silence in the room. Then Dee continued with her questions. "Did you discuss with her the warnings from Bailey?"

"Yes. I told her that some parts of the world did not care about her privilege. That the color of her skin defined who she was. She refused to be afraid."

"That no ignorant redneck was going to make her change her plans," said Dee.

Dr. Oluco nodded.

Dee stood up and offered her hand to Dr. Oluco. "Thank you for taking the time to see us. I'm very sorry for your loss."

"Thank you," Dr. Oluco said softly. "And you, Dr. Edwards, you will stay in Eden County and be a doctor?"

"Yes, ma'am," he said.

Dr. Oluco smiled. "Come and see me again. I think you would enjoy visiting me. We can talk. I am very patient, and I can wait for your words."

Ryan felt a rush of blood to his face, making even his ears probably pulsate with red. "Thank you... I will."

Chapter Twenty

At nearly six o'clock, Jim had gotten payroll approved, the next month's schedule nearly completed, and dealt with a half dozen calls from County Commissioners complaining about the weather. He knew they just needed to air their grievances, but it irritated him that he took the bulk of their calls. Only three of his Captains had enough sense to deal with the Commissioners without making promises that couldn't be kept. The others were good officers but tended to fold under the pressure of the politicians who held the purse strings to the department.

Jim turned off the computer on his desk. He hated the damn thing, but Junior had finally convinced him he had to learn how to use it and the scheduling software. It did cut down on the time it took him to read reports and do the scheduling, once he'd finally mastered it.

The first time he'd come into his office and found the computer sitting there, he'd threatened to fire Junior. Then Junior had reminded him that he was the only one who actually knew how to use the damn software and Jim needed him. He'd retaliated by going to Sweet Ella's and not bringing Junior anything back.

Junior had retaliated by making Jim read the manual on the software.

They'd called a truce after that, and Jim had gotten up to speed. He would never be completely comfortable with the computer, but he had made peace with it.

The phone rang at the front desk and Jim considered slipping out past Junior while he was answering it, but his better side made him sit back in his chair and wait to see if it was for him.

The phone on Jim's desk buzzed and he picked it up. "It's for you, Sheriff."
Jim sighed. "Fine."

"It's Michael."

Jim picked up the line. "Michael, what's up? Need something for dinner?"

"Bailey's gone."

Jim hung up the phone and grabbed his jacket. "Junior, I've got to go. I'm not available to anyone unless it's Dee or Doc Ryan." Jim heard Junior say, "Yes, sir" as he closed the door and headed for his car.

Despite the ice, Jim drove over the speed limit. He slid into his driveway and had to steer into the yard to keep from hitting Michael's truck. Michael stood in the doorway as he hurried up the walk.

"What happened? Where's Waylon?"

Michael pulled his father inside and rushed him down the hall to the master bedroom. He could see Waylon following tracks that led into the woods in back of the house. "Bailey went out the window. He told me he was going to shower. I went into the kitchen to talk to Waylon. When the water didn't cut off after about twenty minutes, I banged on the door and he didn't answer. I opened the door and no Bailey. He turned it on, then slipped out through the window in your room."

"Son of a bitch," said Jim.

He rushed outside and joined Waylon in the search. The frozen grass showed where Bailey had entered the woods, but there was no way of tracking him through the debris under the trees. They both circled in different directions trying to pick up where Bailey might have left the woods, but they couldn't find a trace.

Waylon looked sorrowful. "I'm sorry, sir," he said.

Jim shook his head, "Not your fault. I was afraid of this, but he played Michael. Not your fault at all."

They walked back to the front of the house. Inside Jim found Michael sitting on the couch with his head in his hands.

Jim sat next to him and put an arm across his shoulders. "Any idea why he did this?"

Michael shook his head. "I didn't ask him anything, Dad. We watched a movie and then he said he wanted to take a shower. He's been doing that. I think it warms him up. But I know that we don't have twenty minutes of hot water, so I went to see…and he was gone. Probably gone as soon as he knew I was in the kitchen."

"Hey, this isn't your fault."

"I was supposed to be watching him!"

"So was I!" said Waylon. "The sneaky little shit."

Michael glared at Waylon. "Don't call him that. He's…he's…"

"He's probably gone after whoever he thinks can tell him who killed Noel," said Jim.

Michael covered his face and groaned. "Damn him!"

"Waylon, go to the station and get Junior to let everyone know to be looking for Bailey. Michael and I will go check his apartment and see if we can figure out where he may have gone."

"Yes, sir." Waylon grabbed the keys Jim held out and left.

Michael got up. "I'll get my coat. There's coffee and I washed your thermos. You fill it and then we can head out."

Chapter Twenty-One

The interview with the roommate made Dee smile as they were leaving. Ryan thought it likely she'd been amused at the Rickesha Johnson's rant about sad little white boys and Noel's attraction to them. Bailey was not the first she'd become involved with while at the university. Rickesha had said, "At least the last one had money, even if he was an asshole." The sorority sister's boyfriend's hostile stare had felt like it burned his skin the entire hour they were there. He felt like he needed to shake off the layer of rancor he now wore courtesy of the two. He didn't blame them, but it hadn't been fun.

His phone rang as they got into the car. When he heard Junior's voice, he put it on the speaker.

"Doc, you and Sergeant still together?"

"We're here," answered Dee.

"Bailey Braden slipped out of the Sheriff's house and is whereabouts unknown. The Sheriff and Michael have gone to Bailey's apartment to see if he's been there."

"Call Michael's cell phone and let him know that Dr. Edwards and I are headed back to Warren. Tell Michael to let us know if they find Bailey."

"Will do, Sergeant!" answered Junior and disconnected.

"Michael has a cell?"

Dee nodded. "He didn't want his father to know, but we're letting that cat out of the bag. I need a line to the Sheriff." Dee opened the pocket of the car and pulled out a cell phone and set it on the console next to her.

"You have a cell!" Ryan said.

"Most of us do," Dee said. "The Sheriff may hate progress, but the rest of us are getting pretty damn fond of it."

Ryan shook his head. "I had no idea."

"Yeah, Michael said you'd screw up and say something in front of his dad." Dee put the car into gear and carefully pulled out of the parking space at the apartment complex. The ice on the pavement caused the tires to slip a little, but soon she made it out to 24 and they headed west back to Eden County.

Chapter Twenty-Two

Jim heard Michael's phone buzzing in his pocket as they walked up the stairs in the back of the laundromat. Michael jogged ahead of Jim, acting like he didn't hear anything. Jim wondered if the boy thought him a complete idiot. Jim quickened his pace and caught Michael at the door to Bailey's apartment. The phone continued to buzz.

"You going to answer that?"

Michael looked at his father with horror. "Answer?"

"The phone, Michael. Answer the damn phone."

Michael reached into his pocket and pulled the phone out. He pushed the button to answer it. "Junior! Yeah, he's standing here. Sure." Michael handed the phone to Jim.

"What's up, Junior?"

"I called Dee. She and the doctor are on their way back. I told them that Bailey's taken a runner and that everyone's out looking for him," said Junior.

"Michael and I are going to check out Bailey's apartment. We'll see if he's been here. I doubt he'd go anywhere near his work or the library. If you hear about any bikes disappearing, check where it is in relation to my place and let me know."

"Yes, sir. We'll take care of it," said Junior.

Jim ended the call and handed the phone to Michael. Michael looked embarrassed. "Son, your pants are way too tight for me not to notice a phone in your pocket. You carry your wallet in your back right pocket, and this lump was always in your front pocket."

"Sorry," said Michael quietly.

"You're paying for it, so don't be sorry. We're going to need it to coordinate finding Bailey. I know more than half my deputies have phones, so we'll work with that."

Michael smiled and walked up to Bailey's door. He stopped and pushed at the door with his elbow. "The door isn't latched," said Michael.

"Shit," said Jim and he pushed Michael to the side. He pulled out his service weapon and standing away from the opening, leaned against the door to push it all the way open.

The wreckage of the tiny apartment had not been done by Bailey. His bed was overturned, and the bed coverings were tossed to the side. The card table and two chairs had been overturned as well. A small bookcase had every book pulled out of it and tossed around the room. All the clothes had been pulled out of the closet, and some pulled off their hangers.

In the bathroom, all the drawers to the vanity were pulled out and dumped into the bathtub. The mirror had been pulled off the wall and shattered in the tub on top of washcloths and towels.

"What would anyone be looking for in Bailey's apartment?" asked Michael.

Jim shook his head. "I don't think they were looking for anything. I think this was just destruction for the sheer hell of it. Why pull a mirror off the wall? No reason to throw around the chairs and table. This looks like a temper tantrum, not a burglary."

Michael walked over to the wall next to the bed. A corner of a photo hung by tape to the wall. On the floor next to the broken bed frame were other pieces of the photo. He picked them up and saw a young woman's face. He handed the piece with most of the face to his father. "Is that Noel?"

Jim looked at it and nodded. "Yes. This is the woman who was killed."

Michael walked over to the little sink and hot plate that served as a kitchen in the apartment. He grabbed a paper towel and put the pieces into it. "You might want to check these for fingerprints. Mine are on file so they can eliminate them."

Jim dropped the piece he had in hand into the paper towel and took it. Then he reviewed what Michael had just said. "Why the hell are your fingerprints on file?"

Michael grinned. "Gee, Dad. I thought you knew about the thing with the thing at the thing…"

Jim closed his eyes. He knew damn well Michael hadn't been arrested, so whatever it was, it was something else (after the phone thing) he didn't want to tell him about. "I will find out, you know."

"Sure, Dad."

Jim closed up the paper towel and motioned for Michael to hand him the phone. He hit re-dial and got Junior on the line. "Call over to the FDLE and see if we can get someone to gather evidence in Bailey Braden's apartment. And send someone over to guard the place and keep anyone out until they get here."

"Yes, sir," responded Junior before he disconnected.

Jim handed the phone back to Michael and pointed to the piece of the photograph. "Is this the only thing you touched?"

"Yes."

Jim nodded and motioned for Michael to go out into the stairway. They waited there in silence until the deputy showed up. Bobby Dale was dressed in civilian clothes, but he had his gun and his badge on.

"Hey, Sheriff. Junior said you need someone over here."

Jim sighed. "You're not on duty, are you?"

"No, sir. But he said FDLE will be here in a couple of hours. I figure I can cover until then."

"I'll run over to the minute market and get you a cup of coffee," said Michael, then he disappeared down the stairs.

"Do you have an evidence bag on you?" asked Jim.

"Got one in the car."

They walked down the stairs to Bobby Dale's patrol car and he opened the trunk and pulled out an evidence bag. Jim put the paper towel and the photo pieces into it. "My fingerprints and Michael's will be on the photo. We didn't realize what it was until we both touched it."

Bobby Dale nodded. "I hope it's not the woman Dee didn't like. Manny said she's a stickler."

Jim groaned. "With the way this is going, it will be."

Michael returned with the cup of coffee and Bobby Dale took it gratefully. "Thanks! I owe you one."

"Nah," said Michael, "We touched evidence. If someone yells at you about it, the least I can do is get you coffee."

Bobby saluted them with the coffee and headed back up the stairs.

Michael looked over at his dad. "Where next?"

Jim took a deep breath and let it out. "Who would do that to Bailey's stuff?"

Michael didn't hesitate. "China."

"You're right. Dammit, I'm not supposed to be working this case."

"You turned everything over to FDLE. We were looking for Bailey. This couldn't be helped."

"Yeah, that's not going to fly with a prosecutor."

"I could go see China." Michael faced his father. "I'm not afraid of her."

"I know. I know you've stopped her from rampaging before. But this is different. Noel Williams is dead. Someone shot her."

"And if it was China, I can find out."

"You're not doing this. Michael, we still don't know where Bailey went. We need to find him. If he didn't come home, where would he go?"

Michael turned and looked at the street. Jim watched Michael think. His son knew Bailey better than anyone else. The two of them had been inseparable as small children. Bailey had been Michael's protector until high school when Michael had a growth spurt that made him taller than Bailey. Even when Bailey dropped out of school, they would still hang out together. It had amused him to see how they shared the protection part of their relationship. Michael took on the big guys and China Braden. Bailey took on the troublemakers who had wanted to beat up the Sheriff's kid.

"Is Doc's office open?"

Jim thought about it. "Maybe. Would he go there?"

Michael turned to Jim, "Filly would take him in when China was on the warpath."

"Let's check it out."

Chapter Twenty-Three

Dee offered to drop Ryan off at either the office or his apartment and he chose his apartment. He felt wrung out by the day. It gave him a little more understanding of why sometimes Jim looked exhausted when he'd been out doing interviews or notices to families of injuries or deaths. Dee seemed to take it all in stride, but he also thought that her military background enabled her to mask her emotions.

She pulled into the drive next to Ryan's car. "I guess the Sheriff is still out with Michael," Ryan said.

Dee nodded, "Probably. I'll check in with Junior. Thanks for coming with me. It made it a little easier. I forget that some doctors are good with people."

Ryan smiled, "I...took...workshop. ER called... 'how not to be an asshole.'"

"From some of the doctors I've talked to, I wouldn't think that works all that well."

Ryan laughed. "It doesn't." He got out of the car and closed the door carefully. Dee gave him a thumbs up and pulled away.

Ryan made his way up the stairs and opened the door to his apartment. He stepped inside and didn't see Bonehead, which was odd. Generally, anyone on the stairway brought him to the door. The heat in the apartment blasted out of the vents, but he knew he'd turned it down when he left. Bonehead had thick fur and he liked the apartment when it was cooler.

He walked through the front room and stepped through the bedroom door. Bonehead rested on his bed, draped over Bailey Braden. Bonehead raised his head and looked at Ryan. Bailey snored softly. He had wrapped himself up in the bedspread and still had on a coat and his shoes. The sleeves of the coat covered his hands, so the coat had to be Michael's.

Ryan motioned with his hand for Bonehead to come to him. The dog yawned and put his head back down on Bailey. Ryan stuck his hands in his pocket and looked at Bonehead. He obviously figured Bailey needed him more than Ryan did. Ryan gave it one more shot, taking one hand out of his pocket he waved for Bonehead to come to him. Bonehead closed his eyes.

Ryan stepped back into the kitchen area. Bonehead was never particularly obedient, but he hadn't outright defied Ryan in several years. Ryan took off his coat and tossed it across the kitchen counter. He opened the cabinet where the treats were kept. Ryan didn't know why he felt he needed to get the dog away from Bailey because Bonehead certainly wasn't going to explain to him how Bailey had come to be here. But he did want Bonehead to come out of the room.

He pulled a couple of dog biscuits out of a box and stopped and thought about what he was doing. He didn't have any reason to think that Bailey was dangerous. Especially not if Bonehead had climbed onto the bed with him. In fact, Bonehead wasn't allowed on the bed, so he'd broken one of Ryan's few ironclad rules to lie next to Bailey. Could he be jealous that the dog stayed with Bailey and didn't greet him at the door?

No, that was ridiculous. Bonehead probably hadn't been out to pee in hours, and he needed to be let out.

Ryan walked back into the bedroom and held up a biscuit.

Bonehead opened his eyes, looked at Ryan and yawned again and closed his eyes.

"Dammit, dog," Ryan whispered. "Come here!"

Bailey stirred and Bonehead rolled over, so his body fully rested against Bailey's. Bailey began to snore softly again.

Ryan walked back out and went to one of the stools next to the kitchen counter. He sat down, tossing the biscuits on the counter. They slid across the glossy surface and stopped at the sleeve of his coat. He should call someone and let them know that Bailey was here. He knew that the Sheriff and Michael were searching for him. He didn't have Michael's phone number, so calling him was out. But he could call the Sheriff's office and get Junior to let them know.

"Why…here?" Ryan asked quietly.

Of all the people Bailey could have gone to, why would he come to Ryan?

Ryan got up and walked back into the bedroom. Bonehead raised his head and looked at Ryan. If he hadn't known better, he would have thought the dog was thinking, "So are you finally getting it?"

"Don't…that look," said Ryan softly.

"Hi, Doc."

Bailey sat up slowly. "Boy, it's hot in here."

"Yes… why?…Bonehead, get off the bed."

Bailey straightened out the bedspread as best he could while sitting on it. Bonehead jumped off the bed and headed into the kitchen.

The sound of something falling came from the kitchen. "Crap," said Ryan and he headed into the kitchen. Bonehead had a biscuit in his mouth and Ryan's coat lay on the floor.

"Bonehead, …heathen beast thrust…upon me…by a woman I loved. I did… did not deserve you."

Bailey snickered behind Ryan. "You sound like Sheriff Jim."

Ryan glanced over his shoulder. "He taught me."

Bailey nodded. "He talks like his daddy did. It's funny."

Ryan turned around, "It…is funny."

"'Specially hearing you say it with that Yankee voice."

"Yankee voice?"

"You don't talk like people from here."

"One more thing…grateful for," said Ryan smiling.

"I need your help," Bailey said.

"You want…a drink?" asked Ryan.

"My insides still feel cold. Do you have coffee?"

"…Hot chocolate?"

"You know how?" asked Bailey.

"The Sheriff…taught me."

"Okay."

Ryan picked his coat off the floor and picked up the second biscuit that still sat on the counter. He looked at Bonehead. "Take this to your bed… stop…crumbs…slobber on my…floor."

Bonehead took the biscuit and walked to his bed. He dropped into it and began to crunch his way through the biscuit.

"He understood that!" said Bailey.

"He's smarter than his name implies," said Ryan. "Hungry?"

"Yes, sir," said Bailey.

"Okay, …take care of that."

Ryan heated soup as he went through what he thought was a laborious process for making hot chocolate. Since Bailey knew Jim's way of doing it, he didn't want to disappoint. He took his time with the sugar and the milk and the cocoa powder. It made good hot chocolate, but honestly, he wasn't sure the drink deserved such devotion.

Bailey drank the hot chocolate, ate the soup, and said absolutely nothing. Ryan wondered if Bailey intended to talk. He could see Bailey relaxing, his shoulders dropping from up around his ears.

"I can do the dishes," Bailey offered.

"Later…talk? Now?"

Bailey nodded. "I need your help."

Ryan bit back the immediate response of 'why' and tried to find other words. Bailey responded before he could find them.

"If Michael and Sheriff Jim help me, they'll be in trouble. Not because I want you to help me do anything wrong, but because Sheriff Jim isn't supposed to do that. But you don't have that problem."

"Oh," said Ryan.

"I need to find Finley. I need to know who he told about Noel. I know where to find him, but it's over in Alachua County."

"Oh!" said Ryan. "I have a car."

Bailey smiled. "I know. And you understand."

"I don't…"

"Michael said your wife was killed."

Ryan nodded. "Yes."

"Will you help me?"

Ryan struggled to answer, not because he couldn't find the words, but because he didn't know if he should do this. Would Jim ever forgive him for getting involved and not telling him?

"Let's...a deal. Make a deal."

Bailey nodded.

"I help... But I tell..."

"No, he'll get in trouble!"

"I tell Sergeant Jackson."

Bailey shut his mouth and thought about what Ryan said. He took a long time. Then he looked at Ryan and said, "Okay. You can tell her I'm with you, but you don't tell her where we're going."

Ryan took a long time to think over what Bailey suggested. What he wanted would piss Dee off, but it wasn't illegal. It might be dangerous, but if he was Bailey, he might ask for the same thing.

"Okay."

"Thank you."

"Once we...find..."

"You can tell Dee what he says."

Ryan knew that Dee would let Jim know that Bailey was with him. The agreement made it maybe 30% better than no one knowing. Also, if Finley had told someone who would kill Noel, the potential for them being in danger increased, but possibly they could get back to the house and safely before something bad happened. Ryan gave them a 50-50 chance on that, just because of the unknowns.

"What are you thinking?" Bailey asked.

"Odds...dying...," said Ryan.

Bailey shrugged. "If Finley isn't alone, we can wait until he is."

Ryan nodded. That might improve the odds. He had the feeling that Jim would say this was a stupid thing to do, and the odds of Jim being right were pretty good.

Chapter Twenty-Four

When Jim and Michael walked into the clinic, Doc sat with his feet up on the counter at the front desk. Doc glanced up when he heard the door open and waved to them. "C'mon in. It's warm in here."

"Where is everyone?" Jim asked.

"Sent 'em home. We're getting phone calls that only I can answer. No sense in them being here if there's nothing for them to do. Drag up a chair, join me. I got coffee in the back if you want something hot."

Jim and Michael both pulled chairs from the waiting area up to the desk.

"I'll get us some coffee," said Michael and he walked into the back of the office.

"Bailey's disappeared," said Jim.

"Shit," said Doc.

"Yeah. I was hoping that maybe he'd tried to contact Filly."

"Let me give her a call," said Doc.

Michael came out with two mugs and handed one to Jim. He sat down and they both listened as Doc talked.

"Filly, Bailey Braden's taken a runner. Has he contacted you? I got both Jim and Michael here looking for him." Doc took a long drink from his own mug, and they could hear Filly's voice but not her words.

"Well, if he does get in touch with you, let Jim know. That boy doesn't have any business being out in this weather. He just got over being nearly frozen to death."

Filly spoke some more, and Doc thanked her and hung up. "She hasn't heard from him, but she'll call Michael's phone if she does."

Michael gripped his mug tightly. "I really fucked up."

Jim reached over and took the mug out of his hands and set it on the desk. "This isn't on you. Bailey did this."

"I should have been watching him."

Doc dropped his feet to the floor and leaned forward. "Stop feeling sorry for yourself and remember that Bailey Braden is your best friend and prone to behavior that is not in his best interest."

Michael looked at Doc and his mouth dropped open in stunned surprise.

Jim put his hand on top of Michael's head and shook it. "You know that's true."

Michael's phone rang and he pulled it out of his pocket. It was Dee Jackson's number. He handed the phone over to his father.

"What's up, Sgt. Jackson?" asked Jim. "He what?!"

Jim could feel his pulse racing and he thought his blood pressure must be going up because his ears were ringing.

"Any idea where they're going?" asked Jim.

He looked at Michael and Doc, who both leaned forward, trying to listen to the call. He knew they couldn't hear Dee's voice. He could tell she didn't want anyone to hear what she said. Dee replied with a quick "negative."

"Damn," said Jim. "I'll see what I can find out and call you back. Maybe he had the sense to leave some kind of note or something to tell us where they were going."

Jim ended the call and handed the phone back to Michael. "Ryan called Dee and told her that he and Bailey had some things to check out and they'd be in touch soon."

"Neither one of those idiots has a lick of sense!" said Doc.

"Bailey went to Ryan?"

"He must have backtracked after we left and gone to Ryan's place. I bet the spare key to the apartment is gone."

Michael laid his forehead against the desktop. "If they come back alive, can I kill them both, just a little?"

"Get in line," said Doc.

"Oh, Dee's going to be first in line. Ryan hung up on her."

"Holy shit," said Doc softly. "He's a dead man."

Chapter Twenty-Five

Ryan's all-weather tires handled the icy road pretty well, and since he'd driven on icy roads for most of his adult life, he knew to take his time and not get in a hurry doing anything. Bailey sat in the passenger seat and Bonehead slept in the back seat. His harness was hooked into the seat belt in the middle which hopefully would keep him safe if the car did go into a skid.

He couldn't understand how he'd ended up bringing Bonehead along, other than that Bailey had insisted the dog should not be alone. The argument he'd put up was ridiculous, but Bonehead had trotted to the door and stood there as though he knew he'd been invited to ride along.

Ryan thought he might have temporarily lost his mind. At least he hoped it was temporary because if he continued to follow Bailey's lead, he could not see it ending in any way that would be good.

"I really like your dog," Bailey said quietly.

"I noticed."

"When I opened your door, he didn't bark or anything. He just took me back to your bedroom. I think he knew I needed a nap. I hope you don't mind that I turned up the heat. I'd been hiding out in the woods for a while."

"You need...warm."

"Thank you. You were really nice to me at Doc's, and I needed to get someone's help, but I couldn't let Sheriff Jim or Michael know what I wanted to do. Sheriff Jim has to stay out of investigating Noel's murder because Michael and me are friends. I have to protect them both. Just like I used to protect Michael when he was little. He's my best friend, and I don't want to

94

make trouble for them. They've always been good to me."

Ryan smiled. "They're good people."

As they came to the bridge over the river Ryan slowed a little more. Bridges tended to ice up more than roads, and he didn't think Bailey would survive another case of hypothermia. The car slewed a little as it first hit the bridge, but then the tires caught, and they stayed in the lane and crossed without further trouble.

Ryan's heart rate returned to normal, and he picked up their speed. As much as he wanted to be careful, he also wanted to get Bailey back to Warren and into the care of Jim and Michael. He knew that Jim would not be happy with either of them or this adventure into Gainesville, but he couldn't turn down Bailey's request. If their positions were reversed, he'd want someone to help him find out who'd hurt Danielle.

Once they reached Gainesville, Bailey guided him to a run-down house in an older neighborhood. A battered Toyota sedan sat in the driveway, but the house looked quiet. Ryan pulled up in front of the house and parked. He looked at Bailey. "This guy, right...?"

Bailey nodded. "He hangs out with some people in Warren. I think he's from Dixie County."

Of course, there's a Dixie County in Florida, thought Ryan.

"Lots of people in Eden work in Gainesville. There's a truss company over here that some guys I know work for. I think maybe he works there."

"...He'll be home?"

Bailey tilted his head to think. "It's what, about 5:30? I think maybe so. That's his car."

Ryan reached into the back seat and unclipped Bonehead's harness. "If we're going... let's take Bonehead. He's...people sense, and if...not right, he'll let us know."

The three of them got out of Ryan's car and across the frozen lawn to the front door. Bailey knocked, and they could hear someone moving around inside. When the door opened, Ryan found them face to face with a slender young man who was about 5'6", wearing a down vest over a heavy flannel shirt. His surprise at seeing Bailey and his companions broadcast from his wide eyes.

Ryan did not have time to react when Bailey grabbed Finley by the throat and rammed through the front door, driving Finley across the room, slamming him into the wall. Finley's hands grabbed at Bailey's hands.

While Ryan was startled, Bonehead ran across the room and stood behind Bailey and growled lowly.

"Who did you tell?" Bailey's voice had dropped into a deep gravelly tone.

Ryan rushed inside, closing the door behind him so no one would see what was happening. He went to Bailey and saw that Finley clawed at Bailey's hands, making deep bloody scratches.

"Who did you tell?" Bailey demanded again.

"Bailey, stop, …don't…can't breathe," Ryan struggled to find the words to get Bailey to let go of Finley's throat. "Please…Bailey…"

Bonehead continued to growl. He was backing whatever play Bailey was making.

Bailey dropped his hands and stepped back. Finley gulped air, coughing and rubbing at his throat. He looked terrified.

"You going to tell me?" Bailey asked.

Bonehead stepped forward and growled showing teeth.

"Your mother. I told your mother."

"Fuckhead. I should let Killer tear your throat out." Bonehead took another step forward and growled louder.

"But I'm not a murderer," Bailey said. He reached down and patted Bonehead. "Come on, Killer. Let's leave this piece of shit where we found him."

Bailey and Bonehead turned and walked past Ryan and out the front door. Ryan looked at Finley. There were going to be bruises on Finley's throat. There was also a nasty scratch, probably from when Bailey had grabbed him so fast. "Sorry," he said. Then he hurried out behind Bailey.

Ryan opened the car and Bonehead jumped into the back seat. Bailey reached back and clicked his harness into the seatbelt. Ryan started the car and pulled away from the curb. His hands shook as he grasped the steering wheel.

Bailey pulled a tissue out of his pocket and began to pat at the scratches on his hands.

Ryan shook his head. "What...the hell!"

Bailey looked at Ryan and said, "I'm angry."

Ryan took a deep breath, "I get...you attacked...him!"

"What would you do if you were in front of the man who killed your wife?" he asked.

Ryan pulled over to the side of the road and put the car in park. "He... You could...jail!"

"I can't go to jail, yet. I have to find China now."

Ryan leaned his forehead against the steering wheel. "She wouldn't..."

Bailey nodded.

Bonehead put his head on the console between the front seats and huffed.

"And you...dog!" said Ryan.

"He was protecting me," said Bailey softly.

"I know," said Ryan, his head still resting on the cold steering wheel.

The silence lasted a long time. Finally, Ryan raised his head and looked at Bailey. "Now we call Dee," he said.

Bailey shrugged. "Okay."

Ryan handed his phone over to Bailey, then he put the car in drive and pulled away from the curb. "If she tries...kill me... you both..."

Bonehead raised his head and nudged his nose under Ryan's arm.

"Yeah, you, too!" Ryan said.

Bailey opened the phone and found Dee Jackson's listing. He pressed the call button and waited. When Dee answered they all heard, "I am going to kill both of you."

"Bonehead helped," he said.

"Then I'm going to kill all three of you," Dee said.

Chapter Twenty-Six

The door to the clinic slammed and Jim, Michael, and Doc startled at the sound. Jim turned and saw a tall woman wearing an ankle-length down coat. Her gloved hands clasped in front of her pointed toward them.

"Which of you yahoos left your fingerprints on my crime scene?" she asked.

Doc chuckled and pointed to Jim, "Well, this is Sheriff Yahoo and this one over here is Yahoo's son."

Jim turned and glared at Doc, who grinned with an unrepentant gleam in his eye. He turned back to the woman and stood up. "I'm Sheriff Sheppard."

"I'm Dr. Sullivan and this is the second time I have come to a crime in this county in which there has been interference with the scene. I know your fingerprints will be on file with the state, which will help me eliminate you from my analysis, but it does not eliminate your son."

Michael stood up. Taller now than Jim, he towered over the woman. "My fingerprints are also on file with the State of Florida. I work security in Alachua County for Excellence Security Agency."

"Fine. My next question is this. Does anyone in this godforsaken county understand anything about maintaining a crime scene for forensics? Or am I going to have to continue to eliminate the fingerprints of everyone in the Sheriff's Department routinely?"

Jim's hackles rose immediately. "My department is actively investigating a homicide."

"You have heard of gloves? I suggest you invest in them for you and your deputies, and that your son not accompany you into crime scenes."

"Dr. Sullivan, I suggest you not make enemies of the people with whom you will be required to work. When will I have your reports on the car and the apartment?"

The woman stood up straighter. "I can give you a preliminary on the apartment right now."

"Then please do," said Jim.

"There are three sets of fingerprints on items in the bathroom and the doors. You told the deputy you left at the apartment that you had not touched anything with your fingers other than the torn photograph. The three sets are distinctive, so I'll be looking for matches on them. I can eliminate the murder victim's fingerprints as the Medical Examiner has sent those to me. From the destruction in the apartment, I believe it was deliberate, and caused by someone in an altered state, probably enraged, but possibly also drinking or drugged. It was chaotic and unorganized. Someone wishing to leave a message would have been more methodical and done more damage to personal items than was evidenced at the scene."

"Well, gee," said Jim. "I would have never thought of that. How about you, Michael?"

Michael shook his head. "Nope, Dad. I mean everything tossed around. The mirror in the bathroom pulled off the wall and broken. I would definitely not have pegged that as being an act of anger."

"It probably just fell off and rolled into the tub," Jim said.

Dr. Sullivan turned on her heel and headed for the door.

Jim called out to her, "What can you tell us about the car? Was there any evidence of a struggle?"

Dr. Sullivan stopped at the door and turned around. "No."

"Fingerprints?"

"The victim's. From the scene, I'd say whoever took her was armed. Looked like she cooperated and got into the other car."

"Thank you," Jim said. "Let me know if you get anything else."

"Of course."

The door slammed behind her as she left.

The room was silent and then Doc spoke, "Hoo-boy. You did not make a friend there, Jim Sheppard."

"I have friends already," Jim said. "I need evidence."

Chapter Twenty-Seven

Ryan and Bailey arrived at the Trenton McDonalds in the early evening. Dee Jackson's patrol car was parked outside. Ryan pulled up next to it and hoped that she would not just shoot them on sight. He was hungry, and Bonehead's supper was overdue.

Bailey hadn't said a word since the phone call with Dee, which suited Ryan fine. He didn't know what they'd say to each other anyway. He still felt shocked by Bailey's physical attack on Finley and the way that Bonehead had backed him up, providing him with an extra threat to the other man.

He started to leave Bonehead in the car, but Bailey opened the back door and pulled the dog out by the collar. "It's too cold for him to be out here," Bailey said. Then he walked right into McDonalds with the dog by his side. Ryan just threw up his hands and followed him inside.

Dee sat at a table as far from the counter as possible. Ryan raised a hand to acknowledge her and went to the counter where Bailey stood with Bonehead.

"I'll have a quarter-pounder with cheese, no, make that two, and a large order of fries and a cup of coffee," said Bailey. He pulled loose bills out of his pocket to pay.

Ryan stepped up. "I'll get this," he said.

Bailey shook his head, "No." He paid for his order and stood to one side to let Ryan place his order.

Ryan ordered four cheeseburgers and a large cup of coffee. Two cheeseburgers would hold Bonehead until he could get him home and fed. As he paid for his order, he saw that Bailey had gotten his and walked

101

toward the table where Dee waited for them.

When his order came out Ryan took it and went to the table. Bonehead was gulping down a quarter-pounder with cheese and half of Bailey's fries.

"You didn't... I...got cheeseburgers," said Ryan.

"I owed him," Bailey said.

Dee watched them both as she sipped on her coffee. "What the hell happened?"

"What do you mean?" asked Ryan.

"You two are barely speaking to each other. What happened?"

Bailey stuffed the last bite of his quarter-pounder into his mouth and washed it down with nearly half his coffee. "I kinda attacked Finley," he said softly.

Dee's eyes cut up to Ryan's face. He shrugged and stuffed most of a cheeseburger into his mouth. "Finley hurt?"

Baily rocked his head from side to side. "Might be a little bruised."

"Where?"

"Throat."

"He going to press charges?"

"Nope," said Bailey.

"Why not?"

"He told China about Noel."

Dee's eyes opened wide. "Holy shit."

"Yeah."

"China have a gun?"

"Not that I know of," said Bailey. "Gun's not her style anyway."

Bonehead finished Bailey's fries and looked at Ryan. Ryan pulled out one of the cheeseburgers, unwrapped it, and set it on the floor on the quarter-pounder wrapper. Bonehead had licked up every speck of food from the wrapper, right down to the salt from the fries.

"You're... die... congestive heart failure, dog," said Ryan.

"What do you think happened?" Dee asked.

Bailey sighed. "I think she got someone to kill Noel for her."

"Any idea who that might be?"

"Maybe whoever she's fucking these days," Bailey said.

"You had to go fall for a black woman, Bailey Braden."

Bailey looked at Dee. "Timothy Mackey," he said bluntly.

Ryan held his breath.

Dee shook her head. "Least no one in my family's as crazy as China."

Bailey nodded. "True."

Bonehead finished the two cheeseburgers and sidled over to Dee. She looked down at him. "Don't come to me, dog. I am not feeding you this shit."

"You ate it," said Bailey.

"Shut up, Bailey," said Dee.

Ryan offered the second cheeseburger to the dog and Bonehead took it and laid down on the floor to eat it.

"Okay, I don't know…going on here, …China is Bailey's mother… Not approve of Noel."

Bailey pushed his coffee cup around on the table. "The big surprise with China is that she didn't have whoever did it kill me, too."

Dee snorted. "Maybe that's why the truck came back."

Bailey looked up at Dee thoughtfully. "He chickened out or something?"

"Probably or something."

"What truck?" Ryan asked.

"Jim told me that Bailey heard a diesel engine pull up outside when he was with Noel in that shed. We all figure it was probably the killer."

Bailey spoke very softly. "Kinda wish he had killed me."

Dee kicked Bailey's shin.

"Ow!"

"Don't say that, Bailey. If you weren't here, we wouldn't be getting close to who did this. You need to be here so Noel gets justice."

Bailey put his hand over his mouth and said nothing.

"So, Ryan. What were you doing while Bailey was trying to kill Finley?"

Ryan pointed to Bonehead. "He…backed Bailey up. He…growled."

"So in other words, Bonehead here took action and you stood there with your thumb up your ass not knowing whether to shit or go blind?"

"I told Finley I was sorry…," Ryan said.

Bailey snickered behind his hand. Dee smiled slyly. "I cannot believe you," she said.

Ryan got indignant, "It surprised me, okay? …Bailey …his plan. And I'm not… Bonehead. Okay?"

"All right, all right," Dee said, and she finished her coffee.

Chapter Twenty-Eight

Michael's phone rang in Jim's pocket. He pulled it out and saw Dee's number and answered it. "What's going on?"

"China's involved."

"Not surprising, but what confirmed it?"

"Bailey and Dr. Edwards tracked down Finley, and he talked. He told China he'd seen Bailey with Noel."

"Great." Jim rubbed the space between his eyebrows. Between the cold air and everything that had gone on today, he could feel a band of pain squeezing right across his forehead. He'd never had a migraine, but he thought maybe he was about to. "I wouldn't suggest confronting her."

"That's not the plan. I'm going to find the person she talked into doing the killing for her."

Jim's heartbeat began to race. "Dee, no. This is getting too dangerous. I don't want you going by yourself."

"I'm not," she responded. "I'm going to take the adventure trio with me. I'm dropping my patrol car off at my house and meeting Tim. We're going to use Ryan's car and take the dogs with us. We're going to be very unexpected and unlikely."

"You have a lead?" Jim asked cautiously.

"I have someone who's going to have a lead," said Dee.

"I don't suppose you want to let me in on that?"

"No, sir. I don't think that'd be wise. But I'll let Junior know, and you are going to promise not to ask him unless you haven't heard from us in 24 hours."

"If you get Ryan killed, Doc Markham's going to hurt you."

Dee laughed, "No worries, sir. I promise to keep him well out of the line of fire. That's why I'm taking Tim and Jackie with me."

"His car isn't big enough for all of you."

"We'll be fine. We're getting to know each other real well." Dee ended the call.

Jim considered tossing the phone as far as he could, but then he'd have to replace it and apologize to Michael for losing his temper.

"Dad, please don't throw my phone."

"I wasn't going to."

"You want to."

Jim nodded. "Yes, I do. This is just one more reason I'm never going to buy one of these things." He handed it to Michael. He watched Michael stick it in his pocket, and they started walking toward home again. He let his mind puzzle over who Dee would pick to see to get information on China. It would have to be someone who knew the local gossip. Someone people talked to with ease.

"If Dee calls again, you want me to answer it?"

"Yeah." They walked on, finally turning onto the street their home sat on. He thought through all the places that China Braden and her friends hung out. Most of the time they stayed in Eden County. None of them had the money to go to places in Gainesville. China lived on her father's pension which limited her range of trouble.

"You have Junior's number?" Jim asked.

"I do."

"When we get home, you're going to call Junior and ask him where Dee was headed, and you're not going to tell me. You're just going to take me there."

Michael stopped in the middle of the road. "Why?"

"So you won't have to lie to him."

"Dad...?"

"Just do it for me, Michael."

Michael shook his head, but Jim knew the answer was yes. Michael would help him. His son always would.

Chapter Twenty-Nine

Dee took Ryan's keys out of his hand. "I'm driving. Bailey, you're in the back seat with Tim and the dogs. Doctor, you're riding shotgun."

Bailey got out of the car and obediently got into the backseat. Bonehead and Jackie sat in the middle and Tim Mackey took the seat behind the driver. Tim reached over the two dogs and offered his hand to Bailey. "Tim Mackey. And you're Bailey?"

"Bailey Braden," he answered taking Tim's hand and shaking it.

"And you're Dr. Edwards?" Tim asked reaching his hand out between the front seats.

"Ryan. Call me..."

"Ryan, right. By the way, thanks for going to Tampa with Dee. Sounds like you were the right person for the job. Death calls suck," said Tim.

Ryan nodded. "Yeah... Done more than a few..."

"Right. I'm sure working in the ER was no picnic when it comes to that. I've been lucky. Only had to do two in all my years as a Deputy."

Dee reached out and patted Tim's hand. "This is how we're going to do this," started Dee. "The Cypress will be open by now. Ryan and I will go in and talk to Edna Bass. Tim and Bailey will wait in the car. I don't want anyone seeing Bailey with us. So keep your head low, Bailey."

"Yes, ma'am," said Bailey.

"Why... why...," said Ryan.

"Because Edna knows you and trusts you. She's not going to trust me, so you're going to ask her who China's been hanging out with. We need names, and we need to know if any of them drives a big diesel engine truck. She'll tell you."

"You…stand there?"

"I'm just there to make it official and watch your back while you talk to Edna."

"Be sure you check to make sure China's not in there," said Bailey.

"I'll do that before I have Ryan follow me in."

"Good."

"I think maybe you should let me take the Doc in," said Tim.

Ryan could tell that Dee struggled with the idea of not going in herself. "It's my case."

"I'm not trying to take it. Can't. Don't even work in Eden County. But I'd be a whole lot less conspicuous in there than you're going to be, even if you hold back near the door."

"You don't know China Braden," said Dee.

"Loud?" asked Ryan.

"In the bar? Yeah, they've got a jukebox, and the place will be full of regulars. Two white men walk in, no one's going to think anything of it. Except maybe to wonder who they are, said Tim. "I've been there before."

"They'll know Ryan," said Dee.

"They'll figure I'm a friend of his and we're out getting a beer together."

The silence grew weighted.

"China is easy to spot. Long platinum hair, she'll be dressed in something that shows off her breasts, sheer, no bra. She smokes. There will be at least one man with her, maybe more. No women at her table. She hates competition. She'll eye both of you when you come in to see if you look like you've got more money than whoever she's with. Won't be subtle. She'll take one look at Ryan's coat and peg him as someone from out of town. Might even get up and head in his direction."

Bailey took a breath and grabbed Ryan's shoulder. "Make sure you order a couple of beers to cover your conversation with Ms. Bass. China's not stupid, and she's not afraid to make a scene. She likes it. Tim should go with you to the bar and you should both take seats. It'll cover why you're talking to Ms. Bass. Don't say China's name if she's anywhere near you. She'll want to know how you know it. Won't take no for an answer. Won't hesitate to invite her men friends over to make sure you give her an answer."

"That's what we'll do," said Tim. "I'll cover for you if she gets close, give you time to get your question answered."

Ryan snorted. "You mean...get... get it asked."

Dee laughed and the dogs both stood up. "Sit down, Jackie," she said, reaching back to scratch the dog's ear. "All right. I think that's a plan. I'll find a place to pull over and we'll switch places, Tim. Bailey's right. China's not that hard to spot. It will be safer for the Doc."

Dee swatted Ryan's shoulder. "Introduce Tim and let him ask the question. That way you can both get out of there before China starts something if she's there. If she's not there, no need to rush."

Dee pulled over onto the shoulder of the road out in the open and she and Tim traded seats. He started the car up again and headed for the Cypress. Ryan felt himself relax. He'd never been inside the Cypress, but he'd seen enough injuries from bar fights there on an emergency basis at Doc's to not want to wander in there and look any more out of place than he already would. Tim, in his heavy Carhartt jacket and baseball cap, would fit right in. Edna had invited him to stop by for a beer more than once while she was in the office. This was the time to take her up on the offer.

The drive to the Cypress passed too quickly for Ryan. The next thing he knew, Tim was parking his car on the far edge of the gravel parking lot. Tim gave Dee a quick grin and got out of the car. Ryan swallowed his nervousness and got out on his side. Tim tapped on Dee's window and handed in the car keys.

"If you have to take the car and get out of here. I'll call you when we're done," he said.

Dee took the keys and grinned at him. "Sure you don't need me in there to cover your ass?"

He laughed and headed for the bar.

Ryan stopped when he reached the door of the bar. Tim stepped around him, opened the door, and pushed him inside. They walked up to the bar and Edna broke out in a huge smile when she saw Ryan.

"Doc Ryan! Come sit and get warm! It's colder than a well-digger's ass in the Klondikes out there!" she called out.

She moved down to where Ryan and Tim sat and leaned against the bar. She looked at Tim. "I've seen you before. Been a while, huh?"

Tim nodded. "Yes, ma'am. Ryan here invited me for a drink. Said he knew you personal and that you would treat us right."

"Damn straight," said Edna. "What'll you have, Doc? First one's on the house."

Ryan smiled at her. Edna Bass had lost over 100 pounds in the years since Buddy had died and she'd taken the bar back over. At first, her grief had her eating less, but then as she lost weight and felt better, she'd given up cigarettes and gotten more active. Doc Markham had been right. Buddy had been the source of her problems. She would never be thin, but she smiled more and seemed happy. Even her blood pressure was normal. "I'll have a beer," he said.

"And a beer for your friend?"

"Yes, ma'am."

Edna went to the tap and poured two tall glasses. She brought them back and set them in front of Ryan and Tim. "I got me a guy helps out now, so we're back to beer on tap. It's the good stuff."

Ryan looked at the taps and saw the beer was Budweiser. He swallowed his chuckle. "Thank you, Ms. Bass."

No, Doc. No Ms. Bass here. It's Edna." She reached out and patted his hand. "You and Doc do for me, and in here, I do for you."

"Thank you, Edna," Ryan said.

Edna beamed at him.

"I…have questions…," Ryan said.

Edna leaned closer. "Something wrong?"

"Patient…almost froze…," Ryan started.

Tim patted Ryan on the shoulder. "A kid up here got brought in nearly froze to death. Ryan's worried. Wanted to get to some information on the family."

Edna nodded. "If I can help, I will. I owe you that, Doc."

Ryan smiled, "Ryan...here, Ryan...not Doc."

Edna laughed and the sound was like bells. Ryan loved her laugh. "Go on, Ryan. Ask."

"China...," he said softly.

Edna nodded and moved a little closer. "I heard. What do you need to know about China?"

"Who...who she with...," said Ryan.

"It's been a good month ago she was in here with Buckley Adams. She had a beer in here with Ward Foley a couple of weeks ago."

Tim leaned in a bit. "Either of them drive a diesel truck?"

Edna side-eyed Tim. "You're that deputy from Levy County."

Tim nodded and sipped at his beer.

Edna put her hand on Ryan's. "You be careful. Buckley Adams. Got a Ford F-350. Mean as a snake."

Ryan put his other hand over Edna's. "Promise."

"Drink your beer, Doc. I got customers to take care of." Edna pulled away and headed down the bar.

Ryan picked up the glass and drank it quickly. Tim drank about half of his, then set it back on the bar. Then Ryan pulled out his wallet and set a twenty on the bar under his glass. The two men got up and made their way out of the bar.

When they got back to the car, Bailey stood at the edge of the parking lot as both dogs sniffed around for a spot to pee. Dee rolled down her window. "That was fast."

"We got a name," said Tim. "Buckley Adams."

Bailey shook his head. "That is not good," he said. "If she's back with Buck, means she's pissed off and ready for war."

Dee motioned for Tim to get in the car. Ryan had already gotten in on the passenger side. "You know this guy?" he asked Dee.

"Manny Sota does. He's arrested him about six times."

"What kind of charges?" asked Tim.

"Assault mostly. He likes to beat up his women."

Bonehead and Jackie finished their business and Bailey opened the door to the back seat. Both dogs jumped in and made themselves comfortable. Bailey got back into the car.

"Got any idea where we might find him?" asked Tim.

Before Dee could answer a truck pulled up next to the car. A window rolled down and Michael stuck his head out. "Evening. Want to take a little drive somewhere and get something to eat?"

Jim called out, "My place. Don't wander!"

Michael saluted, rolled up his window, and backed away.

Tim fired up the motor and put the car into drive. "Guess we're going to have some dinner," he said.

Dee muttered under her breath.

Chapter Thirty

J im had set Bailey and Michael to making the sandwiches. Bailey sliced the cheddar into thick pieces as Michael buttered the bread. Jim heated the pan, melting butter for toasting the bread and melting the cheese properly. Ryan had the largest saucepan and heated the milk for hot chocolate. Dee and Tim filled bowls with dog food and water as Bonehead and Jackie sat patiently waiting for their meal. No one spoke, just went about the business of making a meal for everyone, including both dogs.

The dogs were crunching away on their food by the time the sandwiches were delivered to the table. Ryan set down mugs of hot chocolate topped with melting miniature marshmallows.

Jim motioned for everyone to sit down and then took the seat at the head of the table. "After we've eaten, I want to know exactly what you have all been up to, and what leads you have and then, we will decide on the next course of action."

Dee started to object, but Jim raised one finger. "After we've eaten."

She subsided, grumbling a little under her breath, but everyone just dug into the food. Once everyone had eaten, and the dishes had been cleared from the table, they all sat down and faced each other.

Bonehead snored and Jackie had taken up residence under the table next to Dee's feet.

Jim looked at Bailey. "You scared the crap out of Michael. You owe him an apology."

Bailey looked guilty, bumped his shoulder against Michael's, and said,

"Sorry. I didn't want to get you and Sheriff Jim into any trouble."

"And what possessed you to go off with Bailey like you did?" asked Jim, staring right at Ryan.

"Ah...," Ryan started.

"I guilted him," said Bailey. "Knew about his dead wife. Wasn't fair at all."

Jim sighed and rubbed his forehead. "Do I even want to know how you and Tim got involved in this, Sergeant?"

"Bailey found Finley. He and Ryan called me on their way back to Warren."

"From where?"

"Gainesville," said Bailey. "I know where Finley lives."

"And you did not share this information before?"

"Couldn't. You're not supposed to be investigating, and I wasn't going to get Michael to take me there."

Jim shook his head. "You talked to Finley?"

"Yes. He told China about me and Noel."

Ryan held up his hand which made Dee snicker.

"Yes, Ryan?" Jim said.

"Got...a name. Edna...told us."

"Whose idea was it to go talk to Edna?" asked Jim.

Dee raised her hand.

"Smart. China does hang out at the Cypress," said Jim. "Where are you taking it from here?"

"Sheriff, I'm calling Manny and bringing him in on it. He'll know where to find the guy."

Jim took a deep breath. "And none of you are going to tell me who."

"Sir, respectfully, you shouldn't know," said Tim.

Michael put his hand on Jim's shoulder. "Let it go, Dad. We've got Bailey back. Dee and Manny can take it from here."

Jim stared at Dee. "Take Ryan with you."

"Sir...," started Dee.

"I want him with you. If it's someone Manny's dealt with before, he shouldn't be the one going to the door. If you go to the door, I don't want you getting shot. You take the Doc and Manny covers your back. No discussion on this."

"I like it," said Tim.

Dee shook her head. "Of course you do."

"I can't work with you on this. I have no standing in Eden County. Plus I've got to work tomorrow. If you have the Doc with you, there's less likely to be shooting. With Manny as backup, you'll both be okay if there is."

Ryan raised his hand again. Tim reached over and put it down. "Doc, you got to do this for me."

Ryan nodded. "Fine."

Jim stood up and motioned to Michael and Bailey. "You've got dish duty. Ryan, go make plans with Dee. Nice seeing you, Tim."

Jim left the room and headed down the hall.

"Keep an eye on him, Michael," said Dee.

Michael laughed. "He doesn't have a car and I've got the keys to my truck. I'm going to sleep with them under my pillow."

"Good," she said. She got up and Jackie jumped up with her. "Let's go make plans," she said to Ryan.

The two dogs and Dee, Tim, and Ryan went out the back door and headed up to Ryan's apartment.

Bailey turned on the water. "I'll wash, you dry."

Michael grabbed up a dish towel. "No more investigating, Bailey."

"Promise."

The two of them began working on the dishes.

In his room, Jim could hear Bailey and Michael talking quietly in the kitchen. He had a hell of a headache, and he worried about sending Ryan out with Dee. The thing was, Ryan would be good cover for Dee. Anyone seeing him at the door wouldn't jump to conclusions about why. He was known in the community, and he was white. If Dee and Manny were going after someone who was involved with China Braden, they needed a white man. Manny's brown face and Dee's black one would immediately be suspicious. All China's men were bigots, and every one of them was violent.

If China was present, it just raised the odds that there'd be shooting before any talking.

116

But the good-looking white doctor would be unexpected. He would trigger curiosity first.

It was a gamble. But it was the best gamble Jim had. He laid back and put his arm over his eyes. He had to hope that it would work.

Chapter Thirty-One

Dee had talked to Manny Sota and agreed they'd meet in the morning at the Sheriff's office. Ryan stood at the desk with a cup of coffee and chatted with Junior. Jim called in and said he and Michael were taking Bailey to the Chiefland Walmart to get him some clothes. His apartment had been taped off as an active crime site.

"The Sheriff's got you working with Dee," Junior said.

"Sort of," said Ryan.

Manny opened the door and walked in carrying a rifle case. He nodded to Junior and Ryan, and walked on into the bullpen, where he took the rifle out of the case and began to check it over.

"Ah…is…," Ryan pointed at Manny, "normal?"

Junior shrugged. "Depends on who you're looking for."

Ryan felt his stomach flip, and he set his coffee down and pushed it away.

"You all right, Doc?"

Ryan made a see-sawing motion with his hand. "No."

Junior headed for the break room. "I'm getting you a Vernor's."

Manny looked up from the rifle, "This is just a precaution, Doc. Buckley and I have a history. I probably won't need it with you and Dee taking the door."

Junior came back and set an open can of Vernor's ginger ale on the desk. "You drink that up, Doc. It'll help."

Ryan knew it couldn't hurt and he took a big swallow. He was not expecting the strength of the Vernor's and he had to cover his mouth to keep from spitting it out with a cough. He managed to swallow it.

The door opened again, and Dee entered. She saw Manny putting his rifle back together and called out to him, "I thought you said morning would be safer."

Manny laughed. "I said morning was likely to be safer because Buckley doesn't work. That doesn't mean the man won't come to the door with a gun."

Ryan took another sip of the Vernor's.

Dee patted him on the shoulder as she walked past the desk to talk to Manny. "I checked his record. Most of it is domestic abuse."

"He occasionally dabbles in misdemeanor assaults," said Manny. "But if he is the shooter in your case, I've got no idea how he might react."

"He's done some time?"

"County only. His Mama buys him good lawyers."

"Who's his Mama?" Dee asked.

Manny smiled at Dee and leaned back against the table with his rifle butt resting on his thigh. "Charlene Forrest. She claims her Great-Great-Great Grandfather was Nathan Bedford Forrest, the first Grand Wizard of the Ku Klux Klan. Her Daddy raised cattle in Hardee County. Man was a millionaire."

"Great," said Dee. "And you've arrested this guy six times?"

"Yeah. But he was drunk every time. His Mama keeps sending him off to rehab as part of his plea deals. Not that he ever stays very long. She bought some land up here and put a house on it for him to keep him away from home. He was in school at UF in Agriculture, but he majored in fraternity parties. China met him over in Gainesville back when he was in school. They've been on and off with each other for the last 10 years or so."

"How come you keep drawing the short straw?" Dee asked.

"I'm bigger than he is. He beats up women and small men. He's pure coward. First time I arrested him, he took one look at me and put his hands up."

Ryan visually measured Manny's height against Dee's. He estimated Manny at around six feet, but he was thick with muscle. His neck was nearly the width of his head. Dee was a tall woman, and though slender, he knew she carried a lot of muscle. His own height of six foot four inches put him way over either of them. He let out a long breath. If he was bigger than Adams, that made him feel a little more confident.

Dee looked over at Ryan. "You ready to go beard the lion in his den?" she asked.

Ryan finished off his can of Vernor's and set it on the desk in front of Junior. "Let's do this," he said.

Junior raised one eyebrow at Ryan, but Dee and Manny both headed in his direction. Manny slipped his rifle back into the case as he walked. The three of them opened the door to the office and stepped out onto the concrete steps.

"You lead, Manny. I'll follow, but when we get to the house, let me pull up close and you hang back."

"You're the Sergeant, Sergeant," Manny said and went to his car.

"The rifle...?"

Dee kept her eye on the back end of Manny's patrol car. "Manny was a sniper during Desert Storm. He's got the best shooting score of anyone in the department, handgun or rifle. Best man to have covering you— ever."

Ryan felt his confidence grow a bit more. He knew that Dee would position him safely, and Manny would be covering the door with a sniper rifle. He also knew that his white face and no uniform worked in his favor.

They reached a fenced area with a long, two-track drive heading into the distance. Manny stopped just before it and motioned Dee ahead. The drive to the house was easily another mile or more. The house was cedar plank, with a large porch. A huge red truck with an extended cab was parked at one end of the big porch.

"Ford F350 Super Duty," said Dee. "And of course, this guy has it in red."

Ryan had no idea about anything. The only truck he'd ever been in was Michael's pick-up, and it was a second-hand Datsun.

Dee got out of the car and Ryan got out and followed her up to the porch. Fortunately, the porchlight was on because the sun hadn't even considered coming up yet. Dee opened the screen door and banged on the wooden door. Then she stepped back behind Ryan so he would be the first person seen.

About two hundred yards away, Manny had pulled up in his truck. He'd parked parallel to the house, and he had the rifle braced against the trunk of the patrol car. In the dark, it was nearly invisible. Ryan could see it because he knew it was there. He doubted anyone coming to the door would have a clue it was out there, watching what would happen at the door.

"Bang on the door," Dee said, nudging Ryan forward. He opened the screen door and banged on the wood with his fist.

Finally, they started to hear someone bumbling their way through the room behind the front door. They hit something hard and there was loud cursing. The door was flung open, and Ryan stared down into the bullish face of a man about five foot ten. He blinked his eyes trying to see who or what was in front of him. He stared at Ryan's coat, then slowly raised his eyes up. "Who the fuck are you?"

"Dr. Ryan Edwards... Doc Markham's partner," said Ryan.

The man stepped out onto the porch and Dee swung into action. She grabbed his right wrist and swung him around until he was hanging over the porch railing. She had cuffs on him and pulled him back into a standing position before Ryan could count to ten.

"Let's step inside and get warm," she said pulling out her gun and pushing Buckley through the door.

Ryan stood there holding the screen door. He heard Manny's patrol car start up and a minute or two later he was parked behind Dee's car. He got out and put the rifle in the trunk, then came up the steps onto the porch.

"Thanks, Doc," Manny said as he walked inside.

Ryan sighed and then entered the house behind him.

The room they entered stretched the width of the front of the house. Two doors led to other areas of the house, but it was dark, and Ryan couldn't see anything down either hall. The impression was that the place was big.

"What the hell are you hassling me for now?" grumbled Buckley.

"Just need to ask you some questions and didn't want you to get excited and shoot one of us before we got to do that," said Manny.

"Fuck you, Sota." Buckley dropped onto the couch and glared at the three of them.

Dee pulled a micro-recorder out of her pocket, turned it on, and set it on the coffee table in front of Buckley. "Just so we're clear on this and you can be assured that we're on the up and up, I'm going to record this. You agree to that?"

"Yeah, whatever," said Buckley.

"Let it be noted that Deputies Dee Jackson and Manuel Sota have verbally acknowledged with Buckley Adams that we are recording our interview, taking place on December 22nd, 2001, at 7 a.m. This interview is taking place in the home of Buckley Adams. Mr. Adams is not under arrest and may refuse to answer these questions at any time. If Mr. Buckley should decide not to answer our questions, this is to serve as our verbal notice that we will take him into custody and continue this discussion in the Sheriff's Department interview room in Warren. Is this understood, Mr. Adams?"

"Yeah, I got it. You and the Mex here will take me in if I don't agree to talk to you."

"Thank you. When was the last time you saw China Braden?" Dee asked.

Buckley looked confused. "What the fuck does China have to do with this?"

"Just answer the question, Buckley," said Manny.

"I don't know. She was at the Cypress a couple of weeks ago. Saw her then."

"You and China on the outs?" asked Manny.

"China runs hot and cold. Right now, she's running with some kid from up around White Springs. I don't do threesomes with guys."

"Have you seen Bailey Braden recently?" asked Dee.

Buckley stared at Dee like she'd grown another head. "Bailey? Why the fuck would I be seeing Bailey?"

"I asked if you had seen him recently, not if you're dating him, Mr. Adams."

"No."

"Were you aware that Bailey had gotten engaged to a student from the University of Florida?"

Buckley shook his head. "Lord, no. What'd he do? Knock her up? I mean,

I know the boy doesn't have brains enough to use a rubber, but I also didn't think he'd ever have to."

There were footsteps in the southern hallway and Dee and Manny both pulled their guns. "Come on out of there with your hands up," shouted Dee.

A short dark-haired woman wearing a man's t-shirt stepped into the room with her hands up. "Am I being arrested?"

"No, ma'am. We're just here to ask Mr. Adams some questions."

"How come he's cuffed?"

"Yeah, how come I'm cuffed?" asked Buckley.

Manny laughed. "How many times have I had to arrest you?"

Buckley shrugged. "I don't know."

"Six. It makes me think you would not be exactly happy to see me."

"Oh!" said the young woman.

Dee motioned for her to sit down, and she took a seat on the big easy chair near the door. "You can put your hands down, ma'am," said Dee.

"Thank you." She set her hands on the arms of the chair, keeping them in sight of the two Deputies.

"Mr. Adams, getting back to our questions, were you aware that Bailey's fiancé had been murdered this week?"

Buckley's eyes went wide. "Oh hell, no. I met Shana last weekend. We've been holed up here since, what? Sunday night?"

Shana nodded. "Yeah. We ran into each other Saturday night. We went to my place, but I just have a space heater in my bedroom and Buck said he had central heat, so we came over here. His place is real nice."

"You've been together since Saturday?"

"Yeah. I mean, yes, ma'am. Buck said he'd take me down to his mother's for Christmas. I don't have any family around here."

"Ah, Buckley, that's sweet," said Manny.

"It IS sweet," said Shana.

Buckley grinned at Manny. "See, Sota, I can be nice."

Manny shook his head and looked at Dee.

"Shana, may I have your full name, date of birth, and address?"

"Sure! Shana Marie Rickards, June 6, 1982. I live at 11011 Wheatley Road,

Bronson, Florida."

Dee turned off the tape recorder and motioned for Buckley to stand up and turn around. She unlocked the handcuffs and Buckley rubbed his wrists as he sat back down. "That all you needed?"

"Yes, Mr. Adams. You and the Ms. Rickards have a Merry Christmas," said Dee.

"You, too!" said Shana.

Dee left the house first, with Manny pushing Ryan between the two of them so he could exit still keeping an eye on Buckley Adams.

Once outside they stood next to the patrol cars. "Well, that was a bust," said Manny.

"If he takes her to his Mama's maybe he'll behave himself," said Dee.

"This means we start over?"

"We've got a second name," said Dee. "Ward Foley."

"I don't know him," said Manny.

"Maybe he's the guy from Ft. White?"

"Junior?" suggested Ryan.

"Yeah, we'll have Junior run his name and see what he can come up with. Meet us back at the office," said Dee. She opened the passenger door and waved Ryan into it. "Get comfortable, Doc. Looks like we've got a long day ahead of us."

Chapter Thirty-Two

Bonehead lay across Bailey and Michael's laps on the couch. He'd stretched out to his full length so that he could occupy both. He snored softly, which made Bailey snicker. Michael had put on the DVD of Bull Durham after they'd gotten back from Chiefland. Jim peeked over the edge of his book to see how the two were doing. Bailey's soft snicker made Jim feel good. Michael and Bailey had moved closer together when it became clear the dog was determined to lie on both of them. Bailey didn't seem to care about the movie, but Michael kept laughing out loud and repeating certain lines. He loved Bull Durham.

Jim had hopes that Michael's love of baseball would lead him away from returning to Eden County. The coach at UF had told Jim he thought Michael had a good chance of being drafted. Michael's skills at center field and his power hitting were a combination that could take him far if he wanted it.

Jim returned to his book. McCullough's biography of John Adams had been Michael's birthday present to him, but until now he hadn't had the opportunity to really dig into it. He'd deliberately taken the day off so he wouldn't be tempted to try to find out how Dee and Manny's investigation developed. If anything big happened, they'd let him know.

"Sheriff Jim," Bailey said quietly.

Jim looked up from his book. Bailey was stroking Bonehead's ears. "Do you have to have a college degree to be a deputy?"

Jim shook his head. "No. You have to pass the Criminal Justice Basic Abilities Test and then graduate from something like Santa Fe's Law Enforcement Academy. Why?"

"Now that I have my GED, I was thinking about what I might do with it."

Jim tried to imagine Bailey as a deputy. He'd never been in trouble, not even as a kid. He'd worked at the Magnolia since dropping out of high school at 16. He knew that Martin would give Bailey a great recommendation. He'd worked there for four years, never missing a day. He had lived on his own, paid his own rent and utilities. Bailey was a fit and lean 5'10", and twenty years old. If he studied for the CBAT and completed the two semesters at Santa Fe, he'd easily pass the background test and drug testing. The kid didn't even drink. He never had. He'd always said his mother drank enough for the both of them so he'd decided to let her continue to have his share.

"Bailey, there's no reason in the world you couldn't be a deputy," Jim said.

Bailey nodded. Michael's head was on a swivel looking back and forth between his father and his friend.

"Would you hire me?" Bailey asked.

Jim smiled. "I would."

Bailey nodded. "I'm going to think about it."

"You do that," said Jim.

Jim noticed that Michael's mouth had dropped open. "Close your mouth, Michael."

There was an audible pop as Michael did.

"I'm just thinking about it." Bailey elbowed Michael. "I'm pretty sure it pays better than bussing tables."

"I just never thought about you doing something like that," said Michael.

"Yeah, well," said Bailey. "I don't think anyone did."

"Watch your movie, Michael," said Jim as he turned the next page in his book.

Michael elbowed Bailey. "You keep surprising me, Bailey."

Bonehead stretched and rolled over onto his back. Bailey began to rub the dog's stomach. "Yeah, I surprise me, too," said Bailey.

Chapter Thirty-Three

J unior set the file to print as he turned to Dee and Manny. Ryan had pulled Jim's office chair out into the bullpen and propped his feet up on a small waste basket. Thus far, everything Junior had found for them led them further from a suspect than toward one.

"Ward Foley is 56 years old and has enough arrests for public drunkenness to paper the walls of this room. His driver's license has been suspended for years. He lives with a sister that is married and out in McCracken. The only vehicle registered to any of them is a 1980 Dodge van," said Junior.

"That doesn't fit with what Buckley told us," said Manny.

Dee had turned on a small space heater and had it pointed at her feet. She dragged it a little closer with one foot. "That van isn't going to be our diesel engine that Bailey heard. Who is this young kid from White Springs that China's been seeing?"

"That," said Manny, "is the mystery. And if Edna didn't mention him, I'm thinking she doesn't know about him."

Junior finished off his can of Vernor's and dropped it into the bag under his desk. "Would Buckley have told you if he knew?" he asked.

Manny nodded. "Yeah, I am sure he would. He may be making time with a young woman right now, but he has always had it bad for China. If she dumped him for someone younger, that's probably why he went out and found himself a Shana."

"She...seemed nice," said Ryan.

Dee shook her head. "Buckley Adams isn't. First time he gets pissed off at her, he's likely to knock the crap out of her."

"More than likely," said Manny. "He'll do it. Probably not while he's down at his Mama's."

Ryan dropped his feet to the floor. "That's...not good."

"It's not up to us to tell her, and she wouldn't believe us anyway," said Dee. "She's 19 and she's got a man with money that's taking her to his Mama's house, which is a mansion by the way. He'll buy her some fancy thing for Christmas, and she'll be convinced he's going to be the one to put a ring on her finger and take care of her forever."

"But...," Ryan started.

"Ryan, I was a 19 year old girl once."

Manny laughed, "And you were Military Police in Kuwait at the time."

"You weren't ever that dumb, Dee Jackson," said Junior. "You broke Ke'shawn's nose in the 8th grade."

Dee pointed a finger at Junior and Ryan thought he saw the man pale a little. "I knew girls who were like Shana," said Dee. "And none of them listened to me or anyone else."

Ryan sighed heavily. "So...what?"

Manny looked at Dee, "Oh, no. No, no, no. That's a really bad idea."

Junior looked at Dee. "You know she tore up Bailey's apartment. Sheriff said it was her for sure."

Ryan's head swung from Manny, to Junior, and back to Dee. Are...you... really?"

"I think we have to talk to her," Dee said.

Manny grabbed his head with both hands, covering his ears. "I'm not listening to this, I am not listening to this."

"She's likely to be home. It's still early," said Dee.

Junior got up and walked back toward the break room. "If there's going to be crazy talk, I need another Vernor's."

Ryan took out his phone and dialed Michael's number. "Michael...put... Yeah, Jim."

Dee stood up, stepped over to Ryan, and pulled the phone out of his hand. "Sheriff, this is my investigation, and I will handle this."

Ryan could hear Jim's voice, but not what he was saying.

"We know it's not Buckley. He's alibied."

Jim talked a bit more and Dee said, "Not likely Foley either. No license and apparently living with his sister and her family in McCracken. The only vehicle he might have access to is a 1980 Dodge van."

The conversation on Jim's side went on for a bit after that, and finally Dee said, "Ask Bailey if he knows anything about China seeing someone younger from White Springs. If he knows something, we'll follow that lead instead of going to China now. He doesn't, it's the only lead, and it means going to see China."

Jim's response was short and Dee handed Ryan his phone. "He's going to talk to Bailey."

Manny sighed, "I hope Bailey knows something."

Chapter Thirty-Four

J im found Bailey in the kitchen eating a grilled cheese sandwich. He'd already washed the skillet he'd used to make it. "Where's Michael?" Jim asked.

"Outside with Bonehead. It's too cold for me," Bailey said.

Jim sat down at the table. "I need to ask you something about China."

Bailey shrugged, "I'll answer it if I can."

"Dee talked to Buckley. He says that China is involved with a younger man who's from White Springs. You have any idea who that could be?"

Bailey put his sandwich down and thought for a minute. "Maybe. There's a new guy who got a job working at the Cypress. I heard some talk that he had hooked up with an older woman and was living with her. He's supposed to be real good-looking." He blushed. "The women at the Magnolia talk a lot and I hear stuff."

"I'll let Dee know. Thanks, Bailey."

Bailey nodded. "China doesn't have the sense God gave a goose. She took up with Buckley when I was 10 or 11. Mama and Papa were still alive then. She'd show up all bruised and then take off with him again just a few days later. No telling what this guy from the Cypress is like, but if he's younger and good-looking, and he doesn't hit her, that'd be enough for her to dump Buckley. She's got the house and Papa's pension money, so Buckley's money isn't as important as it was when she had nothing."

The back door swung open and Bonehead charged in carrying a soggy tennis ball. He dropped it in Jim's lap.

"Oops! Sorry about that, Dad. I got too frozen to throw to him anymore.

130

He must not be done," said Michael, laughing.

"Well, he's going to have to be done for a while. I've got some work calls I have to make," said Jim, handing Michael the ball.

"I'll make you a sandwich, Michael," said Bailey, getting up from the table.

"Make one for Bonehead, too. If he's eating, he won't be bugging me about going out!"

Jim shook his head. "Do not feed that dog cheese. Ryan will have your head!"

Chapter Thirty-Five

The call from Jim gave them a new direction for the investigation, but it also brought up a slew of new issues. If China had hooked up with Edna Bass' employee, why hadn't she mentioned him? Maybe she didn't know?

"Do we go talk to China? See if this guy is there?" asked Manny.

"I'm not sure it's the best move right now. If the new boyfriend killed Noel Williams, we'll be tipping our hand. I also don't want to panic him, because that's a damn fine way to get one of us shot," Dee said.

Ryan cleared his throat and Dee and Manny looked at him.

"You have an idea," Dee said.

"Yes," Ryan said.

"This going to get you shot by the new boyfriend or by me?" she asked.

Ryan smiled. "Neither...I think..."

Manny laughed. "Out with it, Doc!"

"I...treated Bailey... Don't know her..."

"And?"

"Just go...to...tell her," said Ryan.

Dee nodded. "No reason to suspect you of anything."

"Yes," said Ryan.

"So maybe she doesn't let you in, but maybe she does, and you find out about the boyfriend," Dee continued.

"Yes," said Ryan nodding.

Junior shakes his head, "Doc, no offense, but you can't talk for shit."

Ryan laughed. "Gives me...more time..."

"And while you keep her busy, Dee and I can get a look around for a diesel truck."

Ryan shrugged. "Sure."

"Drive your car," said Manny. "She'll like your BMW."

"That's true. Dressed nice. Doctor with a BMW, she'll give you some time to talk."

Ryan smiled. "Good...plan..."

Dee pointed a finger at Ryan. "You be cautious. We'll be close. If the boyfriend is there and starts anything, you let us know."

"Radio," Manny said. "We give him a radio. You click it twice if something starts and we know you need us."

Dee nodded. "That'll work. Junior, get us a spare radio."

Junior got up from the desk and hurried back to a storage area. Manny got up and went to Ryan. "I'll get it set up so it's under your coat. I can fix it on your belt so you can feel it through the lining when your hand is in your pocket. We'll be listening for your signal, should you need us."

"Undercover!" Ryan exclaimed.

"Dear God, no," said Dee. "You are not going undercover!"

Manny and Junior both laughed.

"Sounds like he is, Sergeant," said Junior.

"Yeah, I think Junior and the Doc are right," said Manny.

"Let me make myself clear," Dee said firmly. "Under no circumstances are any of you to use the words undercover to describe anything the good doctor here does for this investigation. If the Sheriff thinks for one minute that we have sent him into a situation in which he is acting as or for any deputy of this department, we will all be looking for new jobs."

Ryan grinned and said, "Undercover!"

Dee pointed a finger at him. "No."

Ryan nodded.

"God save me," said Dee softly.

It took Manny about 20 minutes to hook up the radio and teach Ryan how to use it to notify them if he needed help. It took another 30 minutes for Junior to print out and mark a map so that he would be able to find

China Braden's house. Junior ordered lunch, and they all ate sandwiches from Sweet Ella's so no one would faint and fall over from hunger during the not-undercover adventure. Finally, after an hour of rehearsal, Dee was satisfied that Ryan had his story down pat.

Manny headed out toward China's house while Dee took Ryan back to the Sheriff's house to pick up his car. When they saw Michael's truck in the drive, Dee stopped well before the house.

Ryan pulled his keys out of his pocket and got out of the patrol car. He had refined this technique when he was still in high school. He opened the car door quietly, released the brake and put the car into neutral. Then he pushed off gently with his left foot and the car rolled quietly out of the paved drive and into the road. He got out of the car and pushed it up the road about 10 or 15 yards.

He started the car and pulled slowly up the road until he was even with Dee's patrol car. He waved at her, pulled out his map, and as he drove away he saw Dee reverse into a nearby drive and then pull out to follow behind him.

As he got closer to China Braden's house, he saw Dee's patrol car turn off the road to the left and head down a double-track dirt road. Ryan took a deep breath. He knew that Dee and Manny would be nearby. He knew he had the radio strapped to his back under his heavy coat and the microphone clipped to his belt next to where his left hand could reach it, through his pocket. He wouldn't truly be on his own, but he would be alone in the house with Bailey Braden's mother—a woman who no one had had anything good to say about since he'd first heard of her.

He reached the drive up to the small frame house. Painted a very faded shade of blue with a concrete porch and a white door, the house looked old. He pulled into the drive and parked in front of the steps of the porch. He got out of the car and reached into his left pocket to feel the microphone attached to his belt. It reassured him. If he got into trouble, Dee and Manny would come to his rescue.

As he stood in front of the door Ryan could hear a tv inside. He knocked on the door and waited, listening for sounds on the other side of the door.

He had raised his hand to knock again when the door opened. The woman standing there holding the door had to be Bailey Braden's mother. She had Bailey's vivid green eyes, but where his were warm, hers were cold. Her platinum hair was natural and fell just above her shoulders. China's head didn't come to his shoulder, and she probably didn't weigh 100 pounds. How did such a tiny person make so many people fear her?

"Hello, …I'm Dr. Edwards… I work with Doctor Markham," Ryan said.

China blatantly looked at him from shoes to the top of his head. She raised one eyebrow and said, "Yeah. I've seen your picture in the newspaper."

Ryan nodded, "I… I treated Bailey Braden for hypothermia."

She shrugged and the sweater she wore slipped over her hands. "So, you looking for money or what?"

"I wanted…to tell you…about his treatment… Not here about money."

She thought for a moment and motioned for him to come in. China went back to her seat on the couch, picked up her cola. On the television, a young man jumped up and down and screamed, "I'm not the father. I'm not!"

"Ms. Braden," Ryan said.

"China. Call me China. Everybody does."

Including your son, thought Ryan. "Yes… China…Bailey was exposed…to freezing…for too long…"

"Is he going to die?" she interrupted.

"Oh…no… But very serious…," said Ryan. He'd already forgotten his well-rehearsed story. He stood in the room, towering over China sitting on the couch. He gripped the microphone tightly, making sure he wasn't touching the button Manny had shown him. "Damage to his…fingers and toes… limited… Some frostbite on his face."

"Okay," she said.

"As his mother…"

"I am nobody's mother. Did Bailey say I'm his mother? He knows better than to say that," said China.

"No… no… Doc told me," Ryan said. Damn, he was doing this all wrong and she was going to throw him out or go after Bailey. He rubbed his forehead with his right hand and tried to remember what he'd been going to say.

"Calm down, Doc," said China. She patted on the seat next to her on the couch. "Park yourself, take a deep breath, and we'll start over."

Ryan felt his face grow hot with a blush.

"Want something to drink? I've got colas, beer, might even be a cup of coffee left if you'd rather."

Ryan waved his right hand, "Water?"

China nodded. "I'll get it." She disappeared through a doorway into a hall.

Ryan sat down on the couch, making sure his right side would be next to China. The last thing he needed was for her to wonder why his left hand stayed in his pocket.

China returned with a glass of water. She set it on the coffee table and stepped over to turn off the tv. She took her seat and picked up her cola. "Want to take your coat off?" she asked.

Ryan shook his head. "No…thanks… I'll try to…make this quick."

China smiled. "Doc Markham doesn't like me much. I imagine that's why you're so nervous. So, Bailey almost froze hisself to death."

"Yes… Sheriff Sheppard found him… brought him…"

"And you treated him."

"Yes."

"Anything else I need to know?"

"…you…have questions?"

China shook her head. "Nope. You must be a good doctor."

Ryan nodded. "I am."

China reached over and touched his coat. "This wool?"

Ryan nodded.

"Must have cost an arm and a leg, long coat like that, wool. You can't be making that kind of money with Doc."

"I do…good… Only me and Bonehead."

"Bonehead?"

"Dog."

She laughed. "Funny name."

"He earned it."

"What kind of dog is he?" a male voice asked.

Ryan looked up and saw a man standing in the doorway to the hall. "Golden…"

"Nice. I like Golden Retrievers. Pretty dogs. I'm Ray," he said holding out his hand.

Ryan stood up and took his hand and shook it. "Ryan…Edwards."

"You're one of Edna's doctors. She talks about you guys."

Ryan smiled. "Edna… She's special."

"She is," said Ray, as he moved into the room and dropped into a nearby chair. "I really like her. She's a good boss."

Ryan sat back down on the couch, a little bit further away from China. China noticed the slight increase in distance. He could see that in her smile and little wave of her hand. Ray had thick, longish hair, and bright blue eyes. His wide mouth showed white, even teeth. Something that Ryan didn't often see in Eden County. Dental care wasn't available in the county, so anyone who could afford it went to Gainesville for it.

"China and I are getting ready to head over to Hamilton County. My folks have a place on the Suwanee. We've been invited over for a late lunch."

"Oh," Ryan said, standing again. "Sorry… I should go…"

Ray nodded. "No problem. We're not rushing. My day off, so we're taking it easy."

China stood up. "I appreciate you wanting to keep me informed," she said.

Ryan was sure he could hear a note of sarcasm in her voice. He wondered if Ray had heard any of their conversation. He didn't seem concerned. China, on the other hand, gave off nothing but mixed signals. He knew he should be afraid of her. Her touch on his coat had been proprietary. Like someone looking at the lines of a horse or judging the color of a dog's coat.

At the door, China stepped out on the porch with him. She rested the fingers of her right hand on his sleeve. "Nice meeting you, Ryan. You ever need to inform me about anything else, feel free to stop by." Her voice had all the warmth of a mortuary.

Ryan said nothing and made his way down the steps and to his car. As he pulled out of the drive and back onto the road, he hoped that Dee and

Manny wouldn't be too far away. He hadn't needed backup, but he damn sure needed to talk to them. Even if neither of them was the murderer, China Braden made his skin crawl.

Ryan had just driven out of sight of China Braden's house when Dee and then Manny pulled up behind him. His phone rang and he answered it.

"We're going back to the office. Head that way. We want to know what you learned."

"Not much, Dee…met boyfriend… China…is scary."

Dee laughed. "We'll talk," she said.

The drive back to the Sheriff's Department seemed shorter than the drive out to China Braden's. When he pulled up in front of the building, Junior waved to him through the window. Dee and Manny had probably let him know they were on their way.

Once settled into their previous chairs, and Ryan had his feet propped up on the wastebasket, Dee and Manny went into reporting mode. They'd found a diesel truck parked in the garage in back of the house with China's 1988 Mist Blue Buick Regal with the white vinyl top. She'd inherited it when her mother died two months after her father had passed.

"Yeah, it's a Ram Turbodiesel pickup. It's a beauty, too. Looks mint. The guy definitely takes care of it," said Manny. "If the engine is half as nice as the exterior, that's a nice truck."

"So just how young is this new boyfriend?" asked Dee.

Ryan thought about it and said, "…Early 20s… Taking her…place on… Suwannee …For lunch. Name…Ray."

"No worries on the rest of the name," said Junior. "I already ran the plate. Truck belongs to Raymond Anderson Sherman the third. I checked out Raymond Anderson Sherman, Jr., and turns out he's a guy who owns a restaurant, a bar, and a campground in White Springs. They have a house in town, and a place out on the Suwannee River."

"What is a kid like that doing in Eden County working for Edna Bass?" asked Manny.

"Yeah, sounds like Daddy has money, which would explain the truck, but not the age of it," Dee said.

"Going…parent's place…," said Ryan.

"Huh," muttered Junior. He began tapping away at the keys of his computer keyboard. For several minutes that was the only noise in the room. "AHA!" crowed Junior. "I got the touch!"

Manny smiled, "Okay, out with it Junior. What have your magic fingers found on the computer this time?"

"There's a big story about the Third in The Suwannee Democrat. Seems like The Third made a deal with his grandfather, Sherman Senior, that if he could make it on his own for five years, then the old man would set him up in his own business. Senior owns a construction company. Junior of course has the restaurant, bar, and a campground. The Third wants to build custom furniture. He didn't have the start-up money, and granddad decided he'd have to earn it by making his own way for five years."

Ryan shook his head. "He…was nice."

"How nice can anyone be who is with China Braden?" asked Manny.

Dee swatted him.

"So maybe we found the truck, but did we find the killer?" asked Junior. "This article says he's 22 and graduated from Jacksonville University with a Bachelor of Arts in Sculpture. He works in wood and metal."

"If China's his first big love, and she wants someone dead…," said Dee.

Manny nodded. "We've seen people do more for less reason than that."

"Why not…China…?" asked Ryan.

Junior shook his head. "China always has a man taking care of things for her. Always. First, it was her Daddy, then it was Buckley."

Dee looked at Ryan. "She is not a nice person, but I don't see her getting hold of a gun and killing someone. She's very good at manipulating people to do what she wants. Buckley's been beating the shit out of people for her for years. Even some of the women he beat up were for her."

Ryan didn't like it, but he knew he didn't have the experience with crime nor the knowledge of China Braden that the Deputies had. It felt wrong.

Dee had obviously picked up on his reticence. "Go on home, Ryan. You've been a big help. We'll take it from here."

Ryan pushed the waste basket away and stood up. "Let me know…," he said and headed for the door. He stopped, turned around, and grinned at Dee. "You…need undercover…, give me…call."

Dee tossed her empty water bottle at him, and he ducked out the door.

He stood in front of the office and pulled on his knit hat. The street had iced up while they were talking. He'd have to take it slow getting back to the house. Bonehead would need a walk. He'd probably been mooching snacks all day from Michael and Bailey. And it wasn't going to get any warmer standing here. He headed for his car.

Chapter Thirty-Six

The tap at the back door made Jim look up from where he had leaned into the refrigerator. Ryan stood at the glass looking like a well-dressed popsicle. "Come on in!" called Jim.

Ryan opened the door and wiped his shoes on the rug. Not that it did any good. Everything clinging to his shoes was frozen.

"Just take them off, Ryan," said Jim.

Ryan looked at him and smiled. "Lost...cause."

"I'd say so."

He slipped out of his shoes and stepped on the linoleum and slipped a little. "Oooo!" he yelped and Jim reached out and grabbed him.

"If you fall and break your neck in here Doc will never get over it," said Jim. "And I'm likely to suffer right along with him."

Ryan laughed. He pulled off his hat and stuffed it in the pocket of his coat, then leaned against the table to pull his socks off. His long bony feet made soft slapping noises as he made his way into the living room where there was carpet.

"Want something to drink?" asked Jim.

"Nothing...cold," said Ryan as he disappeared into the other room.

Jim could hear the clinking of Bonehead's tags and the soft nonsense noises that Ryan made when he greeted the dog. The boys had disappeared into Michael's room. Jim felt sure they were playing video games and that Bonehead had not been allowed to go with them because he had a habit of nosing the controllers out of their hands, wanting to be petted.

Jim poured Ryan a cup of coffee and topped off his own mug before he walked into the living room behind Ryan. He found him sitting on the couch with Bonehead sitting between his feet and his head resting on Ryan's knee as he got cooing sounds and deep ear rubs. The dog looked completely blissed out. He set the coffee on the table in front of Ryan.

Ryan looked up at Jim. "I...want...talk to Bailey," he said. He still rubbed Bonehead's ears, but he was focused on Jim. "Have...questions..." Ryan closed his eyes and shook his head. "I met China."

"Yeah, I can see how that would make you have questions," said Jim. "Bailey will answer you. He has no illusions about his mother."

"She...denies...," said Ryan.

"Being Bailey's mother? I know."

"Creepy," said Ryan.

Jim laughed sadly. "I talked with Mike Braden about China one time. I'd had to arrest her for misdemeanor assault. She attacked a woman in Doc's waiting room for calling her a bad mother. The other woman had to get stitches in her face where China clawed her face. She didn't care about the bad part, but she was madder than a wet hen about being called a mother. Mike told me that she never admitted she was pregnant. They realized she was pregnant when she was about six months along and her mother realized she had a rounded belly. When she went into labor, she insisted she had appendicitis and demanded they take her to Gainesville to the hospital to have it removed." Jim set his coffee mug on the table.

"She was a minor and delusional, so Mike and Abby got the doctor to agree to tie her tubes when he did the cesarean. She wouldn't push, demanded sedation, and screamed at them she wasn't pregnant, so it was a pretty easy thing to get him to agree to do."

"Poor Bailey," whispered Ryan.

"The hospital insisted on having her evaluated because of her behavior when she was admitted. Mike said the doctor told him that she had antisocial personality disorder."

"Sociopath," said Ryan.

"They raised Bailey as their child and protected him from her as much as they could. Mike died first, but he had set up things to take care of Abby and China. Abby died two months later. But China was all set. He knew she'd never be able to take care of herself, and she was his daughter. He loved her. He had a savings account he and Abby had set up when Bailey was born. He put Bailey's name on it before he died."

"He...know?" asked Ryan

"He does. As far as I know, he's never touched it." Jim had watched Bailey grow up. He and Michael spent a lot of time together until Bailey dropped out of school and started working full-time at the Magnolia. Even then, they would find time to hang out together. He had never regretted asking that very sad little boy to watch out for his first-grade son.

Ryan got up. "I should go say hi to Bailey and Michael. Then I need to go crash. I'll take Bonehead with me."

Jim watched him head down the hall to Michael's room. Bonehead trotted along beside him. Over the past couple of years, he'd watched Bonehead and Ryan become more comfortable with one another. Bonehead still had a mind of his own and would refuse to obey when he didn't want to, but he no longer acted like he was the most depressed animal on the planet.

But then, Ryan didn't act like the most depressed man on the planet either. He liked the change in both of them.

Chapter Thirty-Seven

Ryan tapped on Michael's door and heard a clear, "Come in!" along with the sounds of general destruction which turned out to be car crashes on the monitor of Michael's computer. Bonehead quickly slipped past him and into the room, heading straight for Bailey and Michael who sat on the end of the bed with controllers in their hands.

"No!" Bailey said as Bonehead pushed on the underside of the controller knocking it out of his hands. He replaced the controller with his big fuzzy head.

Michael laughed and Bailey stared into Bonehead's eyes and said, "Dog, I know I wasn't winning, but I prefer to be defeated for my own mistakes, not yours."

"He just saved you from losing to me, again," said Michael.

"You're just trying to make me feel better," said Bailey, "and failing at it."

Ryan closed the door and sat on the end of the bed next to Bailey. "Sorry."

Bailey shrugged. "It's okay. I suck at this."

Michael stood up and shut the game down. Bailey rubbed Bonehead's ears, which would do nothing to discourage him from continuing to knock the controller out of his hands in the future.

"How was your day?" asked Michael.

"Met China," Ryan answered.

Bailey's eyes widened in horror, "Oh no! Why?"

"Helping...Dee... Manny."

"I thought they were going to talk to Buckley," said Michael.

"Did...that...," said Ryan.

"What's going on?" asked Michael.

"Buckley...alibied...new boyfriend," said Ryan.

"China has a new boyfriend?"

Ryan nodded. "Dee and Manny...don't see it."

"Don't see what?" asked Michael.

"China...I think..."

Bailey reached out and grabbed Ryan's arm. "China?"

Ryan nodded.

"And the deputies don't see her," said Bailey.

"Not...not like...me."

Bailey turned to Michael. "We have to help."

Michael started to answer. Finally, the words came, "You're not trained to do this, and it's dangerous."

"Death...always around."

"Please," said Bailey. "You know how to do this."

Ryan watched Michael rub his forehead the same way Jim did while he struggled with an idea. "Fuck," he whispered.

"I can...," Ryan said to Bailey. "You said... car... coat..."

"I can't let you do this alone," Michael said. "I completed the EVOC training. I'm better prepared than either of you."

"I don't know what any of that means," Bailey said, "but if you can help...."

"We can't tell Dad. He can't know," said Michael. We won't have any legal standing, but maybe we'll come up with something that will get Dee and Manny to see what Ryan sees. We'll stick together. We'll go to Dee with whatever we find. This is her case."

"I'm good with that," said Bailey.

"Yes...." said Ryan.

"When Dad goes to the office tomorrow, Bailey and I will come up to your place."

Ryan smiled. "We'll plan..." Bonehead stood up and Ryan rubbed his head.

"Yeah....feed you..." He got up and went to the bedroom door. "...Just knock..." He left the bedroom and went down the hall, waving goodbye to Jim as he and Bonehead headed into the kitchen and toward the back door.

Ryan picked up his socks and shoes and sprinted from the back door up the stairs to his apartment. Bonehead thought they were racing and nearly bumped Ryan off the small porch getting in front of him to the door.

"...Dog!..." Ryan put his key in the lock and Bonehead pushed the door open and headed straight for his bowl. Ryan closed the door behind him and thought that if he couldn't keep his own dog from nearly killing him, how could he manage an investigation?

Bonehead picked up his bowl and dropped it noisily onto the floor. He stood looking at Ryan with clear annoyance. Ryan threw up his hands. "You!" he said. Bonehead stood his ground.

Ryan moved around him to the upper cabinet where he stored the food. He pulled out the gallon container of dry food and set it on the counter. Then he picked up the bowl and began to fill it. Bonehead sat. He huffed a little as if to say 'Hurry up!' but otherwise behaved himself.

Ryan knew he had to do this. He had to find something that would make Dee and Manny look at China and not Ray. China reeked of danger. Ray might own the truck, but Ryan would bet money, he wasn't the one who drove it to the DOT shed that morning.

Chapter Thirty-Eight

Dee and Manny sat together at a table when Jim walked in the next morning. Junior industriously typed on his computer. Junior waved at him as he passed by on the way into his office. Dee didn't look up, but Manny nodded in his direction.

Jim shrugged it off and sat at his desk. He pulled up the report that Dee and Manny had put together the day before which covered their talk with Buckley Adams and then Ryan's pre-text meeting with China Braden. Buckley's alibi held up with a confirmation from the girl's roommate that had put them both in Gainesville until late morning on Sunday. The girl's presence in Buckley's house removed the probability of him having communicated with China and then gone off to murder Noel Williams.

The discovery of the new boyfriend's diesel truck in the shed at China Braden's set up a new line of investigation. Edna Bass had confirmed that Raymond Anderson Sherman had started working for her just over a month ago, which gave him plenty of time to come into contact with China. His presence in her house yesterday brought Dee and Manny to the damning conclusion that he was a much more likely suspect than Buckley. Edna had not known where Sherman was living, nor if he was in a relationship. She had his cell number and he had shown up regularly for his shifts.

Edna had supplied them with Sherman's cell phone number, and they were making plans for when it would be easiest to pick him up for an interview.

From the background run on Sherman, Jim wondered whether or not the young man would have gotten himself involved in a murder. He started to call out to Junior when the big man walked past his door to where Dee and Manny worked.

"He doesn't have a concealed weapons permit," Jim heard Junior say.

"That doesn't mean anything. He could still own a gun," Dee responded. "Guns are easy to buy, and only long guns have to be visible in a vehicle."

"He could have a gun. Do we have the report from forensics on what type of gun we're looking for?" asked Manny.

He could hear them rustling through paperwork and the clicking of the keyboard of the computer. Jim knew he hadn't seen a report from Bud Peterson. He waited to hear if any of them had gotten it.

Junior's high whine took over, "Nothing from Bud, yet. You want me to give him a call?"

Dee said, "No, I'll give him a call. I've got his cell number."

Manny laughed, "When did he give you his cell number?"

"He didn't. One of the techs who'd just put in notice a couple of months ago sent it to me. I think he was really pissed off at Bud about something."

"Oooo, you piss off Bud, Jim's going to be very unhappy with you," said Junior.

Jim snorted. He sure as hell would be. They needed Bud. He'd done them a lot of favors over the years.

"She just doesn't want to call the office and get Dr. Sullivan," said Manny.

Jim had the sudden urge to bang his head on his desk. He'd met Dr. Sullivan. If she had also been the female tech who'd come to Warren and checked out the Noel Williams' car, she and Dee had already butted heads. That would explain her exasperation at his and Michael's contamination of the crime scene in Bailey's apartment. She probably thought no one in Eden County knew anything about maintaining the scene of a crime.

Jim got up from his desk and quietly closed the door to his office. He sat back down and quickly dialed Bud's home number from memory. He'd arranged more than one fishing trip for the two of them with Doc Markham.

The phone rang twice and was answered with a gruff, "What do you want, Sheppard?"

"Dee's about to call your cell."

148

"Ha! It's turned off. I don't go back on duty until the day after Christmas and I am not answering it."

"Is that why you got caller ID?" asked Jim.

"Yes, sir. This number is too damned available to suit me. So other than telling me that, what do you want to know, 'cause I know you're not calling me about going fishing."

"Does you not answering your cell mean Dee's going to have to talk to Dr. Sullivan?"

Bud started laughing, "Oh, that's too sweet to stand. Yes, it does. How much do they hate each other?"

"Manny thought Dee might shoot her."

"I'm sure the feeling was mutual. Sullivan's prickly. She thinks she's too good to be stuck in North Florida with all us hicks from the sticks. Her degree is from the University of Albany. Her husband got a job teaching at UF. She hates it here."

"What's he teach?"

Bud cackled. "Creative writing. The over/under's one year. I'm taking under."

Jim found himself grinning. "Well, I'm not allowed to be involved in the case."

"You have a good Christmas, Jim."

"You, too, Bud. Your daughter coming with the grandkids?"

"Nah. Roads are too bad. We're going to try for New Year's."

"Ryan bought a turkey. Want to join us?"

"No thanks. I promised a certain lady we'd go see Ocean's Eleven Christmas Day. She's making dinner afterward."

"Oh," said Jim. "This wouldn't be the lovely...?"

"Enjoy your turkey," interrupted Bud and the line went dead. Jim chuckled and went back to work on the schedule for the second half of January 2002. He decided that leaving his door closed would keep him from hearing anything he shouldn't.

His line rang and he picked up the phone. Junior spoke quietly, "China Braden is here to see you." Jim's heartbeat quickened. He hadn't spoken to

China in years. "I'll talk to her."

Before he could get out of his chair there was a tapping at the door. Jim sat back down and called out, "Come in."

The door opened and China Braden stood there. "Want me to close the door?" she said, smiling.

"Leave it open, China."

She laughed and pushed it all the way open. "So you don't want to be behind a closed door with me, Sheriff? Now that's just being a coward."

Jim kept his face blank. "What do you want, China?"

"I can't stay long," she said, "Ray's waiting to take me to his parent's place." She stepped into the office and sank into one of the chairs in front of his desk. Her hair was swept up into a messy bun on her head, and her make-up understated. She looked human, and the friendly smile on her face didn't reach her eyes. She even had on a modest outfit, a long gray sweater and jeans.

"Trying to impress the parents?" asked Jim.

China tilted her head in a practiced way that made her green eyes catch more light. "Ah, Sheriff, you're too kind."

"Why are you here, China?"

Her smile disappeared. "Bailey. He with you? I stopped by his place and he wasn't there."

"I know," said Jim.

"He's at your house?"

Jim shook his head. "Bailey's safe."

China huffed and put her hand on his desk. She kept her voice soft, not wanting anyone outside the office to hear. "He in Gainesville with Michael?"

"China, I'm not going to tell you where he is."

"You're protecting a killer," she said.

"Who did he kill?"

China leaned forward, "You know who he killed. You think of him like he's a kid, but he's a man, with a man's needs. She says no, and he loses control."

"How do you know this?" Jim leaned back into his chair and tried to look relaxed.

"I know men," China said softly.

"So you don't actually know anything."

"Stop being deliberately dense. You know damn well what I'm talking about."

"I really don't."

"Fine. I don't give a fuck about that girl or the dummy anyway." China stood up and brushed at her clothes as though being in the Sheriff's office was dirtying her in some way. "I'm going to go have some fun."

"I hear you have a new...friend."

China shrugged. "Men just like me, Sheriff. They always have. Except you, which probably means you ain't much of a man."

"Right, China," Jim said. He smiled. "Definitely not the kind of man for you."

China let a faint grin cross her face. "I hear that new doctor lives in your daddy's old apartment at your house."

Jim didn't answer and the silence brought out China's anger. "Maybe I'll just go see him sometime. I got lots of space at my house. He might like it better than that shabby shit hole you're renting him."

Jim stood up and stepped around his desk. He let himself loom over her, "He's got a dog, China. Dogs don't like you."

"Fuck you," China said and turned and walked out, moving at a slow pace to let him know that he hadn't intimidated her. She opened the front door and looked back, "It's not healthy for a white man to associate with coloreds like you do. No wonder no good white man wants to work for you."

She went out of the building and slammed the door closed behind her.

Junior, Dee, and Manny looked at Jim. Dee snorted, "She's a piece of work."

"That she is," said Jim quietly.

"What did she say?" asked Dee.

"She wants me to think Bailey killed Noel Williams."

Everyone was silent for a moment, absorbing the statement.

Dee took a breath, "She knows who did it."

Jim nodded. "Yeah. And you have to find out who that is."

Chapter Thirty-Nine

"Does China have access to a gun?" Bailey echoed the question Ryan had attempted to ask. "Wow." Bailey rubbed Bonehead's ears and thought about it. "I've never seen her with a weapon, other than her personality. I know Mama and Papa never had a gun. Papa said he got rid of his shotgun when China was a kid. She shot at a cow with it."

Michael snorted. "Of course she did."

"How old?"

"I think maybe ten or eleven. She got it out of the garage. He had it locked up in a storage room, but she picked the lock on the door."

"Okay," said Ryan. "So...she could..."

"She doesn't have much money. She lives on Papa's pension."

"Maybe Buckley bought her one?" said Michael.

Bailey grinned. "Buckley isn't stupid."

"But...not ruled out...gun," said Ryan.

"No," said Bailey.

"What happened to the cow?" asked Michael.

"Ran away. Papa said she missed it by a mile."

Ryan leaned back against the counter on his stool. The counter pressed against the small of his back uncomfortably. So far, their avenues of investigation didn't seem promising. China didn't have friends to confide in. Finley did say he'd told China about Noel, but that didn't put her with Noel with a gun in her hand.

"It's Saturday. I think we all hit Edna's and have a beer. Do it early. When

153

all the geezers from the VFW go before bingo. I'm betting her guy works set-up and will be there," said Michael. He pointed at Ryan, "You ask Edna if we can talk to him. She likes you."

"Braden and Sheppard...ask to speak to...the guy...," said Ryan.

"She didn't mention him the other night when she told you about Buckley and that other guy," said Michael.

Ryan tilted his head to acknowledge that. "May not...yet..."

"We go early, no chance of China being there." Bailey sat back on the couch, pulling Bonehead up into his lap. Bonehead immediately rolled over, so his belly faced up. "She'll get there around ten at the earliest. If we see her car, we can always bail."

"Yeah, no missing that car," said Michael.

"88 Buick Regal," he said to Ryan.

Ryan nodded. "Good...time?"

"The geezers get there around 7. Bingo's at 8:30," said Bailey. Bailey squinted at Michael, "You're not old enough to drink."

Michael shrugged. "If I order a soda, Edna won't throw me out."

"You hope," said Ryan.

Michael blushed. "I'm not sitting in the car while you guys talk to him."

"You?" Ryan asked looking at Bailey.

"21 on the 25th of November."

"C'mon, Ryan. I won't drink, I promise."

"We go...5:30... No one drinks," Ryan said.

"Fine," said Michael. No one will be there at that hour except a bunch of old people who play bingo. One drink and they're out of there."

"Edna...and Ray..."

"Nice and quiet. Good time to talk to the guy," agreed Bailey.

"Fine! We meet at the car at 5?"

Ryan nodded. "Good."

Bonehead raised his head and looked at Michael. Michael dropped his head back. "All right, Bonehead. I'll throw tennis balls to you."

The dog scrambled off the couch and Bailey's lap and found a tennis ball in his bed. He brought it to Michael and dropped it at his feet.

Michael stood up and grabbed the ball off the floor. "I swear, Bonehead, I'm going to need Tommy John surgery before New Year's." Michael walked to the door and threw the ball into the backyard. Bonehead raced down the stairs, with Michael clomping along behind him.

Bailey got up and went to the door. "Thank you."

"For what?"

Bailey turned around and closed the door behind him. Ryan puzzled over him. He found it difficult to imagine how Bailey had grown up to be who he was. He thought how odd it was that some people became someone good no matter what they went through, and others could have everything and still be worthless. Life was a genuine mystery.

Chapter Forty

When Jim arrived home at 6, he turned over the keys to Bobby Dale's patrol car. Bobby had the TV on in the living room and watched a children's Christmas movie. Jim didn't recognize it, but his deputy seemed entranced.

"How'd things go today?" he asked Bobby.

Without looking away from the TV, Bobby explained that it had been quiet. "Michael and Bailey took off with Doc Ryan a little while ago. They said they'd be back for supper."

Jim sat down in his chair. "Any idea where they were going?"

"No," said Bobby. His eyes still followed everything going on in the movie.

Jim found himself smiling. Michael had bought this DVD when they'd been out buying clothes for Bailey. He'd seen Bailey looking at it and decided they needed to have it for the holidays. Bailey had watched it, as it turns out, mostly in horror. He had fond memories of the story from childhood and the movie simply didn't echo his memories.

Bobby seemed fascinated, which Jim found entertaining.

"Any idea when they'll be back?"

Bobby shook his head.

"What do you think of the movie, Bobby?"

Bobby didn't turn away from it. "I don't think I understand it."

Jim struggled to keep from laughing. He swallowed hard. "Did you ever read the book?"

Bobby shook his head. "Never was much for reading," he said.

"It doesn't really follow the story in the book," said Jim.

Bobby sat back on the couch as The Grinch carved the roast beast. "I wouldn't show that to a kid," Bobby said.

Jim made his face more serious. "Yeah, Bailey thought the same thing. He liked the animated movie better."

"I hope you don't mind. It was in your DVD player, and they'd gone out," said Bobby.

"It's fine. You couldn't leave until I brought your patrol car back."

Bobby got up and Jim handed him the car keys. "You need anything before I leave, Sheriff?"

"Nah. Head on home, Bobby. I'm sure you've got gifts to wrap." Bobby Dale's brother and sister had six kids between them, and Jim had watched him struggle with what to get each child. He'd polled the opinions of everyone in the department about his potential gifts. The man took Christmas very seriously.

"Oh, I got that done. I'm making stuff for Christmas morning now. I always make cookies for the kids to have instead of breakfast. It's a tradition."

Everyone in the station had heard of this tradition. Bobby brought cookies in for his fellow deputies, and Jim generally got his own box for Michael. "Anything new this year?"

Bobby smiled. "I'm making peanut butter cookies with chocolate chips, along with the usuals."

"That sounds good."

"I tested it on Andy. He loved them."

Deputy Andy Driscoll and Bobby Dale had become close friends ever since they'd worked together on the Libby murder. Andy's approval of any new cookie recipe would be a sure vote for the taste of the cookie as far as Bobby was concerned.

"I will look forward to tasting them."

"Yeah, the secret is to not use too many chips. You just want a taste of the chocolate, or it overwhelms the sweetness of the peanut butter cookie."

"You are definitely the master of Christmas cookies. Even Dee looks forward to them."

Bobby lit up like a floodlight. "If the Sergeant likes these, I'll know I've struck gold."

Bobby got his coat, gloves, and hat and headed for the door. Jim called out just as he opened the door. "Oh! I gassed up the car for you. Noticed you were getting low."

"Thank you, Sheriff!" Bobby smiled big.

Chapter Forty-One

The parking lot of the Cypress had four vehicles in it. One big pickup truck, two small sedans, and one giant older sedan. Ryan recognized the giant Cadillac as Edna's. Her son had bought it for her in the mid-1990s when she had been extremely over-weight and he'd wanted her in a car that she could comfortably drive. Ryan had never met Buddy Bass, but he believed that despite the man's reputation, he must have loved his mother.

He pulled up and parked near the door and Edna's car. He wanted to be able to make a quick getaway. Bailey climbed out of the back seat and Michael got out of the passenger seat. The three of them settled themselves and walked in.

Edna looked and saw Ryan and waved. "Ryan! Come on in! Let me buy you a beer!" she said.

"Let her buy you a beer," said Michael. "One of us should get a drink out of this. I'll drive home."

Ryan gave Michael the side eye. "You just want to drive my car."

Michael grinned. "Guilty."

They walked to the bar and took three seats in a row. Edna filled a glass with a draft and then filled two glasses with cola and set them in front of Bailey and Michael. "I know damn well neither of you is 21, so drink your colas and I won't toss you out," said Edna.

A very tall, shaggy-haired young man brought two trays of glasses and set them behind the bar. Edna tapped him on the arm. "Ray, let me introduce you to Doc Ryan. And these two troublemakers are Michael Sheppard and

159

Bailey Braden."

Ray smiled at them. He reached out to shake Ryan's hand. "Heard a lot about you, Doc. Miss Edna's real fond of you."

"I'm real fond of her," Ryan said.

Ray looked at Michael and Bailey. "Braden? Any relation to China?"

Even the music seemed to go quiet.

"I was raised by her parents," Bailey answered.

"I've been renting a room from China. Must have been your room once upon a time," said Ray.

Edna's eyebrows raised almost to her hairline and she looked between Ray and Bailey. "I didn't know that," she said.

Ray shrugged. "Yeah, China said you might not like it. She seems to think you don't like her."

Edna smiled. "Yeah, that would be China."

"How is China doing these days?" Bailey asked.

"She's all right. It's been tough, Christmas without her parents, and her and her boyfriend breaking up a few weeks ago. I took her to my parent's place on the river. She had a good time. Seemed to cheer her up pretty good."

Ryan could feel the gears in his head trying to take in this information. Rented a room? Not the boyfriend? He looked at Edna and she reached over and patted his hand.

"Ray ain't dumb enough to date her," she whispered.

"That big pickup in the parking lot yours?" asked Michael.

"Yeah! You like trucks?"

"I've got a little pick-up. Nothing fancy like that. Is it diesel?"

"It is, and it's sweet. Automatic transmission, comfortable seats. Gets great mileage."

"Sounds sweet."

Bailey leaned towards Ray. "You ever driven that tank China has?"

Ray threw his head back and laughed. "God, no. Belonged to her parents, right?"

"Yeah, it was her Daddy's pride and joy. I helped him wash and polish it more than once."

"It is in mint condition."

"Ray, honey, could change out the keg for the Budweiser?" Edna asked.

"Sure thing," said Ray. He nodded toward the three men. "Nice meeting y'all." He disappeared into the back of the bar.

Edna rested on her elbows on the bar. "That's some slick interrogation. Why are you doing it?"

Bailey took a sip of his cola. "China's trying to snag him. Mama and Papa been dead since 1997."

"Yeah, I noticed that. Don't worry. I'm going to fix it."

"How?" asked Ryan.

"Going to rent him Buddy's place. It's closer to the bar than China's and the last renter moved a couple of months ago. It's all clean and ready."

Bailey laughed loudly. "I love it. You do that, Edna."

"So you thought our interrogation technique was slick?" asked Michael.

Edna patted Michael's cheek. "Honey, you were born to be a deputy. Now get the hell out of my bar before your daddy decides to arrest my ass for underage customers."

"Yes, ma'am," said Michael.

Ryan drained his beer, handed Michael the keys to his car, and stood up. "Merry Christmas!"

Edna made a shooing motion, and they filed out through the door and got into Ryan's car.

"He's not involved," said Bailey as he fastened his seat belt.

"Still, has the truck," said Michael.

"China...drove...?"

Michael shook his head, "I can't see him letting her borrow it."

"She might have taken it, and he doesn't know," said Bailey. "She's done that before. Took off in Buckley's truck once and went to Ocala. Pissed him off bad."

"No way.....to check...."

Michael nodded. "We need to find out about a gun. Then find out if China has one."

Bailey shook his head. "Can't see it. China doesn't like to get her hands dirty."

"Find…..gun…..see where…..leads."

Chapter Forty-Two

The phone rang and Jim answered it. Michael and Bailey had disappeared as soon as they came in. He thought they were in Michael's room, but he'd been reading when the phone rang.

"Give me the phone, please."

"Ms. Bass, give me just a minute to be sure I have the Sheriff on the line, all right?"

Jim wondered what the hell Dee had done now.

"Excuse me, ma'am, I will give you the phone!"

Jim leaned against the wall and waited for the two women to come to an agreement. Finally, Dee said, "Sheriff, Ms. Bass wants to speak to you."

Before Jim could even answer, Edna Bass was on the line, "Why are your people harassing my barman?" Edna said.

"I have no idea, Edna, but they are working a case. May I please speak with my Sergeant again?"

"Of course, Sheriff," said Edna.

Dee came back on the line. "Sorry, sir," Dee said.

"What is going on? Who's her barman?"

"Ray Sherman, 22, from White Springs. Drives a diesel truck. Lives with China Braden."

"Rents a room from her!" shouted Edna.

"He and Edna swear he's not dating China," continued Dee.

"And this is how you came to be outside the Cypress."

"How'd you know where we are? Oh, duh. Saturday night and Edna Bass."

"Yep," replied Jim. "Is Manny there with you?"

"Yes, sir. He is mangasming over Mr. Sherman's truck at the moment."

"Mangasming? I don't think that's a word, Sergeant."

"It should be."

"All right, let's move on. What happened?"

"Truck has an alarm system on it."

"And?"

"Manny may have triggered it by climbing up into the bed of the truck to see if he could look into the cab through the slider window. It was part-way open."

"So, let me see, you and Manny wanted to talk to Ray Sherman and you knew he worked at the Cypress. It being Saturday night, you figured he'd be working. So you went to the Cypress and triggered the alarm on his truck, possibly while looking for a weapon hidden somewhere behind the seats. Mr. Sherman and Ms. Bass came outside when they heard the alarm and found the two of you looking at his truck. Edna wanted to know why and you and Manny declined to be forthcoming about your suspicions about Mr. Sherman, so she insisted that you call me and let her talk to me."

"Yes, sir. That would be a relatively accurate summary."

"Put Edna back on the phone."

"Sheriff, what the hell is going on? First Doc Ryan's in here with your son and the Braden boy, and now this. Ray Sherman has been working for me for almost a month. He's a good boy. And I mean good. He's been renting a room from China, but he and I have talked and he's moving into Buddy's old place on Monday. So he's not going to be associating with that woman any more, and I will personally see to that myself. Also I'm freezing my fanny off out here, so if we could get this straightened out so I could get back inside, I'd appreciate it."

"Wait a minute, Ryan, Michael, and Bailey were at the bar tonight?"

"It was real early. Michael and Bailey drank cola and Ryan had a beer, but Michael drove the car back to your place. I have to tell you Michael did a real slick job of talking to Ray and getting the information out of him. You need to make that boy a deputy."

"I'll take that into consideration, Ms. Bass. I want to apologize to you for the deputies and Ryan and the boys. I'll have a talk with them. They're following some leads on a case, and they're looking for a diesel truck that would have been out on Highway 27 early last Tuesday morning."

"That explains Sota having the top half of his body through the slider on the truck," laughed Edna.

Jim considered banging his head against the wall. "Yes, ma'am. I guess it did. Would it be all right if I spoke to Ray for a moment?"

"Of course! He's got nothing to hide. Hang on here."

Jim could hear voices in the background and then a young man's voice was on the line. "Sheriff?"

"This is Jim Sheppard, yes."

"I'm Ray Sherman. Miss Edna said you asked to speak to me."

"I was wondering if you'd mind coming by the office tomorrow and having a conversation with Deputies Jackson and Sota."

"Be happy to, sir. Not too early, I hope?"

"Would sometime around 1 pm work for you?"

"Yes, sir. I'll see ya'll then!"

Dee came back on the line. "I'm sorry, sir."

"Don't worry about it. I didn't know that Ryan and the boys had been at the bar earlier, and that will be something I'll deal with. Mr. Sherman is coming by the office tomorrow to talk with you and Manny. Let's make sure we've got our ducks in a row before that. I'll see you around 10 am."

"Yes, sir. We'll be there."

Jim hung up the phone and then walked back to Michael's room. The door was open and no one was there. He turned around and headed back down the hall, through the kitchen outside in the biting cold, up the stairs, and banged on Ryan's apartment door.

Bonehead didn't bark, which meant he knew it was Jim on the other side of the door. He only barked at strangers. Jim smiled and wondered how high his son's heart rate was right now. The door opened and Ryan gave a little wave.

"Hi, Jim!"

"Uh-huh," Jim replied and walked into the apartment. Bailey and Michael sat together. Bailey petted Bonehead, who was luxuriating in the attention.

"Hi, Dad!" said Michael.

Jim grinned. "Quite the adventure this trio had tonight."

Michael and Ryan spoke at once, "It was my idea."

Bailey, being the most intelligent one in the group at the moment, kept his mouth shut.

Ryan shut the apartment door and motioned for Jim to take the chair. Jim shook his head. "No, I think I want a stool. I have the high ground here."

Ryan sat down and Jim pulled a stool away from the counter and sat down. He smiled at the three of them. "So, the three of you went to The Cypress tonight to question Ray Sherman. How did that go?"

"Ms. Bass said we were pretty slick about how we got the information we wanted," said Michael.

"Good to know you were slick about it."

Ryan raised his hand.

"Ryan, stop raising your hand."

"I think China killed Noel."

Bailey spoke up. "I told him it wasn't like her. She doesn't like getting her hands dirty. She always finds someone else to do her dirty work."

Michael said, "So we figured we'd go see what Ray Sherman was like and see if he might have been the one to do the dirty work."

"I don't think he did it," said Ryan.

"Turns out he's renting a room from China. Probably met her at the bar," said Bailey.

"I know the three of you realize this is not a game of Clue because none of you are stupid. But at the same time, I find myself wondering if a moment of idiocy didn't strike everyone except me, Edna Bass, and Ray Sherman since it got dark. Because we're the only three who don't seem to have mistook the idea of a legal investigation."

"That's on me," Michael said.

"No, no, you three aren't the only ones who were at The Cypress this evening. Turns out that Dee and Manny had the same idea. Only they accidentally triggered the alarm on Sherman's truck and ended up with

Sherman and Edna standing in the parking lot freezing their butts off wondering what the hell was going on."

"Oh," said Bailey.

"Edna had Dee call me and let her talk to me. Fortunately, she is not angry about any of this, which is good for all of you. Sherman is coming into the office tomorrow morning, and they will question him. And by the way, Edna's convinced Sherman to move into Buddy's old place, so Sherman will no longer be living with China. Which leads me to believe that he is unlikely to have been manipulated into killing Noel."

Bailey nodded. "She's definitely not sleeping with him. I've been told she gives a very convincing..."

"Let's stop there," interrupted Jim.

"Yes, sir," said Bailey.

"Ryan, I can see why you would think China is involved. And I wouldn't put it past her to be, in some way. I'll have Dee and Manny ask questions that might give us some lead towards that."

Ryan nodded. "Thanks."

"I suggest that you two," said Jim nodding toward Michael and Bailey, get your butts down to the house and stay out of trouble."

"Yes, sir," said Michael.

"All right. Let's see if we can't all just be normal, at least for tonight. It's cold, I'm tired, and I'd like to get a good night's sleep. All right?"

All three nodded at Jim.

The dog rolled off Bailey's lap and sat down looking at Jim.

"I take it back. There were four of us who had good sense tonight. I forgot Bonehead."

Jim pushed the stool back under the counter and he went out the door.

Chapter Forty-Three

At 8 am on Sunday morning, Jim walked into the departmental office and pointed to his office. Ryan, Michael, and Bailey moved past him, Michael grabbing an extra chair on his way past the bullpen so they would all have a place to sit.

Junior held up some copies to Jim. "Thought you might be interested in seeing the reports from FDLE and the Medical Examiner."

"That's Dee's case."

Junior grinned. "I've got copies for her."

"Do we have a report on the woman's car or Bailey's apartment?"

Junior got up from his chair, "Let me copy those for you."

"Thanks, Junior."

Jim walked into his office, moving around the three men sitting in front of his desk and dropping into his chair. "When Dee and Manny get here, I want you to tell them everything that was said while you were at The Cypress. None of you will investigate again on your own. If Dee and Manny want your help, I'll consider it. Otherwise, once you've told them what they need to know, you will go back to the house and stay there. Do I make myself clear?"

They all nodded, and Michael said, "Yes, sir."

Jim began to read the reports, happily letting the three sit there uncomfortably while he did. The first report he read was the one on Noel's car. There had been a second set of tire tracks for a vehicle that had parked next to the VW. The tread marks were P205mm tires that indicated a European sedan, not a large, diesel truck. Footprints indicated there was no struggle and that Nicole had gotten into the other car. Jim felt sure this meant whoever was in the other car, the gun had been used to coerce her.

Jim looked up at Bailey, Michael, and Ryan. They were all watching him read the report. He would wait for Dee and Manny. She would decide what, if anything, to tell them. It was not his place to share the information. Not right now.

He continued reading, but the report and found one big surprise. Bicycle tracks. A bicycle had been at the scene. It crossed over the car tracks, so it had been there after Noel had been taken. Everything else had been in Dee's earlier report. The one that had the thinly veiled frustration Dee had experienced with Dr. Sullivan of the FDLE. The terms "reluctant cooperation" and "information withheld until final report" had been peppered throughout the document.

Jim realized, looking at the report, the one question that he'd never thought to ask Bailey. He should probably wait for Dee to ask it, but he couldn't. "Bailey, how did you find Noel in that shed?"

The surprise on Ryan's and Michael's faces matched Bailey's. Jim watched Ryan and Michael turn to look at Bailey.

"I followed the tracks on the road from the car that was next to hers at the library. It was really early, and the street was pretty clear except for Noel's car and that one."

Jim shook his head. "I can't believe we never asked you that."

Bailey shrugged. "I never thought about it."

"How long did it take you to get out to the DOT shed?"

Bailey thought about it. "I got to Noel's car around six and probably looked around for about 15 minutes. I saw the footprints and the other tire tracks and decided someone had to have taken Noel. I got on my bike and followed them. I probably got to the shed around 8 or 8:30. I rode as fast as I could, but I didn't get there in time."

"She was still breathing when you got there," said Jim softly.

Bailey nodded. "I put her head in my lap and I talked to her. She stopped breathing, and I just kept holding her. I didn't want her to be there alone."

"When...you find...him, Jim?" asked Ryan.

"11 am. We're lucky it was that fast."

"Damn," said Ryan. "Very…"

Jim heard the front door to the department office open and close and Junior call out, "Morning, Sgt. Jackson."

"Good morning, Junior. Why is the Sheriff's office full?"

"You'll have to ask him," replied Junior.

Jim faced the door and the three with him swiveled their heads around to see as Dee Jackson walked up and looked over the group. "Sir, did you decide to throw a party and not invite me?"

Jim smiled. "No, Sgt. Jackson. I brought these gentlemen in to tell you what they did last night so you would have the full story. Also, I asked Bailey a question this morning that has led to having a timeline for the crime."

Dee frowned at Jim. "Sir, are you participating in my investigation?"

"Absolutely not. I just asked him a question that hadn't occurred to me before. I'm going to let you talk with him now and confirm our discussion."

"Then I approve, sir. I'd like to read over the reports first and then talk with Bailey if that's all right with you."

"He'll be here," Jim said.

Dee nodded and headed into the bullpen to read the same reports that Jim had on his desk.

Michael raised an eyebrow and nodded to the reports. "You going to let us in on what those reports say?"

"Nope," said Jim.

Michael sat back in his chair with a huff.

A short time later Jim heard Manny come in and greet Junior, get his copies of the reports, and go to sit with Dee. He could hear the soft sound of their voices, but could not hear what they were saying, so he continued to be quiet and read the reports.

Noel Williams's car had no other fingerprints than hers on or in it, which made sense according to the footprint information. He moved on to the report on the apartment. Fingerprints were all over the apartment. Three sets had been identified—Noel Williams, Bailey Braden, and China Braden's. That didn't surprise him at all. Dr. Sullivan's report indicated the lock on the door to the apartment had been forced open with a tool, probably a large screwdriver. The damage to the lock and the door was extensive.

Jim reviewed the report from the scene of Noel Williams's death. A badly deformed bullet had been found in the cement block cut out of the wall. The bullet had gone into the block in such a way as to indicate that it was moving in an upward direction when it came through the woman's skull. The frozen pool of fluids on the floor beneath the body included blood and urine, but not from the same individual. The blood was type O- and the urine indicated type A+ blood.

The damage to the bicycle indicated a heavy vehicle with wide tires. Red paint on the pedal from the bike indicated the vehicle was a Dodge Ram truck. The paint sample on the bike matched the manufacturer's paint code PS2. Once the vehicle was found it was probable that the damage would be to the front or back bumper, depending on how the vehicle had hit the bicycle as it ran over it.

According to the trio sitting in front of him, the truck Ray Sherman owned was a red Dodge Ram. Jim would lay money that there would be some minor bumper damage on that truck that would account for the paint on the bicycle pedal. This would be something that Dee and Manny could check when Sherman came in to be interviewed at 10 am.

Finally, Jim began to read the medical examiner's report. He always hated reading these. He hated attending an autopsy more, and he wondered who had gone into Gainesville to be present for it. He hadn't caught up on Dee's and Manny's reports from Friday, yet. And though he'd spent much of the day in the office with them, he had kept his door closed to allow them to discuss the case without him hearing. He'd given the case to Dee and he damn well intended for her to be the one to finish the investigation.

She'd worked some murder cases with him, but she had never been the lead in an investigation. It was time that she had the opportunity. Probably past time, but murder wasn't all that common in Eden County, except in cases of fights that turned into murders. Mostly these were bar fights where a grudge got carried on into the next day. On a few occasions, the cases had been domestic abuse that had resulted in the death of one partner or the other. In all of these cases, there was generally very little mystery about who had done it.

Jim took a deep breath and began to read through the report.

The trajectory of the bullet that had struck Noel Williams entered the skull through the left side of the forehead. The beveling of the bone defined this as the entrance wound and the fragmenting and shape of the exit wound indicated the bullet traveled in an upward path through the brain. Bone fragments had been carried into the cranium from the entrance wound and a massive cavity created in the frontal lobe of the brain. Damage to blood vessels on the path of the bullet indicated a trajectory of the bullet rising through the brain until exiting out of the parietal bone at the fibrous joint approximately 2.54 cm higher than the entrance wound. Cause of death was autonomic dysfunction from intracranial hemorrhage. It was noted that the blood loss through the exit wound was estimated to be approximately two pints.

The distance of the gun from the victim was estimated to be two feet and the size of the wound matched the casing size of a 9mm handgun.

Jim set the report down on his desk and covered it with the other reports. He wanted to be sure that Bailey did not get the opportunity to see it.

A tap on the door frame made Jim look up.

"I'm ready to interview the three amigos now."

Jim smiled. He knew that Dee was referencing the movie from years ago. It was one of several movies that was frequently quoted among the deputies in his department. He was pretty sure that none of the three sitting in front of him would get it. "They're all yours," he said.

"Gentlemen?" said Dee indicating that she wanted them in the bullpen area.

"You want to use my office?" asked Jim. "It will be a little more private."

Dee considered this a moment. "You don't mind?"

Jim shook his head. "I'm going to walk up to McDonalds and get some hash browns."

"Dad!" exclaimed Michael. "No fair!"

Jim smiled. "Yeah, it's the price you pay for foolish actions," he said.

CHAPTER FORTY-THREE

He got up from his desk, grabbed his coat, and left the room.

Chapter Forty-Four

Dee and Manny made themselves comfortable at Jim's desk, with Dee taking Jim's chair and Manny pulling one in from the bullpen. Dee set her recorder out on the desk and turned it on.

"All right. Let's start with the question that Jim asked that got him a timeline of the crime," said Dee.

"He asked me how I found Noel. I told him I followed the car tracks. I got there sometime between 8 and 8:30 and she…she was lying on the floor. She was still breathing, so I put her head in my lap, and I talked to her. She stopped breathing after a while, and I stayed there holding her."

"What time did you start following the tracks?"

"Must have been around 6:15 maybe. We were supposed to meet at 6, but when I got there, she was already gone. I was too late. I was too late everywhere."

Michael reached over and put his hand on Bailey's shoulder. "I'm sure she heard your voice. She knew you were there."

Bailey whispered, "I hope so. I hope she heard me. I couldn't let her die there alone."

"Dad said you got there around 11," said Michael.

"We were late, too, Bailey," Dee said. "I'm sorry."

Bailey nodded.

"So, she was there before 6," said Dee.

"She must have gotten there a little early. We planned to meet at 6, and I got there right at 6."

Manny shook his head, "If she was a little early and the person was waiting for her, it would have been fast."

"Her keys weren't in her car. They were found in the shed. They'd been kicked over toward the wall. She probably had them in her hand, maybe planned on using them as a weapon," said Dee.

Bailey nodded, "She'd do that. She'd fight."

Manny looked at Bailey's hands and pointed to the scratches on the back of both. "Where did you get those?"

Ryan blushed bright red, remembering Bailey's hands around Finley's throat. He felt fresh embarrassment that he had been so shocked by Bailey's behavior that he had not tried to stop it. Bonehead backing Bailey up had been another surprise. The dog had taken Bailey's side immediately.

"And why are you blushing, Dr. Edwards?" asked Dee.

Ryan covered his face with his hand. Of course, Dee would notice his reaction. He heard Bailey say, "Finley."

"Finley?" repeated Manny.

Dee snorted and Ryan looked up at her. "So explain to us how you got the scratches."

"I scared Finley into telling me he'd told China about Noel," said Bailey. "Doc Ryan didn't know I was going to do it. He was pretty freaked out."

"Exactly how did you scare Finley?"

"I grabbed him by the throat when he opened the door and slammed him into a wall. I'm pretty sure he thought I was going to kill him."

"Would you have killed him if he hadn't told you?"

Bailey shook his head. "I wanted him to think I would."

"Is Finley bruised," asked Manny.

Ryan nodded. "...Yes...marks...there..."

"That wasn't the smartest thing you ever did," said Manny.

Bailey shrugged. "Not the dumbest."

Dee stared at Ryan, and he felt the color drain from his face.

"If you were a deputy, I'd have Jim pull your badge."

"I'm...a..."

"Doctor. Yes, I know. Did you say anything to Finley?"

"Said...sorry," said Ryan.

Manny started laughing. "I kinda love it, Dee."

"Of course you do. Es todo muy machista."

"¡Es! Bailey es el hombre."

"I know what that means!" Michael said.

"What?" asked Bailey.

"Shut it, Sheppard. If I didn't need to know information, I would throw all three of you out of here right now."

Ryan saw Michael close his mouth with an audible click. Bailey mouthed, 'Later,' to Michael.

"All right. Let's move on. Finley told China about Noel. What prompted the visit to The Cypress?"

"Let me tell them," said Michael to Ryan. He nodded, thankful that he wouldn't have to struggle to get the words out that would make Dee and Manny understand.

"Ryan really didn't like China. He came back after you'd had him go to see China on pretext. He knew you'd found a truck, but he didn't think Ray Sherman had done the killing. He wanted to investigate more about China. She creeped him out. He knew that Sherman worked at The Cypress, so he thought if we went there, maybe we could talk to him and get some information. Bailey and I convinced him to take us with him. Bailey knows China better than anyone, and I lied and told Ryan I was licensed and could protect them."

"You're an idiot," said Dee.

"Yes, ma'am. But I thought if he believed I could protect them, he'd let me go with them."

Ryan felt worse with each minute that passed. He hadn't taken Michael with him so someone would have a gun. He'd done it so Bailey would feel safe.

"We got to the bar, and Edna gave Ryan a beer, which he had like two sips of, and she gave Bailey and me colas. We did meet Ray Sherman and turns out that Edna did not know he was renting a room from China. They're not together, not like we thought. Which means he probably didn't have anything to do with Noel's death."

Bailey spoke. "China's got a way with men. They do things for her. Edna says he's too smart for that."

"Ray Sherman is coming in for an interview with the two of us today," said Dee, waving her hand between herself and Manny.

"You think he did it?" asked Michael.

"Don't know, but there's a good chance it was his truck that Bailey heard at the shed. We've got a report that says a red truck ran over his bicycle," said Dee.

"How do you know?" asked Bailey.

"There was red paint on the pedal of the bike. Must have hit the bumper or something when it was run over."

"Can we stay for the interview?" asked Michael. "We'll stay in Dad's office, won't make a sound."

"No!" said Dee. "You three are not getting anywhere near this investigation again. Is that clear?"

Ryan nodded, and Michael and Bailey both said, "Yes, ma'am."

Dee sat back in Jim's chair and sighed. "Look, I know that you were trying to help, all of you." She looked at Ryan. "You were a great help going with me to Tampa and to visit witnesses in Gainesville. I appreciate that. But I really need you to not take this any further. We'll consider China's role in this, I promise."

"Thanks," Ryan said.

They all got up from their chairs and moved out of Jim's office. The door to the office opened and Ray Sherman walked in. Before Junior could greet him, Ray started laughing. "I have no idea what is going on, but I'm starting to connect the dots here," he said.

Dee huffed and stepped forward. "Mr. Sherman, I want to apologize for all that went on last night."

Ray shrugged. "Don't worry about it. It got me out of China's place. I'm happy and Edna's happy, and I'm paying the same amount of rent and getting a house to myself. I cannot complain about the results."

"These three are about to leave, and then Deputy Sota and I have a few questions for you."

"Sure," Ray said. "But I also have some questions, mostly for Bailey, if you don't mind. Edna explained to me a little about China."

Ryan watched Dee throw up her hands. "That's fine, Mr. Sherman. Why don't we all just have a seat out here in the bullpen and get to know each other." Ryan couldn't help but be amused. Poor Dee was losing the battle to keep the investigation to herself. He felt sure that at some point they would all pay for her aggravation, but until then, he knew somehow his involvement would help.

Junior got up from the front desk and asked if anyone would like a soda. "We've got cola and ginger ale in the back. I'd be happy to bring you one," he said.

"I'll help you, Junior," said Michael, and they disappeared into a back hallway.

Manny smiled and Ryan thought that he might be enjoying Dee's frustration. Dee went to retrieve her recorder and reports from Jim's office. Manny winked at Ryan, then pulled out several chairs and sat down near one of the bullpen desks.

Once they all had settled in their chairs, and Junior had returned to the front desk, Dee turned on her recorder and began her questions. "Mr. Sherman," she said.

"Ray, please," he said.

"Fine, Ray. How long have you been living at China Braden's?"

"I moved out this morning, which China probably doesn't know, yet. But I'd been at her place about two weeks. I got the job at The Cypress and started there on December 6th. I was living at the Bambi and looking for a place. China was in the bar on the 8th and offered to rent me a room at her house. It was better than the Bambi, so I took it."

"How did you and China get along?"

Ray shrugged. "She's been pretty down. She broke up with her boyfriend earlier this month. That's why I invited her to come with me for brunch at my parent's place on Saturday. Thought maybe if she got out she'd feel better."

"Has she said anything other than about her boyfriend that was making her unhappy?"

Ray shook his head. "Not to me. I work from 5 until 3 am or so. She comes into the bar, and that's pretty much the only time we see each other. But I'm working then, so it's not like we're hanging out together."

"And you've moved out," said Dee.

"This morning. Edna gave me the keys to her son's old place. It's pretty nice and a lot closer to The Cypress than China's place. Also, it doesn't have China."

"You and China didn't get along?" asked Manny.

"China's China. Not exactly warm and fuzzy. But I needed a place to live, and the rent was reasonable, so I took it." Ray looked at Bailey. "Edna explained about you and China last night. That really sucks."

Bailey nodded. "China's China," he said.

Ray smiled. "I can't imagine growing up with her."

"I had Mama and Papa. That made it better."

Dee interrupted them, "Mind if I get back to my questions?"

"Sorry," said Ray.

"Did China ever ask to use your truck?" she asked.

Ray looked surprised. "Asked? No. But she did. Didn't say anything to me about it either. I was not happy. I went to get into it to go to work and the seat was so close to the steering wheel I couldn't get in it. I knew damn well she'd taken it and hadn't said anything. Truck seemed fine, though, so I didn't say anything to her. I've seen her get riled up and I did not need to be dealing with that."

"When did this happen?"

"Last Tuesday."

"You haven't noticed any damage to the truck?"

Ray's eyes narrowed. "Why?"

Manny stood up. "Let's go take a look at it." Everyone got up and followed Manny and Ray outside. Dee motioned for Ryan, Bailey, and Michael to stay in their seats, but they ignored her. Ryan knew they were taking their lives in their hands doing it, but his curiosity got the better of him.

Outside Manny walked around the truck, followed by Ray. After one

179

circuit around, Manny knelt down and checked the front bumper more closely. Then he went to the back bumper and knelt down to examine it. As everyone followed him, Manny pointed to some scrapes along the bottom edge. "Right there," he said.

Ray dropped down and looked more closely, "Damn. What the hell did she hit? Is that blue paint on the axle?"

Manny leaned down further. "Oh yeah, that's blue paint all right. Your bike is blue, right, Bailey?"

"It was. I don't know what it looks like now," said Bailey.

"The red paint was on the bicycle pedal. It was the color of your truck, and the scrape on your bumper looks like it was caused by something like a pedal.

Ray looked at Bailey. "She ran over your bike?"

"Bicycle, yeah," said Bailey. "Least that's what Sheriff Jim told me."

"Let's get back inside," said Dee. "I'm going to have to call FDLE to come get your truck."

"Wait, why? I mean, she ran over a bicycle, why do they need to take my truck?"

"Bailey's bike was at the scene of a murder," said Dee. "Looks like your truck puts China there, too."

All the color drained out of Ray's face. "Murder?"

Manny patted Ray on the shoulder. "Come on back inside. We'll explain."

Chapter Forty-Five

J im walked into the office and dropped a bag on the front counter for Junior. He hadn't expected to see a full house sitting in the bullpen, but he figured the young man he didn't know must be Ray Sherman. He held on to a can of Vernor's with both hands and looked more than a little shell-shocked.

Dee walked out of Jim's office. "FDLE's going to send a flatbed tow over to get your truck." She looked over at Jim. "It's definitely his truck that was there."

"He didn't know?" asked Jim softly.

She shook her head. "Doesn't seem like it. Stay out of the men's room for a bit. He vomited."

Jim shook his head. "You carry on. You want me to take these three off your hands?" he asked, nodding toward Ryan, Michael, and Bailey.

"I think Bailey needs to get somewhere more private," she replied.

"Okay, everyone outside. Ryan, you're driving."

Ryan stood up and gathered his coat. Bailey and Michael stood up. Michael put his arm over Bailey's shoulder. Jim dropped the bag of McDonald's hash browns on the table in front of Manny. "Maybe you and Dee can eat these later."

Manny nodded.

Jim followed Ryan outside where he unlocked the car and let Michael help Bailey in. Jim opened the front passenger door and Ryan got into the driver's seat.

"I'm sorry, Bailey," Jim said, turning around to speak to him.

181

Tears rolled down Bailey's face. "I always knew she didn't love me, but I don't think I ever thought she hated me," Bailey said softly. "I wonder if she knew I was still alive?"

Michael hugged Bailey.

"Why would she drive to that shed?" asked Bailey.

"To confirm Noe...dead," said Ryan. "She didn't... Someone...told her."

Jim rubbed his forehead, but he knew the mild headache he felt starting would not go away. "She went to see if it was true and left when she realized Bailey was there. She didn't want him to see her."

Bailey sighed loudly. "I really, really hate her."

"What do we do now?" asked Bailey.

"I need to talk to Dee and Manny," said Jim.

Ryan slowed the car and stopped. Then he began to make a U-turn.

"What are you doing?" asked Jim.

"Going...back," he answered.

The slow U-turn brought them around and they headed toward the Sheriff's Department office. No one said a word as Ryan drove.

Chapter Forty-Six

E dna was getting out of her car as Ryan pulled up beside her. She had a stormy look on her face, and Jim thought it a damn good thing that they had turned around when they did. Her expression did not bode well for Dee and Manny. Jim got out of the car quickly.

"What the hell is going on, Sheriff? Why is Ray calling me to come pick him up?" Edna had her fists on her wide hips. She wore a knit cap and multiple sweaters. Jim would have offered her his coat, but he felt sure she'd throw it to the ground and spit on it.

"Let's get inside, I can explain."

She evil-eyed the car that contained Ryan, Michael, and Bailey. "They involved in this?"

"It's bad, Edna," said Jim.

Edna pointed to Ryan, "Doc Ryan, I thought better of you! Ray Sherman didn't do anything."

Ryan got out of the car. He took off his coat and put it over Edna's shoulders. "We...know," he said.

Edna pulled the coat around herself as much as she could. "Good." She stomped toward the office door.

Michael and Bailey scrambled out of the back seat and followed Ryan and Jim into the office behind Edna. Once everyone entered the warmth of the office, Edna pulled off Ryan's coat and handed it back to him.

She went directly to Ray who still looked stunned. When he saw Edna, he reached out to her and she pulled him into her arms. "Don't you worry about a thing. I'm here now. I'll take care of you," Edna said.

Ray leaned his face against Edna's shoulder. "Thanks, Miss Edna."

Dee and Manny stared at Jim and the trio behind him.

"We had a realization," said Jim.

"Sheriff..." Started Dee.

Jim held up his hand. "Let me explain. The truck. She took it to go see if the woman was really dead."

"What woman?" asked Edna.

Jim and Dee both spoke at once, "That's not public information...," said Dee as Jim said, "Bailey Braden's fiancé."

Dee glared at Jim.

"You think he wasn't going to tell her?" Jim asked.

Dee huffed. "Fine."

"China took my truck. I knew she'd driven it somewhere, but I didn't know... I swear, Miss Edna, I didn't know."

"Of course you didn't," said Edna.

"We know that," said Dee.

Manny wisely kept quiet. Jim turned and saw Junior's eyes wide with surprise. Junior very quickly made the sign that his lips were sealed, and the key thrown away.

"You better keep this quiet," said Jim. "Senior does not need to know. Not right now."

"Yes, sir," said Junior.

"Ms. Bass, we have to send Mr. Sherman's truck to the forensic lab in Jacksonville. There's evidence on the truck that indicates it ran over Bailey's bicycle at the scene of the murder."

"Ray sure as hell wouldn't drive that truck over a damn bicycle. That must have tore-up something on the undercarriage. This man babies that truck like it was a child. He washes it every damn day, except right now with the freeze. He's afraid the temperature would screw up the finish," said Edna.

"Miss Bass!" Ray whispered.

"It's true, Ray. You're a sweet boy, but you have an unnatural relationship with that truck."

Jim bit the inside of his mouth to keep from smiling. He looked at Manny and saw him doing the same thing.

"Thank you for confirming Mr. Sherman's relationship with the vehicle in question," said Dee, looking serious, but Jim knew the tone. She'd just dissed Ray Sherman bad. "If you wouldn't mind taking him home, we'd appreciate it. I'll call as soon as we know when the truck will be returned."

"No problem, I can give him rides back and forth to work. I'll make sure he's taken care of until then." Edna patted Ray on the back. He stood up and the two of them started for the door.

"Edna," said Ryan. "Do...my coat?" He held it out to her.

She shook her head. "I got good heat in the car. Don't you worry about me, Doc Ryan. Buddy bought me a damn fine car and it heats and cools like a champ. I got the best at home, too. My boy took care of me."

Ryan nodded, "I'm...glad."

Edna and Ray Sherman left the office together. Jim pulled a chair out from the table and sat down. Ryan, Michael, and Bailey stood awkwardly.

Dee waved toward the chairs. "Sit down. You're making my neck ache looking up at all of you."

Everyone sat down, pulling chairs away from the desks in the bullpen. No one sat in the chair where Ray Sherman had been. Manny stuck out a leg and moved the chair away from the table where he and Dee sat. Her recorder was off and lying on her notepad.

"You know everything we know," Dee said. Her voice sounded tired. "From what Bailey has told us and Ray Sherman's statement, we know the truck was at the scene and that it was likely driven by China Braden."

"Likely?" asked Michael.

"Until forensics finishes with the truck, we're not taking anything as a given," said Dee.

"But knowing China as we all do, it's unlikely she cleaned up behind herself in the truck. She didn't even change the seat position back. We'll hope for hair, maybe even fingerprints."

"If we definitively put China Braden in the truck at the scene, that could open the investigation to other avenues. Such as how did she know about the murder?" said Manny.

Jim shook his head. "It gets all kinds of complicated tying her to the murder."

Dee stood up. "I'm going to go home and get something to eat."

"You didn't eat any of the hash browns I left?"

Dee shuddered. "Manny ate the hash browns. You know I hate fast food." She picked up her recorder and her notepad. "I'll write my report tomorrow. And you four need to butt out of my investigation."

She went to a desk, grabbed her coat and hat, and walked out of the building.

Manny grinned at Jim. "I like hash browns," he said. Then he got up, picked up his jacket and cap, and headed out as well.

"Okay," said Jim. "Think we can make it back to the house this time?"

"Better…," said Ryan. "Bonehead needs…out."

They all got up from their chairs and headed for the door. "Who's relieving you, Junior?" asked Jim as he got to the front desk.

"Maynard," said Junior. "He wants Christmas Eve, so I'm taking his double that night and he's taking mine on Christmas."

"I'll see you tomorrow, Junior."

Ryan put his coat back on and they went out to his car, once again taking up their respective seats. Ryan carefully backed out of his parking space and turned toward the east and home.

Chapter Forty-Seven

Bonehead was miffed. When Ryan came into the apartment, he had draped himself across the couch like a courtesan lying naked across a narrow bed. His head was closest to the door, and he looked up at Ryan, then turned his head toward the back of the couch. He didn't move at all, just his head.

"Want…walk?" asked Ryan.

No response. Definitely miffed. When Ryan left in the morning Bonehead had expected to be invited along. When Ryan refused to take him, he could have sworn the dog looked shocked. He obviously had the opinion that some social rule had been violated by leaving him alone in the apartment when interesting things were happening with other people.

"No?…Fine," said Ryan. Two could play this game. He tossed his coat over the chair, walked into the bedroom, and turned on the TV. He pulled off his tuque and dropped it on the bed and went into the bathroom. The apartment felt warm, and he'd been cold in the car. He turned on the hot water and washed his face and hands.

He came out of the bathroom and looked out into the big room. Bonehead was still on the couch.

Ryan took off his shoes, grabbed both pillows and laid down on the bed. He picked up the remote from the bedside table and began to flick through the channels. Christmas movies flashed across the screen as he flicked through the channels. Nothing seemed very interesting.

He turned the tv off and tried to consciously relax his body, starting with his feet and working his way up his legs to his hips, then his torso, then arms and hands. He rolled his head from side to side trying to get the muscles in his shoulders and neck to relax. He'd been tied up in knots all day.

He heard the clicking of Bonehead's nails on the wood floor and waited to see if he would come into the bedroom.

Bonehead sauntered into the bedroom and headed straight toward the sliding glass doors. Ryan had pulled in the potted azalea that Claire had given him. It looked bare and pathetic in the dim afternoon light.

Bonehead walked up to the azalea, then raised a leg and pissed on it.

Ryan sat straight up, his mouth opening and closing, but nothing coming out.

Bonehead started back toward the bedroom door.

"Dog!" shouted Ryan. Bonehead didn't pause but continued out through the bedroom door into the larger room.

Ryan looked over at his azalea. There was a puddle on the floor and piss dripping from the branches of the plant and the wall behind it. Oh, it was so on, thought Ryan. He got up from the bed and stormed out into the kitchen/living room combination. Bonehead was lying on the couch again, his head turned toward the bedroom, waiting for Ryan's appearance.

"You!" he shouted. He went to the couch, pushed Bonehead off it, opened the door to the apartment, and pushed him outside onto the landing. Then he slammed the door.

He got paper towels and spray cleaner out from under the sink and went into the bedroom and began cleaning up the puddle of dog urine from the floor, the pot and the wall. The whole time he cleaned he swore, muttering obscenity after obscenity, and wondering if he should water the azalea or repot it or what. He had no idea if it would start to stink or if the urine would kill the plant. He liked the plant. It had pretty dark pink blossoms and it had bloomed almost all spring and into the summer.

He managed to clean up all the urine, scraped away the top layer of soil in the pot, watered the plant, and then sprayed the stuff that was supposed to remove the scent. He hoped it worked. Right now the smell was in his head and not going anywhere.

He dumped everything into a garbage bag and left the apartment to go put it in the garbage downstairs. He'd gotten all the way to the cans before he realized that Bonehead wasn't in the backyard. Oh, shit, he thought. Had he managed to get over the gate and take off? He wouldn't put it past Bonehead to do that, and he had thrown him out into the cold.

Crap, he thought.

Chapter Forty-Eight

Jim heard scratching at the back door and opened it. Bonehead pushed past him into the house and headed straight for Michael's room. Huh, he thought. He looked up at Ryan's apartment and saw that the lights were on, and the door closed.

He closed the back door and stepped into the hall just in time to see Bonehead scratching at the door and Michael opening it.

"What are you doing here?" asked Michael.

Bonehead wagged his tail and pushed past him into the bedroom. Michael looked out into the hall and saw Jim. "What's going on?"

"No idea. He was scratching at the back door."

"Ryan isn't here?"

"Nope."

"You think something's wrong?"

"I think if Ryan was hurt or something Bonehead wouldn't have come inside."

Michael nodded. "No, and he'd have been barking."

"Suppose the dog's mad at him?"

Michael laughed. "Wouldn't be the first time."

Jim started to laugh, too. "That is true. Well, hang on to him in there. I'm sure Ryan will come looking for him at some point."

Michael stepped back into his bedroom and closed the door.

Jim went into the living room and sat down again in his easy chair, picking up his book. Michael had bought him several books for Christmas, but he was fascinated by this one, Life and Def: The Autobiography of Russell

Simmons. This one he'd given him early. He said it didn't fit with the others, and he thought Jim would enjoy reading it as a "palate cleanser." It had cracked him up. He found the book interesting. Not that he would ever try to connect with any of his young black deputies by quoting hip-hop. That would do nothing but make Dee Jackson laugh her ass off.

Michael had been trying the last few years to introduce something other than history into his reading. Or as Michael put it, history of something besides history. He'd given him some biographies of artists and writers, and now he was dragging him slowly toward the current century.

Several sharp knocks at the back door had Jim putting down his book again. He saw Ryan through the glass as he walked through the kitchen. The door wasn't locked, but Ryan refused to let himself in other than for an emergency. The young man would never get the hang of Southern visiting.

"Is Bonehead here?"

"Yes."

Ryan sighed with relief. Bundled up in his coat and tuque, with a bright red face, he'd obviously been out looking for the dog for a while.

"Come on in, get warm. He's back in Michael's room."

Ryan followed him into the living room and dropped onto the couch.

"He came over and scratched on the door a while ago. Did he get out?"

"I threw him out."

Jim bit his lip to keep from smiling.

"He… he pissed…the azalea," said Ryan. "I…like…the azalea."

Jim burst out laughing. He covered his face with one hand and shook his head. "I'm sorry, but you two are hysterical. It's like the Odd Couple."

Ryan frowned, "…He's Oscar!"

Jim howled with laughter. Bonehead definitely was Oscar.

"…S…Stop laughing."

Jim covered his mouth and desperately tried to get his laughter under control.

Michael came down the hall followed by Bailey and Bonehead. "What is going on in here?" He saw Ryan and smiled, "Looking for your dog, Ryan?"

Ryan hung his head and didn't respond.

191

"Ask him what Bonehead did," said Jim laughing.

"Don't...," said Ryan.

Bonehead walked around the side of the couch and stopped next to Ryan.

Ryan raised his head and looked at Bonehead. "I'm...sorry."

Bonehead stuck his nose under Ryan's hand and bumped his hand on top of his head. "...Apology...accepted?"

Bonehead wagged his tail.

Ryan rubbed Bonehead's ear. "No...pee...azalea," said Ryan.

Bonehead huffed, but he stayed next to Ryan.

"He peed on your azalea!" said Michael. "Oooo, bad dog!"

Jim started laughing again. "Bonehead is Oscar."

"Who?" asked Michael.

"I know that!" said Bailey. "I've seen the reruns! The Odd Couple! Mama and Papa loved that show."

"You are truly a man out of time, Bailey," said Michael.

Bailey flipped Michael off, which made Jim start laughing again.

"Come on...trouble," said Ryan to Bonehead. The dog and Ryan stood up.

"Are you warm enough up there?" asked Jim.

Ryan nodded. "It's...good."

"Don't pee on Doc's azalea," Bailey instructed Bonehead seriously. "It's not nice."

"C'mon, Bailey. I haven't finished kicking your ass."

"Game?" asked Ryan.

"Halo. I am winning," said Michael.

Bailey shook his head. "He's evil," he said to Ryan.

Ryan smiled. "Tomorrow?"

Jim shrugged. "I'm taking tomorrow off." He pointed to the Christmas tree. "I've got gifts to wrap and cooking to do. I'm going to cook that turkey you bought. Want to eat around one?"

"Thanks...yes."

Bailey and Michael wrestled each other in the race back to Michael's bedroom and the game. Ryan and Bonehead made their way out through the kitchen. Jim picked up his book and wondered if they'd get to enjoy any of Christmas Eve or Christmas Day.

Chapter Forty-Nine

Christmas Eve day Jim answered the phone trying to catch it quickly enough so it wouldn't wake Michael and Bailey. Once he heard Dee's voice he set down the cake pan he'd carried into the living room with him and sat on the couch.

"Wanted to give you an update. We're applying for a Frankenstein warrant to get China Braden's phone records. Forensics found China's fingerprints on the inside of the driver's door of Ray Sherman's truck. It's enough to put her at the scene of the murder. The murderer would have had to call her to tell her where the body was, and the only phone she has is her cell."

"Sounds solid. Who are you going to try to get to sign it?"

"Manny and I both think Judge Thurman will sign it. She's signed warrants for both of us before."

"Make it happen. We won't get anything before Christmas, but if we get it in now, maybe we'll have something after New Year's."

"Yes, sir. We're going to keep working the case. There's a tech examining the truck who apparently thinks getting this truck to examine is his early Christmas present. He said he'd have more for us on the evidence on the undercarriage by tomorrow."

"Nice. You never know what's going to make someone's day."

Dee laughed. "There's one other thing. Manny and I want to talk to this Finley that Bailey found in Gainesville. We'd like to try to do that today. We'll be by your place after we've dropped off the warrant."

"I'll make sure he's prepared for that. Ryan may have a good idea of the address. I think Bailey just finds places by landmarks."

"Yeah, bring him in on it. Thanks."

Jim hung up and thought about who he should talk with first. Bailey and Michael had been up late. The game sounds had ended around 11, but he'd been able to hear the murmur of their voices much later. It didn't seem like anyone in the house could sleep well.

He picked up the cake pan and carried it back into the kitchen. He grabbed his down jacket that was hanging next to the back door and slipped his feet into his boots. Outside he went up the stairs to Ryan's apartment. He'd have been up early to let Bonehead out and was far more likely to be awake than either of the boys.

When Ryan answered his knock, he looked wide awake. "Morning! I've got a question for you from Dee."

Ryan grinned and opened the door to let him in. He could hear Bonehead crunching his way through his breakfast.

"...Coffee?"

"Yes!" He hadn't made coffee this morning. He'd gotten up determined to get some baking done before Christmas and so far had managed to not have coffee or start the baking. Once he had the hot mug in his hand and had taken a few deep gulps he felt warm to his toes.

"So...Dee?"

"She and Manny want to interview Finley. She wanted to know if you could give them the address, or maybe help them get there?"

"Sure," said Ryan. He sat down on one of the stools at the counter and Jim dropped onto the couch. Bonehead came around the kitchen divider licking his lips.

"Hey, Bonehead," Jim said. The big dog dropped his head on Jim's knee and allowed his ears to be rubbed. His coat was still cool from having been outdoors already. "You get a good walk this morning?"

Ryan laughed. "He...disappointed...too cold for...squirrels."

"If you go to Gainesville with Dee and Manny, I can walk Bonehead this afternoon."

"Don't...tell...Bailey."

"Dee wanted to talk to him."

195

"Not...good."

"I trust your judgment, but can you tell me why?" asked Jim.

"Scratches on...hands? ...Finley...Bailey...hands on throat."

"Bailey tried to strangle Finley?"

"No...scare him."

"And Finley is who scratched up his hands."

"Yes."

Jim rubbed his face with one hand and took another deep drink of his coffee. "Okay. You sure you can find the place again?"

"Yes."

Jim nodded. "Then I'll get with Dee and set a time for you to go with them. I won't talk about it to Bailey or Michael. Have you eaten?"

Ryan shook his head. "Wrapping...gifts."

"Want to come down with me? I'll make some breakfast and maybe you can keep me on track, so I get the damn cake started."

"Cake?"

"My mother made red velvet cake every Christmas. When Michael was a kid he called it Christmas cake, because it was the only time she ever made it. She said it was too fussy to make except for special occasions."

"I...eat...cake."

"I know. I figure between you, Michael and Bailey, I need to make a big one."

Ryan smiled. "Okay!" He got his coat out of the closet in the living room and Jim reluctantly put his coffee down on the counter.

"You make the coffee and I'll make breakfast," said Jim. "You make better coffee than I do."

Ryan held up one finger and stepped back into the kitchen. He opened a cabinet and took out a bag of coffee. "Better...coffee."

"I need to find out where you get your coffee," said Jim.

"Not...grocery," said Ryan smugly.

They headed out of Ryan's apartment with Bonehead running down the stairs in front of them. Bonehead took a moment to mark the gate that led into the backyard. Jim heard Ryan sigh when he saw Bonehead lift his leg.

196

CHAPTER FORTY-NINE

He muttered, "Dog!"

Jim said nothing and opened the back door to his home.

Chapter Fifty

Ryan found Dee Jackson and Manny Sota sitting at a long table they'd dragged into the bullpen and covered with notes and reports and photographs. They both stood, moving slowly back and forth with concentrated looks.

"Hello," he said.

Manny looked over his shoulder. "Hey, Doc. Pull up a chair. We'll be with you in just a minute."

Junior snorted.

Ryan looked at him.

"They've been looking at that stuff for over two hours, just like that. If the answer hasn't jumped out at them yet, I don't think it's there," said Junior.

Ryan took one of the rolling chairs from a desk. He pulled off his coat and tuque and sat down. He might as well be comfortable if he had to wait. Dee amused him as she touched whatever she studied. He wondered if she thought she could sense something through her fingers. Manny had his arms crossed and leaned close. He couldn't help but think that Manny would regret his positioning later. It could not be good for his back to bend over the table that way.

"The answer has got to be in her phone," said Dee.

"And we aren't going to see those records until sometime in January if we're lucky," said Manny.

"You suppose Jim would let us arrest her as an accessory?"

Manny laughed. "Sure. Right after he runs buck naked through the streets singing Christmas carols."

Dee laughed. "We have proof she was there."

"Which a good lawyer would tear apart in a heartbeat. It's circumstantial."

"Circumstantial doesn't mean not true."

"Weapons of Mass Destruction," said Manny.

Dee shook her head. "This is a lot more substantial than that. And don't you go getting political on me, or we're going to end up in a smack down and I will kick your ass."

"You may be better at close combat, but I will take you out later on, and you'll never see me."

Dee reached out and swatted Manny's arm. "Asshole," she muttered.

"Let's talk to this Finley. If that gives us nothing, we go to Jim and tell him we want to apply for a warrant to arrest China."

"Fine," said Dee.

They both turned around to Ryan. Ryan backed his chair away from them. Junior started laughing.

"Why the hell are you backing up?" asked Dee.

"You...," Ryan started.

"Stop scaring our help," said Manny.

Dee swatted Manny again. "Sorry, Ryan. We were just thinking out loud. Didn't mean to make you nervous. Jim says you can find the place Finley lives."

"Yes."

"All right. We'll take my patrol car and Ryan can ride in the back."

"No."

Dee looked surprised and Manny chuckled. "He may have a point. We turn up in a Sheriff's Department car, the guy might not answer the door."

"Yes...my car."

"Fine. Your car, you drive, but we're staying in uniform."

Ryan shrugged. "Fine."

Dee and Manny grabbed their jackets, checked their weapons, and Dee made sure the batteries in her recorder were working. Ryan stood up, put on his coat and tuque, and pushed the chair back to the desk.

"Time to roll," said Manny.

199

"Drive careful," said Junior as they walked past his desk.

"Promise," said Ryan.

Junior gave him the thumbs up.

Dee and Manny argued for a moment about who would ride shotgun, but as Ryan expected, Dee won and Manny climbed into the back seat. As Ryan drove, Manny kept up the conversation. Dee said very little. She seemed to be deep in thought. The drive to Finley's with Bailey had felt long, but this time, knowing where he was going, Ryan thought it went a lot faster.

They pulled up in front of the house where Finley lived in just over 60 minutes. Finley's black sedan sat in the driveway, and an even sadder-looking pick-up truck was parked behind it. Ryan parked behind the two vehicles and couldn't help but think that would at least keep Finley from trying to drive away before they could talk to him.

Ryan deliberately got to the front door first and knocked, forcing Dee and Manny to stand to one side and slightly behind him. After a couple of minutes, the door opened, and Finley stood in the doorway. He looked at Ryan and shook his head. The bruises on his throat stood out on his fair skin, yellow and green in color.

Dee pushed Ryan aside and stepped into the doorway so Finley would not be able to close the door. "Sergeant Dee Jackson, Eden County Sheriff's Department. I have some questions for you.

Finley's eyes went wide with surprise. "Why?"

"Regarding the murder of Noel Williams," she said.

"Who the hell is Noel Williams?" he asked.

"The black woman you saw with Bailey Braden."

The color drained from Finley's face. "Oh shit, she's dead?"

Ryan knew Finley's surprise had to be real. No one could fake going that pale, which meant that Finley had not known that Noel was dead when he and Bailey had shown up.

Finley stepped back and let Dee and Manny come in. Ryan followed behind. Finley didn't sit. He just stood, dumbly, his eyes wild with fear. "I don't know anything about murder. I don't."

"We have some questions. Will you answer them?" asked Dee.

"Yes, ma'am," Finley said.

"Let's sit down."

Finley dropped into an easy chair that butted up next to the couch facing the television. He sat bent over, his hands gripped together in his lap. The color had not returned to his face.

Dee took a seat on the couch and Manny remained standing a short distance away. Ryan dropped onto the other end of the couch and just watched. Manny and Dee made a good team. He had kept mobile so if Finley tried to run, he would be able to intercept him. Dee sat near him, radiating calm.

"You saw Bailey with Noel Williams."

Finley shrugged. "I don't know her name. I just saw Bailey with this black woman. He was kissing her. They were standing in the library parking lot next to a blue Bug. I didn't know who she was. I don't know if she was this Noel person."

"Bailey has verified that he was with Noel Williams when you saw him."

Finley nodded. "Okay."

"Bailey Braden came here."

"Yes. He...he was angry. He wanted to know who I had told about him and the... the woman."

"That's how you got those bruises on your throat."

"Yes, ma'am. She was already dead?" Finley asked.

"Yes. Her body was found last Tuesday."

"Wow. I...I thought he was just pissed because I told China about them."

"When did you call China and tell her about Bailey and the woman?"

Finley shook his head. "I didn't call her. I don't have her phone number. I met her through a guy I know in Warren when we were at the Cypress, and she was there. He had told me about Bailey and introduced me to him when we saw him at McDonald's."

"How did you tell her?"

"Saw her at the Cypress that same night. She's in there most nights, so I went there to find her."

"Why did you tell her?"

Finley's face flushed with color. He hung his head. "I thought she might... well, talk to me more if she thought I could give her information about the woman. I heard..."

"You heard what?" asked Dee.

"I heard she rewards guys with sex for things she wants."

"And you thought she'd want to know about this woman."

"She did, but I didn't know anything else, and she got all huffy and told me to fuck off."

"Who's the guy you know?" asked Manny.

"Euler Wynn," said Finley.

Ryan knew that name. Euler brought his mother into the practice regularly. She'd had surgery for breast cancer in the spring and then several rounds of chemotherapy. Marie Wynn also had diabetes and they'd done regular testing and adjusting of her medication to be sure that it stayed well-regulated during her treatment.

"Did Euler tell you that about China?"

Finley nodded his head. "Yeah. He said she likes young guys or guys with money. If you have both, she's real easy."

"Does Euler know this from experience?" asked Manny.

"No. Euler said his mama would kick his ass if he slept with China. His mama doesn't like her, and he's real good about not upsetting her."

Ryan broke in, "She...not well... Euler brings her... Believe that's true."

"How do you know Euler?" asked Dee.

"We work together. We both work at the truss factory."

"If we need to talk to you again, can we find you here?"

Finley nodded. "I'm going to Hawthorne to my parents for Christmas morning and lunch, but I'll be back here tomorrow night. I have to work Wednesday."

Dee handed Finley a card. "If you think of anything or hear anything about China or the woman who died, call me."

"Yes, ma'am." Finley took the card. Ryan thought he would call. Realizing that Noel had been murdered had really shaken him. He looked scared and maybe a little sick.

Dee and Manny headed for the door. Ryan looked at Finley. "You…may…caused…death."

Finley looked up at him. He spoke softly, "I hope not."

"Think…on it," said Ryan. Anger rose up inside him and he couldn't find it in him to say sorry this time.

Ryan followed the two deputies out to his car.

He unlocked the doors and the three of them got into the BMW. He turned the heat on immediately and set the fan to run on high so Manny would be warm in the back seat.

"Hold on for a minute, Ryan," said Dee.

She pulled out her notebook and began to flip through the pages. "There's something that's been niggling at me. Something that's been said more than once about Noel Williams."

Manny leaned forward, propping his chin on the back of Dee's seat. "You think it could be connected to her murder?"

"Maybe. We've run out all the lines we had."

"No," said Ryan.

Dee shook her head. "China didn't shoot her."

"You…don't know…that."

Manny rolled his chin on the back of the seat. "It's not likely. Why would she go back to the scene?"

"Hide…body?"

"If we hadn't seen Bailey's bike, both of them wouldn't have been found until God knows when. No reason for DOT to be out at that empty shack. It's used during the summer and hurricanes," said Dee.

Dee kept looking. "Sad little white boys," she said. She flipped back a few pages more, "White, cute, and damaged."

"What's that about?" asked Manny.

"Dr. Oluco," said Ryan.

"And the sorority sister, Rickesha Stephens."

"What are you thinking?" asked Manny.

"What about the boy before Bailey?" asked Dee.

Ryan groaned.

"Someone connected only to Noel," said Manny. "But how would he know about China?"

"You find out about Bailey Braden, what's the first thing someone in Warren's going to tell you?"

Manny sighed. "China."

Dee nodded. "China Braden. Everyone in town knows China. Maybe she wasn't pointing a finger at Bailey for no reason."

Dee looked at Ryan, "Remember the way to Dr. Oluco's home?"

Ryan nodded.

Dee dialed Dr. Oluco's number and put her phone on speaker.

"Hello, Sgt. Jackson."

"Dr. Oluco, I know this is short notice, but I wondered if I might stop by and speak to you again about Noel Williams."

"Of course. I don't celebrate Christmas, so you're not interrupting anything here. When will you be here?"

"I'm in Gainesville. We can probably be at your place in 15 or 20 minutes?"

"Fine. I'll make tea. I'm assuming Dr. Edwards is with you?"

"Yes, and Deputy Manny Sota. He's my partner in the investigation."

"I'll look forward to meeting him."

"Thank you," said Dee.

They disconnected and Dee patted Ryan on the shoulder. "Let's get moving."

Chapter Fifty-One

T he iced cake sat on the kitchen table. The turkey was in the oven. Michael and Bailey had come out of the bedroom, grabbed wrapping paper and ribbon, and disappeared back into the bedroom.

Jim had wrapped his gifts with the not-so-helpful help of Bonehead, who had insisted on inspecting each step to ensure that Jim performed to his level of approval. He'd finally resorted to bribery by bringing some cold cuts and cheese into his bedroom to distract the dog. It had worked as long as he gave it out in sufficient amounts.

He'd gone into the attic and pulled down the box with the Christmas tree in it. He'd given up on real trees years ago when it had taken him most of a month to get the pine needles out of the living room carpet. Michael swore he didn't care if they even put up a tree, but Jim's conscience would not allow him to fail to do it.

Bailey had taken great care in stringing the lights on the tree. He seemed especially fond of the blue lights and had let Michael take care of the small white ones.

Now with the living room decorated and all of Jim's gifts under it, the place had started to feel like Christmas. He'd put an old album of Christmas carols on the stereo his parents had owned and left in the house when they moved into the apartment over the garage. He loved the old vinyl records that his mother had insisted on buying each year. The Firestone Christmas albums had been her favorites, and he loved listening to them as he got ready for Christmas Day.

Bailey came down the hall singing Silent Night and Jim couldn't stop smiling. He doubted Bailey had celebrated many Christmases since his grandparents died. He and Michael had always had Bailey over for Christmas dinner, but he'd never decorated the tree with them.

Jim remembered the first time they'd invited him over. He'd moved out of his grandparent's house and into the little apartment above the laundromat. They knew he would be without a Christmas now that his grandparents were gone, so they decided to have him over for dinner and a little Christmas celebration. They'd even waited on cutting the red velvet cake so he'd get to see it decorated.

Bailey had taken one look at the tree in the living room and gasped. "That's beautiful! Mama and Papa just had a little one they set on the table." Michael and Jim had each bought and wrapped a gift for him. He'd thanked them for the gifts, but it was the tree and the food that he'd been enamored of that day.

When Jim had put some leftovers into containers for Bailey to take home with him he'd hugged them. Jim could see that Bailey was close to crying. "I never had a Christmas like this. China always wanted everything to be for her, so Mama and Papa would save my gifts for later after she'd left to go out with her friends. This was the best Christmas I ever had!"

Jim had decided then that Bailey would have Christmas with them as long as he wanted.

"Sheriff Jim?" Bailey said as he sat down on the couch next to Jim's easy chair.

"What's on your mind, Bailey?"

"Would it be all right if I called Noel's parents tomorrow?"

"Of course. Do you have their number?"

Bailey nodded. "Got it memorized. I know it will be sad, but I feel like I owe it to them to call."

"I'm sure they'll appreciate it," said Jim softly.

"Thanks. I'm going to miss meeting them with her. Her father sounded real nice when I talked to him that one time."

"Find out when they're going to have Noel's funeral. Michael and I will go with you."

Bailey nodded. "Thank you. Does it take long for them to get her body?"

Jim shook his head. "I think the medical examiner released her body on Friday. I imagine the funeral will be sometime this week, after Christmas."

"I'll ask them tomorrow. I want to be there."

Bailey stood up and Bonehead got up from the floor next to Jim's chair.

"You think you could take him outside, see if he needs to pee or something?" Jim asked.

Bailey nodded, "Sure. C'mon, Bonehead. Let's go see how fast it takes for us to freeze our nose hairs."

Jim laughed as he watched Bailey and Bonehead head through the kitchen. There were warm jackets hanging near the door, so he knew that Bailey would grab one before he went out. Bonehead would probably find a frozen tennis ball out there and want Bailey to toss it for a while.

He hoped that Bailey would be able to embrace the gift Noel had given him of helping him learn to read and get his GED. He would love to see Bailey go on with his education. He had never been stupid. He'd been crippled by the demands of a woman who wanted to punish him for existing.

He closed his eyes and saw that little boy on the roof of the school, confused and sad because he couldn't move forward with his class.

Chapter Fifty-Two

D r. Oluco had the tea out and cookies to go with it. She shook hands with Manny and waved the three of them to seats in her spare but warm living room. She took her own seat in an overstuffed chair that was bright yellow with a blue blanket lying on one arm.

"Pour yourselves some tea and tell me what it is that brings you back to speak with me."

Ryan poured the tea, letting Dee take the lead with the questions.

"When we were here before, you mentioned that Noel had a 'type.' You used the words 'white, cute, and damaged.' You'd met Bailey Braden?"

Dr. Oluco smiled broadly. "Oh yes, she always brought her young men to meet me. I think she felt that if I approved of them, then it verified her judgment."

"So Bailey was her type."

"He is a very nice young man. His hunger for love was very evident, and that she had discovered his learning disability and assisted him in overcoming it, made her very special to him."

"Noel worked with him for eight months?"

"I would say that's right. Yes. She met him when she was doing her practicum at the elementary school in Eden County. She was testing children in the first through third grades for learning disabilities. It was her goal to become a specialist. She had already applied for a PhD program. I believe she'd decided to go to University of South Florida so she could be closer to her family."

208

"Had her previous relationships been with white men?" asked Dee.

"The serious ones, yes."

Ryan watched Dee carefully as she asked the questions. In light of her relationship with Timothy Mackey, he couldn't help but be uncomfortable. He looked at Manny who very purposefully was not looking at anyone in the room.

"Was there anyone who was upset about Noel's relationship with Bailey Braden?"

Dr. Oluco smiled. "Someone who might want to harm Noel? I believe this is the direction you wish to take with these questions."

"I'm not known for being subtle," said Dee.

Dr. Oluco laughed. "I don't know the answer to that question. I do know that she had been dating a young white man. He was not happy when she ended it. He demanded to know if she'd met someone else, and accused her of finding some tall, well-endowed black boy. His comment made her incredibly angry."

"Do you know the name of the man she was dating before she met Bailey?" asked Manny.

"Matt Wetherford. He is bright and ambitious, and I think he believed that Noel would make the perfect accessory to the life he had planned," said Dr. Oluco. "Noel broke up with him during her practicum."

"He doesn't sound damaged," said Dee.

"Oh, he was damaged. His father had been married multiple times and kept custody of him through each marriage. I'm not sure he'd ever known his biological mother. He also is short, and she said his stature was different from his father's, and his father commented on it frequently."

"She wanted to fix him?" asked Manny.

"She thought she could."

"Do you know if he is still in the area?"

"I'm sure he is," Dr. Oluco said. "He's in medical school."

"Thank you. We appreciate your time, Dr. Oluco," said Dee.

As Dee and Manny prepared to leave, Ryan went to Dr. Oluco who reached out and grasped his hand. "She loved Bailey, Dr. Edwards. At first, she thought she could help him, but he charmed her, made her laugh, and he worked so hard. Once he began to read, she said he blossomed into this even more remarkable man."

Ryan nodded. "Bailey…loves….whole heart…"

"I'm glad she found him. She deserved to be loved that way."

Dr. Oluco hugged him lightly and quickly. "Now go, your friends have work to do."

"Yes, ma'am," said Ryan.

Chapter Fifty-Three

Jim heard a tapping at the back door. Bonehead ran from the living room to the door when it started. Jim followed him and found Bonehead standing on his hind legs and smiling at Ryan through the door. Ryan tried to wave him off so he could open the door, but Bonehead wouldn't have it. Jim laughed and pushed around Bonehead so he could open the door for Ryan.

"Dog!" Ryan chastised as he came in.

Bonehead jumped up and licked Ryan's mouth. He began to spit and wipe his lips making choking sounds.

"Got you good, didn't he?"

Ryan laughed. "Dog...kisses... yuck!"

Bonehead jumped up and licked his mouth again.

"Yuck!" Ryan shouted.

"I don't think that's working, Ryan."

Ryan pushed the dog away and pulled off his tuque. "...Danielle..."

"Liked dog kisses?"

Ryan nodded. He pulled off his gloves and wiped his mouth with the back of his hand. "Not...me..."

"Go wash your face."

Jim got a beer out of the refrigerator, twisted off the cap, and tossed it in the garbage. When he walked into the living room, Ryan's coat, gloves, and tuque were draped across the back of the couch. He looked down the hall and saw Bonehead's butt hanging out of the bathroom door, tail wagging.

Jim heard Ryan making noises and Bonehead backed out of the doorway.

He tried to hand Ryan the beer when he reached the doorway to the kitchen. Ryan shook his head and then smiled. "On call….."

"Dee and Manny make any progress?"

"Finley…deadend… New possible… Writing warrant…"

"They have a new lead?"

"Yes."

Ryan sat down on the couch. "Tree…nice…"

"Glad you like it," said Jim as he sat down. "We're opening gifts at 9 am tomorrow. Be here with Bonehead."

"I…bring coffee," said Ryan.

"I'll furnish the cream and sugar. We're having pancakes for breakfast."

"Nice…."

Bonehead sprawled across Ryan's feet. "He…looking for…gifts?"

Jim laughed. "Bonehead is spoiled by all of us. He does have a few gifts under the tree."

"Toys?"

"I'm not telling."

Ryan laughed.

"What's the new lead?"

"Med student…former boyfriend."

"Huh. Let's not share that with Michael and Bailey."

"Got it."

"Want to eat with us tonight?"

Ryan shook his head. "Walk…dog …then read."

"Burned out, huh?"

"Long…day."

"I hope you have a quiet night."

Ryan rolled his eyes.

Jim nodded. "I'll see you in the morning?"

Ryan nodded and nudged Bonehead to get up. "9…gifts… pancakes."

"See you then!"

Ryan grabbed up his coat and hat. Jim heard the back door open. The sound of Bonehead's clicking nails disappeared. Jim leaned back in his chair, took a sip of the beer, and picked up his book. He glanced over at the tree. It did look good.

Chapter Fifty-Four

Christmas day had turned even colder than the week had been. The day after, Jim let himself into the office early. Michael and Bailey were still asleep when he left. He'd found himself unable to sleep, and not very hungry. He'd made himself a fried egg sandwich on toast and bottled up his regular thermos of coffee. No one at the department liked their coffee as sweet and milky as he did, so he always had the whole thing to himself.

Junior was at the desk and the smell of fresh coffee filled the air. Junior had on a jacket, despite the warmth in the building. When Jim walked in Junior seemed to shrink back into his jacket.

Jim closed the door quickly. "Sorry, Junior. Should we get you a space heater or something?"

"I think the only way I'd stay warm is to set this desk on fire and have it between me and the door," said Junior. "First shift is already out on the roads. Bobby Dale radioed that it was pretty dead on 27. Might be the quietest day we've had in years."

"We live in hope. I didn't get any calls yesterday."

"Dee says everyone is too busy huddling up to stay warm to be getting into trouble. We did not even get a call out to the McCarty's place this year."

Jim shook his head. The McCartys were notorious for their family brawls. At Thanksgiving he'd had four of them in holding cells overnight, just to keep them from killing each other. They'd shouted at each other and one had actually pissed into another's cell just out of sheer meanness. "That's got to be a first. We've never had a holiday without a McCarty being brought in."

"Dee is driving into Gainesville. She got her warrant, and she said the office was open that had the records on the students."

"The medical student records."

Junior nodded. "Manny got food poisoning. That girl he's been seeing didn't cook the bird all the way through, and the fool ate it trying to not hurt her feelings."

"Oh, good Lord," mumbled Jim. "He okay?"

"Yeah, he called Doc Ryan who went over to take care of him and the girl. They're both sick as dogs. Doc Ryan's the one called me and told me Manny wouldn't be in."

"You let Dee know?"

"She knows. She went by to pick Manny up and the Doc was there."

"Poor Ryan."

Junior got up and went to the coffee maker. He poured two mugs full and carried them back to the desk.

"You drinking two-fisted this morning?"

"Just trying to keep my hands warm," Junior said. He sat back at his desk and held a mug in each hand.

Jim rolled his eyes and went on into his office. There were reports to be read and he needed to get working on the schedule for February. He might have to re-organize the first couple of weeks of January. It didn't look like he was getting Dee or Manny back any time in the next week, and he wanted to figure out coverage for New Year's Eve and the first few days after it with that in mind. The fact that the freeze had worsened on Christmas Day and didn't seem to be warming up anytime soon had him concerned.

Some of the smaller farms and houses out off the beaten track didn't have central heat. He wanted to start arranging welfare checks, especially on the homes of the elderly. They had some power outages where tree limbs had fallen on lines. So far the utility company seemed to be keeping up with repairs, which was nothing short of a miracle. He knew Gainesville had lost power to about half the city on Christmas Day. The fortunate thing in this area was there were fewer neighborhoods with tree cover, and the power demands in Eden County were far less than those in the heavily populated city.

He could probably have the patrols on the county roads stop by the houses along the way and make sure their pumps hadn't frozen and that they had a way to deal with the cold that didn't involve burning their houses down.

For just a moment he considered just closing the door to the office and laying his head on his desk for a while. Hurricanes he could deal with. Thunderstorms, lightning strikes, the river rising, all were a part of normal business in Eden. Extended heat waves, drought, even wildfires, he knew how to cope with those.

But freezing temperatures in Eden were so far out of the norm that he couldn't even think of anyone who had experience with them. There had been one freeze when his Dad was Sheriff, but it had lasted a couple of days. Moving into the second week of weather in the 20s didn't fit any emergency plan he had.

He picked up the schedule. He had to keep the roads covered. If someone had an accident in this weather, they'd need to be found sooner rather than later. During patrols he'd encourage them to check on anyone they thought might need help. He knew the churches were keeping an eye on people who'd gotten food baskets for the holiday.

Eden County would survive this freeze, just as it had survived all the other bad luck and trouble that had happened over the last couple of hundred years.

Chapter Fifty-Five

Ryan had just finished removing the IVs from Manny and his girlfriend. He'd dosed them well with Metoclopramide through their lines to help with the nausea. They both seemed better now, and he felt like it was safe to leave them on their own. He'd taken out the turkey, the dressing, and the gravy that the young woman had made so that neither of them would have to smell it again. He knew how the smell of what had made you sick could often trigger nausea, so he'd bagged it up tightly and taken it outside to the garbage. It would freeze in this weather which would keep it from smelling there.

Dee showed up to pick up Manny and was surprised to find Ryan there. She had talked to Manny and given him more than a little grief about being sick when they had the warrant for the information from the medical school.

"Ryan, you're working today?" Dee asked.

Ryan shook his head as he put the sharps into the container he carried in his medical bag. "Just...off call...now," he said.

"Want to take a ride with me over to Gainesville?" she asked.

Ryan checked to see if she was serious. "...Why..."

"You're a doctor. I know you went to Harvard Medical School. Maybe having a fancy degree will impress the people at UF and they'll cooperate more quickly."

Ryan rolled his eyes. "Yeah...right..."

"All right, I don't want to drive over there alone. It's boring."

Ryan laughed. "You...like me."

Dee rolled her eyes. "Don't flatter yourself, Doc."

He finished wrapping up his trash and left some oral medication for Manny and Triana. They'd both returned to the bedroom, and he felt sure they would fall asleep now and get the rest they needed.

He and Dee left the house, and he dropped off another bag of trash. She headed for her patrol car and Ryan stopped and pointed to his car. "Mine?..."

Dee shook her head. "Official business. Otherwise, we have to park in a visitor's lot and pay for it."

He took his medical bag with him. He didn't want to trust it to his empty car. He got into the passenger seat in the front. At least he wasn't having to ride in the back where the doors didn't open from the inside.

"You...this guy...killer?" Ryan asked as Dee was driving east toward Alachua County.

"We are running out of suspects," said Dee. "I agree with Bailey. I don't think China shot Noel Williams. I think she went to see if she was dead. We know Buckley didn't do it. I don't think Finley did it. I know Bailey didn't do it. I can't see any reason to think that Ray Sherman would do it. So that leaves us with Matthew Donaldson Wetherford III. Former boyfriend, current medical student, and the man who got dumped for Bailey Braden."

"Wetherford?"

"Yeah, apparently Daddy's a UF Med School alumnus and he has a very successful surgical practice in Boca Raton."

"Oooo...," said Ryan.

"Says the legacy physician from Harvard," said Dee.

"...Harsh..."

Dee laughed.

"...Mother...surgeon... I'm wrong...practice," said Ryan.

"I'm sure she's horribly disturbed by that."

"...She is...," he said.

Dee shook her head. "Yankees are weird."

They kept the harassment going as they drove through the countryside and into Gainesville proper. Ryan figured Dee wasn't bored.

She drove past the hospital and the parking lots and pulled up next to the Harrell Medical Education Building. Ryan didn't say anything, but she had parked illegally. Thus, the reason for the patrol car.

The admissions office was open, and Dee walked right into it. The first person she saw responded to her uniform by standing up.

"May I help you?" the woman asked.

Dee stepped up and handed the woman a copy of the signed warrant. "Sergeant Dee Jackson, Eden County Sheriff's Department. This is a warrant for the address and phone number of a current medical student."

The woman's surprised look disappeared quickly, and she reached out to take the papers from Dee. She looked through the warrant carefully. "Matthew Wetherford."

"Yes, ma'am."

"Just a moment." The woman disappeared through a closed door and Ryan wondered if she'd gone to call someone about the warrant.

According to Dee the permanent address for Matthew Wetherford was readily available online, but his address in Gainesville was not. Dee wanted the local address. She and Manny had discussed it and both felt that questioning Wetherford at his father's home would not be an advantage. They planned to wait until he would be in Gainesville to question him.

Ryan felt sure that no matter where they questioned Wetherford the Third, there would be a lawyer involved. He knew that if law enforcement had tried to talk to him about anything when he was a student he'd have called his parents' attorney immediately and arranged for representation. People who grew up in his world never spoke to law enforcement without an attorney.

The woman returned carrying a sheet of paper. "I assumed you probably had his home address, but I've printed it out as well, just in case."

"Thank you," said Dee. "I appreciate your help."

They left the building and once they were near Dee's patrol car, she looked over at Ryan and grinned. "What do you say to taking a run past the building? We can see if Mr. Wetherford went home for Christmas or not."

"Not safe..."

"I'm with you, I've got a gun."

"I...don't... Not safe...you," said Ryan.

"I'll be fine."

Ryan reached out and grabbed Dee's shoulders. "…Same thought… Noel."

Dee looked surprised. She touched one of Ryan's hands. "Thank you for worrying, Ryan. But I'm prepared in a way Noel wasn't. I know someone's dangerous."

Ryan dropped his hands. "…Never forgive…me."

"You wouldn't forgive yourself?"

Ryan nodded.

"I'm going to go there, with you or without you," said Dee. "I'm not your wife, and I'm not Noel. I have a gun and I'm a trained officer. I've been to war, Ryan. I promise I wouldn't suggest this if I thought I'd get hurt."

Ryan realized that he could feel tears forming. He blushed.

Dee hugged him, her head coming just under his chin. "Trust me, Ryan. I promise not to get shot or get you shot. If he is here, he'll probably refuse to talk to me and lawyer up. Isn't that what rich white boys do?"

Ryan hugged her back. "…Yes…"

Dee dropped her arms and stepped back. "Don't make me do that again."

Ryan nodded. "…Okay…"

Dee unlocked the patrol car and they both got into it. Dee turned the heat on and let it blast them both. Despite her heavy jacket and his coat, the car felt like the inside of a refrigerator. She folded the sheet of paper she'd been given and handed it to Ryan.

"It's a street address, no apartment, so he must be renting a house. 1301 SW 12th Avenue. It's not that far from Shands, which would make it handy for anyone in medical school." Dee took the patrol car back the way she'd come, then turned left on Archer Road. "The great thing about Gainesville is it's a grid system. Pretty damn hard not to find what you're looking for if you understand that."

She headed east on Archer Road and then took a turn right onto 441. In less than 15 minutes they found themselves turning onto 12th Avenue and pulling into the driveway of the house. It was an old home, white, and one car was parked in the driveway. Dee had pulled up next to it. The bright blue BMW was a 4-door sedan. Dee shook her head. "What is it with you young doctors and blue BMWs?"

Ryan grinned. "Mine...newer."

Dee snorted. "Let's go knock on the door, Dr. Edwards. You can compare cars once you've met him."

They walked around the house to the front door. Dee pulled the screen door open and banged hard on the wood with her fist. Ryan caught himself almost thinking, 'typical cop knock' and then quickly looked over at Dee. He wouldn't be surprised at all if she could look at him and know what he was thinking. The woman had scary skills for reading people.

Her eyes were focused on the front door. Her right hand rested on the butt of her gun and her holster snap was open. Dee prepared for the worst-case scenario. She thought like a cop, never taking for granted that the door of an unknown would be opened by someone who was a bad guy or someone who was innocent.

People panicked when they saw the police or a deputy at the door. Even people who hadn't done anything wrong might panic, wondering what bad news awaited them on their doorstep. Until Ryan had moved to Eden County, he had never had any contact with law enforcement that didn't involve something wrong. Now that he knew Jim and Dee and Manny, he saw them in a different way.

He wondered now since he'd moved from Eden County if the sight of an officer at the door would make him think of the people he knew, or of talking to the detective who had investigated Danielle's murder. He didn't know.

The door opened and a short young man dressed in dark sweats faced them. Dee's hand dropped to her side, and she spoke to him in a neutral way. "I'm Deputy Dee Jackson and I'm looking to speak to Matthew Wetherford."

"I'm Matthew Wetherford. What is this about?"

"Noel Williams."

"What about her?" he said.

Ryan didn't like the tone of voice that Matthew Wetherford had. It was dismissive, as though Dee was a nuisance.

"I understand that you used to be involved with Ms. Williams," said Dee.

Matthew Wetherford shrugged. "Old news. I've moved on."

221

Ryan saw the faintest shift in Dee's head. She didn't like Wetherford's tone either.

"I would like to speak with you about your relationship with Ms. Williams."

He shook his head. "I've got nothing to say to you people," he said and started to shut the door. Dee's foot stopped the door from moving.

"I'm sorry that I'm inconveniencing you, but I do need to speak with you about Ms. Williams."

"Come back with a warrant," he said. Then he kicked her foot, trying to move it away from the door. Her foot didn't move.

"Mr. Wetherford, you're suggesting I have a warrant before you'll answer questions?"

"You heard me, Deputy. You are keeping me from my studies and not allowing me to shut the door to my home."

Ryan stepped back.

"And don't bring lookie-loos with you," he said pointing to Ryan. "Get a warrant. I'll get an attorney. You can talk to the attorney."

Dee moved her foot and Wetherford slammed the door. Dee walked away, heading for her patrol car. Ryan quickly followed her. She already had the car started when he closed his door.

"Back...to..."

"Yes," said Dee.

Chapter Fifty-Six

Dee Jackson didn't react to anger the way people expected she would. Jim knew the minute she walked into the office that she wanted to kick someone's ass, but her calm demeanor would have fooled most people.

Junior felt the sudden need to go out and pick up lunch for everyone when she walked through the door. He sent Jim an email asking him to listen for the phones and took off through the front door, barely taking the time to grab his keys and jacket.

Jim could hear her typing furiously at one of the computers in the bullpen, and he gave serious consideration to not leaving his office to speak to her. However, not doing so would only lead to a more pointed confrontation later, so he took a deep breath and got out of his chair. Dee didn't look up when he walked out of his office, nor did she raise her head when he made his way to where she sat.

"What happened?" he asked quietly.

"Exactly what I expected," Dee said.

"Meaning?"

Dee continued typing, letting his question die in the quiet of the room. The clicking of the keyboard continued.

"You scared Junior off, but you can't make me leave."

Dee's hands stopped on the keyboard. "I took Ryan with me."

"And?"

"Have you ever heard someone with aphasia rant?" asked Dee looking up at Jim.

"No."

"It took him the whole trip back to Warren to finally get it out."

"That must have been annoying."

"Surprisingly profane, mostly."

"That was probably more the aphasia than the actual rant. He gets frustrated."

"No shit." Dee went back to furiously typing.

"That a warrant?"

"Yes."

"What's it for?"

"He said not to come back unless I had a warrant. I think that's an invitation I should take him up on."

"It's a search warrant?"

"Yes, sir."

"Do you think he knows that you don't have to have a warrant to question him?"

Dee grinned. "He's lawyering up."

Jim nodded. "Want me to call Junior and have him bring you some lunch?"

"No, I think I'll just chew on a bullet for a while."

Jim laughed. Dee continued the furious typing.

"The good thing is Manny is feeling better and this guy is going to need his lawyer."

Jim turned and started to head back to his office. "I'm calling Ryan and having him come sedate you."

Dee looked over at him. "Just don't have him try to talk to me."

Jim laughed out loud. "What do you want Junior to bring you for lunch?"

"Chicken sandwich from Ella's."

"You got it."

Jim called Junior's cell and had him pick up a sandwich for Dee and one for him as well. Food would do her good and give him time to talk Dee into waiting for tomorrow to serve her warrant. The last thing he needed was for Dee to go back to Gainesville today.

Jim called Manny back and explained what was going on with the medical student in Gainesville, and Manny promised he'd go with her to serve the warrant.

"Make the interview happen here. I want you and Dee both on it, and I want it recorded. He's going to have a lawyer, but I'm sure you can craft some questions that the attorney won't object to that will give you some answers that will lead to something."

Manny agreed with Jim about how to handle the interview. Now it was up to Jim to get Dee to agree to it.

He waited until Junior had brought back lunch, and Dee had eaten hers. Then he casually walked out of his office and pulled up a chair next to her.

"I'm all right," said Dee.

"I'm glad. Then you won't mind what I'm going to ask you."

Dee squinted at Jim.

He ventured on anyway. "Get the warrant signed today but wait to serve it tomorrow. Go with Manny. I'm sure he'll call the attorney. You then bring him in for the interview. Then you squash him like a bug in the interview."

Dee burst out laughing.

Jim grinned at her.

"You're just trying to appeal to my natural desires."

"Yes, I am."

"Manny said he'll be back tomorrow?"

"Yes. You get the warrant signed today you serve it tomorrow. You get lucky, you arrest him because of what you find."

"I have to get the search warrant first."

"What do you have?"

"Former boyfriend. Dropped when she took up with Bailey Braden. She kept a journal and wrote that he didn't take the break-up well. Dr. Oluco said he'd accused her of becoming involved with a tall, well-endowed black boy."

Jim cringed. "He used the word 'boy'?"

"I don't think Dr. Oluco would have used it if she hadn't. Dammit. We focused on the truck. It kept us here, and he was just an hour away from Warren."

"Use the proximity in the warrant. It wouldn't be hard to get to Warren and find out what was going on."

Dee sighed. "Let me get this written up and get it signed. Then I'll wait for Manny and execute it tomorrow."

"Thank you. I think you'll be glad you did."

"Well, I'd hate to disappoint him and not show up with a warrant," said Dee smiling.

The front door opened and Jim looked up expecting to see Junior, but instead, Tim Mackey walked in. He was still in uniform, but driving his own truck, which Jim could see parked out in front of the office. He waved and Jim and walked up to the desk where Dee was still furiously typing. He leaned on top of the monitor and dropped his head so his face covered the screen.

Dee looked up. "What are you doing here?"

"I have the late shift. I thought I'd come see my lady and maybe take her away for a bit. What you typing up?"

"Search warrant."

"Ooo, who's getting searched?"

"Suspect in the Williams murder."

"Whoa! Need some inter-county cooperation?"

"It's in Alachua County."

"I know you're always short-handed over here. No offense, Jim."

"None taken," said Jim. He'd rolled his chair back a little so he could watch them better.

"Not serving it until tomorrow."

"Well, damn. Here I am with the afternoon available."

"You could go let Jackie out and take her for a walk," said Dee.

Tim shook his head. "I'm feeling very unwanted, and slightly used."

Dee stopped typing and stood up. "Tim, I'm going to get this warrant signed. I'm sorry."

Tim's face dropped into a pout. "Now I'm sad."

Dee started laughing. "You are the silliest man I know."

"Once you get that warrant signed, your shift is over," said Jim.

Dee and Tim both looked at him and then at each other again.

"I can take Jackie for a walk and wait for you at the house once your warrant is signed. I'm not on until tonight."

Dee leaned forward, "Think you can wear Jackie out so she'll take a nap?"

"Oh, yes ma'am. I am sure I can do that."

"Just don't wear yourself out."

"Oh, no worries about that, ma'am. I'll be awake and waiting." Tim leaned forward and kissed the tip of Dee's nose. "See you shortly." He nodded to Jim and headed out to his truck.

Dee sat back down and started typing up her warrant again.

"Want me to get Junior to bring another sandwich?" asked Jim.

"Dee shook her head. "No thank you, sir. I don't believe we'll have time to eat."

Jim laughed out loud. "Sgt. Jackson, finish up that warrant, get it signed and have a good afternoon. That's an order."

Dee shook her head as Jim headed for his office laughing loudly.

Chapter Fifty-Seven

At 7 am Thursday morning, December 27, 2001, four Eden County patrol cars pulled up next to the house at 1301 SW 12th Avenue. Sgt. Dee Jackson and Deputy Manny Sota got out of their cars and walked up to the front door of the house. Dee banged on the door. She banged on the door again after five minutes, and then again after five more minutes.

The blue BMW Coup still held its place in the driveway. Sheriff Jim Sheppard had gotten out of his borrowed patrol car and stood next to it facing the front door. Deputy Bobby Dale stood next his patrol car. They stayed back. Bobby would participate in the search. Jim and Bobby both would serve as witnesses to Matthew Wetherford's response and behavior while his house was being searched.

The door finally opened after Dee banged on the door for the third time. Matthew Wetherford looked surprised to see the two deputies. Manny handed him the warrant and announced they would be searching the house and his car. He asked them to provide the keys to the car, and Bobby Dale would do that search.

They requested that he step outside and wait for them to finish.

"The fuck I will!" Matthew said loudly. "You're not tearing apart my house." He started to slam the door and Dee and Manny both stepped forward and stopped him. "Get the fuck away from my door. You are not coming in!"

Jim nodded to Bobby Dale who quickly moved up to the house and helped Manny and Dee pull Matthew Wetherford out of the doorway. Once he was outside, Dee and Manny went inside. Bobby Dale cuffed Wetherford's hands and led him to his patrol car. He put him in the back seat, made sure the seatbelt was on him, and closed the door. Then he followed Dee and Manny into the house.

Jim leaned against his car and watched Wetherford. The car would still be warm from Bobby driving it to Gainesville. But with the temperature being around 20 degrees Fahrenheit, it wouldn't be long before the car turned cold. Wetherford didn't have shoes on, and he wore a short-sleeved t-shirt. It wouldn't take him too long to get cold.

Jim had worn long johns under his uniform and had on a thick jacket, gloves, and a black tuque. The tuque had been his Christmas gift from Ryan. It definitely beat the baseball-style cap he normally wore all to hell. In fact, he felt downright toasty.

Wetherford noticed him standing and started yelling at him. Jim smiled pleasantly. He was an observer here. The seatbelt on Wetherford would keep him from turning his body to kick at the window. The man continued yelling and Jim continued ignoring him.

Suddenly Jim heard a loud sound. He looked over at Bobby Dale's car and Wetherford had slammed the side of his head against the window. Wetherford was a medical student. Certainly, he had enough sense to know that his head wouldn't break the glass. As Jim watched he slammed his head against the window again

Jim pulled his radio and called into the house. "10-55, I've got a 10-24 out here."

Dee responded. "10-55, Will Bobby Dale do?"

"That's who I need."

"10-5, I'll send him out."

Wetherford continued to bang his head against the window. Bobby Dale ran out of the house and to his car and opened the back door just as Wetherford went to slam his head against the window. The seatbelt kept him from falling out of the car. "What are you doing?" shouted Bobby.

"That officer over there came over here and hit me," said Wetherford. "I need an ambulance!"

Bobby put his hands on his hips and looked at Wetherford. "Sir, that's the Sheriff over there. I know he did not hit you, but I can see where your greasy hair has been up against this window. When was the last time you took a shower, man? You've got the whole back seat stinking worse than a farting dog."

"I tell you this is police brutality. That man opened this door and slammed his fist into the side of my head. I've got a concussion. I need an ambulance."

Bobby Dale looked at the young man. "Mr. Wetherford, I can tell you for a fact that the Sheriff over there did not come and open this door and hit you."

"You don't know that."

Bobby Dale gently touched the man's head and tilted it to look at it. "That's not a fist mark, sir. I've pulled enough people out of bare-knuckle bar fights to know what that looks like. I can take you to the emergency room and have you looked at, but I'm still going to be taking you to be booked after that."

Wetherford spit on Bobby Dale's jacket. Bobby Dale took a deep breath. "Mr. Wetherford, you just added assault to your misdemeanor attempting to prevent an officer of the law from performing his duty as ordered by a warrant. You're digging the hole deeper here, sir."

Jim called out, "Bobby, do Dee and Manny need you on the search?"

Bobby called back, "No, sir. I believe I'll take Mr. Wetherford over to the emergency room and have his head checked out before he does anything else stupid."

"Sounds like a good idea, Deputy."

Bobby pushed Wetherford back into the seat and closed the door quietly. He waved to Jim. "See you in Warren, sir!"

Jim watched him get into his car and pull away. The hospital was less than fifteen minutes away, and it would be better for Matthew Wetherford to be seen by a physician. The young man seemed determined to make everything more difficult.

Dee came out of the house. "We've found a gun. We need to get FDLE here. Manny and I don't want to compromise any evidence there might be on it."

"Call it in."

"Where's Bobby?"

"He took Mr. Wetherford to the emergency room. He slammed his head against the car window and tried to convince Bobby that I had opened the car door and hit him."

"I thought you had to be smart to go to medical school."

Jim grinned. "Evidently not."

She made the call to FDLE and Manny came out of the house to stand with them. "That place is a pigsty. Actually, that's probably an insult to pigs. There are dirty dishes, food rotting in the garbage, and the bathroom. It would gag a vulture off a gut wagon," he said.

Dee slipped her phone into her jacket pocket and muttered a curse word. Manny looked at Jim surprised. Dee walked back to them. "Dr. Sullivan happens to be in Gainesville today and will come and collect the gun and any other evidence we've found."

"I'm sorry," said Manny.

Jim moved toward the driver's side of his car. "I think that's my cue to leave," he said.

"Coward!" said Dee.

"If you shoot her, I'd like to have reasonable deniability."

Manny smiled.

"Very funny, sir," said Dee.

"I will see both of you back in Warren. I ought to go check on Bobby and Wetherford, anyway."

Jim got into his car and escaped before either of them could guilt him into staying. His one contact with Dr. Sullivan had convinced him that he should avoid her at all costs. Dee and Manny were strong and had thick hides. They'd be able to handle the abrasive forensic specialist. Jim, on the other hand, was glad to escape another meeting with her.

As he headed into the parking lot next to the ER, Jim saw three local police cars pull up to the entrance of the building. The possibility that this had anything to do with Bobby Dale and Wetherford seemed distant, but then again, Jim had developed a sort of sixth sense when things were about to go sideways—and this case had been going sideways all day.

He quickly parked and ran toward the doors to the ER. Just as he got to the building, a car pulled up with an elderly man and woman in it. As the man opened his door, Jim saw Wetherford run out from one side of the building and head for the car.

Jim ran to intercept him and tackled him to the ground just before Wetherford grabbed the door. His right shoulder hit the pavement hard as he rolled onto his back with Wetherford in his arms. The young man's head scraped the pavement and he screamed, but Jim did not let go of him.

Within seconds the three GPD officers came out of the building and ran straight to where Jim lay with the struggling Wetherford. A huge black man dressed in the dark uniform of the GPD cuffed the fighting Wetherford and pulled him out of Jim's grasp.

Jim let him take him, dropping his arms and taking a deep breath. He had been lucky and only hit his shoulder. With Wetherford slightly under him, he'd taken the brunt of the fall, even though Jim had rolled trying to not crush the smaller man.

Another officer helped Jim get up. Wetherford had quit fighting the minute he'd gotten a good look at the size of the officer who had put the handcuffs on him. He certainly wasn't yelling about police brutality.

"You all right, sir?" asked a younger officer.

"Yes, thanks for your help."

"That was a hell of a tackle," said the large man. "You played football?"

Jim laughed. "Yes, at UF. I'm glad it's not something I do regularly anymore."

The elderly man at the car had been calmed by the third GPD officer, and together they were now getting his ill wife into the ER.

Jim followed the two officers into the ER. He and the GPD officers were quickly taken back to a room where the nurses could get them out of sight of the people in the waiting room. A young man in scrubs with a stethoscope asked the group who was in charge, and Jim spoke up. "This is a man one of my deputies had in custody. Do you know where he is?"

"This way," said a nurse. The GPD officers were taken into another room with Wetherford and Jim was led into an open area with curtains closing off the beds. The nurse pulled back a curtain and Bobby Dale lay on a bed, unconscious. "He's all right," said the nurse. "The nurse went to sedate the prisoner. He'd been handcuffed to the bed. He grabbed the syringe from the nurse, stabbed him with it, kicked your deputy to the floor, jumped out of the bed and stabbed your deputy with the same syringe, got his keys, and unlocked himself.

"Damn," said Jim. "Deputy Dale is sedated?"

"Yes, but he's been checked over. He's breathing fine and it shouldn't last too long. He didn't get the whole dose. It was pretty much split between him and the nurse."

"How is the nurse?" asked Jim.

"Pissed off, but fine."

Jim heard Wetherford screaming 'Police brutality!' from the room he'd been taken into. "That guy is a pain in the ass," said Jim.

The big GPD officer appeared in the curtained area. "I'm Sgt. Johnson. We were responding to a call from the hospital about your prisoner escaping. You're from Eden County?"

Jim stuck out his hand and shook Sgt. Johnson's hand. "Sheriff Jim Sheppard. My deputies served a search warrant on Matthew Wetherford this morning and he's been very uncooperative. He slammed his head into the window of the car while he was restrained in the vehicle, so I had Deputy Dale bring him over here to be checked."

The Sergeant looked at the sleeping man on the bed. "I heard he stabbed your deputy with a syringe."

"Nurse...," Jim looked at her name badge. "Nurse Tanner was just explaining to me what happened."

"The nurse here is fine and doesn't want to press charges. He's mostly just pissed off. I'm supposing you'll want to press charges for him sedating your deputy."

"Yes. He's a person of interest in a murder investigation. I have two deputies at his house who found a gun, so we have forensics from FDLE

233

coming."

"That would explain his desire to get away from your deputy."

"Yes. We don't even know that the gun is from our case, but his behavior is leading me to think there is a connection. We're going to have to get it figured out."

"We're happy to let you take him to Eden County for booking."

"Thanks," said Jim. "It would be nice to get him into County until we can get all this sorted."

Sgt. Johnson nodded. "We're having him checked out right now. He's in four-point restraints, so he should be secure."

"I'll take him and my Deputy at the same time. I don't want Bobby driving. I'll send someone back to get his patrol car. I do appreciate your help. I'm not sure how long I could have held onto him out there in the drive."

Sgt. Johnson said, "For a little guy, he's got a lot of fight in him. I'll have one of the officers remain here with him until you're ready to go. I'll do my report and get our paperwork straight."

"I appreciate that," said Jim.

"Sheriff?"

Jim looked over and saw Bobby Dale blinking at him. "How are you doing, Deputy?"

"My mouth tastes like last year's bird nest, but I think I'm okay. Did Wetherford get away?"

"No, we got some help from GPD."

The Sergeant laughed. "Don't let him get away with that. He caught your man outside the ER. We just helped him up off the ground and cuffed the guy."

"Way to go, Sheriff!" said Bobby Dale.

Jim patted the deputy's leg. "Let's get you awake enough that we can ride back together and take Mr. Wetherford to be booked."

Bobby Dale nodded. "Sounds good, sir. I can't believe I'm saying this, but it may take the two of us to get him back to Warren."

* * *

Jim got his patrol car and pulled it around to the front of the ER. Sgt. Johnson and another officer brought Wetherford out with his hands and feet restrained. Bobby Dale followed along, only slightly wobbly from the sedation. Fortunately, the cage in the back of Jim's car had a plexiglass partition that kept the prisoner from being able to spit or vomit into the front of the vehicle.

Sgt. Johnson had buckled Matthew Wetherford into the seatbelt, making sure he wouldn't be able to change positions or slide across the seat. Jim thanked him again for his help.

He slid the middle of the partition open about an inch so he could hear Wetherford if he decided to be vocal. He hoped that the man had worn himself out and would just sit back and be quiet for the ride out to Warren. They had a good hour to travel, and he really didn't want to listen to him screaming 'police brutality' all the way to the Eden County Jail.

His radio buzzed and clicked, and he heard Dee Jackson's voice. He reached over, grabbed the mic, and responded, "Sheriff here, Sgt. Jackson."

"Does Deputy Dale still have a 10-15?"

"10-4. I have Deputy Dale with me and the 10-15. We're headed to County for booking."

"Booking?"

"10-4, Sgt. Jackson. You need something?"

"Can you hang on to him at County until we're finished here?"

"10-4. Take your time."

"Excellent, sir. We'll see you at County. It's going to be a couple of hours at least."

"I'm sure we'll still be there. Yell if you get delayed."

"10-4, Sheriff."

Bobby Dale sipped at the bottle of water he'd been given at the ER. He swallowed and said, "I'm awful sorry about what happened, sir."

Jim shook his head. "You did the best you could. I saw that nurse he stomped. That guy is twice your size. Wetherford's like some dwarf ninja or something."

"Fuck you!" shouted Wetherford in the back.

"He is nimble," said Bobby.

"Fuck both of you!" shouted Wetherford from the back.

"Nasty mouth on him, too," said Bobby.

Bobby reached over and slid the plexiglass closed. "I don't think we need to listen to him, sir. I guess the good thing about what happened is we have something to hold him on."

"I'd have been tempted to leave him with GPD if the nurse had pressed charges."

Bobby laughed. "He has been trouble."

"I think GPD just didn't want to have to deal with him."

Jim could hear Wetherford yelling in the back seat, but the plexiglass was thick enough that it muffled the words. He was pretty damn sure that the man wasn't saying anything new.

Chapter Fifty-Eight

At the County jail, Wetherford still hadn't run out of steam. He'd spit on the jailer who'd taken him to holding and ended up in a restraint chair with a spit hood on his head. Jim had watched them get his fingerprints and photo as he completed paperwork. Bobby Dale had turned over a report from the ER on the drug that had been injected into him and agreed to let them draw blood to see if he still was under the effect of the drug before he completed his paperwork.

The technician seemed to think that there would still be traces of the drug in his system. Jim thought about calling on Ryan to come out and check him over. The doctor at the ER had been pretty hands-off about the whole thing. He'd sent the nurse off to get the drug because Wetherford had been aggressive with him during the examination. That had not turned out well at all, and Jim thought the man just wanted Wetherford and the Deputy out of the hospital as soon as possible.

The technician had taken a blood sample from Wetherford as well. Not because he'd been drugged at the ER, but because his behavior was erratic. He suggested to Jim that he might be under the influence of something, and if they checked now, there might be additional charges.

Jim looked at his watch and saw that it was noon. It felt like it should be much later because he'd definitely done a day's full work in the last five hours. His shoulder hurt and he hadn't eaten, and he felt irritable.

Wetherford had not calmed down at all. He hoped that the blood work gave them some answers about that. One of Bobby Dale's sisters had come and picked him up. Jim told him to go home and take sick leave for the rest of his shift. He'd been kicked in the chest and then drugged. He had to feel at least as bad as Jim did.

Jim found a seat in the front lobby and sat with his head leaned back against the wall. He'd had an early morning and more excitement than he needed. He'd promised to wait for Dee and Manny here at the jail, so he would wait for them. Hopefully, Dee would have avoided shooting Dr. Sullivan, and his wait wouldn't be too long.

* * *

"Sheriff?" said a voice, and someone gently shook his shoulder. The movement made the shoulder throb and Jim snapped awake to see Dee standing over him.

"Ow!" he said softly.

"Sorry," she said.

Jim shrugged. "It's all right. I landed on that shoulder when I tackled Wetherford."

"When the hell did that happen?"

Dee and Manny sat down on either side of him. "Oh, yeah, you don't know. Wetherford managed to escape the ER. I saw him outside getting ready to hijack some old man and tackled him to the ground in the driveway."

"Are you all right? Is Bobby Dale hurt?"

Jim shook his head. "I'm fine. Just sore. He stabbed Bobby and the nurse at the ER with a syringe full of a sedative. Knocked both of them out and then got Bobby's keys and unlocked himself from the cuff on the bed. GPD had been called in, but the nurse didn't want to press charges, so they let me bring them both back here. Oh, I need to send someone to get Bobby's patrol car from the hospital."

Dee patted Jim's hand. "I'll call Junior and get him to take care of that."

"Thanks. I sent Bobby home. He's fine. He took a pretty good kick to the chest, but nothing's broken. The sedative wore off before we left the ER."

"Good to know."

"How'd things go with Sullivan?"

238

Manny laughed. "She was very impressed that we'd stopped our search when we uncovered the gun. It was under a bunch of garbage in the kitchen."

"Yeah, you said the place was a sty."

"I think Wetherford is having a breakdown or something. I can't imagine he lives like that all the time," said Dee. "He'd set his medical books on fire in the fireplace."

"That does not sound normal," said Jim.

"The gun's the right caliber for the Noel Williams' murder. Probably can't match the bullet to the one that hit the concrete, but Dr. Sullivan said there might be trace on the gun that would help us," said Dee. "She's going to try to get a report to us by Saturday.

"Did you want to question Wetherford?"

"Not yet."

We're going to need to get him arraigned.

"I think we should request a psych eval, sir," said Dee.

Jim nodded. "All right. Let's see what we can do. Mind if I leave the two of you to that and I head back to the house? I need food and coffee."

Manny stood up. "We got this, Sheriff."

"Good," said Jim. He groaned as he stood up. "I'll be back in the office later. Let me or Junior know if you need me. Junior always finds me."

"Yes, sir," said Dee.

Jim put on his jacket, gloves and tuque and headed out of the jail. It was still cold enough to freeze the balls off a brass monkey when he got outside. But a meal, some coffee, and maybe a talk with Michael would help him get awake enough to finish out his day. He looked at his watch. It was 2:30. No wonder he'd fallen asleep. He walked toward his car. The nap in the chair had maybe helped a little. He was at least awake enough to drive home.

Chapter Fifty-Nine

Ryan had gone into the office to see a couple of patients. Filly had come in, but Claire had opted to stay home since the roads were still bad. Doc Markham had gone into Gainesville to check on the patients in the hospital but hadn't come into the office to see anyone.

Fortunately, everything had been simple. A patient getting a routine check of sugar levels, one case of minor frostbite, and an earache. He and Filly had taken care of everyone and gone home.

Bonehead had gotten a long walk and a couple of extra treats. Ryan justified it by deciding that the dog probably needed a little bit of extra fat during the severe cold snap. Bonehead certainly wasn't arguing about it.

Jim came in around 3 pm as Ryan was coming back with Bonehead from the short walk that served as his bathroom break before dinner. Jim looked tired, so he expected him to wave and go on inside, but he'd stopped and waited for Ryan and Bonehead to meet him.

"This tuque is great," said Jim.

"Good!" said Ryan.

"Got a little time to talk?"

Ryan nodded. "Sure... my place?"

"Yeah," said Jim. "I need to talk about today, and I don't want to do it with Michael and Bailey in hearing range."

They walked up the stairs to Ryan's apartment over the garage. Bonehead went straight to his water bowl for a long drink. Ryan shook his head. "Refill...," he said.

Jim sat on the couch and slipped off his jacket, gloves, and tuque. "Dee and Manny executed a search warrant on the medical student's house today. We had a couple of unexpected results, but they did find a gun."

Ryan dropped his coat on the end of the coach and sat down. "Every...one okay?"

Jim rolled his eyes. "Questionable. Bobby Dale got stabbed with a syringe of some kind of sedative. Didn't get the full dose and seemed okay once I got him back to Warren."

"What!"

"The student, Wetherford, has either had a breakdown or is trying to make a case for being insane. He refused to cooperate with the search. Had to cuff him and put him in the back of a patrol car. Then he started bashing his head against the window. I had Bobby take him to the ER, and he put up a fight while handcuffed to the bed. Got his hands on a syringe, stabbed a nurse and Bobby, and escaped. When I drove over to check on things, he tried to hijack an old man for his car. I tackled him. The local police had been called and they helped. We got him back inside in restraints and once Bobby woke up, I brought them both to the County jail. Wetherford is still there."

"Dee and Manny?"

"Called FDLE in when they found the gun. Stopped their search and let her take over."

"Dr. ...Sullivan? ...Dee...like...that?"

"They got along okay this time. Now we're waiting on the forensic report on the gun and a couple of other things."

"Phone?"

"They didn't find one."

Ryan thought about that for a moment. Bonehead wandered over and dropped onto the floor at Jim's feet.

Jim reached down and began to pet the dog's head.

"Not...right."

"Yeah. They may have to continue processing that house. I didn't see it, but they all said it was full of garbage and that Wetherford had burned his medical books in the fireplace."

241

"Weird."

"I agree. I have a feeling that there will be a team going over the house, and the car will be towed to FDLE. Maybe the phone is in the car."

Ryan nodded. "Want…check shoulder?"

Jim moved his shoulder and winced. "It's probably just bruised."

"Yeah… yeah…," Ryan got up and pointed to Jim's shirt. "Off."

Jim surrendered, unbuttoning his shirt and pulling it off. He pulled off the long underwear shirt and kept it in his lap. Ryan touched the bruised skin on his shoulder and gently manipulated the joint. Jim couldn't stop wincing whenever he moved the shoulder backwards.

"Bruised…bu…not clicking…or hanging."

"That good?"

"Yes." Ryan went to his refrigerator and pulled out an ice pack. "Use this…now."

"Ryan, I'm not putting ice on my shoulder."

Ryan slapped the ice pack on Jim's shoulder. "Yes… make coffee."

"I don't think coffee is going to counteract the damn ice," grumbled Jim.

Ryan pointed at him, as though telling him to stay.

"And I am not Bonehead."

Ryan smiled. "You…mind better."

Jim nudged Bonehead with his foot. "That's true. You don't mind worth a damn, do you?" Bonehead rolled over and exposed his belly for rubbing. Jim rubbed his belly with his foot. "Why would a medical student burn his textbooks?"

Ryan set up the coffee maker and filled it with water. "Quitting."

"He was aggressive. Yelling about police brutality and spitting at people. He stunk like he hadn't showered in weeks."

Ryan leaned against the counter. "Confusing… fighting…. quitting…" Ryan shook his head. "No self… care …odd."

"Dee wants a psych evaluation."

"Good…parents?"

"Legally he's an adult so we haven't contacted them."

"Should… maybe problem…there."

"I'll have Dee call them."

The coffee maker signaled it was done. Ryan poured Jim a cup, filled half the cup with milk, and spooned sugar into it. He came around the counter and handed it to Jim. "Drink."

Jim snorted at the command but drank the coffee. Ryan noticed that he wasn't moving the arm with the sore shoulder. "Ice...later... fifteen minutes... aspirin..."

"Got it. Is it okay if I use a heating pad on the rest of me at the same time?"

Ryan shook his head. "Im...possibl....you..." He saw Jim grinning at him and made a shooing motion. "Out...go home... drive..Michael...crazy..."

Jim set the ice pack down, pulled on both shirts, and grabbed his jacket and the ice pack. "Thanks for looking at my shoulder. I'll let you know how things go."

Ryan watched Jim go out the door and heard his boots clomping down the stairs. He sat down on the couch and reached down to scratch Bonehead's exposed belly and let his mind roll over all the things Jim had told him.

Chapter Sixty

Manny and Dee made it back to the office around 5:30. Jim had gotten back to the office around 4. He'd tossed Ryan's ice pack into the freezer at home, gotten something to eat, looked in on Michael and Bailey, and then headed back to the office. He'd been on tenterhooks waiting for his deputies to return to the office.

"What happened with Wetherford?" he said, standing in his office door.

"I haven't even taken off my jacket!" said Dee.

Junior had turned around on his chair. "He's been like that since he got here. I'm glad you're back."

"Matthew Wetherford is booked and had his arraignment. He's being held over for a psych evaluation."

"Which he protested loudly," said Dee.

"They transporting him somewhere or bringing someone in?"

"The judge decided he's too aggressive to keep at the jail. He's had him taken over to state hospital in MacClenny for psychiatric evaluation. He's being transported now," said Manny.

Jim sat down in the bullpen. "Dee, you need to call his parents and inform them of his arrest and where he's been sent."

"I can do that."

"See how they react and if they had any idea something was wrong."

"All right."

"Have you talked to Sullivan?"

Manny and Dee both sat down, dropping their things on the table. Manny answered, "Dr. Sullivan called us. They found a phone in the car. They

244

think it's Wetherford's but can't be sure until they get into it."

"Ask the family if they know his password."

Dee nodded. "You're worried."

Jim rubbed his face. "Let me just put this out there, what are the odds that we've got two sociopaths involved in this crime?"

"China and Wetherford," said Dee.

"Yeah."

"Wait, I know China's a sociopath, but this guy Wetherford? He's in medical school. He's got a college degree," said Manny. "Wouldn't someone notice this during the selection process?"

"If he's a legacy at UF, and Daddy has been taking care of all his problems until now…" Dee let that thought hang.

"Noel Williams was smart. Older than Wetherford."

"His family is rich, and she was something he wanted," said Jim.

"Shit," said Manny.

"Call Sullivan, Manny. See if you can get anything by tomorrow. We know China was at the site of the murder in Ray Sherman's truck. That means she had to know that Bailey and Noel Williams were in there."

"Yeah, okay," said Manny. "I'll call her."

Dee reached out and took Jim's hand in hers. "You're cold."

"It's the weather."

"Sir, that's bullshit and you know it. Who is with Bailey and Michael?"

"Wilcox."

"Go relieve him. We'll let you know whatever we hear. You go home and take it easy. We're going to need you."

"Make those calls," said Jim as he stood up and went back into his office.

Chapter Sixty-One

Ryan's cell phone rang. He followed the noise and found it in his coat pocket. He answered and heard Edna's voice.

"Doc Ryan, I need your help," she said.

"What's...wrong?"

"I'm at Buddy's house. Ray ain't here. His truck's still out with the people up in Jacksonville, so I know he ain't got no way to get anywhere. I'm scared."

Ryan felt his heartbeat speed up. "Edna, ...I need ...Jim..."

"I don't know about the law..."

"Edna, I...can't..."

He could hear her breathing. "Yeah, all right. I get that. Yeah, you bring Jim with you. But I need you. I feel all spinny, and I know that ain't good."

"I'll...be there...soon."

Ryan ended the call and grabbed his coat. He ran out and down the stairs. Jim pulled up in the driveway as he started to go to the back door of the house. He rushed through the gate.

"I...need you!" he shouted to Jim.

Jim got out of the patrol car. "What's wrong?"

"Edna...crap...my bag..." Ryan ran back through the gate and up the stairs. He opened the door and grabbed his medical bag off the kitchen counter. Then he ran back out again, not even bothering to lock the door this time.

When he reached the patrol car Jim had the motor running. Ryan got in the front seat and Jim pulled out of the drive. "Edna's house?"

"Buddy's... Ray gone."

"Oh hell." Jim turned on the siren and took off to the southwest and Buddy's place. When they reached the house, Edna's Cadillac was parked in the drive. They both ran up to the house. Ryan tried the door, and it was open. When they got inside Edna was sitting on the couch trying to take deep breaths and failing miserably."

"I'm here…," said Ryan. He took out the blood pressure cuff and helped her pull her sweaters off.

Jim stood back and didn't ask any questions. He didn't want to make Edna's blood pressure go any higher if that was the problem.

Ryan kept talking to her softly. Edna kept trying to take deep breaths. Soon he had the pressure read. "It's…not high …Edna," he said.

"You're scared," said Jim. "Tell me what's going on."

Edna reached out and grabbed Jim's hand. "Ray ain't here. He's supposed to be here. I pick him up for work. He ain't got his truck."

"Have you tried to call him?"

Edna covered her mouth. "Oh Lord, I'm an old fool." She pulled out her cell phone and quickly punched in Ray's number. The phone rang and rang and rang, and just about when Jim thought he was going to hyperventilate he heard Ray answer.

"Oh, God, Ray, I was so worried!" said Edna. Jim sat down beside her. Ryan stayed by her on the floor.

"Hi Edna, I'm fine. I decided I'd just go out for a while since you gave me the night off."

Edna looked confused for a fraction of a moment, then she answered. "I swear, Ray, I'm just getting old. I had totally forgotten that. You going to do something exciting?"

"Out taking a drive. It's colder than a witch's tit out here, but it is beautiful. It's a nice afternoon for going somewhere. I'm thinking I'll wander towards home, maybe make a stop in Baker County."

"Baker? What's there?"

"I've got a friend over there that's a little on the crazy side, but he's a hell of a cook. I'm figuring the two of us can have a good dinner and then see if we can stay out of trouble. The two of us usually end up in trouble, you know!"

"You're not a troublemaker."

"No, but he is. I may even run into him on the way there. He's always out doing something crazy."

"Okay, Ray. You take care of yourself."

"Yes, ma'am. I've got an old roommate here…"

Ray disconnected and Edna looked at Ryan.

"He's in trouble. Baker. Shit, he's headed for MacClenny," said Jim. "Old roommate, I think China's got him."

Ryan hit speed dial for Dee Jackson and handed Jim the phone. "Dee, get on the radio. Get anyone you can pull and get them headed to MacClenny. Ray Sherman's in someone's car headed that way, and not willingly."

Edna grabbed Ryan's hand. They both watched Jim. "Get someone to check China Braden's place. See if her car is missing. I think she's got Ray Sherman and is headed to go get Wetherford."

"Oh my God," whispered Edna.

Chapter Sixty-Two

J im had Junior call and let the deputy at his house know he needed to hang tight and make sure that Michael and Bailey didn't go off anywhere. Dee and Manny were both coordinating deputies from the roads of Eden County to go up to County Road 129 and head for MacClenny. They wanted to get on the road themselves, but Jim had deemed them necessary to get people out looking for Ray.

Jim had sent Ryan to The Cypress with Edna to help her open the place. Also because that way he could be sure that Ryan stayed out of trouble and Edna didn't keel over with a stroke.

Bobby Dale had had his radio on at the house and he'd gotten his sister to drive him out to China Braden's place to check on her car. After a tortuous twenty minutes, he'd confirmed that China's car was gone.

They'd called out her make, model, and tag number to the deputies.

Jim had just put down his phone when it rang. He answered it and shouted out to Dee and Manny, "One of the MacClenny ambulance crew just called in to say they've been hijacked."

"What?!" Dee and Manny both said.

"Yeah, he was on his cell. He said he and the other attendant had been stopped by a big blue car in the middle of the road and a guy with a rifle told them to get out of the ambulance and run."

"This is so fucking balls up," muttered Manny.

Dee and Manny could hear Jim telling them he had deputies out looking for the car and the people in it. That the guy with the rifle may have been kidnapped and should be considered a possible victim. They saw that Jim

249

was listening and then he ended the call. He came out of his office. "They've got highway patrol out on the roads looking for them."

"What do you want to bet that damn rifle Ray Sherman was holding wasn't even loaded," said Dee.

"I'm not taking that bet," said Manny.

"Stay on the radio. Our guys need to find them before the highway patrol does," said Jim.

He stood in the middle of the room looking pissed off.

Junior began to wave his hands at them frantically. "Yes, ma'am. Yes, this is the Eden County Sheriff's office. Oh, yeah, put him on, please!" Junior hit the speaker on the phone.

"Hello? This is Ray Sherman. This nice lady let me use her phone to make a call. I'm just off... Where am I, ma'am?" They could hear a woman's voice in the background. "I'm just outside of Branford."

"Ray, are you all right?" asked Jim.

"They kinda pushed me out of the car, so I've got a little road rash and I'm bleeding all over hell, but I don't think anything's broken. This nice woman let me in her house. Oh, shit, Sheriff, you gotta call Edna and let her know I'm okay."

"We will. Listen, we need to get the address where you are, and we'll have one of our deputies pick you up. We've got people out on the road. We'll get someone to you quick as we can."

"Thank you, Sheriff. It was China. There was some guy in the ambulance. She made me let him loose and then we all drove off, well until the guy from the ambulance pushed me out of the back seat."

"All right, we'll get you. Give Junior the address and we'll send the nearest deputy."

Junior cut off the speaker and picked up the phone to get the information.

Jim went into his office and picked up his phone to call Edna's cell. Manny helped Junior figure out who was closest to Branford and got the address to them.

Dee sat at the table and shook her head. "I always knew China Braden was crazy, but this just beats everything she's done all to hell."

"How did she know where he was?"

"Call the jail and find out."

Manny picked up the phone and called the jail. Dee got up from her chair and walked into Jim's office. When he hung up, he looked up at her, "Edna's relieved. I bet she makes him move into her house now.

Dee laughed. "Lord, we have definitely got two crazy people, because this was double the crazy of anything I think I've ever heard of in Eden County."

"Edna's teaching Ryan how to hook up a keg."

Dee sat down across from Jim and they both started laughing. "Where do you suppose they're going?"

"I don't know. But I think we put someone on China's house 24/7 until we figure it out."

"Sounds like a plan. She's likely to just go home."

Jim leaned on his elbows on his desk. "Thank God, Ray's okay. I don't think Edna would survive if Ray had gotten killed. She's kind of taken him on as a surrogate son."

"She'd have to adopt Ryan, and I don't think he'd move into Buddy's old place."

"Yeah, I don't think so either. God knows, Bonehead would object."

Manny leaned into the doorway. "I've got someone on the way to pick up Sherman and take him into Gainesville to the ER. We ought to make sure he's not hurt. He's probably got so much adrenaline running right now, he wouldn't know if he was or not."

"Thanks, Manny. I don't know what I'd have done without you two here," said Jim.

"Wetherford asked for his one call while he was at the jail. He must have called China before they took him in the ambulance," said Manny.

"This is going to shit," said Jim. "I think you and Dee need to take a break. We've got China's house covered, and there's nothing we can do until we hear if someone's spotted her. You'll be called the minute any word comes in."

"Thanks," said Manny. "I think I need food and a nap."

"Go walk, Jackie," Jim said to Dee.

"Thanks, sir. I'm sure Jackie will appreciate that."

Chapter Sixty-Three

Ryan had changed kegs at the bar, brought out clean classes, and done set up. He'd stocked the refrigerator with bottled beer and juices and brought up bucket after bucket of ice. He wasn't sure his arms were going to function tomorrow. He'd worked up enough of a sweat to take off his sweater, and the bar wasn't that warm. He'd just worked that hard.

Once all of that was done, Edna told him to have a seat at the bar and she set a large glass of ice water in front of him. He drank it gratefully.

"The first thing a good bartender learns is that you don't drink while you're serving. That's a sure way to end up free pouring too much and giving away more drinks than you sell," said Edna.

"Too...tired to drink...," said Ryan.

Edna laughed. "Yeah, you may be a bit long in the tooth for this job, Doc. I do appreciate your help."

"Welcome," said Ryan.

Edna poured out some pretzels and nuts into a bowl and put it in front of him. "I'll keep that filled up. It's probably going to be a slow night, being Thursday and all."

"Good," said Ryan. He finished off his water and Edna filled the glass again.

Edna's phone rang and she answered. "Ray! Are you all right?" She stepped away toward the end of the bar that was not occupied.

He could hear bits and pieces of her conversation over the music and conversation in the bar. He hoped that Ray wasn't hurt enough that Edna would need help over the holidays. He knew that he wouldn't be able to keep setting up. New Year's tended to be a pretty busy time for doctors. Some idiot always managed to drink too much, eat too much, or nearly blow his hand off with fireworks. Both Ryan and Doc Markham would be on call for New Year's Eve and the next day.

Edna came back to Ryan. "He's got road rash and they had to stitch one of his ears back on. It near tore off when he got tossed out of the car by that asshole with China."

Ryan shook his head. "Glad…okay."

"Me, too. I was afraid I'd have to have you helping me out. No offense, Ryan, but you're one damn slow barback."

Ryan laughed. "Good!"

Edna patted his hand. "You need to, you can go on home now. I shouldn't need anything else tonight." She pointed to the paltry crowd in the bar. "I'm not likely to make enough money to be worth being open."

"Stay…a little," said Ryan.

"All right. Wish I had something better to feed you than pretzels and peanuts. You take it easy. I don't think we'll have to change the keg again, but I may need to restock glasses."

Ryan nodded.

Chapter Sixty-Four

One of the Captains had come in to take over the night shift, and Maynard had shown up to relieve Junior. Jim had sent another deputy out to relieve the man who was watching China Braden's place. He let both men in the office know to be sure to keep someone on the house until further notice.

Jim felt worn to the bone. The highway patrol hadn't been able to find China and Wetherford. They'd probably gone to ground in some motel somewhere further north. Jim didn't doubt that they'd be back in the area sooner rather than later. China never believed that she'd suffer any consequences for her actions. The months she'd spent in County lock-up just pissed her off. She never got the point that breaking the law meant serving time.

Jim had no idea what Wetherford might be thinking. The man hadn't been rational during the search or while at the ER. Now with China rescuing him from the psychiatric hold at MacClenny, he didn't have any idea what he might think he could do.

Dee had talked to his father. Apparently there was currently no step-mother in the picture, and Dr. Wetherford had told Dee that he would arrange for an attorney for his son. Otherwise, she said he seemed rather unconcerned. Jim figured the attorney would show up tomorrow wanting to know what charges were likely. At the moment Jim didn't have any idea in hell, other than the attack on Bobby Dale.

The deputy at the house had been relieved by someone on the evening shift. Jim had a patrol car he could take home and then the deputy would go on to his regular duties.

Jim needed to sit down and talk with Michael and Bailey. He knew that Michael owned a handgun. He'd show up with it in a case and a trigger lock on it. As much as he hated the idea, he thought it might not be a bad idea for him to have it ready for use. One deputy against two sociopaths made him nervous. China had been pretty predictable before Wetherford, but with him, he had no idea what she might try.

He'd heard from the highway patrol that the rifle Ray had held on the ambulance was not only not loaded, but not even a real gun. It was a BB gun. If the ambulance driver had decided to run over him, a damn BB wouldn't have even broken the windshield.

Two officers had interviewed Ray Sherman at the ER in Gainesville and he'd told them China had the BB rifle in the backseat of the car and told him to use it to stop the ambulance. She'd had a handgun herself. He said it looked cheap as hell and he'd been afraid she'd shoot him by accident with it.

Sherman had a mild concussion from hitting the road and rolling, and it had torn his ear badly enough to need stitching. He had a lot of road rash, but considering he'd been pushed out of a moving car he'd been damn lucky.

Taking his jacket, gloves and tuque, Jim stopped by the front desk to say goodnight to Maynard. Then he pulled on his cold weather gear and went outside to get into the patrol car. His breath made a heavy fog around his head as he walked into the parking lot. It was bitterly cold.

He got into the patrol car, turned the heat on high and pulled out of the lot. He was not done for the night, yet. He still had to break the news to his son and Bailey.

Chapter Sixty-Five

Ryan had just put out another tray of glasses when Ray Sherman walked into the bar. Edna saw him and ran to him, hugging him hard. Ryan was amused because Edna was so short and Ray so tall her hug caught him around his waist. She made a big fuss over the young man and brought him to the bar. He sat on one of the stools and Ryan got a better look at his injuries. He had on a scrub top so Ryan figured his own shirt had been ripped beyond repair. Bandages stuck out from beneath the short sleeves and one side of his head was covered with a huge bandage over his ear.

"I…can check…tomorrow," said Ryan.

Ray nodded. "Thanks, Doc. I'd appreciate that. Right now everything's numb, but I figure tomorrow I'm going to hurt everywhere."

"Give…pain meds?" Ryan asked.

"Yeah, they gave me these." Ray handed him the bottle from the little bag that seemed to have some additional bandages and instructions.

Ryan looked at the medical label. They'd given him something pretty mild. "Antibiotic?"

Ray pulled out a second bottle. "They said they got all the gravel out, but I should take this for a week."

"Skin?" Ryan nodded. It was amoxicillin-Clavulanic. It would work fine.

"Told me to get some Neosporin and use that."

"Good…need more…I'll help…"

"Thanks," said Ray. "I'm kind of crashing now. I think adrenalin kept me going until now."

Edna had her arm around Ray's waist. "Ryan, would you use my car and take him to my place? I don't want China Braden showing up for him again."

"Sure..."

Ray leaned against Edna. "I'll be able to work tomorrow, Miss Edna."

"Don't you be worrying about that. I can always get one of the guys in here to bring out a keg if I need it. You just see how you're feeling."

"Yes, ma'am."

"Go on, Ryan. Get your things."

Ryan smiled and headed to the little office. He'd tossed his coat and things onto a chair in there when he and Edna had come in to open the bar. When he came back out, Edna was back behind the bar.

"You...get home?"

Edna waved him off. "I'll catch a ride. Don't you worry about me. Thanks for your help tonight. You've been a lifesaver of a whole new kind!" She laughed.

Ryan smiled at her and he and Ray went out to her car.

* * *

Ryan decided he would walk back to his place from Edna's. The distance was only a couple of miles, and though he was tired and it was cold, he thought he'd like the alone time. Once he got back to his place, he'd have to get Bonehead back from Michael and Bailey, and he just didn't feel like dealing with the dog's scrutiny at the moment.

Having a dog, especially one like Bonehead, came way too close to having a disapproving parent or an annoying child. There were times they got along fine, and then there were times when the dog made it clear he just didn't much care for Ryan.

Moody damn beast.

And honestly, there were times Ryan didn't care all that much for Bonehead.

Bonehead and he had both loved Danielle. This commonality caused them to live together under the same roof. Over the past three years, they'd managed to find an equilibrium in their relationship. But when either of them felt tired or out of sorts or ignored by the other, they had the bad habit of pissing each other off.

Or in Bonehead's case, literally pissing on something to let Ryan know he didn't like the way things were going.

Filly had assured him that an azalea could survive being pissed on.

He understood why the dog did it. He could admit that there were times when he wanted to piss on something of Bonehead's in retaliation. But he tried to be more mature than the six year old dog.

Right now he just wanted to go home and lie on his bed and not think about anything. But Bonehead would need one last trip to the great outdoors to pee, and then he would want a biscuit, which he would take and slobber and crunch in his bed, making a huge mess, which Ryan would feel obligated to clean up before he went to bed so that it wouldn't be like cement on the tile floor the next morning. Sometimes he just didn't want to deal with it. This night qualified as one of those times.

Ryan crossed the street and cut across an empty lot which put him one house up from his place. Michael's truck was in the driveway. His own car was parked in front of the garage. With Jim's patrol car gone, he couldn't tell if there would be a deputy inside or Jim. With everything that had happened today and Ray's late arrival at the bar, Jim could still be at the Sheriff's office.

He walked up to the gate between the house and the garage and let himself in to the back yard. The light was on in the kitchen, which meant that someone was still up. Ryan walked up and started to tap at the glass.

Jim sat at the table with a sandwich and what looked like hot chocolate. Jim had a book on the table and hadn't noticed anyone coming through the gate. Ryan's stomach growled. Ice water, pretzels and peanuts did not a dinner make. He tapped at the glass.

Jim turned and saw him. He motioned for him to come inside.

"You...lock...door!" Ryan said as he came inside.

"I don't think China Braden's going to come here," Jim said. He set his sandwich down.

Ryan pulled off his tuque and unbuttoned his coat. "Bailey....here."

Jim started to say something and stopped.

"That…guy…shoot Bailey," said Ryan.

"FDLE has his gun."

"Not…China's!"

Jim thought about that for a minute. "I wonder where she got a gun?"

Ryan threw up his hands. "Who…cares?!"

"Well, evidently you do," said Jim.

Ryan wanted to bang his head on the table. Bad things happened everywhere.

"Sorry. You're concerned and I'm being a smartass."

"No shit!" Ryan exploded. Ray had been hurt. Noel had died.

Ryan heard Bonehead's nails clicking on the wood floor of the hall. The dog stuck his head around the door frame and stared at Ryan.

Ryan flipped a bird at the dog.

"You're really upset," said Jim.

Ryan put his hands over his face and tried to calm down. He'd managed to get himself worked up since he dropped Ray off at Edna's house. Seeing Ray in pain, the raw skin on his face, knowing he had more wounds like that under the scrub shirt, Ryan realized his crankiness about going home to Bonehead had been generated by his anger at China Braden and the medical student.

"I'm…angry…about… everything," said Ryan.

Jim pushed his cup of hot cocoa over to Ryan. "Want a sandwich?" he asked.

Ryan sighed. "Yes."

Jim got up and made another sandwich. He set it the plate in front of Ryan. Then he poured another cup of cocoa from a thermos on the counter and sat back down at the table.

"Tell me what happened."

Ryan took a bite of the sandwich and chewed on it for a minute. Then he took a swallow of the hot cocoa. "Saw Ray…"

"He's home?"

"Brought to…Cypress…at Edna's."

"That's good. I'd rather he not be alone."

"Yes," said Ryan. He ate more of the sandwich. He held it up and said, "Thank…you…"

"Yeah, you probably didn't get dinner being at the bar with Edna. How'd you get home?"

"Walked…"

"From the Cypress?"

"Edna's."

"That's not too far."

Ryan finished the sandwich and drank the rest of the cocoa.

"I've got China's house under 24-hour watch. The highway patrol is looking for China and Wetherford. Someone will find them."

"Bailey…know?"

"Yes. I told him and Michael everything. I figure it's better that he knows."

Bonehead had slowly worked himself into the kitchen. He suddenly put his head on Ryan's knee.

Ryan reached down and stroked the dog's silky ears. "Sorry," he whispered.

"If it will make you feel better, the front door is locked," said Jim.

Ryan nodded. "Yes."

"I just didn't think about the back door. The only person who ever comes that way is you. Put those things in the sink and go get some sleep. You can leave Bonehead here if you want. I know that Bailey wouldn't mind."

Ryan shook his head. "No. I…got…him…" He slowly rose from the table and Bonehead followed him to the door.

"Take care of yourself, Ryan. Bonehead needs you, and the rest of us just like having you around."

Ryan grunted and shook his head, then he went outside.

Bonehead sniffed around a bit and finally peed. Then they went up the stairs to his apartment. He reached into his pocket for his keys and realized he didn't have them. He turned the knob on the door and it was unlocked.

Bonehead nosed his way in first and headed straight for the spot where the treats were kept. Ryan followed him and got out a couple of biscuits. He gave them to Bonehead, then went back and locked his own door. He dropped his coat onto the couch, then made his way into the bedroom. Frost coated the sliding glass doors out to the balcony. He knew those were locked. He never unlocked them unless he was going out to sit on the balcony. With the current weather, that had not been an option he'd wanted to pursue.

He kicked off his shoes, pulled off his sweater, and stretched out on the bed. The apartment felt warm and safe.

A few moments later he heard Bonehead come into the room. He curled up on the rug next to the bed and went silent. Sometimes he did seem to understand that Ryan was just exhausted by the whole world outside their little home.

Chapter Sixty-Six

The house phone rang and Jim grabbed the extension next to his bed, hoping it wouldn't wake anyone else.

"Good morning, Sheriff."

Jim recognized the woman's voice. "What do you want, China?"

"Oh, Sheriff Jim. Always acting like some guardian angel. I want to make a deal with you."

"China, I don't make deals. You know that."

"You want to make this deal. You get what you want. You get the murderer of that poor black girl that was stupid enough to fall in love with Bailey."

"Wetherford isn't going to get away with killing Noel Williams."

"Wrong. Wrong. Wrong. Wetherford didn't kill Noel Williams. He wanted to make her come back to him. She was going to, you know. She was going with the rich boy. She wasn't stupid. Marrying Bailey, now that would be stupid."

Jim didn't respond.

"The gun I have? The one I used to get Ray Sherman into my car? That's the gun that killed Noel Williams, and I found that gun in Bailey's apartment."

Jim bit his lip. The one thing he was sure of in this case was that Bailey Braden did not kill Noel Williams.

"She was going to leave with Matt, but Bailey showed up and killed her. So Matt ran off and, well, you know what happened from there."

"Florida Department of Law Enforcement has Matthew Wetherford's gun. They've already matched it," Jim lied.

He could hear China breathing. "Why did you use Sherman to stop the ambulance?"

China laughed. "He wanted to do it. For me. He begged. He said that we'd get Mattie back and then Mattie's father would help us get away."

"Then why did Matt push him out of the car?"

"He got jealous. What can I say, Sheriff Jim? They all want me."

"I thought Matt wanted Noel?"

"Well, he did, but once Bailey killed her, he decided I would be as good a wife as she would have been. Probably better. His parents wouldn't really want him to marry some piece of black trash like her. I mean, she slept with Bailey. If that's not lowering your standards, I don't know what is."

"China, what do you want?" Jim spoke through gritted teeth.

"I want to give you the gun Bailey used to kill Noel Williams, and then I want you to leave me alone."

"That's not going to happen, China. You kidnapped Ray Sherman. You used him to get Matthew Wetherford out of that ambulance. Wetherford was under arrest."

"I'm going to leave the gun for you. You have it tested and you'll see that it's the murder weapon, not that other gun. Then we'll talk again. I left the gun in the bed of your precious Michael's pick-up truck. I know you don't want to disappoint me any more than Mattie or Ray did. Be a good boy and get that gun tested."

The call ended and Jim got up. He quietly left his room and went into Michael's bedroom. Michael slept like the dead. His cell phone was sitting on his dresser. Jim took it and left the room. He went into the living room and used Michael's phone to call Dee's cell.

"Michael?" said Dee.

"It's me, Dee."

"Sir? What's going on?"

"I need you and Manny here as quickly as you can get to my house. I'm going to call FDLE. We're going to need their forensic people. China Braden just called me and said she left the gun that killed Noel Williams in the bed of Michael's truck."

"Damn. I'll call Manny. We'll be there in 30 minutes or less."

"Thanks, Dee." Jim went to his home phone in the living room. He knew the FDLE number by heart. He dialed it and explained he needed a forensic officer at his home address as soon as possible.

Jim pulled on his jacket and tuque, and wearing just his slippers and pajamas beneath them, went to Michael's truck. The bed of the truck was empty except for a beat-up Tec-9 with an extended magazine. He'd only ever seen one before, and it had been taken off some dumbass who'd come to Eden County thinking he was going to bring the drug trade into the area.

He'd lasted less time than the high from his drugs. He'd been shot and left in a cow pasture on the far north side of Eden County. He'd had a Tec-9 that had jammed lying next to him. The stovepipe in the ejection port had probably gotten him killed. Everyone in the department had wanted to see the thing before forensics took it to Jacksonville. Bud Peterson had been patient and let everyone get a look at it. He'd even left the stovepiped casing in it so they could see what had caused the problem that got the guy killed.

This had to be the gun Ray Sherman had talked about. He said it looked like it would explode rather than fire. Where the hell had China gotten her hands on this thing?

Jim's feet were freezing. He left the gun where it was. It wasn't light enough for anyone to see it. If it hadn't been for his porch light, he wouldn't have been able to see it in the bed of the truck.

He hurried back inside. He turned on the coffee maker as he headed back to his room. He'd set it up the night before so he could fill his thermos before he went to work. In his bedroom, he quickly pulled on his uniform and thick socks and boots. The coffee hadn't finished by the time he got back to the kitchen, so he pulled on his jacket, gloves and tuque back on and headed outside to the truck.

He saw headlights from the east and Dee pulled up in front of the house. She got out of her patrol car and walked over to the truck. She took one look into the bed and snorted. "Where the hell did she get that piece of shit?" Dee asked.

"Hell if I know," said Jim. "She's trying to convince me this is what shot

265

Noel Williams. She says Bailey did it."

Dee looked at him. "China Braden is so full of shit her eyes should be brown."

"She says Bailey shot Noel because she was leaving with Matthew Wetherford."

"Oh hell no," said Dee. "I can't even believe she dated that guy."

Manny's patrol car pulled up and parked behind Dee. He walked over. "What do we have?"

Dee made a presentation of the back of the truck, waving her hands like Vanna White.

"Is that a Tec-9?"

Jim nodded. "Yep."

"Where the hell?" Manny turned to Dee. "You said China Braden left this gun."

"She did."

He looked between Dee and Jim. "Where did she get this? I mean, I can see having one in Miami, or hell, maybe even Gainesville. But Eden? Plus no one in the right mind would use one of these things."

"I know," said Jim.

"Get this, she says Bailey used this gun to kill Noel."

Manny looked at both of them again. "You know, I've arrested China before, and she has had some sorry excuses for what she was doing, or what she'd done, or what she said someone else did and did not do to her, but this makes no damn sense at all."

Jim held up his hand. "Oh, that's not the best part. She says she found this when she tossed Bailey's room."

"But Bailey was in your house when she tossed that room," said Dee.

"So Bailey killed Noel with the gun, took it back to his room, and then rode his bike back out to the DOT shed where you found him," said Manny.

"Be the only way it could happen."

"China thinks everyone is dumber than she is," said Manny.

"You got any coffee made, Sheriff?" asked Dee.

"There's probably a full pot in there now. It wasn't finished when I came out here,"

Manny headed for the front door. "I'll bring everyone coffee, just the way they like it, because I'm a nice guy," he said.

"And he's also afraid to ask me to go get the coffee," said Dee.

Manny called out, "I'm smart as well!" He disappeared inside.

Dee stood away from the truck. "This case has taken more left turns than anything I've ever worked on."

"Welcome to my world," said Jim.

"China was here. Right outside your house."

Jim nodded. "No telling where she is now. I wonder if she still has Wetherford with her."

"Someone should probably check on whoever is at her house."

"Yeah, Lee Hauser will know. Maynard will be gone, and Junior's not on until 7."

"I'll give him a shout."

Dee went to her car to get on the radio. She finished the call to Lee Hauser and came back to where Jim stood. "Is he gathering the coffee beans?" asked Dee.

Jim laughed. "I don't know, but he is taking a while."

Finally, Manny came out of the house with three mugs. He handed one to Jim and to Dee. Jim tasted his, expecting it to not be what he liked. "It's perfect!" said Jim.

Manny smiled. "I see all and know all."

"Yeah, right," said Dee.

They'd finished their first cup and Jim had gone and gotten the second servings. He had no plan to ask Dee to get the coffee either. He had to ask how Manny took his. He knew Dee's regular order.

Finally, as the sun started to peek over the horizon enough to make it not pitch black outside, the van from forensics pulled up in front of Jim's house. All three watched as the door opened and Dr. Sullivan stepped out. She looked at the three of them. "Do you not have anything to do besides make work for me?" she asked.

"Your scene is pristine," said Dee. "We didn't even breathe on it."

Sullivan shook her head and walked over to the truck. She had several boxes for the evidence. She looked for a place to set them down and Manny stepped up and said, "I'll hold them for you."

Sullivan looked surprised, but she handed him the packaging. "Thank you."

She pulled off her heavy gloves and put on gloves for handling the evidence. She took several photos of the gun lying in the truck bed. "Has anyone touched the truck?"

"No, we just looked over the edge. There may be fingerprints from the owner of the truck, but you shouldn't find any from us."

"Thanks," said Sullivan. Once she had her photos, she reached over and picked up the gun. She released the magazine and looked surprised. "It's empty!" She held where they could see. Then she cleared the chamber and nothing came out. She then released the slide and pulled it off the gun. She set the gun down and dismantled the slide, taking the barrel and the spring out. "I don't think this gun has ever been fired," she said.

Jim groaned. "That's China. She probably never bought any ammunition. She got the gun."

Sullivan looked surprised. "Why did she turn this over to you?"

"She's trying to convince me it belonged to Bailey Braden and that he used it to kill Noel Williams."

Sullivan laughed. "The gun found in the search of the house was fully loaded and had been fired recently. It's a nine-millimeter. The casing found at the site of the murder matches that gun. It's definitely the murder weapon."

"Thank God," said Jim. "I was afraid this one might have been used."

"We'll check it for fingerprints and other trace but it's not the murder weapon. We already have that. I just haven't had time to get the report out to you. There was a lot of evidence at the house, but I tested the gun first." Sullivan put the gun back together and placed it in one of the boxes. "I'm going to try to raise some prints from the sides of the truck and the area where the gun was lying. I don't know how successful I'll be, but at least it hasn't frosted, yet."

She closed up the box with the gun and handed it to Manny. "I bought evidence boxes for the ammunition, and I am definitely not going to need them."

They watched Sullivan print the sides of the truck and the area of the bed where the gun had been laid. When she finished, she put all the evidence in the van. "Who owns the truck? Do I need to get elimination prints?"

"No, it belongs to Yahoo's son," said Jim. "You already have his prints."

Dr. Sullivan blushed, which surprised Jim. "Sorry. I was out of line that day."

Jim smiled. "Don't worry about it. You gave Doc more material to use against me. He was thrilled."

"Thank you," she said. She turned to Dee. "And this scene was pristine."

Dee nodded to her.

"I'll get back to the lab and add this to the things to be tested. I'll let you know what I get on the prints."

"Thanks, Dr. Sullivan," said Jim. "Want a cup of coffee before you leave?"

Sullivan shook her head. "No, thanks. I've got a thermos of tea in the van. Coffee and I don't get along too well."

She went back to the van and after a moment drove away.

Dee looked at Jim. "I think she's starting to get used to us."

A call came over Dee's radio. "Hey, Junior."

"I'm sending Forest over to China Braden's to take over the watch."

"10-4. Thanks."

She turned to Manny. "I think we need to take a look at the house. That property goes back to those woods. I'm wondering if she's parked off one of the roads nearby and walked up to the house."

"No telling how many ways China knows to sneak into that place," said Manny.

"Get at least two more Deputies with you," said Jim. "I don't want you going in there with less than four people."

"Yes, sir, we'll let you know what we find."

Manny and Dee handed their coffee mugs to Jim and took off in their cars.

Jim went into the house and found Michael in the kitchen. He was scrambling eggs and had sausage cooking.

"Saw you were out at the truck. Figured I'd make you some breakfast," said Michael.

"Thanks. Bailey up, yet?"

"No. Checked on him, but he's buried under a couple of blankets and had a pillow over his head."

Michael served up the food and they sat at the table. "What was in my truck?"

"A gun. China Braden left it in the bed of your truck. Claimed it was the murder weapon."

"And?"

"Unloaded and probably never fired according to Dr. Sullivan."

Michael raised an eyebrow. "I hope no one had touched anything."

"We were all very well-behaved, and Dr. Sullivan apologized for calling us yahoos."

"No kidding?"

"No kidding."

"Is it okay if I use my truck?"

"Yeah, she took prints. It's all yours."

"Good. I think I'm going to have Bailey shag balls for me over at the high school."

Jim shook his head. "Don't. China's out and about, and I do not want her seeing Bailey anywhere. She's bound and determined to lay the murder on him."

"Shit," said Michael.

"I hate to keep you guys housebound."

"What if I take him over to Gainesville? There's a couple of open areas on campus where he and I could bat some balls around."

Jim nodded. "That would be fine."

"Good. I think we're both a little stir-crazy."

There was a knock at the front door. Jim got up and answered it. The Deputy for the day was Buck Neville. Jim let him into the house and Buck handed Jim his keys. "I filled the tank this morning, so you'll have gas for anywhere you need to be."

"Thanks, Buck," said Jim. "I'm letting Michael take Bailey to Gainesville. They're going stir-crazy. I'd like you to stay at the house and keep an eye out here."

"No problem, Sheriff. I can do that."

"There's coffee in the kitchen. I'll be heading out to the office soon."

"Yes, sir."

Jim heard Buck and Michael chatting as he walked to the bathroom. Time to brush his teeth and shave, then he needed to get to the office.

Chapter Sixty-Seven

Ryan had already seen three earaches, a sore throat, and talked to two people he diagnosed with flu by telephone. Neither of them felt well enough to come into the office, but both had family with them, so he didn't think he needed to worry about them. He'd suggested some over-the-counter medications that would lessen the symptoms and let them know they could call him on his cell if they felt worse after hours.

Doc Markham had referred one patient to the hospital for chest pains and done a breathing treatment on an asthmatic patient.

Filly had run her butt off helping Ryan and working with Doc and the asthmatic. The morning had been very hectic.

Claire had come in because the roads weren't as bad. Her sister had dropped her off and she planned to drive her own car home. It had been parked at the office since just before Christmas.

They were all taking a break, sitting around the waiting room with their feet propped up when the door opened, and Edna walked in with Ray. She had Ray wrapped in a blanket.

"Hi, Ms. Edna," said Claire. She eyed Ray Sherman appreciatively. Filly elbowed Ryan to see if he noticed.

"Hi, Claire. I know we don't have an appointment, but I figured Ray's bandage on his ear ought to be changed out. We're not in a hurry. Don't have to be nowhere until tonight when we open up."

Doc waved Edna and Ray over and pointed to two chairs next to each other. "Have a seat. We're just taking a lunch break. Give us a few and I'll be glad to get a look at that ear."

"Thanks, Doc," said Edna. They both sat down. Ray looked tired and the side of his face that had the road rash was bruised and swollen. "We're going over to Buddy's house to get him some clothes and a jacket. China took him out of the house in nothing but shirtsleeves. I swear that woman has no sense at all."

"Do…have a…coat?" asked Ryan.

Ray nodded. "I've got a good jacket at the house. I'll change clothes and pick up some things for the next few days. Edna's letting me stay with her until I'm feeling better."

"Can…you…work?" asked Ryan.

"I'll be fine. I'm just sore. They did x-rays at the ER and nothing's broken. Just bruised up and a little bloody."

"A little bloody? This boy has no skin at all from his right shoulder down to his elbow. It's just raw."

"I'll take a look at that as well," said Doc.

"What happened?" asked Claire.

"Got pushed out of a car," said Ray.

"That's awful!"

"He was lucky. It was that old Buick of China Braden's. I don't think it can go faster than about 30," said Edna. "She doesn't take care of that thing at all. It'd break her Daddy's heart to see the kind of shape it's in these days."

Doc looked at Ray. "Ryan said they gave you antibiotics and some pain pills. What kind of pain pills?"

Edna shook her head, "It's damn Motrin. I could have given him that."

"It's prescription strength," said Ray.

"That's like four of them regular Motrins. It's nothing," said Edna.

Ryan hid the smile that wanted to break out. Edna did not like to see her friends suffer. She had a soft heart.

"Might not want to be taking Motrin if you're still having a tendency to bleed," said Doc. "I'll take a look at you and see if there's something else we can do."

"Thank you, sir," said Ray.

Edna looked at Claire. "Ain't he the most polite man you've ever seen?"

Claire nodded.

Filly elbowed Ryan and whispered. "Money on Edna playing match-maker."

Ryan shook his head. "No...bet."

They finished up their food and Filly led Ray back to an examination room. Edna stayed and continued her conversation with Claire.

Ryan went into the med closet and found some Tylenol 3. He caught Doc before he went into the room and handed it to him. "That'll do," said Doc.

Filly looked at Ryan, "Time to go walk Bonehead?"

He nodded. "Be... back."

He put on his coat, gloves, and tuque. The temperature had gotten higher, which would make taking Bonehead for his midday walk better, but it still felt damn cold compared to normal temperatures in Eden.

At the house, Michael's truck wasn't in the driveway. As Ryan went through the gate the back door opened and a deputy stepped out.

"Afternoon!"

"Hi," said Ryan.

The deputy lit up a cigarette. "You letting the dog out?"

"Walk...time."

"I'm bored to tears," he said. "Mind if I walk with you?"

Ryan shook his head. He went upstairs and let Bonehead out. The dog ran down the stairs and headed straight for the gate. Ryan grabbed the leash from just inside the door and when he got to Bonehead clipped it on his collar.

The Deputy put out his cigarette and stuck the butt in his pocket. They walked out to the road and headed down the street. The Deputy carried the conversation, mostly just requiring Ryan to nod or grunt. Bonehead took his time, sniffing at things and peeing on things. They walked about a half mile and then turned around and went back to the house.

"Thanks for the company," the Deputy said. "Michael's due back around two, so it won't be quiet much longer."

"Good," said Ryan.

"I can keep the dog down here. I know the Sheriff lets him in the house."

Ryan looked at Bonehead. He seemed to be fine with the man. Bonehead didn't hide his feelings when he didn't like someone. "Okay." He took the leash off and handed it to the man. Bonehead bounced.

"Oh... ball," said Ryan.

"Ball?"

"Thinks...you...throw."

"Hell yeah!"

Ryan looked under the stairs for the bag with the tennis balls. Jim had put a hook on the underside of the stairs to the apartment, so they didn't have to hunt for a tennis ball. Ryan took one out and tossed it to the Deputy.

The man looked delighted to have something to do. He reared back and threw one to the far end of the backyard. Bonehead took off after it.

"Enjoy!" said Ryan, and he left them to play.

Chapter Sixty-Eight

Dee and Manny had gone out to the Braden place, but nothing indicated that China Braden had been there. The Deputy on watch confirmed that he hadn't seen anyone or any lights on in the house. The garage was empty and the tall grass in the backyard hadn't been disturbed. If someone had walked through it to the house, there would be a sign of it somewhere.

They'd left the deputy watching the place and gone back to the office.

Sullivan had faxed them the reports on the two guns. The brass that Bud Peterson had found at the scene of the murder definitely matched the gun found at Wetherford's house. It'd been wiped of all fingerprints. Testing on the Tec-9 showed that the gun was clean. The only fingerprints on it were China's, which surprised no one.

China never had been particularly smart, but even this seemed too dumb for her. Did she honestly believe that they would think this gun had killed Noel Williams? Or did she have some other game going on?

Manny thought China was that dumb. Dee wasn't convinced. She thought there might be some other purpose to it. But then Dee had never arrested China, and Manny had. She might be giving China more credit than she was due.

Jim listened to them argue about it. He just wished they could find China and Wetherford and get both of them booked for the crimes they knew about. They had the gun. That and China's stunt of helping Wetherford escape the ambulance gave them plenty to get them both locked up for a while.

The front door slammed open and Edna, wearing at least three sweaters, and Ray Sherman, wrapped in a blanket, came into the office. Jim got up from his desk and walked to the door to see what they wanted.

Edna saw him and pushed Ray through the office to him. "You got to do something, Sheriff."

"About what?"

Ray pulled the blanket closer around him. "China's at Buddy's. We went over there to get me some clothes and we saw her car in front of the house."

Dee and Manny both jumped up from their seats and came to Ray and Edna. "She's at Buddy's?" asked Dee.

"Sure as shit is. I guess she thinks we didn't find Ray," said Edna.

Manny turned to Dee. "I told you she was that damn dumb."

Jim pointed to chairs in the bullpen. "Edna, you and Ray have a seat. Talk to Dee and Manny. It's Dee's case."

"Why the hell aren't you working it?" asked Edna.

"Because I know Bailey. I'm too close to it."

Edna snorted. "Well, that's just bullshit." She sat down and patted the seat of the chair next to her. Ray sat down in it.

Dee and Manny both took seats where they could talk to Edna. "Ms. Bass," said Dee. "It's a legal thing. Jim asked me to take the case because the court would think he had a personal interest that would override his ability to be impartial."

Edna wasn't having it. "Jim Sheppard wouldn't let his personal feelings affect his job for nothing. You know that."

"Yes, ma'am, I do. But the courts don't, and they would look askance at him investigating something that was this personal to him."

Jim watched from the door of his office. Edna was offended for him.

"So you saw China's car at Buddy's house?"

"Yep. And there was lights on. She's there."

Manny leaned forward. "Did you see anyone else?"

"We didn't go look in the windows or nothing. I got the hell out of there. That woman's just damn mean, and I wasn't about to let her see us. She had a gun when she took Ray. She's liable to shoot someone. She hasn't got the sense God gave a goose."

Dee looked at Ray. "Do you know what kind of gun China had when she took you?"

Ray shook his head. "I don't know shit about handguns. I can tell you that it had one of those long ammunition clips."

"Magazines," said Manny automatically. "Sorry. That's what they're called. Not clips. So it had a long magazine on it."

Ray nodded. "Yeah. Like I said, I don't know shit about handguns."

Manny looked at Dee. "Sounds like the gun she left at the Sheriff's."

"She was at the Sheriff's house! Is everyone all right?" Edna asked.

"We're all fine, Edna," said Jim. "She left it in the bed of Michael's truck. Called me to tell me where it was."

"Edna, did Buddy have a gun?" asked Dee.

Edna thought about it. "He could have. Why?"

"Would it be in the house?" asked Manny.

Edna thought about it a minute. "I got no idea."

Dee and Manny looked at Ray. "Have you ever seen a gun there?"

Ray shook his head. "All his stuff is still in his bedroom. I've never even opened the door."

Jim stepped up to Edna. "Did you go through his room after he died?"

Edna shook her head. "I locked the door and pulled it shut. I couldn't bring myself to go in and look through his things. I had a tenant in there for about a year, but it was that new teacher at the high school. I don't think she ever went in there. I told her it was Buddy's personal stuff and I didn't want it disturbed."

"So we have no idea what might be in the house, other than Ray's things," said Jim.

"I guess not," said Edna.

Manny looked like he wanted to bang his head on something.

"Do you know something, Manny," asked Dee.

"I stopped Buddy once for speeding and he had a gun on the passenger seat of the car. I told him to take it home and lock it up. That if I ever saw it again, I was going to bust him for it. He didn't have a permit for concealed carry, and it wasn't in a case."

"Oh Lord," said Edna. "That sounds like Buddy."

Everyone in the room went quiet.

"China would bust into that room," said Jim.

"And she gave up the gun she had when she took Ray," said Edna.

"If that gun's in the house, she could have it," said Dee.

"Fuck," said Manny.

Ray said nothing.

Junior had turned his chair so he could see them. "How many deputies you going to need?" he asked.

Chapter Sixty-Nine

Ryan got the call from Edna around 3 pm. She needed clothing for Ray, and she wondered if they could borrow some from Ryan. Doc told him to go ahead and go home, since it was Friday. He would cover the office until 4 pm, and then he had call that night.

Ryan met Edna and Ray in front of Jim's house. Michael's truck sat in the driveway. He felt sure that Bonehead would be fine with the deputy, Michael, and Bailey until he got Ray set up.

They walked up the stairs to his apartment and Edna sat on the couch while Ryan took Ray into the bedroom and they went through his closet. They found several shirts that would fit and Ryan had a couple of pairs of jeans that would work for Ray.

Ryan pulled a light jacket and a sweatshirt out of the closet and handed them to Ray.

"Sorry...nothing warm..."

Ray shrugged. "I'll be inside."

"T-shirts...boxers?" Ryan asked.

"A couple of pairs of boxers would be great. I can't get into my house, yet."

"Why?" asked Ryan.

"Guess where China and that creep are hiding out?"

Ryan could not believe it.

"Yeah, we were driving up to the house and China's car is parked off to the side. Thank God we saw it before we stopped.

"Crap!"

"I went with something a little stronger than crap," said Ray.

"Sorry…"

"Listen, I'm just happy someone has pants long enough that I'm not walking around with high waters. I hate it when my ankles show."

They packed up the things into a small backpack that Ryan had. Ray put on the sweatshirt and jacket. He folded the blanket. "I was getting awful tired of looking like some homeless guy wandering around in a blanket."

"Glad…to help," said Ryan.

When they walked back into the main room, Edna stood up and went to hug Ray. Then she hugged Ryan. "I can't thank you enough for all you've done," she said.

Ryan patted her shoulder. "Welcome…"

"Walk…you out…," said Ryan. "Bonehead…at house."

"Who's Bonehead?" asked Ray.

"That's his dog," said Edna. "I've seen him, but never met him."

"Come with…," Ryan said.

They trooped down the stairs and went to the back door. Ryan knocked on the door, more as a warning than waiting for someone to answer. He found Michael and Bailey in the living room watching television, Bonehead draped across their laps as usual.

The dog rolled his head and looked at them as they walked in. His tongue hung out of his mouth and all four legs were relaxed as Bailey rubbed his belly.

"That is a comfortable dog," said Ray.

Michael started to get up, but Edna waved him back. "We just came in to see the dog. We're heading right out."

"Nice to see you, Ms. Bass," Michael said.

Bailey looked at them and waved, "Hi!"

"Deputy…?" Asked Ryan.

"Dad sent someone over to pick him up. They're calling in a bunch of people," said Michael.

"They're going over to Buddy's old house to get China and that boy from Gainesville," said Edna. Then she slapped a hand over her mouth.

Bailey looked at them. "What's going on?"

Ryan looked at Ray and Edna.

Edna went and sat down in the chair next to the couch. She leaned forward and spoke to Bailey, "I'm sorry. I'm a thoughtless old woman."

"It's okay," said Bailey. "What did she do?"

"She kinda kidnapped Ray yesterday. Used him to get this guy that Dee and Manny arrested. He was in an ambulance on his way to MacClenny, and she made Ray hold a gun on the ambulance and help her get him out of it."

"I know about that. Who's the guy?"

"He's from Gainesville. None of us know him," said Ray. "He and China have some connection."

Bailey thought about it for a moment. "Sheriff Jim told me about China grabbing you and wanting some guy. I thought it was some new boyfriend. It's not, is it? It's about Noel."

"I think so," said Edna.

"Is Sheriff Jim going after her?"

"I think it's Dee and Manny. Something about him not being involved in the case."

Bailey continued rubbing Bonehead's stomach. Bonehead leaned up and licked his arm. "Thank you, Ms. Bass, for telling me. I know how China is, so I don't take offense. Okay?"

"Thank you, Bailey. I am really sorry."

Edna got up. "I'd better get Ray back to the house. Doc gave him something for the pain and I know he wants to take it and get a nap in before we open tonight." Edna took Ray's arm and the two of them went out through the front door.

Ryan sat in the chair Edna had vacated.

"We're watching X-Men. We just started it. We can start it over if you want to watch it with us," said Michael.

Ryan looked at Bailey who continued rubbing Bonehead and keeping his eyes down. "Yes... Halle Berry... hot," said Ryan. Bailey peeked up at Ryan.

Michael used the remote to restart the movie. "I like Mystique myself," he said.

The movie started again, and Bailey looked up to watch it. "You like the blue girl?" he said.

Michael nodded. "Always been partial to blue girls."

Bailey laughed.

Chapter Seventy

J im stood in the doorway of his office watching as Dee and Manny ran the plan by the gathered deputies.

"Okay, Dee's said China's car is parked in the side yard. It's out of sight unless you're coming from the west. I want someone to come in from woods behind the place. There's no houses on either side, so if you keep low, you should be able to get right up on the passenger side of the car. I want the tires flatted all the way around. If, and only if it's safe. You think you can keep out of sight from inside, you do the driver's side. If not, just the passenger side."

Tom Wills raised his hand. "I've got a buck knife. I'll do the tires."

Dee nodded. "Thanks, Tom. Now, moving on, there are only two entrances to the house. The one right off Blue Heron Road, and the one at the back of the house. I want a team coming from the woods behind the house, and two teams coming from the Blue Heron. With no houses on either side and only a church down at the corner, we shouldn't have to worry about civilians. Everyone wears a vest, everyone wears a helmet. Got that?"

The deputies murmured an agreement.

Manny stood up. "The Sheriff has asked me to remind everyone that this house is owned by Edna Bass. He does not want it shot all to hell if we can avoid that. Homeowners insurance does not cover damage done by law enforcement. Do not shoot out windows unless there is someone there firing at us. It's a furnished rental, so the furniture and appliances and such are owned by Edna Bass. If you want to shoot something, shoot China's car."

Everyone laughed and Manny grinned. "The place is heated by propane and there is a tank in back of the house. Do not shoot the propane tank. This will cause an explosion, and the house will catch on fire. Also, if you're close enough, it might catch you on fire. Understood?"

There were nods and murmurs again.

Dee held up two keys. "We have keys to the doors. The same key opens the front and back door. Edna had it keyed that way when she started renting it out. There will be no reason to kick in the doors. If we get really lucky, they won't realize we're there until we are already in the house. We're going in after dark, and if you are quiet, we may get into the place before either of them realizes we're there."

Dee set the keys on the table. "The team from the back will go in just slightly ahead of the team on the front of the house, as long as the kitchen is not occupied. Manny will give three clicks on the radio if the back team is going in first. If that happens, the front teams will wait on my signal and then move. If Manny gives two clicks, the people in the back will go in on Manny's signal which will be on the count of three. The teams in the front will also be going in on the count of three. I will be the person counting to three. Watch me and go in on my signal."

Jim felt every muscle in his body tightening. He wanted to go with the deputies. He would not, though. He would be waiting with the EMTs. If all went well, they would take China and Wetherford to County for booking. If it didn't, well, he didn't want to think about that.

Junior had reached out to the EMTs and they would be on the main road before Blue Heron. They would not go in until they were called.

"Does anyone have any questions?" asked Dee. No hands were raised. "All right. It's going to be cold, so do wear your jackets over the vests. Hopefully no one will get shot and need to replace their jacket when this is all over."

"Everybody have shooting gloves?" asked Manny.

A couple of guys raised their hands. "No gloves. Lord, people. Get your butts over to Favor's now. I don't want numb fingers on the triggers of those shotguns."

Three guys got up and left the office. Manny looked at Dee. "I despair sometimes."

Jim stepped out of his office.

"I will be waiting with the EMTs. Manny's going to be with the team from the back, and Dee is leading the two teams from the front. Listen to them, watch them. Don't do anything until they signal. They've both got the experience for this, more than I have. We want to take China Braden and Wetherford in alive. So pay attention and do your best."

This time there were a lot of 'Yes, sirs' and Jim hoped like hell these guys would pay attention.

Jim went back to his desk and sat down. He'd checked with the jail and no attorney had ever shown up for Matthew Wetherford. Dee had tried to call the father again once they'd learned he and China were in Buddy's house. She'd left messages at his office and at his home. Neither had been answered.

China's only family was Bailey, and she did not acknowledge him. The times she'd been arrested since her parents died she'd either had Buckley bail her out or bonded out with Frank Delano who ran the only bail bonds business in Eden County. She always put the house up for her bond and always showed up in court so she could get the deed back. He couldn't help but wonder if she would behave any differently this time. These charges were a whole lot more serious, and she likely wouldn't be eligible for bail. He rubbed his neck, trying to get the muscles to stop aching. He'd had a headache since the phone call this morning.

He hadn't told Bailey about the call. He knew that Michael wouldn't have mentioned it. If anything, Michael was more sensitive about the way that China treated Bailey than anyone else. He'd recognized as a child how she affected Bailey's life. He had told Jim once that he would be glad when she was gone because she made Bailey sad. Jim hadn't even called him on it. Michael was right. China had spent all of Bailey's life making him sad.

Chapter Seventy-One

Ryan took Bonehead for his before-dinner walk after the movie finished. He had not seen it in the theater, and he'd been surprised at how entertained he was. Though part of that was listening to Michael and Bailey debate who among the X-Men they'd prefer to be.

Michael had firmly come down on Wolverine. He liked the idea of the healing factor. "Dad wouldn't be worrying about me being a deputy if I had that healing factor. That would be great."

Bailey thought Wolverine's claws were cool, but he wanted to be a character who wasn't even in the movie. Apparently some guy named Quicksilver was far cooler than Wolverine. Personally, Ryan couldn't figure out why everyone was so hot for Jean Grey. While he could see that she was pretty, he thought being with a woman who could read your mind would be creepy as hell.

Bonehead finally took his evening crap, and Ryan dutifully cleaned it up, bagging it to take back with him. He doubled bagged the poop to keep it from smelling up Jim's garbage cans too much. It did seem to help.

When he and Bonehead came around to the house, he saw that Michael's truck wasn't in the drive. That didn't make sense. He went around to the back door and found it locked. He knocked on the glass, but no one answered. He knocked again, harder and still didn't get an answer. He went back around the house and tried the front door. It was locked, too. He walked over to Michael's bedroom windows and looked in. Michael was on the bed. Ryan knocked on the window and Michael didn't respond. He knocked louder and Michael still didn't move.

He used his cell and called the Sheriff's office. Junior answered the phone, and he asked him if Jim was in the office. He said he'd get him. Jim picked up the phone. "Jim, I can't get into your house, and it looks like Michael's unconscious. His truck isn't here, and that worries me.

"I'll be there in ten minutes," Jim said.

Bonehead picked up on Ryan's anxiety and began to whine. Ryan knocked on the window again and there was no reaction from Michael. He went back to the front door and started pacing back and forth. Bonehead whined louder and louder, and Ryan couldn't get him to stop.

Jim pulled up in front of the house driving a Lincoln Navigator. He got out of the SUV and went straight to the front door with his keys. He opened the front door and Ryan and Bonehead followed him in and down the hall to Michael's room. He bent over Michael and gently tried to rouse him. Jim moved him and Ryan saw blood on the pillow.

"Wait!" Ryan said and he pushed past Jim and very carefully felt around the back of Michael's head. He felt the blood and there was a bump. He felt Michael's neck to be sure there wasn't an injury there and, finding nothing turned Michael's head to one side. There was swelling on the back of his head and the skin was broken and bleeding.

"What is it? What's happened?"

"He...needs...ambulance...," said Ryan. He handed Jim his phone and Jim called for an ambulance.

Ryan opened Michael's eyes. Neither pupil was blown, which was a good sign. "Not...broken... unconscious."

"So it's not a fracture?" asked Jim.

Ryan nodded his head. "Bump... skin broken... pupils good..."

Jim's relief was palpable.

"Bailey...?"

Jim went to the guest room, but it was empty, as was his room. "Bailey doesn't drive. He wouldn't take Michael's truck. He'd take the bicycle from the garage. He knows it's there," he said as he came back into Michael's room.

He used Ryan's phone to call the office. "Junior, put Dee on." He sat at the foot of the bed, his hand on Michael's leg. "Dee, Bailey's gone and Michael's unconscious. We've called an ambulance."

Ryan could hear Dee's voice but not what she was saying. He watched Jim.

"Yeah, all right. I'm going to send Ryan to the hospital with Michael. I'm coming back to the office. We need to get eyes on Buddy's house."

Jim spoke to her a short time and then handed the phone back to Ryan. "When the ambulance gets here, go with him to the hospital. I'm going to see if I can find out where Bailey is."

Ryan nodded. "I'll...stay with..."

"Thank you. I'll take Bonehead to the station with me."

"Feed..."

"I'll make sure he gets fed."

Jim grabbed Bonehead's leash. "Come on, Bonehead. I'll get Junior to feed you." Bonehead looked at Ryan and then obediently went with Jim. Ryan sat on the side of the bed and waited for the ambulance to arrive.

Chapter Seventy-Two

At the office, Junior fed Bonehead leftover barbeque pork and french fries. Jim decided to pretend he hadn't seen it. Dee and Manny had gone to check the site of where all the deputies would gather that evening. He knew they had a deputy watching the house, but Junior hadn't heard anything about a change for breaching the house to get China and Wetherford.

Junior gave Jim Dee's cell phone number and he went to his office to call her. When she answered he filled her in on what Ryan had found at the house. According to the deputy watching Buddy's house, he couldn't see inside. China's Buick hadn't moved, and no one had come out of the house.

Something didn't seem right. Who would have taken Michael's truck? Jim felt certain Bailey hadn't taken it. He'd never had a driver's license and in the years he'd known Bailey, he'd never learned to drive. It didn't make sense that he would take the truck and leave Michael injured and alone.

Dee didn't have any suggestions for what could have happened, but she and Manny were deep into the planning of the raid on Buddy's place. She suggested that maybe Ray Sherman or someone had come by the house and borrowed the truck and that maybe Bailey had gone with him to help at the bar.

Frustrated by Dee's split attention and confidence that the explanation for the missing truck would turn out to be something innocent, Jim finally ended the call.

Jim left his office and pulled a chair up near Junior. The two of them tried to brainstorm about what might have happened.

"Could Michael have fallen or hit his head and then gone unconscious when he went to lie down?" asked Junior.

"God, I hope not. That sounds worse than finding him the way we did."

"Why don't I call Edna and see if Ray's still with her? We can at least get that out of the way."

Jim agreed. As Junior made the call, a very satisfied Bonehead came out of the break room and walked up to Jim. He leaned against Jim's legs. "Feeling fat and sassy?" Jim said to the dog as he stroked his head.

Bonehead burped and Jim had to lean back because of the sudden smell of barbeque on the dog's breath. "Damn, if this end of you stinks now, I don't want to be around later for what comes out the other end," said Jim.

Junior had gotten Edna on the phone, and he could hear him asking about Ray. It didn't sound like either of them had been out of the house so far that day. He hung the phone up and shook his head. "Sorry, sir."

"There has to be someone who came to the house and took the truck and possibly Bailey. If we didn't know that China and Wetherford were still in Buddy's house, I'd think it might be them. But how would they have gotten to my place if they didn't take China's car?"

Junior shrugged. "It doesn't make sense."

"How long until it gets dark?" asked Jim.

Junior checked his computer and noted that sunset was supposed to be at 5:38 pm. Jim looked at his watch. It was about 30 minutes before it got full dark. The Deputies would be meeting Dee and Manny soon.

"Is anyone still on the Braden place?" asked Jim.

Junior shook his head. "No, I heard Manny call that guy off before their meeting. He's going to be with them when they go into Buddy's place."

"I've got a very bad feeling. I'm going to check out the Braden place."

Junior shook his head. "You are not going alone."

"I'll be fine."

"Dee finds out I let you go out there by yourself, I'm going to be lucky if she doesn't hang me up by my balls. You know how she is."

Jim nodded. "I do, but we can't just close up the office."

"I'm calling Maynard. You're not going anywhere without me."

Junior went back to his phone and began to make a call.

Jim went into his office and got his gun out of his desk drawer. He checked it, made sure it was loaded, and then pulled out two extra magazines. He might be chasing phantoms, but his gut was telling him that they weren't covering all the bases. Something had been missed. He didn't know what it might be, but he would look for it until he found it.

"Maynard's on his way," said Junior from the doorway.

"Get your vest and a shotgun," said Jim.

Junior headed toward the armory. He rarely if ever went into the field, but Junior was a full-fledged officer. Like all the deputies he did a retraining with weapons three times a year, and he had completed his last training in early December. Junior might not be a marksman like Manny Sota, but he always had high marks on his retraining courses.

Jim had done his last retraining in October. He spent time on the range every month for the simple reason that he'd never liked using a gun, and he wanted to be sure he kept his skills as sharp as he could.

The shotgun from his patrol car had been destroyed when it'd been pancaked by the semi, but he could take one of the guns out of the armory. When it came to confrontations, he preferred the shotgun. The spray of a shotgun didn't have to be aimed as finely as a handgun. He considered his handgun a backup to the shotgun.

Junior came back into Jim's office with two boxes of shells. The shotguns they used in the department were 12 gauge and could hold 10 shells. They generally used buckshot because a shotgun worked best at close range. Jim and Junior loaded both guns with ten 12 gauge shells. Junior opened the third box of shells.

"I'm going to carry extras in my pockets. You just never know what you might need," said Junior.

Jim reached into the box and took five of the shells, leaving five for Junior. He set them on his desk. He would put them in his jacket pockets, so they were easily reached for reloading.

"I'll need a flashlight," said Jim.

"I'll bring two out. We got that 500-lumen one that Dee likes."

CHAPTER SEVENTY-TWO

"Sounds good."

By the time Maynard arrived, Jim and Junior were kitted out in their vests, had their jacket pockets filled with shells and were both wearing their handguns on their duty belts. They had pepper spray, two pairs of handcuffs, a Taser, their radios, and surgical gloves. Junior had on a pair of black shooting gloves. Jim wore leather that he'd had for decades. They were worn-in perfectly, and he always felt he could feel the gun better with them on.

Maynard took one look at them and asked, "You going hunting for bear?"

"Bad guys," said Junior.

"I thought it was all deputies going to sneak up on Buddy's old place tonight."

"They are," said Jim.

Maynard's eyes went wide. "You two sure about this?"

"We're sure. We'll radio if there's trouble," said Jim.

Maynard nodded, "Yes, sir. I'll keep an ear to the radio."

Bonehead wandered out of Jim's office. Maynard pointed at the dog. "Is he going with you?"

"No. Need you to keep an eye on him. He's Doc Ryan's dog."

"What if he needs to poop or pee or something? It's just me here?"

"Try newspapers," said Jim, then he and Junior went out the front door.

They got into the Lincoln Navigator, making sure their shot guns were secured. Junior started the SUV and pulled away from the office.

"I bet we come back and the whole floor's got newspaper on it," said Junior conversationally.

"I just hope that pork doesn't work its way through him while he's inside."

Chapter Seventy-Three

Ryan sat in a chair next to Michael's bed. He'd come to in the ambulance, according to the attendants. Once at the hospital, they'd done x-rays and an MRI. There'd been no bleeding in the brain, and the fact that he could speak, and answer questions led them to believe that he could be discharged soon.

Ryan had followed the ambulance in his car so that they would have a way to get home. It seemed like that would be possible from everything the doctor had said. They were still in the emergency room which indicated to Ryan that they had not arranged for a hospital room and didn't intend to keep Michael overnight.

Michael had not thrown up or had any dizziness on regaining consciousness. He did have a sore head. When the doctor had asked what happened he either couldn't remember or had been hit from behind and hadn't seen anyone. Even Michael didn't seem to know which was true.

"Why don't I give your father a call?" said Ryan. "He's probably worried sick by now."

"Maybe he knows what happened to Bailey," said Michael.

"You don't think Bailey took it?"

"Bailey doesn't know how to drive."

Ryan thought about that. "I knew how to drive, or at least the basics when I was a kid."

"Yeah, Bailey has been riding his bike for years. He'd ride with his grandfather some, but that was in the old truck. It had a manual transmission. Bailey was scared of it."

"Why?"

"It was really old and broke down a lot. His grandfather carried all kinds of hoses and parts for it and fixed it himself."

"That would put me off driving. I don't want to know how to fix my car."

Ryan called the Sheriff's office and someone he'd never spoken to answered. "Hi… Jim there?"

"He's not here. Is this an emergency?"

"Uh…," said Ryan.

Michael held out his hand and motioned for Ryan to give him the phone. Ryan handed it over. "Hey, this is Michael. I'm at the hospital in Gainesville. They're going to let me go home tonight and I wanted to let Dad know."

"Oh, hey, Michael! It's Maynard!"

Michael rolled his eyes. "Hi, Maynard. You're on early."

"Your Dad and Junior took off around dark. They had shotguns and extra shells. I asked them if they were going hunting for bears!" Maynard laughed.

Michael's eyes were wide when he looked over at Ryan. "Maynard, do you know where they went?"

"Yeah, they were going to the old Braden place."

"I thought the deputies were going to raid Buddy Bass' place."

"Yeah, that's still on. I'm not sure what they thought was going on at the Braden place, but they were fully loaded!"

"Okay. So, Junior's with Dad?"

"Yeah. You could probably reach Junior. You know that number?"

"I do. Thanks, Maynard. You have a good evening."

Ryan cut off the call. "Dad and Junior left the Sheriff's office just before dark. It sounds like they were expecting trouble."

Ryan looked confused, which Michael understood because he himself felt confused. "I'm going to call Junior."

Michael dialed Junior's number. It rang longer than usual, but then Junior picked up. "Sorry, Ryan. Had my phone on mute. Took me a minute to notice it was vibrating."

"Junior, this is Michael. I'm using Ryan's phone. Is my Dad with you?"

"Oh, he's going to be glad to hear your voice! Hold on!"

"Michael?"

"Dad, I'm doing fine. The ER is discharging me and letting Ryan take me home."

"Good! You let Ryan take care of you. And would you tell him that Bonehead is at the Sheriff's office? He might want to go get him. I don't think Maynard is sure what to do with a dog."

"Dad, what are you and Junior doing?"

"Nothing. We're fine. You just let Ryan take you home. I'll see you there later."

"Dad, Maynard said you and Junior were armed for bear."

There was a long silence on the line. "Eh, you know Maynard. He exaggerates," said Jim.

"You're not going to try to go with Manny and Dee and the others into Buddy's place, are you?"

"No, of course not. They've got that all handled."

"Why is Junior's phone on mute?"

"No particular reason. I think it was so we could talk without being interrupted."

"Dad, are you on a stake out?"

Michael put the phone on speaker and held it out so Ryan could hear.

"Dad, where are you and Junior?"

Michael and Ryan could hear some whispering and it sounded like Jim had his hand over the phone's speaker. Finally, Jim came back on the line.

"We're just following up on something. Nothing to worry about."

"Oh, shit," said Junior suddenly.

"Call you back," whispered Jim. Then the line cut out.

Ryan and Michael stared at the phone and then at each other. Michael said, "That was weird, right?"

Ryan nodded. "Very…"

"We need to get out of here." Michael swung his legs over the side of the bed.

"Whoa!" said Ryan.

"Ryan, Dad, and Junior are somewhere, fully armed, and it's not at Buddy's place."

"China's?" asked Ryan.

"Maybe. I think he's looking for Bailey, and I think he thinks China has him. Which means she's not at Buddy's house."

"Oh, boy...," said Ryan.

"We need to leave now."

Ryan stood up and helped Michael off the bed. "Okay?"

Michael nodded. "I'm okay. Let's go."

Chapter Seventy-Four

Junior saw Michael's pickup truck drive up to the barn-like garage at the Braden place. He reached over and grabbed Jim's arm as he talked to Michael. Jim looked up in time to see the door to the truck open and China Braden step out of it.

"Oh, shit!" said Junior.

Jim got off the phone and watched carefully as China opened the door to the garage. She stepped inside and then the lights came on. She went back to the truck and pulled it into the garage.

Once she parked the truck, she got back out and the passenger door opened, and Matthew Wetherford got out. Wetherford stepped up to the bed of the truck and pulled a tarp out of it. Then he reached in and dragged a tightly bound Bailey Braden out of the bed and dropped him onto the dirt floor of the garage. He pulled a gun out of the waistband of his pants and pointed it at Bailey.

"Jesus, Matt! Don't kill him, yet. We need to follow the plan." China walked over to Bailey and pulled a knife out of her pants pocket. She cut the rope around his ankles. "Just keep your eyes on him."

"I'd rather just shoot him."

"Yeah, and we both know how well that went the last time you said you were going to shoot someone. You chickened out and I had to do it for you."

"I loved her! That's why I couldn't do it. She loved me, too, until this asshole came along and ruined everything."

"That's why we have to follow my plan. We do this right he takes the fall for killing her and we walk away clean."

China walked over to a ladder that went from the floor to a loft above them. She climbed up, and then she walked out onto a beam that ran across from the loft on the left to the loft on the right.

"Was this place a barn?"

"Back when the Bradens used horses, yes. But once my granddaddy got hisself a car, he took out the stalls and cleaned it up so he could park in here."

When China reached the center of the beam she bounced on it a little. "Yeah, this will hold him. He ain't that much bigger than me."

"Probably outweighs you by about forty pounds."

"It'll hold. The building's old, but it's strong."

China made her way across the beam and climbed back down the ladder.

Jim and Junior made their way up to the garage and stood behind the opened door. They waited silently. They didn't want to make a move that would cause Wetherford to shoot Bailey.

China went to the truck and grabbed a coil of rope out of the bed of the truck. The braided rope looked dirty and worn. She pulled the coil over her shoulder and then went back up the ladder. She walked out to the middle of the beam, sat down and began to uncoil the rope.

"How long is it?"

"Fuck if I know," said China. "I gotta see. You keep that gun on him."

Wetherford watched China but pointed the gun at Bailey.

Bailey shifted, trying to get his hands out from under him. He got his hands under his butt and slowly curled his legs up toward his body. Once he had his hands under his legs, he pulled his legs up to his stomach and slipped one leg, then the other through the loop of his arms to get his hands in front of him.

China looked up and shouted, "Matt! Look at him!"

Matt saw that Bailey had his hands in front of him and he stepped over and kicked Bailey's shoulder hard. Bailey cried out, but the gag over his mouth muffled the sound.

"He's not going anywhere."

"If you have to shoot him, then they'll know someone was here with him and he didn't kill hisself. It's got to look like he killed hisself."

"How are we going to do that?" Wetherford asked.

China muttered something to herself and went back to the rope. She let out a length of about six feet and then she wrapped the long side of the rope around the beam. She tied it in a double knot against the beam and dropped the longer side of the rope to the floor.

She got up and walked back across the beam to the loft and came down the ladder. She stood over Bailey. "Probably just as well he got his hands in front of him. I'm going to need him to go up the ladder."

"Why can't we just stand him in the bed of the truck, tie it around his neck and then drive out of the garage. He's not tall enough for his feet to reach the floor. That will take care of it."

"Oh my God, for someone that's been to college you are really stupid."

China went to where Bailey lay and pulled him to his feet. "You're going to climb the ladder."

Bailey shook his head.

"If you don't climb the ladder, I'm going back and killing Michael. I might even shoot his daddy, Sheriff Jim."

Bailey shook his head.

China tried to drag him over to the ladder, but Bailey planted his feet and used his weight to pull himself away from her. China slapped him. "You want me to kill Michael? 'Cause I will. I will do it just because it will make me happy."

Jim started to go around the door and Junior dragged him back. Jim nodded. Junior was right. They needed to wait. Needed China to get Bailey away from Wetherford so they could keep him from shooting Bailey.

"Stop it. Let me do this," said Wetherford. He grabbed Bailey around the throat with his arm and locked his elbow. He dragged Bailey toward the ladder. When he got him to the ladder, he put the gun to his head. "If I have to shoot you, and you ruin China's plan, I will not kill Michael. I will go back to the house, and I will shoot him in the spine, and I will cripple him. I will let him live, but he won't ever play baseball and he won't ever be a deputy. See, I know about him. I've seen him play baseball. He's really

300

good. I think that being a cripple will make his life a living hell, and I would so like to do that. But I will make a deal with you. You go up this ladder and do what China wants, I'll leave him alone. All I want is for you to die here and take the blame for Noel's death so that I can go on with my life. You're worth nothing. You're a fucking busboy. No one cares if you're gone. You're not going to save anyone's life unless you climb this ladder."

Bailey looked at Wetherford. Then he put his hands on a rung of the ladder, and he started climbing.

"You are good," said China. She walked up to Wetherford and swatted him on the butt. "I might even fuck you after this."

China followed Bailey up the ladder. When she reached the loft she told him to step back. He did and she climbed into the loft. She pointed to the beam. "Walk on out, Bailey."

Jim watched through the crack in the door. Wetherford moved so he could see them both on the beam. He raised the gun and pointed it at Bailey.

China had Bailey in front of her on the beam. He was shuffling, dragging his feet. China gave a little push, "Stop taking so long. We don't have all night." When they reached where the rope was tied to the beam, China grabbed Bailey's ankle and then grabbed the rope. As she stood, she kept her left hand holding to him. If he pushed her, he'd go right off the beam with her.

When she wrapped her arms around his shoulders and brought the rope up and tied it tightly around his neck. "I'm doing it real tight, because I think that might make your neck break when you step off. That'd be quick. Quicker than hanging there and slowly strangling. Isn't that nice of me?"

"Shit," whispered Jim. "She's tied the rope."

Junior shook his head. "Only one thing to do," he said, then he stepped into the open doorway, walked forward and fired the shotgun at China. China fell back and dropped to the garage floor.

Wetherford screamed and turned toward Junior, pointing his gun.

Junior did not hesitate. He fired the shotgun again and Wetherford fell back, the gun still in his hand. Neither China nor Wetherford moved.

Bailey stood on the beam staring at Junior. Jim walked out behind him.

"Don't move, Bailey!" Jim shouted. He dropped his shotgun and ran to the ladder.

Junior picked Jim's shotgun up and put it under one arm. He walked forward and saw where China lay on the dirt floor. His blast had hit her right in the chest. Her eyes were open as though she was surprised.

Jim went up to the loft and stepped out carefully on the beam. He hoped that it would hold his weight. He tried to think light.

Junior walked to Wetherford. The blast had hit him in the chest. Junior could see Wetherford was dead, too. He stepped back, away from the body.

Jim had made it to the center of the beam. He took out his knife and cut the end of the rope that looped back down to the beam. There was still a tight loop around Bailey's neck, but he would not hang.

Jim cut the ropes on his hands and pulled the gag down over his chin. Bailey spit out the cloth that had been stuffed into his mouth. Jim took Bailey's hand and they walked carefully back across the beam.

When they reached the loft, Jim pulled Bailey into his arms and held him. Bailey sobbed against his jacket. "I've got you. I've got you, Bailey," he said softly.

Chapter Seventy-Five

Dee stood with her two teams in the dark on the other side of the road from Buddy's place. She didn't know what the temperature was, but she knew they were all freezing their asses off. She waited for the signal from Manny and his team.

They moved across the road just outside of the front door house. Dee put the key in the lock on the door and turned it gently. The lock let loose, and the door just began to crack open. Dee listened for the signal and there it was. Three clicks. Dee began to count silently and put her hand up, raising one finger for each number.

On three the teams from both sides of the house rushed through the open doors. They quickly began to clear the rooms. No one in the living room. No one in the kitchen. No one in the hall. No one in the bathroom. No one in the bedroom. They looked at the one closed door and Manny kicked it open. The room had been tossed. Clothing, shoes, bedclothes, everything had been thrown around. The mattress had been slit open, as had the pillows. Feathers lay on top of pretty much everything in the room.

The room was empty except for the mess.

Dee and Manny walked around the room, kicking at things and Manny saw the gun case. He picked it up. It was empty. A gun cleaning kit lay on the floor not far from it.

Manny let his gun down and Dee did as well.

"What the hell?" said Manny.

"Don't look at me," said Dee. "I thought they were here. Her car's here."

Tom Wills spoke up. "I slashed all four tires."

Everyone looked at everyone else.

"This is a letdown," said Buck Neville.

Dee's phone vibrated in her pocket. She pulled it out and saw that the call was from Junior. She answered it.

"Jackson here."

"Dee, we need you and Manny and the ambulances over here at the Braden place."

"What?"

"We got a crime scene over here for you. Sheriff and I can't investigate this."

"Hold on a minute." Dee put her phone on speaker and everyone stood close to hear it. "Can you repeat that, Junior?"

They heard Junior take a deep breath. "Me and the Sheriff are at the Braden place. This is your case and you need to get here and bring the ambulances with you. I already called FDLE, and I do not want to face that Sullivan woman by myself."

"You said the Sheriff is there?"

"Yeah, but he's not in any place to handle a crime scene. He's sitting on the back of Michael's truck with Bailey and they're both crying."

"Yeah, okay. 10-4. We will make our way over to you. Hang tight."

"Thanks, Dee. I appreciate it."

Dee hung up the phone.

"Our crime scene is over at the Braden place," said Dee.

Manny shook his head. "Does that mean China and Wetherford are there?"

"Maybe."

There was a lot of muttering from the deputies. Manny looked at them and yelled out, "All right. I need you guys to get back to your cars and go back to the office. Be sure whoever is at the desk has your name and knows you were here with us. We'll verify your time when we get back, though it looks like it may be a while."

Everyone made their way out of the house and back up the road to the intersection where they'd all parked.

Manny went and locked the back door, then headed out the front door

304

with Dee. They turned out lights as they went. As they started up the road to make contact with the ambulances and get them directed to the Braden place, they each kept their peace.

Once again the case had taken a left turn that no one could have seen, except for the Sheriff and Junior, apparently.

The ambulance attendants took the address but decided they would just follow Dee and Manny out to the Braden property. One of the attendants was new and seemed pretty excited about getting to her first crime scene. Dee and Manny had come in her patrol car. They pulled off their vests and put them and their shotguns in the trunk.

It was going to be a long night, but not the one they'd planned. Dee worried out loud about how Jim was doing. If he was crying with Bailey, had something happened to Michael? They'd find out, but she hoped like hell that Michael was okay.

Then there was the matter of Dr. Sullivan. Though she'd mellowed a bit with their last contact, Dee thought she was not going to be happy about whatever had happened.

"Lord have mercy," said Dee.

Chapter Seventy-Six

Jim heard the sound of a motor outside the barn. Dee or Manny had probably gotten ahead of everyone else. He tried to wipe the tears from his face, but his leather gloves weren't being very effective. Bailey still had his face buried against Jim's chest. He'd stopped crying, but he hiccupped a little as he tried to get his breath.

Junior had gotten them both down the ladder and sitting on the back of the truck. He stepped up and handed Jim a handkerchief. Jim wiped his face and pulled Bailey closer. He still had the circle of rope around his neck, but Jim had cut his hands free. Bailey's fists held onto the fabric of his jacket. "Want to wipe your face," Jim asked softly.

Bailey nodded but didn't let go of the jacket or raise his head.

"Dad?"

Jim looked up and saw Michael standing in the doorway of the barn. Ryan, looking very pale, stood with him.

Bailey turned his head and when he saw Michael, he reached one hand out to him.

Michael hurried across to them and threw one arm around Jim and the other around Bailey. "Oh, God, I was so scared," he said. "Maynard said you and Junior had gone off looking like you were loaded for bear."

Ryan moved past the truck and saw the two bodies on the floor. He moved toward both, stooping to check each for a pulse. Junior went to Ryan. "Doc, they're both dead."

Ryan nodded. "Had... to check... doctor."

Junior pulled him away from the bodies. "I understand. You might want to be over here. There's an ambulance on the way, and Dr. Sullivan from forensics."

"Yahoos…Sullivan?"

"Yeah," said Junior. "I haven't met her, yet."

"Oh boy," said Ryan.

Jim called out, "Ryan, is he okay to be here?"

Ryan turned and saw that Jim pointed to Michael's bandaged head. "Discharged…," he said.

"Concussion?"

"Yes."

Jim shook Michael's arm. "You have to stop getting hit in the head!"

Michael leaned against him. "I don't do it deliberately."

"His head's hard," said Bailey.

Jim pulled both Michael and Bailey close. "You're both a couple of hard heads. Doesn't mean I like seeing you get hurt."

The sound of several vehicles came from outside the garage. Jim started to get up and Junior waved him back. "Stay there, sir. I'll take care of it."

Junior walked outside and Jim could hear Dee's voice over the motors of the cars and ambulances. She walked into the garage and saw Ryan, Jim, Michael and Bailey and just shook her head. "It's just not possible to keep you people out of trouble, is it?"

Jim shook his head. "Sorry, Dee. Junior and I couldn't be sure, but we had a hunch."

"A hunch," Dee said, "And you brought them with you?"

"No, Ryan and Michael just showed up. Bailey here arrived with others."

"And the others?" asked Manny as he walked into the garage.

Junior stood beside Manny. "Dead. Doc already checked."

"Jim?" asked Manny.

"Me," said Junior.

Dee looked at Junior and then at Jim. She settled her eyes on Ryan. "You called the deaths?"

Ryan nodded.

"Hell, I might as well go home," said Dee.

"Oh, no," said Jim. "Sullivan's on her way. This is your case. We're going to give you our statements and go home."

"Like hell you are," said Dee. "You're going to be right here with me when Sullivan comes. I am not dealing with explaining this to her."

"I'll leave Junior with you," said Jim.

"What?" said Junior.

Four paramedics came into the garage and rushed past them to the two bodies on the ground. They checked for pulses, looked at the wounds and one young woman stood up and exclaimed, "Damn! They're both dead."

One of the others stood up, stripping off his gloves. "Yeah, that happens at crime scenes."

"Can I at least call it in?" she asked.

"Go ahead."

She pulled at her microphone and began the call into the base and let them know they would have to stay at the crime scene until they were released. Her voice expressed her disappointment at not having anything exciting to respond to on the scene. The paramedics went back out to the two ambulances to wait for their notice to leave.

Dee put Jim into her car with Bailey and Michael. Ryan sat in the passenger seat of Manny's patrol car. They both took in the scene, making their notes and drawings of vehicle placement, where the bodies lay, and the rope that hung from the beam above them.

Dr. Sullivan showed up with her van. Once the paramedics had spoken with her, they headed back to base, and she went into the garage. Dee and Manny had not touched the bodies or the truck. Manny had taken possession of both of the shotguns and had initial statements from Jim and Junior.

Dee had recorded Bailey's statement, making notes as he spoke. He'd been able to tell her what had happened at the house when China showed up with Wetherford in tow. The two of them had walked from Buddy's house to the Sheriff's so that no one would know where they would be or what they planned.

Bailey had spent the bulk of his time tied up, gagged, and hidden under a tarp in the bed of the truck, but China and Wetherford talked openly about China's plan for killing him and making it look like suicide.

Once he was dead, they planned to haul ass for South Florida and get Wetherford's father to get them an attorney. They were sure that once his father saw them, he wouldn't have any choice but to try to keep them from being arrested for the death of Noel Williams.

Jim and Michael sat on either side of Bailey. Jim knew nothing they did would remove the trauma he'd been through, but Bailey would know that they were not going to abandon him. Listening to how he'd laid under the tarp in the back of the truck, cold to the bone and sure he would not survive, Jim wanted nothing more than to take him home and let him use up all the hot water getting warm again, and filling him with grilled cheese and sweet, milky coffee.

Michael seemed to be on the same page. He kept his hand rubbing Bailey's back.

Jim had gotten out of Dee's car to give his statement to Manny and to be sure that the shotguns were identified correctly. He'd been shocked when Junior stepped out from behind the door and shot China Braden and Matthew Wetherford. It never occurred to him that Junior would do that.

Junior had looked at him and said, "I didn't want you to have to kill."

Jim didn't know what to say. Department shootings were rare in Eden County, and Jim had never fired his gun at another person in all his years in law enforcement. Junior, like Manny and Dee, had served in the military. He'd been in Kuwait in 1990. Unlike Manny and Dee, nothing about Junior ever reminded Jim of his military years.

Junior ran the office, kept Jim on time and in place for events, meetings, and did virtually all the computer work for their statistical reports. Jim always told everyone that Junior was the brains of the outfit. He was just the public face.

He didn't think he'd ever forget again that Junior had also been a frontline soldier.

Sullivan cut the rope from around Bailey's neck and photographed where it had marked his throat when China tied it. She photographed his wrists and the marks on his face from the gag.

She ended up also photographing the wound on Michael's head when she realized it had continuity to how Bailey had ended up with China and Wetherford.

Two techs had come with her and they called for an ambulance to transport China and Wetherford's bodies to the Medical Examiner in Gainesville.

Fortunately, she'd released Jim to take Michael and Bailey home before that. It didn't matter that China had never been a mother to Bailey. Bailey knew that the woman who had decided to push him off that beam and be hanged was his mother. Jim didn't want his last view of her to be a body bag being carried out of the Braden garage.

Ryan had driven them home with a stop to pick up Bonehead at the office.

Chapter Seventy-Seven

Ryan couldn't hide his surprise when Bailey Braden showed up at the clinic the day of his mother's burial. Jim and Michael had said they would go to the cemetery with him, but Bailey had told them he didn't plan on going. He would be putting his apartment back together, making repairs on it for his landlord.

Bailey, dressed in a shirt and tie, showed up at the clinic and asked for Ryan. They had taken their conversation to Doc Markham's office, and Bailey had asked him if he would take him to the cemetery for the burial.

Ryan got Doc to cover for him and the two of them drove to the local cemetery. It turned out that China's parents had arranged for her to have a burial place next to theirs. They'd even paid for a headstone.

"Taking care of her right to the end," said Bailey. "Mama and Papa loved her."

Ryan stood next to Bailey as the funeral home crew lowered her into the ground. Bailey watched it with dry eyes. No one spoke, as it was just Bailey, Ryan and the funeral crew.

The crew had asked if Bailey wanted to say something before they put the casket in the ground, but he'd said no.

Once the casket was lowered, a man Ryan didn't know began filling in the grave by hand. The crew cleared up their equipment and left.

"Coffee...I...buy," said Ryan.

"Thanks, if you have the time," said Bailey.

They went to McDonalds, which was as close to a coffee shop as Warren had. Bailey ordered the coffee. Ryan paid. They each doctored their coffee

311

as they liked it and sat down near the side windows. It had warmed up and was in the low 40s outside. After the days of the 20s during the freeze, it almost felt pleasant.

"Want...talk?" asked Ryan.

Bailey smiled. "Not about China."

"Noel?"

"Not yet."

"Anything....?"

"I'm thinking about applying to school," said Bailey. He drank the too sweet, milky coffee in his paper cup.

"Need...help...?"

Bailey shook his head. "I already checked about it. I'm going to apply to the Santa Fe Community College for the Public Safety program. I want to be a deputy."

"Here?"

Bailey smiled. "Sheriff Jim already promised me a job."

Ryan covered his eyes. "Michael..."

"He knows. He's annoyed that his Dad will hire me and keeps trying to talk him out of applying."

"Not...surprised..."

"If Noel had lived, I'd have gone where she got a job. But now I think being a deputy is what I want to do. I understand why Sheriff Jim doesn't love it. I understand why Michael wants it. I know what it's like to be a victim. I think I can be a good deputy, someone who is like a cross between Sheriff Jim and Michael."

"I...see...that," said Ryan.

"You understand being a victim, too," said Bailey. "It sucks."

"Yes...sucks big...," said Ryan.

"I'm going to have to study to get into the program. And I'm going to need to be strong."

"I...help...you...," said Ryan. "Let me?"

"Yeah."

"Good." The money that sat in an account Ryan refused to touch would easily put Bailey through his program.

"I need to learn to drive," said Bailey. "Will you teach me?"

"Yes! ...My car...," said Ryan.

"Sheriff Jim said he could help me get China's car fixed up," said Bailey.

Ryan shook his head emphatically. "No, no...drive better..."

"I can't...," started Bailey.

"Need...," Ryan struggled for the word. "Afford! ...good gas... no breakdown."

"Ryan, I don't have enough. I'm going to sell my grandparent's place and use the money to go to school and get a place to live."

"I can... Danielle...life insurance."

"I can't take your money!"

"Not mine..."

"No."

"Yes... Danielle... Noel...say yes."

Bailey shook his head and covered his eyes. "You're a crazy man, Ryan."

Ryan reached over and pulled Bailey's hand off his eyes. "Rich...crazy."

"Crazy for sure."

"Sell house...get place....pay school," said Ryan. "I buy...car ...used." Ryan gloated. He knew that 'used' would win Bailey's agreement.

Bailey threw his head back and laughed. "You're not going to buy me a BMW?"

Ryan blew a raspberry at Bailey. "Not...that rich..."

"You lie like a rug," said Bailey. He finished his coffee and took their empty cups to the garbage. He brought back a napkin and handed it to Ryan. "You need to wipe up the table. That raspberry you blew got coffee all over the place."

Ryan very obediently wiped up the bits of spit on the table.

"Not bad. You'd make a decent busboy," said Bailey.

Ryan tossed the napkin at Bailey, who caught it and tossed it to the garbage.

"First lesson!" said Ryan. He tossed Bailey the keys.

Bailey's eyes opened wide. He looked out at the BMW parked at the curb. "Now?"

313

Ryan put his hand on Bailey's shoulder and pushed him toward the door. "Now….."

Chapter Seventy-Eight

Dee walked into Jim's office and pointed to the computer. "The reports are all in the system. China Braden died of a broken neck. Matt Wetherford died quickly. Some of the shot went through his jugular. He bled out really fast."

"Does Junior know?"

"I gave him a copy of the reports."

"Thanks."

Jim reached over to the keyboard and brought up the computer program to check on the status of the case. The file was closed, with a final report outlining what had happened in the garage at the Braden's place and the reports verifying the gun used to kill Noel Williams, her cause of death and the reports Jim and Junior had written on what they'd heard China Braden and Matt Wetherford say to each other.

China and Matt Wetherford conspired to kill Noel Williams to prevent her marriage to Bailey Braden. Wetherford purchased the gun and it was his car that had parked next to Noel's in the library parking lot that morning.

They could only speculate why China had gone back later in Ray Sherman's truck, but Jim suspected she planned to plant evidence that would lead to Bailey as the killer. Or maybe she had just planned to move the body in the hopes it was never found.

Whatever had been her plan, she'd recognized Bailey's bike and made sure that he wouldn't be able to get back to town or go for any kind of help.

Wetherford probably did believe that he loved Noel Williams. Wetherford had a breakdown after Noel Williams' death. The burning of his medical textbooks and the filth in the house where he lived indicated he had not functioned in a constructive manner. Certainly not one of someone who had really planned on what had happened in that DOT shed.

Dee Jackson and Manny Sota had pieced together as much as was possible from the forensic reports and what Jim and Junior had heard. The interview with Bailey had reinforced the things said in the garage that night. But he'd been traumatized and hypothermic again. To some degree they all recognized some aspects of the case would always be unknown.

"The autopsy report on Noel Williams has been sent to her parents as they requested," Dee said.

"Thanks for taking care of that."

Dee shrugged. "Won't be much comfort. We don't know if she was aware or suffering. She never spoke. The volume of blood loss indicates that she died slowly."

Jim closed the program. "Yeah. I'm glad Bailey doesn't want to see it."

"How is he doing?"

"I don't know. He insisted on going back to his apartment. Michael and I helped him replace some things and get his new clothes into it. China, of course, didn't have a will, but the property will all go to Bailey once it gets through probate. There isn't anyone else."

Dee put on her cap. "I'm going to head out. Jackie will be wanting her walk and then dinner."

"Timothy going to be around tonight?"

"Sheriff, that is none of your business," said Dee as she walked out of his office.

Jim grinned. Timothy Mackey had already sent Jim an e-mail that he would be having dinner with Dee tonight. He'd mentioned it when he asked Jim if he was willing to write him a recommendation for a job with the highway patrol. Jim had agreed to write the recommendation. He figured the sooner Tim Mackey moved to Eden County, the sooner Dee Jackson would stop biting everyone's head off when they asked about him.

Junior appeared in the doorway. "Sweet Ella's is having a special on shredded pork sandwiches. I'm ordering for me and Daddy. You want anything?"

Jim's mouth watered, but he knew that Ryan would manage to find out that he'd broken his diet. His cholesterol had been high at his last check-up, and Ryan and Doc Markham had given him an ultimatum. Lose ten pounds or they were putting him on medication.

"Yeah, can you order four sandwich platters for me? Michael's still home and I can invite Ryan and Bailey over for dinner."

Hell, Jim thought. One pill a day wasn't that big a deal. As long as Michael didn't find out about it.

Acknowledgements

No book gets written without support and assistance from wonderful people. David Putnam made excellent suggestions for this book, and also taught me the problem with the word "then". Albert Waitt pointed out things the reader really wanted from the book and gave me insights that made the story infinitely better. Pat Payne read it and found all my typos and turned it into a clean manuscript. I had wonderful support from my editor Shawn Reilly Simmons and it is appreciated more than I can express. I would also like to thank the wonderful people who read *Burning Eden* and told me they wanted more.

About the Author

Sarah Bewley has been a private investigator, a freelance writer, and is an award-winning playwright. Her love of mysteries inspired her to write her first book *Burning Eden*. She lives in North Florida with Pat Payne, a visual artist. She rock climbs, takes boxing lessons, and loves reading and dogs.

SOCIAL MEDIA HANDLES:
    FB: Sarah Bewley
    Threads
    Instagram
    X(Twitter) - @wpadmirer

AUTHOR WEBSITE:
    www.sarahbewley.com

Also by Sarah Bewley

Burning Eden (Book 1 of the Eden County Mysteries)